About the author

Marina Stepnova is a Russian no... ... er and journalist. Her first novel *Chirurg* (*The Surgeon*, 2005) was received with great critical acclaim and nominated for the Russian National Bestseller Prize. In 2012, her novel *The Women of Lazarus* won third prize in Russia's prestigious National Big Book Prize and was finalist for the National Bestseller Award, the Russian Booker Award and the Yasnaya Polyana Award. Her latest novel, *The Italian lessons* (2014), will also appaer at World Editions. Marina Stepnova lives in Moscow.

About the translator

Lisa Hayden is a literary translator who lives in Scarborough, Maine. Her translations from the Russian include Vladislav Otroshenko's *Addendum to a Photo Album* and Eugene Vodolazkin's *Laurus*, as well as pieces of short fiction that have appeared in journals and anthologies. Lisa writes a blog, Lizok's Bookshelf, that focuses on contemporary Russian fiction. She received an MA in Russian literature and lived in Moscow during 1992-1998.

Lisa wishes to thank Marina Stepnova for answering questions about the text of *The Women of Lazarus*, Liza Prudovskaya and Anne O. Fisher for their many editorial suggestions, and the Scarborough Public Library for its collection of books about ballet.

The Women of Lazarus

Marina Stepnova

The Women of Lazarus

Translated from the Russian by Lisa Hayden

World Editions

Published in Great Britain in 2015 by World Editions Ltd., London

www.worldeditions.org

Copyright © Marina Stepnova, 2011
English translation copyright © Lisa Hayden, 2015
Cover design Multitude
Image credit © *Ritratto di ragazza* (Portrait of a young woman),
Amedeo Modigliani, 1916

The moral rights of the author and translator have been asserted in
accordance with the Copyright, Designs and Patents Act 1988

First published as *Zhenshiny Lazarya* in Russia in 2011 by
AST Publishers, Moscow

British Library Cataloguing-in-Publication Data
A catalogue record for this book is available on request from
the British Library

ISBN 978-94-6238-019-6

Typeset in Minion Pro

Published with the support of the Institute for
Literary Translation (Russia)

The publication of the book was negotiated through Banke, Goumen &
Smirnova Literary Agency (www.bgs-agency.com)

Distribution Europe (except the Netherlands and Belgium):
Turnaround Publishers Services, London
Distribution the Netherlands and Belgium: Centraal Boekhuis,
Culemborg, the Netherlands

All rights reserved. No part of this publication may be reproduced, stored
in or introduced into a retrieval system, or transmitted, in any form,
or by any means (electronic, mechanical, photocopying, recording or
otherwise), without the prior written permission of the publisher.
Phone: +31 (0)76 523 3533. Email: info@worldeditions.org.

Contents

Chapter One: Barbariska	9
Chapter Two: Marusya	33
Chapter Three: Lazar	72
Chapter Four: Galochka	164
Chapter Five: Galina Petrovna	200
Chapter Six: Lidochka	295
List of Main Characters	445

Chapter One: Barbariska

In 1985, Lidochka turned five and her whole life went down the tubes. They never, ever met again, Lidochka and her life, which is exactly why all the smooth, slightly salty, damp details of their last happy summer together settled in their memories so firmly that their heads buzzed.

The Black Sea (it's black because it never washes its hands, right?). A resort's guest house that looked like spilled matchboxes. A beach strewn with softened little cardboard cups from fruit and berry ice cream (ice cream where the price is a dream, Papa liked to say). Huge, scorching-hot bodies. The morning walk to the chosen spot and all those tiny polite steps to avoid snagging a heel or towel on someone else's luxuriating, vacationing flesh. Lidochka would quickly lose her patience and then all Mama had to do was get distracted for a second—by a neighbor at a cafeteria table or a roaming seller of forbidden cotton candy—and Lidochka would break free of her tight visual leash and rush off toward the sea with a piercing squeal, her fat, round heels haphazardly pounding the sand.

Alarmed vacationers raised themselves up a little, as if they were sea lions, shaking large, barley-like grains of morning sand out of damp crevices and synthetic creases, smiling in response to the parents' apologetic ritual lamentations, It's fine, let the child have some fun! Just look at that, galloped off, what a fidget! You've got to understand, it's her first time at the sea... And where might you be from? From Ensk. Oh, you've come a long way. We're from Krivorozhe, got this holiday trip from the factory, that right, Manya? Manya nodded cheerfully with a kind mouth generously loaded with gold ore. She shifted all their junk into a heap so it was easier for Lidochka's papa to spread out a towel. You vacationing at Sunnyside? Yes, we are. Mama quickly extricated herself from a sundress crackling with artificial silk's static electricity and weak stitches. And we're at Red Banner. Nice to meet you.

The long-term friendship ready to spark—complete with greeting cards on major holidays and reciprocal cross-country visits—was hindered by intense heat and Lidochka, who was golden-brown, ear-splitting, smooth, and glistening in a small surf for all Soviets. Mama just couldn't tear herself away from Lidochka, not for the sweating watermelon that made a sugary crack under the peaceful Krivorozhe proletarian's predatory pen knife, not for the ongoing beach game of fool, *And what do we have as trump here? No, hearts were last time!*, not for the ever-intricate monologues from enticing, unfamiliar lives, *And then Petrovich, that's my brother, he says, So you take the kids, Lariska, and move in with me, there's enough room. And the government really did just give him a room, twelve square meters, you could hold a wedding there, you could ride a motor scooter in there!* But Mama just smiled absentmindedly, even as fate's tentative dotted line for some Petrovich nobody knew threatened to transform itself into a solid line of full-fledged human happiness.

At any other time she would have been delighted to try on someone else's unachievable fate, if only to convince herself how cleanly and cleverly her own had been cut out. But the thread of the story slipped away hopelessly as soon as it took on a new plot turn filled with communal poverty and babies begotten in sin—meager Soviet life somehow always provoked unprecedented, downright Byronic passions—because Lidochka jumped away from a tickly wave, laughing. The horizon, dimly visible and quivering from the surging heat, was blinding and Mama squinted, frightened when she didn't see her daughter's familiar sun hat among peeling shoulders, titanic rear ends, and exultant shrieks. There she is, thank God. Lidochka waved in reply and, without taking off her red and blue inflatable beach ring, crouched down to mold an appetizing cake of a house with termite towers that she pressed out of her hot little fist.

Lidochka's white sun hat cast a lively perforated shadow on her tanned cheeks but the shadows of her eyelashes were even longer and more transparent, oh and your daughter is so sweet, knock on wood, not to jinx anything, and Mama graciously accepted the praise like a special gift, not just feeling but secretly knowing with an exultant, bubbling certainty that Lidochka was singular, not just 'so sweet.' Inimitable. The most wonderful child on earth with the most wonderful and flawlessly fortunate fate. Mama looked at her little daughter with a quiet stunned smile and then at her own stomach—young, tight, and not at all disfigured from her early pregnancy—not believing herself that at one time Lidochka, now as wide-eyed as a puppy, with silky, warm shoulder blades and weightless adult curls on her dark, chubby neck, had fit inside there, all of her, and hadn't even existed before.

Then Mama's thoughts reached the limits of the comprehensible and began spinning dangerously, like a truck hanging over a precipice: the hacking wail of an agonized motor, two wheels vainly spinning bald tires in thickening air, the other two tires spewing little clumps of gravel that seemed to explode from pressure. With just one second before the fall (one second, one second) a translucent little plastic devil toy jumps in front of her eyes, *Vovka made it out of IV tubes, owes me three rubles, the pain in the ass, now it definitely won't get paid back, so there it is, you know,* that's how it is, that's how people die, there's what I'll never be able to tell anyone... But why does non-existence before birth scare me more than the emptiness after death? Why isn't it scarier to die, Oh-dear-Lord-have-mer-cy-and-save-me?

'You look a little pale, Ninusha,' Papa said, worried. He kissed Mama on the shoulder. The skin under his lips and tongue was hot and dry, as if lightly starched. 'Have you been in the sun too long?'

Mama smiled guiltily. The dark thoughts let go of her and her soul lightly crossed itself and steered onto the main road: it was saved, soaked in sweat from horror and exhausted, but still feeling a little despondent not to have learned what was over there on the other side, just beyond that final second, after which there's only a tumbling flight that races with soundless metal wreckage and then the crack of straining muscles, and... and... and... Mama felt lost trying to imagine the impossible and rubbed her forehead on her husband's merciful arm, a strong arm with large freckles and familiar, dear reddish fluff. Yes, it's hot, sweetie. I'm dizzy.

Lidochka, still just a little creature at five years old, sensed an unsettling little draft of otherworldly air and ran right to her mother. She was hot and agile, wearing remarkable imported day-of-the-week panties. Each day a new color, each day a silly new appliqué. Monday: pink panties with a strawberry. Tuesday: light blue with a bristling bunny. Wednesday: yellow with a gap-toothed sunflower. Ma, what's wrong? Mama's delicate lips touched her daughter's eyelids, one little eye, then the other, everything's fine, Barbariska, you're not going to get sunburned on me are you? Nah, and Lidochka, now calm, slipped out of Mamochka's affectionate arms and tore off for the sea again, and their new beach friends grinned affably. Lida, Lidochka, Little Lozenge, Barbariska—little family nicknames that were the cooing patter of parental passion. No one would ever be so intense again. No one, ever.

'Don't sneak off, you little partisan,' Papa said. He gathered Lidochka up in his arms, agilely flipping her over, which made her laugh uncontrollably: the sea and sky had smoothly changed places; biting fishes, sea horses, and little ships on the horizon were just about to fall into the clouds; everything was swimming, slipping away; deafening seagulls hung on invisible threads; and Lidochka herself hovered between sea and sky.

And this was happiness: beloved, hot hands that would never let you go or drop you even if the whole world turned upside down. She grasped that later. Much later.

'You sit with Auntie Manya and Uncle Kolya for a bit,' Papa said, setting Lidochka on the sand. The sea was on the bottom again and the sky was on the top. Like usual. 'Will you sit for a bit? Mamochka and I are going to swim out and back, she's boiling hot already.'

'Go on, go on, don't you worry,' Auntie Manya said in her rich honking voice, 'I got my own two on their feet and the third granddaughter's on the way—I won't take my eyes off your little charmer. You go swim as long as you like.'

'We won't be long,' Mama promised, sounding guilty and pressing Lidochka with her soft, burning-hot cheek. 'Do what Auntie Manya tells you. I love you very, very much.'

Lidochka nodded inattentively as Auntie Manya energetically dug around in her purse, like a plotter—it was clear she was preparing to extract something very, very interesting. Uncle Kolya looked intrigued, too: his life with his wife had obviously been filled with young, exciting surprises thus far. 'Ta-da!' Auntie Manya said with circus-like intonation as she presented Lidochka with a huge, warm peach, softly fuzzy and overflowing with tigery-pink color. A cool wave pawed at Mama's stomach and goose bumps instantly dashed along her back and shoulders. Lidochka sniffed the tickly peach and squinted. Shall we see who's fastest to the buoys, Nina? Mama jerked her head and smiled trustingly. Eat, hon, Auntie Manya affectionately instructed Lidochka. Uncle Kolya had already knocked a boiled egg (procured from the same purse) on his knee and malformed 'oxheart' tomatoes had appeared one after another on a newspaper as if by magic, along with sausage, slices of bread expropriated from the cafeteria, and grapes from the market that were golden through and through. Auntie Manya bragged that she'd haggled them down to eighty kopecks, then, with identically nonthinking tenderness, she stroked first Lidochka's sun-warmed little head, then the close-cropped, degenerate back of her proletarian husband's, oh, Marusya, you're good as gold, what a wife, I'm jealous of my own self, swear to you...

Lidochka ate almost half the peach, taking deep breaths and moaning a little with pleasure, the sticky juice dripping down her chin and chubby, tanned stomach. No, no, don't smear it all over, hon, I'll wash you off in the water later, you'll be all nice and clean, just like a little apple, And where does your mommy work? Whoa, and does your daddy draw plans, too? And how many rooms do you have? Hear that, Kolya? I told you, didn't I, how engineers get three-room apartments right away up north but then you thought, why the hell does Genka need technical school, he should go straight to work at a factory? And that's how he and his family's going to croak, in that dorm. So do your mommy and daddy make a lot of money? Don't know? Just eat, hon, eat, may God give you health and your mommy and daddy, too…

The shriek came up suddenly, as one terrifying note— AAAAAAAA! Lidochka choked and dropped the peach, immediately coating the most delectable pulp with large-grain sand: there'd be no washing it, only throwing it away, too bad really, but the shriek got closer and closer, working itself to such inordinate heights that the picture of the beach—which looked like it had been drawn on thick, translucent glass— instantly dimmed and transformed into a web of frightened cracks. Vacationers slowly got up from their towels and chaise longues like sleepwalkers; some had already run to the shore, jostling the rest aside.

AAAAAAA! HELP! HELP!

Auntie Manya crossed herself, scared, Lord Jesus, Kolya, take a look, see what happened, just don't you howl, hon, someone's head obviously got baked, let's us go have a look, too. Lidochka kept turning to look at the fallen peach, which was hopelessly ruined. She wasn't even thinking of howling. Quite the opposite. This was all terribly interesting.

Papa was kneeling at the very edge of the beach: his arm was being pulled as if he were a little boy by a tall, wet guy, one of the brigade of muscle-bound lifesaving Atlases who usually hung around for whole days at a time in wooden watchtowers, stuffing themselves with ice cream and flirting with female vacationers, but mostly, of course, bored silly.

'You all right, comrade?' the guy asked Papa, sympathetically leaning in so that his rear end, in blazing swim trunks, jutted out behind him.

One of the curious in the crowd answered in a reproachful deep bass, 'What do you mean, "all right"? Can't you see, a man's drowned!'

'It's his woman's drowned,' someone corrected the bass voice. Papa finally tore his arm away from the lifeguard, groaned softly and dully, and then fell facedown, like a toy accidentally jostled from a familiar place by an elbow.

The lifeguard straightened up and looked around, bewildered, but a shouting woman doctor, as white and brisk as a motorboat, had already broken through the ring of vacationers. A motorboat that was just as white and brisk—but real—was already spinning around the buoys, cutting anxious circles as the other lifeguards dove off the boat into the smooth waves with a noiseless splash, their distant young voices pealing as they shouted back and forth.

'Look at that, his wife drowned but he's in one piece,' said someone in the naked, sweaty, babbling crowd. He was invisible and indistinguishable; maybe he was reproachful, maybe envious. Papa got right up as if he'd heard those words: he was all covered with heavy brown sand, just like Lidochka's unfinished peach.

Then he suddenly lifted his head to the sky and threatened someone above with his fists in a gesture of such ancient and frightful power that it wasn't even human. A mischievous little wave decided to lick at his pink, somehow childlike heels but then got scared and threw itself back into the sea, returning to its own. Papa's naked, wet eyes surveyed the vacationers.

'No,' he said, completely calm. 'None of that's true. It's time for us to eat lunch. We'll go have lunch now. Where's my daughter?'

Lidochka pulled her little hand, all sticky with peach juice, out of Auntie Manya's fist and rushed away, hotly and unsteadily, sinking into something hot and unsteady. Her head was bursting inside with frequent little explosions, as if tiny fuses were burning out, one after another, unable to withstand the voltage. Until everything that had to be erased had been erased.

(It wasn't until thirty years later, watching a leisurely BBC documentary about a family of orangutans, that Lidochka mentally paused when a male who'd barely recaptured his young from an alligator jumped on shore, hoarsely began howling like a human, and then lifted his mutilated dead baby toward the sky, maybe punishing, maybe reproaching, maybe trying to understand. Lidochka winced and then her head clouded with an oily murkiness, as if she were looking at the world through glasses—but they were someone else's glasses, with someone else's dioptres, hurriedly grabbed with greasy fingers from someone else's desk. They didn't help. Not at all.

(And then the male cautiously placed his young on the ground and all the orangutans took turns sniffing the motionless, mutilated little body as if they were saying goodbye. They filed away, awkward and stooped by evolution, instantly and happily forgetting everything because forgetting means living for them. 'Awfully sad, isn't it?' said Luzhbin, blinking a lot. Like all deliberately harsh people, he readily shed tears about trivial things. Lidochka nodded in agreement. She'd been broken of crying from pity back in school, when she was nine. 'Want a peach?' Luzhbin stretched, flustered, for the fruit bowl, and damn if he wasn't sniffling like a girl. No, Lidochka said, Sorry. I'm allergic to peaches.)

Children are constructed sturdily, very sturdily. No matter how the grown-up Lidochka tried to remember the summer of eighty-five—after July 24, rather than before—all she could get were vivid, painful flashes. A white and light blue flowered coverlet on the bed in the room. Papa lying the whole day on the next bed, face to the wall; the unprotected pink skin on the back of his head showing through reddish fluff. On the airplane—Lidochka was flying on a plane for the first time in her life!—a very nice pretty lady in tight-fitting dark blue brought around a tray of 'Takeoff' hard candies that were surprisingly itty-bitty, only half the usual size. Lidochka took one and quietly said thank you, like Mama'd taught her. Have another, the stewardess said. Very human, sympathetic wrinkles made their way through both her cordial professional grin and her 'Ballet' foundation makeup so thick you could spread it on a sandwich. Thank you, Lidochka whispered again, taking another. It was interesting to be on a plane but it was stuffy and smelled like pine air freshener and the ghost of someone's long-ago vomit. Papa cried the whole six hours they flew to Ensk. Without stopping. Six whole hours.

Who took on all the unbearable tasks, who gathered the documents and procured the coffin, who helped transport it across the whole country? Who? Lidochka never found out. They didn't bring her to the funeral so she stayed at home, sedately playing with her dolls under the watch of a taciturn neighbor equipped with knitting needles. The dolls made soup and went visiting, and East German Lelya with the squeaky golden hair even married a rabbit. Lelya was almost as tall as Lidochka herself and Mama had even altered one of Lidochka's dresses for her: it was white, for special days, and had a horrible burn on the chest from a careless iron. Mama had hidden the burn under a big bow, dooming the white-silked Lelya to eternal matrimonial aspirations. What do you do for work, Lelya? Me? I'm a bride!

When the doorbell rang, Lidochka was pondering who to appoint to be Lelya and the rabbit's child: a bug-eyed puppy or a plastic Hurvinek figurine whose little arms moved. The neighbor lady attempted to extract herself from her chair in four maneuvers—remove glasses, set down glasses, drop yarn ball, rub small of back—but Lidochka was already dashing to the front door, jumping for joy, it's Mamochka, Mamochka came, I just know it! The neighbor lady finally broke free from the captivity of her furniture and furtively crossed herself. Outside the door stood an unfamiliar woman wearing a dress of an improbable and troublingly nocturnal color. She was very pretty, very, forget the stewardess. She was almost as pretty as Mama, but her lips were way too red. The woman came in after moving Lidochka to the side without looking, as if she were a small and not particularly valuable object.

'But where's Mama?' Lidochka asked, stretching her mouth so she could began howling as artfully as possible.

'She died,' the woman very calmly said. The neighbor crossed herself again.

'But what about Papa?' Lidochka didn't know what 'died' was but she'd called off the howling, just in case.

The woman's lips trembled a tiny bit, as if she'd intended to kiss the air but reconsidered.

'Your papa will be back soon,' she said, finally looking at Lidochka.

The woman's eyes turned out to be blue-gray, translucent, and smooth, with some kind of complex graphite tint in their very depths. But Mama's eyes had been tawny. Tawny and cheery, like a tawny, cheery dog. Later—for the rest of her life—Lidochka was most afraid, more than anything in the world, she'd forget that.

'And who, may I ask, are you?' The neighbor lady finally came out of her fog after gazing mistrustfully at the double strand of pearls around the mysterious guest's neck: the individual pearls were large and completely identical, and they went together with the wonderful modesty of very expensive, very simple things.

Probably artificial, the neighbor lady reassured herself: she was a professional market researcher and inspired envier, now on a much-deserved pension. Her hope was unfounded: the pearls were genuine pink-gray saltwater pearls patiently cultivated in a tender, living, oystery darkness. Just about everything of Galina Petrovna Lindt's was genuine: only the very best and most expensive. With the exception of her own life, but nobody knew that, thank God.

'Who am I?' Galina Petrovna raised her eyebrows sympathetically, as if the neighbor lady were insane and didn't know the reigning personage whose portrait hung in every home's holy corner, wrinkly from the incense of admiring love and an ever-boiling samovar. 'Who am I? Are you serious?'

The neighbor lady instantly shrank and retreated back into her pathetic life, into her crowded one-room apartment with angular village-themed patterns stenciled on whitewashed walls.

'Let's go,' Galina Petrovna said. She nudged Lidochka toward a door nobody had thought to close. And Lidochka obe-

diently stepped over the threshold of her own life.
Lidochka figured out, though not immediately, that her grandmother had inherited her.

Her grandmother's name was Galina Petrovna and she was to be addressed in formal terms. Lidochka tried a variation—'Grandma Galya'—for a while but it was rejected. In the first place, it sounded far too provincial and, in the second, someone might think you had a hundred grandmothers and didn't know which one you were talking to. This was true: Lidochka didn't have a hundred grandmothers or grandfathers, either, for that matter. She did, however, have a grandmother and grandfather who lived in Mama and Papa's bedroom. Mama sometimes took them off the wall and affectionately ran a finger across a black-and-white man in a high-collared military jacket and a curly-haired woman who'd placed a light, round hand that even looked happy on her husband's captain shoulderboards. The woman had dimples on her cheeks and a long strand of beads, and the man had a moustache like a frowning little brush. And these, Barbariska, are my mother and father, said Mamochka, your grandmother and grandfather. Where are they, Lidochka asked: she knew the answer in advance, like in a fairytale, and was as happy as any child to know in advance, once and for all, the natural order of things. Far, far away from here, in a wonderful and fantastic land, her mother said sadly, meaning maybe heaven or maybe the Far East Military District and a snow-covered bridge. A truck dove off that bridge when its not-so-bright driver, a soldier with big ears, dozed off at the wheel, populating his intricate final dreams with a platoon chilled to the bone in the back and a captain who'd hitched a ride at the edge of the city of Bikin and gotten into the truck's cab with his wife, who even in death clutched to her chest a table lamp and bright, sunny lampshade they'd purchased at the commissary.

But why don't Grandma and Grandpa come visit us? Lidochka impatiently tugged on Mamochka's arm as if she sensed it was wrong to think too much about the ice breaking under wheels or the black water, silent from the cold, that rushed up to meet the truck. But why, tell me. Why? Because it's very far away, Barbariska. Will we go see them? Absolutely, Mamochka promised, all serious. First Papa and I, then you. But it won't be for a long, long time. In a thousand million years? Lidochka even went breathless from such a grand figure. Even longer, Mamochka promised and stepped off an ottoman that looked like a plush strawberry on thick little legs. Here, let's go cook up some donuts, how about that? Lidochka squealed triumphantly, already feeling the promise of a fresh jar of jam and playing with flour; her grandmother and grandfather went back to the wall. They didn't honestly look much like a grandmother and grandfather.

But Galina Petrovna, well… Galina Petrovna wasn't like anyone else at all!

In the first place, she lived all alone in a huge apartment that looked like the picture of the castle in the big crackly book of Charles Perrault stories.

In the second place, running, jumping, and screaming weren't allowed. Meaning those things were no longer allowed at all, particularly in the apartment.

In the third place, a special woman came over every morning: Maryvanna put on an apron and tidied up all the rooms with the soulless, taciturn dispatch of a genuine machine. Mama had always been mad or singing when she tidied up. Maryvanna cooked meals, too, something new and fresh every day, and then she put yesterday's lunch or supper leftovers into special little containers for carrying food and took them away with her. She didn't speak with Lidochka, it was as if she didn't exist.

'Why does Maryvanna need the food?' Lidochka asked Galina Petrovna. She couldn't hold back, though she knew all too well what happened to curious Varvara, whose nose was torn off for putting it where it didn't belong. Mamochka and Papa hadn't allowed her to bother grownups she didn't know by asking questions. But if there weren't other adults, people she knew, that meant she was probably allowed to ask.

'What food?' Galina Petrovna tore herself away from the television, absentminded from her surprise. 'Oh, that food. I don't know, she probably takes it for her grandchildren.'

Lidochka quietly pondered for a minute. 'Is Maryvanna our grandmother, too?'

Galina Petrovna finally surfaced from her movie, *Bracelet-2*. About some foolish horse. Nobody knew how to make movies these days. 'What makes you think Maryvanna is our grandmother? And don't pick at the chair. You'll ruin it.'

Lidochka obediently stopped stroking the velvety upholstery. Maryvanna came every day, cooked, cleaned, made the beds, and did laundry. She took care of Lidochka and Galina Petrovna just like a grandmother's supposed to. Furthermore, as had just been revealed, she brought Lidochka and Galina Petrovna's leftover food to her grandchildren. Therefore, Galina Petrovna and Lidochka were also Maryvanna's grandchildren and they were, moreover, her very favorites. Lidochka didn't see a single hole in the logical chain of her reasoning. Everything was correct. Wasn't it?

Galina Petrovna shrugged her shoulders, annoyed. 'Your

head is so stuffed with silliness! Maria Ivanovna is my housekeeper. Why don't you go read or draw? You can read, can't you?'

Lidochka got down from the chair, offended. She could read. She'd been reading for ages. And even by herself, by the way.

Something else was strange: Lidochka'd never had any idea that Galina Petrovna so much as existed. It was incomprehensible. Because either you have a grandmother—even if she's only a wall grandmother—or you don't have a grandmother. Of course she could demand an explanation from Papa but for some reason Papa wasn't coming back even though Galina Petrovna'd promised he'd come soon. Lidochka vaguely remembered Papa had been at Galina Petrovna's the first night she'd spent there. She'd been put to bed on a leather couch that felt alive and all elephant-like to the touch. Papa had knelt by the couch, softly whimpering like a puppy and wobbling a little. Even through thick layers of sleep, Lidochka could sense his homey, warm scent, a wonderful mix of tobacco and a cologne Mama said made him smell like bay leaves in soup; sometimes she even called him Little Bay.

'Little Bay,' Lidochka muttered, turning over. The pillow was unfamiliar and too soft. Mamochka said sleeping on a soft pillow was bad for you. Papa went silent, scared. 'Sleep, little girl, sleep, little bunny,' he whispered, trying with unseen, blind hands to find Lidochka amidst the couch's many outgrowths. 'Just look, nobody unbraided your hair for the night, your grandmother hasn't figured that out but don't be mad at her, she'll learn, you'll see…'

Lidochka tried to lift her heavy eyelids but nothing worked. But where's Mama? she asked in an unsatisfied voice, shaggy from sleep. Get Mama… Papa was quiet, as if he were gathering strength, and then he buried his huge burning face in Lidochka and she could feel his teeth jumping and knocking through the thin fabric of her pajamas.

'Knock off the hysterics, Boris,' Galina Petrovna ordered, appearing out of nowhere in the doorway. A ghostly white nightgown, a robe with firm silk dragons woven right in. 'You're acting like a girl.'

The side of Lidochka's pajamas was soaked through with tears when Papa lifted his head.

'You always hated her,' Papa said quietly. 'Always.'

Galina Petrovna shrugged her shoulders and disappeared and then Papa disappeared, too, melting into the slow night air after Lidochka turned over, no longer strong enough to resist the gentle pressure of sleep that drifted in from all sides…

Papa was nowhere to be found in the morning and Lidochka paced around the unfamiliar apartment for a long time, slapping her heels on the floor until she wandered upon Galina Petrovna standing at a window in a halo of hot tobacco. Mama had never smoked. Papa did, but Mama didn't.

'Where's Papa?' Lidochka asked sullenly.

Galina Petrovna turned. The cigarette in her fingers was astoundingly long.

'He left,' she said.

'What about Mama?'

'Mama died.'

Lidochka silently tried on this impossible fate. 'I want to go home,' she said.

'This is your home now.'

That wasn't true and both Lidochka and Galina Petrovna

knew it perfectly well. But they had no choice, so Lidochka and Galina Petrovna began living together.

Galina Petrovna got started by bringing Lidochka to the doctor. In a long white car with a flowing name: 'Volga.' Galina Petrovna even got behind the wheel herself, which was surprising, too, because in Lidochka's former life only nice, sweet men with huge calloused hands drove cars. Taxi drivers. Mamochka always raised indignant eyebrows at their fingernails, demonstrating to Lidochka what happens if you don't wash your hands before eating: drivers' fingernails were black, cracking, and covered with grimy uncultured layers. Buses, however, essentially drove along on their own, but on buses you could stick your nose into the stuffy sheepskin tails of someone's fur coat or touch the bright crisp hem of a stranger's dress-up skirt. Lidochka loved buses.

Galina Petrovna settled Lidochka, all fresh and dressed-up like a doll, on the front seat, tightly strapping her in with the safety belt as if she were tying up a holiday bouquet with a ribbon. 'Don't squirm,' she commanded, and then the street came at them like a happy puppy, all light and smooth, with long shadows and blindingly sunny-green squares. Lidochka almost immediately felt queasy because the utility poles quickly changed into tree trunks, and then the tree trunks changed into sunny, mirror-like windows: the effect was like running your hand over a piano keyboard. Beyond that, the Volga had a strong, sweet stench of gasoline and Galina Petrovna's perfume, which was as thick and unbearable as currant preserves that explode in the heat and rudely ooze from the jar. It was Dior's Poison, an aroma that hadn't yet become legendary. It was still a novelty, released in 1985 and incredible even in

Paris, the very same year that—just now—the Volga flowed along the Ensk streets with Lidochka strapped into her seat, swinging her little legs, and trying to touch the car's rattling floor with a sandal. Futilely. Utility pole, tree trunk, window, turn. Tree trunk, window, turn, utility pole.

Galina Petrovna spent three hundred rubles—three hundred!—for Poison, which was more, a lot more, than the monthly salary of many citizens of the huge Soviet Union. But the more money you spend, the more money you'll have, that was a very simple and very understandable rule. Besides, who determines the cost of an ounce of happiness? Or what monetary units can quantify the sound of the glassine wrap as it broke and then slipped off a green box that looked like it might even be malachite? And the purplish-blue vial as round and smooth as a young female breast. The transparent prism of its tight cap. Galina Petrovna drew the vial's cool, damp neck along her own hot, pulsing neck. Orange tree honey, raspberry, ambergris, opoponax, and coriander. The Ferula Opoponax plant is mortally wounded to yield its resin. The tears and blood of that herb smell of a spicy poison, the purest. I don't think anyone else in Sovietdom has this perfume yet, purred the faithful Norochka, secret supplier of the Ensk elite, a small rat in the big black market and diplomatic routes. She thrust Galina Petrovna's three hundred rubles into the half-opened pink maw of a show-offy purse as if it were a bra, using a petty thief's quick and efficient motion, a motion that didn't fit with either her imported outfit, intricately designed down to the last dart and yoke, or her drawn-out, offhand air of a wealthy lady who's seen it all.

The car bounced over a treacherously gaping manhole cover and Lidochka barely managed to swallow a gigantic wooly gob of impending vomit. 'It smells,' she complained, looking straight ahead. She complained without much hope, just because. Galina Petrovna bent over, extending a strong hand (the reek of Poison and gasoline became tangible, as if Lidochka had been dunked in inky black, sweet snot) and then the rapid outside air agilely shoved its cool, tensed paw through the window glass like a tomcat, painlessly batting at Lidochka's lips and round, sweaty forehead. It was already a little easier to breathe. But now a dreadful rumbling roar had joined the dangerous monotony of the rhythm of utility pole, tree trunk, window, turn. All the city's noises rushed past, hurriedly pushing one another aside as they tried to elbow their way through the open window: they got stuck instead and, of course, began wailing on just one completely unbearable, raging note.

Lidochka looked sideways at Galina Petrovna to distract herself a little but Galina Petrovna was caught up in endless, very mechanical motions. That made matters worse: Galina Petrovna's strong knees moved quickly under a skirt the color of delicate, fresh-baked milk, as if she were kneading something stubborn, resistant, and evil with the unseen soles of her feet. Her right hand (with a large, ripe ruby cabochon on one finger) kept lowering onto a handle that stuck right out of the floor. The handle twitched with a predatory crunch as if some sort of important but invisible bone was breaking, the car roared sorrowfully in response, and Galina Petrovna's hand returned to the wheel to complete its flowing, turning motion: it all resembled some strange mechanical dance that was unbearable for both the audience and the dancer. The motion Galina Petrovna made with her head was particularly torturous: she looked into three mirrors in turn—above, left, right—and a sculpted honey-brown curl above her forehead jerked each time, falling out of the overall, set rhythm for a hundredth of a second.

At some point her complex rhythmic pattern arrived at the same resonance as the unceasing flashes outside the window and the smell in the car intensified, becoming almost festive, choral, and ear-splittingly loud. Lidochka already knew it was too late of course but she still tried to free her arms from the seatbelt or at least squint. 'Don't squirm, I told you,' ordered Galina Petrovna, angry as she squealed the brakes and then—oopsy!—Lidochka vomited.

Her dress (light blue and new, with a satin waistband and a finely ruffled flounce on the hems) hardly suffered, but a sobbing Lidochka washed out her own little white socks with tiny little pompoms in the clinic bathroom under Galina Petrovna's supervision. Good God, what is with this child! Rinse them better. Now squeeze them out properly. Don't hold your hands like that. Not like that! Galina Petrovna grabbed the defiled socks from Lidochka's hands and quickly—squeeze, squeeze—wrung them out over the sink. The cabochon on her finger caught the faucet's spiral trickle and, now liberated, filled the whole bathroom with a damp, crimson blaze. Smooth pink patches of light galloped over tiled walls and disappeared. Rinse out your mouth, ordered Galina Petrovna, and Lidochka obediently rolled a cool ball of chlorine-scented water around her mouth. And set it free. She picked a strand of bitter, sticky drool off her chin. She wasn't nauseous anymore, other than a little turning in her stomach, but that was more from shame. Galina Petrovna rolled the laundered socks into a tight, damp little ball and quickly tossed them in her purse. Let's go, she ordered. And they went.

The lady doctor looked like a round white meringue cookie glued together from two light, crunchy, sugary halves. And who is this doll that's come to see me, she said, stretching her words with the sweet, meringue-like voice of an experienced pediatrician and crouching in front of Lidochka. Lidochka backed up a bit just in case, expecting something awful like a tongue depressor or a syringe: she obviously couldn't expect anything good from a person with a voice like that. But the lady doctor's smooth fingers palpated nimbly and painlessly, and now say aaaah, what a smart little girl, lift up those arms, good, now let's have a listen to you. The disc of a stethoscope so icy it was almost even hot, then the hurried pattering of anxious, tickly goose bumps. Lidochka drew together her shoulder blades, now covered with goose bumps, and giggled. Don't breathe, ordered the lady doctor, serious. Now breathe. Lidochka giggled again and Galina Petrovna, annoyed, threatened her with a finger.

'A perfectly healthy little girl,' the sugary lady doctor finally said, helping Lidochka on with her dress. 'And what a cutie, she's like a copy of you, Galina Petrovna. Do you have any specific concerns? Maybe Lida isn't eating well? Or sleeping? That would be completely understandable after all that stress. And how are you feeling?' The lady doctor delicately lowered her voice as if she were inviting Galina Petrovna for a spin in an intoxicating verbal waltz. Like many other doctors for the institutional elite, she spent the greater part of her days stupefied from producing an insufferable, well-paid elation for the benefit of high-ranking patients, and only gossip kept her sane.

Galina Petrovna angrily jerked her shoulder. She didn't intend to gossip, particularly about herself.

'I'm absolutely fine,' she said, cutting off the lady doctor. 'Relax. But examine the child properly. Maybe she has worms?'

'Oh, come now, Galina Petrovna, what worms?' The lady doctor even seemed a little offended for Lidochka, who was still sitting right on the chair, swinging her little sandals. There was a telltale spot from the washed-out vomit on the flounce of her blue dress and her left heel smarted a bit. 'The little girl is perfectly healthy, thank God. Of course we can do tests if you want but…'

A wooden-faced older nurse came out from behind a screen as if the word 'tests' had called her to life.

'Olga Valeryevna, write up a referral. Fecal worm and egg. Lidia Borisovna Lindt. Lidochka, your papa's Borya, isn't that right?' Lidochka didn't even have a chance to nod before Galina Petrovna stood, took her by the hand, and left the office without saying goodbye.

'Well, now, she is foul,' the nurse said to the closed door with unexpected fury. 'Worms. As if she'd dragged a kitten home from the dump.'

The puked-in Volga, all hot from the sun but carefully cleaned inside, was waiting for them by the guard booth, where Galina Petrovna had left it. The guard had gone all-out for them; he was a fat, cheery man charged with protecting the elite clinic from rank-and-file fellow citizens with ulcers and sinusitis that were of no interest to anyone. Oof, you sure got carsick, you little bug, the nice man said to Lidochka, sympathizing and slipping a Barbariska candy into her slack hand. The candy had practically lost its original confectionary appearance after a long stay in his uniform pants. Though she was stunned and dispirited about the mysterious word 'worms' and seeing the Volga again, Lidochka obediently mumbled a thank you she extracted from Mamochka's eternally stuffed pedagogical storage bins.

'LazarIosich's little granddaughter?' the guard asked brightly, attempting to pat the hot crown of Lidochka's head before Galina Petrovna nimbly pulled Lidochka out from under his affectionate hand, thrusting the earned three-note into it instead so he'd shut his mouth and not get too familiar.

One car door slammed, then the other, and Lidochka again found herself in the unbearable interior of an automobile with a familiar stench, a sharp blend of the scents of hot plastic, chlorine, and fresh vomit.

'And who is that, LazarIosich?' she asked, trying to breathe with her mouth and not move, so as not to disturb the live vomit gob that was again establishing itself inside her.

Galina Petrovna lifted her brow a tiny bit and looked at Lidochka with unexpected respect, as if she were looking at a very adult and very brave person.

'Lazar Iosifovich Lindt was an academician,' she said, slowly, incomprehensibly, and a little sing-songy, though of course that wasn't an explanation for a five-year-old child or even much of an explanation in general: it was more like a spell that killed a memory, or maybe a prayer that exorcised demons. Lidochka opened her mouth a little, not understanding. 'He's your grandfather.'

Chapter Two: Marusya

He turned up in Moscow out of nowhere, as if God had brought him to life right at the doorstep of the Second Moscow State University on a November morning in 1918 that crunched with frost. Your obliging imagination has probably already fanned out gloomy daguerreotypes that have darkened over time: cold, hunger, ruin, unbridled cannibalism, horror, fratricide, and typhus.

Things weren't actually that bad in Moscow, though. The city had been declared the capital again as of March 1918 and though it wasn't quite clear which country's capital it was, at least the government's hasty move from Petrograd guaranteed crows weren't feasting on corpses in the streets. The public that crowded the Komissarzhevskaya Theater for Aristophanes's *Lysistrata* was by no means bloated from hunger, the Zamoskvoretsky Sports Club's soccer team won the city championship, and the Petrovka tennis courts were ruled by Vsevolod Verbitsky, an actor at the Moscow Academic Art Theater, a real sweetheart, and the dandy who'd taken first place in revolutionary Moscow's first tennis championship that very same year, 1918. Pleasantly squeaky leather jackets for both genders were coming into style thanks to Sverdlov's light hand, anything could be obtained through a private sale, and brunettes with high cheekbones teased with their eyes and their knees just as in former, peaceful times that might have even been rather dull. Intermittent food supplies, the proximity of the Germans, and crowds of soldiers in various degrees of drunkenness didn't seem like undeniable forerunners of the apocalypse: they were more likely the unavoidable costs of a great turning point, things as closely and vexingly linked as mosquitoes and a marvelous evening at the dacha, marriage and being in love, or Shrovetide and greasy heartburn cozily curled up behind the breastbone.

Plenty of guileless human garbage and wreckage of individual fates ended up in Moscow, too: the newly minted revolution had uprooted nothing less than entire social classes and nations. There were, in particular, many Jews—now that's who Soviet power certainly gave everything to, in the beginning, in the heat of the moment. Crazed, awkward, and restless without their usual Pale of Settlement, they made their way to the capital, perhaps to experience some of their own impossible Jewish happiness or to personally assure themselves that, yes, of course, their suffering was over. This time for sure. The wiliest and sharpest had already fit in, adapted, and acclimated, as if from habit: some were in trade, some in rapidly devaluing money, some in positions never seen before, taking things slowly, a little at a time. Treading softly, as the zoological anti-Semite who was also a great Russian writer used to say.

For some, though, there wasn't the slightest reason to adapt since they themselves, the best sons of the Jewish people, participated in and inspired the Russian rebellion. Its futile participants and relentless inspirations, it must be said. It was they, by the way, who became the very first victims of the demons that were set loose a few vivid and faltering years later when the gigantic imperial pig grunted, rose from its century-old puddle, and took to chomping indifferently on its own piglets, not making much distinction between kosher and not-so-kosher. But oh, what a holy and frenzied army they were in the early Soviet years, those youthful commissars, those ancient sons of Abraham! Incorruptible, fanatical, ruthless, and wonderful in their idiotic heroism, it was they who brought the Russian Revolution its distinct Jewish flavor, a flavor that decades later caused Jews themselves to spit furiously, some with venom, others with the realest of blood. Which one, as academician Lindt said, depended on which side you came down on.

Lindt himself, however, didn't belong to either the merchant or commissar class and, truth be told, he generally found very little use or benefit in his Jewishness. He considered Jews a timid and peaceable little nation with an extremely unfortunate historical fate. And, well, think about it: small-scale trade for centuries and being made to feel small, living with your bags packed, shivering and huddling at night, knowing that no matter how you try, you could be kicked to the curb with all your worldly possessions at the very first sign of trouble. Just like that, so you don't get under foot and reek of your garlic.

'You know, Lazar,' Chaldonov said, wrinkling his brow, 'the Jewish anti-Semite is even more repulsive than the slutty nun.' Chaldonov was one of the fathers and founders of contemporary hydro- and aerodynamics, an academician, a beaming pillar of Soviet science, and such a fundamentally genuine Russian that he didn't need any passport to prove it. Just a glance at his doughy nose, colorless brows, and the general contour of his simple-hearted, log-like physiognomy was like an instant high-speed screening of the entire simple history of Russian tillers of the soil, along with all that history's whooping, whistling, forced labor, and equally forced, almost compulsory, merriment.

'Come now, Sergey Alexandrovich, what kind of anti-Semite am I?' Lindt said, grinning and displaying big, crafty teeth. 'I'm just speaking up for the truth. How can anyone call a people great and chosen if it's hopelessly fucked up everything on earth including its own Temple, and then nourished itself for thousands of year on just tear-stained memories? They haven't even managed to create a decent cultural legacy!'

'For heaven's sake, Lazar, but what about the Bible?' Chaldonov asked, frightened. He'd been around since 1869 but even toward 1934 he still hadn't forgotten the pedagogical persuasiveness of a deacon who used his strong fists and gift for enlightenment to ram theology and love for God into a dense-headed village congregation. 'How about the Bible?'

'What Bible, Sergey Alexandrovich, I beg you!' Lindt was openly laughing now. 'Just about everybody wrote it, you might as well cite the Upanishads and the Torah as examples, too! I'm talking about cultural legacy, not religious ravings. Where is your Jews' great literature? Where are the paintings? And the architecture?'

Chaldonov mentally crossed himself and just as mentally muttered to himself, Give us this day our daily bread—dear, familiar, and calming words that meant almost nothing but nourished the spirit's most calloused sorrows and wounds like holy oil. Generations of Lindt ancestors prayed in unison with Chaldonov, praying unseen, unheard, and in another language but to the very same God. They were quiet wanderers, desperate eternal Jews who truly hadn't created either labyrinthine palaces or large-scale canvases or fat-assed sculptures, nothing anyone would be sorry to abandon if exiled. But it was that prayerful striving, both unending and bitter, that had seeped so far into all of world culture that melancholy Jewish eyes or equally melancholy Jewish noses stuck out of every corner. They—meaning, oh, good Lord, you, yes, of course you—are the divine First Cause and spiritual origin for everything rational and civilized. Can you swallow that, Lazar?

Lindt shrugged: he hadn't swallowed anyone's unpleasantries, particularly religious ones, ever in his whole life.

Sometimes Chaldonov thought the Creator had just been in a rush to cram the essence of Lindt's genius into the first available earthly body, as if He himself lacked the power to hold that essence in His hands. Rather like a charred, burning-hot baked potato with bursting sugary sides: you start off just honestly trying to toss it from hand to hand, trying to cool it, but then you drop it in grass you can't see at night anyway, and to hell with it, it's so hot you couldn't handle it, but at least it didn't fall in a cow patty, thanks for the small things.

Lindt's body was so humiliatingly small, frail, and sinewy when it randomly turned up at the Second Moscow State University in November 1918 that the freezing young soldier with the big ears who guarded the entrance initially took Lindt for a street urchin: the rags he wore were absolutely outstanding, as if they'd come from the Imperial Maly Theater. It dawned on the Red Army man that Lindt would go around begging, so he ordered him, almost affectionately, 'Go on, get out of here, you dirty little Jew boy, there's nothing to fucking snatch up here. It's just scholarlyish gentlemen. They don't got anything to feed on, either.'

'I'm here to see Chaldonov, Sergey Alexandrovich,' the dirty little Jew boy politely said, like an adult. And then he firmly requested, 'Announce me, please.'

The secretary of the Physics and Mathematics Department (which had natural, mathematics, and chemistry-pharmaceutical divisions) brought Lindt to Chaldonov. In reality, however, the department and the secretary didn't quite exist because the department as a whole—with all its divisions— still belonged to the future, though the secretary chronically remained in his cozy past as a university privatdozent so as not to lose his mind, since in the past there'd been a reliable salary as well as spiritual and moral pursuits appropriate to his title. Lindt, however, wasn't aware of the circumstances and didn't sense anything remotely wild or Hoffmannesque about the situation: he generally kept a distance from hysterical and esoteric whims or empty reflection on the futility of everything. In that respect he wasn't Russian and he wasn't, of course, from the intelligentsia. He was simply a genius firmly standing on earth, a genius, moreover, in the most biological sense of the word: a classic brain pathology. Honestly. It was probably some sort of rare mutation. It's not my fault things worked out that way.

Sergey Alexandrovich Chaldonov groaned with dissatisfaction when he heard scratching sounds, much like a stray dog, outside the door, sounds that usually preceded a downcast appearance from the department secretary.

Sergey Alexandrovich Chaldonov was pressed for time.

Chaldonov had been pressed for time for almost thirteen years now, since about 1905, when he (a brilliant mathematician, by the way) agreed to direct the Higher Women's Courses, bringing only trouble upon himself. All hell broke loose: firewood, trustees, expansion, papers, female students gripped by hormonal turmoil: Get married, you fools, get married right away! Now, however, all that fuss felt like a pleasant, postprandial nap to Chaldonov. Being the director of the Higher Women's Courses is one thing under the Tsar-Father but just you try, my dear sir, to turn those very same Women's Courses into a second Moscow State University in a month, especially under a new revolutionary government that's inexperienced and doesn't know itself what it wants but makes demands anyway, heaps of them. Assisted by a Nagant revolver.

The secretary thrust his bald head into the office after delicately scratching at the door with his claws. Chaldonov despondently set aside protocol No.77/113 of the session of the Board of the People's Commissariat on Education. The protocol ordered 'reorganizing the Higher Women's Courses into II Moscow State University, making it a mixed educational institution but not considering it a newly established higher educational institution.'

Everything about this sheet of paper categorically disgusted him: its yellowish color, its roughness, and its plebeian, official tone, unbearable for a descendent of peasants ('allocate for financial support of the courses in the form of an advance of 1/12 of the estimate given by them'). Most terrible of all was a list of those on the board, people absolutely unknown to Chaldonov. D.N. Artemyev, V.I. Kalinin, M.N. Pokrovsky, V.M. Pozner, and D.B. Kalinin were at least somewhat bearable. But the name Lengnik, which immediately smacked of both a toothache and Swift's unpronounceable Houyhnhnms, caused Sergey Alexandrovich nothing short of physical suffering. Fortunately, a considerate guardian angel had saved the chronically sleep-deprived Chaldonov by removing the completely intolerable details: Lengnik's first name and patronymic (Fridrikh Vilgelmovich) and his Party nicknames

(Kurz and Kol). Without that assistance, the future academician and laureate would have been lying on the parquet of his unheated director's office with a self-inflicted gunshot wound to the head. What are you waiting for? Pavel Nikolayevich? Come in. What is it? Yet another order from on high?

'No, Sergey Alexandrovich, no orders. Someone's come to see you,' the secretary said, remaining between the corridor (his back side) and Chaldonov's office (his head). In some sense, this was his usual position between past and future, too.

'Well, who the hell is it?' As a human being, of course Chaldonov couldn't help but sympathize with a secretary who hung between two worlds, but he couldn't contain himself because one must work at work, after all, my dear gentleman! Indeed! Work! No matter what!

The secretary lingered, unable to decide quite how to classify the raggedy adolescent who carried himself with the wonderfully cheery calm of a person born rich and free, despite his obvious stench and lack of washing.

'Tell Sergey Alexandrovich that I have questions about the dynamics of nonholonomic systems,' Lindt said quietly. His down-at-the-heel shoes stood out so much it was best not to even think about his feet.

'Ehhh,' the secretary said, definitively deciding the fate of Soviet science because the bored Lindt entered Chaldonov's huge office unannounced after agilely pushing aside the privatdozent's rear end, which had been blocking his path to a bright future.

It was more like a conspiracy than anything else. Or perhaps some children's game where the rules are made up and changed on the go, so the only thing you remember is a feeling of fanciful happiness that's only accessible in an early childhood that doesn't even realize yet that it's childhood.

Lindt and Chaldonov sat at the conference table and deftly tossed a small notebook back and forth to one other. Lindt had extracted the notebook—so greasy it was nearly edible—from under the heap of rags he was wearing. On its empty pages Chaldonov quickly wrote some letters, figures, and words incomprehensible to the normal human, then Lindt accepted the pass and wrote his own figures above those letters. Both players sometimes even quacked from an almost physical pleasure, as if they'd actually gone at it playing volleyball, heh-hehing, tensing their resonant, healthy, ideal muscles, and sending each other a ball that was just as resonant, healthy, and ideal.

Then Lindt finally got stuck for a few minutes on some sort of unheard-of formula that looked more like an intricate insect bristling with a dozen grasping pedipalps and chelicerae. Chaldonov tapped on the table with a short, impatient drumming.

'So?'

'I don't know,' Lindt admitted. He covered the formula with his hand as if he were afraid it would creep out through his fingers, which were all swollen from the cold, and hide with a quiet, dry rustle in the unearthly air of a darkening world.

'What did I tell you, colleague?' Chaldonov happily said, summarizing as he and Lindt suddenly began laughing from joy as if it weren't November 1918, crunching with icy mud, but June of peaceful, sunny 1903, and it wasn't a little notebook lying in front of them but an unswaddled, satisfied, pink-bottomed baby twisting its chubby little legs, and the two of them had just saved the baby from inevitable misfortune. Perhaps even from death.

'Will you take me on as a student, Sergey Alexandrovich?' Lindt quietly asked. Somehow it suddenly became clear that the blotches and streaks on his gaunt, boyish face weren't from dirt, weren't from hunger, and weren't even from thousand-kilometer tiredness because, you know, he'd had to walk most of the distance... It was the twilight of his fate, the shadow of a large gift, a very large and frightfully distant gift under whose shelter Lindt had already had to live eighteen years of his vast and solemn life, and would need to live a minimum of sixty-three more.

'Student?' Chaldonov repeated in a threatening tone. 'Fuck that! He wants to study, just take a look at this goose! You're going to work with me, work! That's what we're going to do!'

Chaldonov laboriously got up from his desk, opened his office door, and brayed out into the depths, into the distance, into an indefinite personal future, 'Pavel Nikolayevich, Pavel Nikolayevich, register our new co-worker right now! What's your name, colleague?' Chaldonov said, catching himself and turning to the wondrous foundling.

Lazar. Lazar Iosifovich Lindt.

Chaldonov nodded—maybe memorizing, maybe saluting—and went off himself in search of the lost privatdozent, without waiting for a response from the future. When Chaldonov returned an hour later, laden with cards, certificates, and questionnaires, Lazar Iosifovich Lindt was sound asleep after dropping his lousy, uncombed head right on his open notebook. Floating on his face—at last!—were not the shadows of demonic wings but the quick ripples of short and seemingly completely childlike dreams.

That evening, Chaldonov brought Lindt home to Ostozhenka Street and his huge professorial apartment, all dusky and creaking, with the appetizing smell of books in nice bindings and sedate home-cooked dinners with four courses for five guests. When Chaldonov hesitated with his thoughts for a moment at the door, Lindt quickly touched him gently on the sleeve.

'Are you sure this is all right, Sergey Alexandrovich? I do have somewhere to spend the night.'

'What do you mean? Stop with the silly ceremony, colleague,' Chaldonov growled, taken aback as he tugged the doorbell. What the hell, does he read minds or something? With abilities like those and considering the electromagnetic nature of radiation… Oh and Marusya will give me the what-for, Lord-help-us-and-have-mercy. The what-for, that much is more than certain.

The front door swung open—without the clarifying questions or bolt clanging that were completely forgivable in the city where the Great October Socialist Revolution had just taken place—and a woman appeared on the threshold along with a light so bright and dense that Lazar Lindt squinted for a second. The light was too alive and too strong for him to write it off to the mundane kerosene lamp that Maria Nikitichna Chaldonova (known familiarly as Marusya) held in her hands. Even much, much later, whole years after, Lindt associated Chaldonov's wife and their whole family with that particular light.

Maria Nikitichna had the gentle and unusually lively face of a coarse and somewhat common type that went out of fashion in the second decade of the twentieth century and now lives exclusively on pre-Revolutionary photocards. There was no doubt she'd been pretty in her youth, also in a way that's already forgotten, back when a sedate allure went along with female beauty and a girl from a good family was most certainly supposed to cry profusely at trifling matters, have skin as fresh as cool milk, and spend whole days in bed during menstruation, lying about in skirts specially made for the purpose. All those gentle requirements and conventions receded into the background in Chaldonov's wife, subdued by the light she seemed to radiate all by herself, as if it were even against her will. Lindt searched his whole life for similar glistening reflections in the faces of many women, a great many. But he never did grasp that a woman just does not exist on her own. She is a body and a reflected light. But there, you took my light and left. And all my light left me. A quote. The year nineteen hundred thirty-eight. Georgy Ivanov. Nabokov would have confirmed that an attentive reader would know where to place the quotation marks.

'Marusya, take a look at who I found,' Chaldonov said, cheerfully and a bit afraid, as if he were a little boy and Lindt was a shivering, flea-bitten puppy that was already tremendously beloved, and the only person deciding if he could stay to live in the house—or if they were going back to the dump together—was Mama, who probably still hadn't forgotten yesterday's behavioral demerit. Maria Nikitichna looked questioningly at her husband.

'This is Lazar Iosifovich Lindt, my new colleague,' Chaldonov said, attempting to introduce his guest. The scheme to bring the foundling home felt less and less successful with each passing second. Like all well-bred people, Marusya possessed a temperament that generally stayed nicely under control but was also capable of exploding with remarkable speed.

Chaldonov knew this perfectly well: he couldn't possibly have known it better. When Lindt attempted to politely bow, the stairs, door, and lamp immediately began softly, quickly spinning around a dizzying axis. He wanted so very much to eat. Marusya was silent for another long second.

'Lice?' she asked Lindt, businesslike, as if she were asking his price at the market. Lindt nodded as if doomed. He had nothing, really, but his little notebook and his lice. 'Then be patient while I clean you up. We won't eat until after that, all right?'

An hour or so later they were already sitting in the dining room at a dinner table set according to rules that were becoming relics of the old regime even as they ate. Napkins crackled, silverware jingled heavily, and Lindt's head, shaved bare and emitting exultant flashes of light, protruded from the roomy collar of one of Chaldonov's shirts as if it were poking through a hole in the ice. (Chaldonov had sacrificed an excellent razor from the Aron Biber Manufacturing and Industrial Trading House in Warsaw, a pre-Revolutionary luxury, just perfect for your impenetrable thickets, colleague.) Real carrot tea with real saccharine glistened in Kuznetsov china cups and Marusya Nikitichna put a third potato (with melted butter!) on their guest's plate and affectionately persuaded him, eat, Lesik, it's scary to look at you, you're like some sort of head on legs, nothing more.

'And what a head, Marusya, what a head!' Chaldonov said, satisfied and boasting as he raised his knife and fork to the heavens. 'This young man is a genius, trust me. And you know I don't throw around words like that!'

'He might be a genius, but he's still very underfed,' Marusya laughed.

Lindt squinted: he was flustered, sated, and trying with all his might not to doze off. He'd already heard 'genius' more than once. But nobody had ever called him Lesik, either before or after. Ever.

He courageously refused a fourth potato, I'll return the favor as soon as I have some rationing cards, Maria Nikitichna. The Chaldonovs' protesting hands waved him off immediately. This was, of course, his winning ticket. Undeserved and unexpected. As if he'd been walking along the street, picked up a little gold key, and released a trapped fate. Lindt himself knew things didn't happen that way. But then there you go: his eyes dreamily close and everything quivers and blurs in the wet radiance of simple human happiness.

Maria Nikitichna stood to clear the dishes from the table and Chaldonov jumped right up to help her though of course he couldn't have been more tired but still he said, good Lord, Marusya, sit down, I'll do it myself, I'll do it. And because he looked at his wife with hungry adoration and because she smoothed an unattractive whitish curl over his forehead in passing, it was obvious that even thirty years of marriage might be something God needed, especially if you believe He really does exist. Lindt swallowed a bitter lump that had arisen out of nowhere. I'll have a life like this, too, he swore to himself. Just like this, no different. Love just like this, a Marusya just like this, a family just like this.

Maria Nikitichna Chaldonova was the biggest success of Chaldonov's life and the fact that they both knew this perfectly well lent the whole tenor of their family life that essential flavor of marvelous adventure without which a marriage quickly turns into a horribly dull and barely digestible dish, something like fried potatoes rewarmed thrice. Marusya was smarter, stronger, and morally loftier than Chaldonov, but the most important thing was that she was of a completely different and better human stock. Her whole family was marvelous: it was an old priestly family with roots extending to such an early Christian, apostolic age that it was immediately obvious why their home was so pleasant for adults, children, cats, a canary in its cage, and all the holy fools, stray, destitute, and itinerant folk without whom it's impossible to imagine either Russian life or service to a Russian God.

Marusya's family, however, had its own special relationship with God. Even their surname was wonderful, delicious, seminarian, and completely of God: Pitovranov. Even now, at age forty-nine, Chaldonov remembered the serious look on young Marusya's face when she explained to him, a twenty-year-old blockhead, that the Pitovranov name honored the prophet Elijah, who was fed by the ravens, the 'vran' in their name. Do you understand? Chaldonov nodded his tangled pale hair but understood only the dimples on Marusya's cheek and the gray polka dots on her smart, fitted cotton print dress, which was unbearably shameful to even think about, even if there was no way not to think about it.

'And the Lord said,' Marusya continued, importantly, '"Get you from here, and hide yourself by the brook Cherith, that is near the Jordan, and you shall drink of the brook; and I have commanded the ravens to feed you." Ravens, vran, like in our name. How could you not remember?'

'I remember very well,' Chaldonov sharply said, far sharper than usual, feeling like some damned village idiot. For some reason the thought that he was supposed to graduate from the Physics and Mathematics Department of Moscow University in about a year with an applied mathematics specialty only intensified the torturously sharp pain of the sweaty shirt under his arms and the general physical awkwardness he experienced from the very presence of this girl, the top of whose head barely reached the button loop on his lapel.

'Then go on, if you remember!' Marusya demanded but Chaldonov's only response was to mutely and beseechingly spread his hands. He knew he'd failed the most important exam of his life, shamefully, pitifully, and for forever, with no right to take it again.

'But Papa said you're a person with an outstanding mind,' said Marusya, disenchanted. She continued the quotation simply, as if it were verse, without even the slightest bit of a churchly lilt. '"So Elijah went and did as the Lord told him: he went and dwelt by the brook Cherith. And the ravens brought him food in the morning and in the evening," for God can do miraculous things to take care of those who serve Him faithfully and depend on Him.'

Chaldonov nodded again and submissively followed Marusya into the next room, where the large Pitovranov family had already settled in at the dinner table, banging chairs and happily squabbling with one another: Alyoshka's sneaking in by the pies again, Pa, tell him, will you, once and for all, the insatiable Mammon! Pitovranov Senior, a theology professor at the Moscow Theological Academy, merely derisively fluffed his well-groomed, fully secular, cologned beard in response. Contrary to all notions of the fustiness of an ecclesiastical education, Pitovranov—adorer of his wife and progeny, man about town, wit, and thinker—knew nine languages (five of which were, however, hopelessly dead), had defended a brilliant dissertation about pagan cults (about which he fiercely argued with his eternal enemy-and-colleague Vvedensky), and yet still contrived to remain, sincerely and artlessly, a religious believer. On the other hand, how could one not believe when God himself—rustic, cozy, and the only Lord possible, hopelessly anthropomorphic with solid peasant heels and a curly beard resembling a curly cloud that completely took the place of His sofa, chair, and the foundation of the world—lived and breathed each day and each hour in the clinking cutlery, crying babies, creaking floorboards, and every note of every voice in the Pitovranov home.

The family was huge, noisy, and friendly, but it was obvious to even a chance guest that this friendship wasn't based on some empty, chance blood kinship but on a completely conscious, intelligent human amity, meaning each newly born Pitovranov and each stray cat or dinner guest had to attempt to win the love and amity of all the others. Once becoming part of this peaceful, many-voiced symphony of great human happiness, however, each received in return more than enough wondrous bodily coziness and warmth to last an entire lifetime on earth and even beyond the grave.

It was the senior Pitovranov, a greedy and fastidious hunter and collector of human souls, who brought Chaldonov into their home. Pitovranov had promptly pegged the lanky student—who admittedly looked rather awkward and plebeian—not as a future academician and not as a luminary of fundamental science but rather as a person of that high, uncommon moral standard that Count Lev Tolstoy so long and furiously sought in people. Tolstoy himself, as was God's will, completely lacked that unnamed delicate organ, that unique vestibular apparatus of the soul that infallibly permits even a small child or a dog to distinguish good from bad, kindness from evil, and sin from upright intention or deed. It was the first time Pitovranov senior had seen with his own eyes such convincing and original proof of the Tertullian axioms—that every soul is by nature a Christian—and this despite Chaldonov's religious journey having likely never progressed further than the creeds, or even Our Father. Unlike many theologians, though, Pitovranov, a thinker, was fully capable of distinguishing the church from God and so after two long discussions with the bright student, he invited him for dinner at his own home, Pyatnitskaya Street, number 46. We will welcome you, my dear Sergey Alexandrovich, and I won't accede to any objections. You'll meet my progeny and members of my household and have something home-cooked as well. The food's always delicious at my house, that's a strictly observed rule, and you're probably sick and tired of taking your meals in taverns anyway.

And Chaldonov, who was generally agonizingly shy about everything on earth except his own mathematics, not only agreed, but actually arrived, all dressed up, pomaded, clumsy with excitement, and bearing candied cherries from the fashionable Einem confectionary company. The show-offy little silk-covered box for those cherries was emptied that very evening and moved in with the Pitovranov girls, where it became a refuge for buttons, silk ribbons, bugle beads, and other little things, odds and ends that were extraneous but eternally dear to any little girl's heart.

The Pitovranovs had six children but Chaldonov never seemed to remember them all by name because it was Marusya he saw right away, as soon as he walked into their crowded entryway: she was holding a huge, fluffy smoke-colored angora cat by the scruff. 'Don't take off your galoshes,' Marusya angrily ordered Chaldonov. 'Sarah Bernhardt, this mangy girl, decided to make a mess again!'

Marusya shook the accused cat, who squinted her insolent blue eyes and did what she could to feign the atoning sinner. Her show wasn't, in all honesty, very convincing, and Marusya shook the limp cat again as a warning.

'But,' mumbled Chaldonov, lost, blushing, and unsure where to put the candy. 'But how can I, well, come in, wearing galoshes? I can't do that, can I?'

'That's true,' Marusya said. 'Mama would probably be upset. Take off your galoshes. I ought to put Sarah outside, let her get some air. You must be Chaldonov, right? Sergey Alexandrovich?'

She offered a hand that clutched the cat in a fist and Chaldonov responded by awkwardly holding out the box of candy.

'Yes, indeed, miss,' he mumbled, cursing himself for the high-flown vocabulary from who knew where. Yes, indeed, miss! Like a lackey, like a steward! Oh, God, the shame! I'm done for, most completely done for!

'And I'm Marusya, meaning Maria Nikitichna, of course.' Marusya smiled easily and joyfully. There was a small, deep-brown beauty mark above her upper lip.

The cat used all the confusion as an opportunity to plop heavily on the floor like a ball of dough and cautiously slip away.

'And there you have it, I let her go again,' Marusya said, distressed. 'Now she'll probably tear up the gardenias, too. Let's go, don't be shy, they're all tired of waiting. Papa talks about you all the time: we all think he's completely in love with you.'

That was Marusya's favorite word: 'completely.' She again offered Chaldonov a small, warm hand—now empty—and he cautiously held it in his sweaty fist.

That was on November 28, 1888, and it was on April 9, 1889, Easter Day, that Sergey Alexandrovich, pale to the point of fainting and barely able to string his words together, proposed to Marusya. Holiday hyacinths that even looked tight and damp cast an overpoweringly loud scent through the whole room.

'Will you, Maria Nikitichna?' Chaldonov asked. In the event of a refusal he'd firmly decided to shoot himself or, at the very least, throw everything aside and leave for the country, a monastery, or a bender.

When Marusya walked right over to him and looked up into his eyes, her very simple, homey, and slightly apple-like scent immediately displaced the hyacinths and filled the whole world.

'Well, of course I will!' she said, happy. 'Especially since Papa and I have a bet about you, a whole ruble! He said you would most certainly ask for my hand at Easter Week. And I said you wouldn't be ready earlier than Trinity Sunday, no matter what. Do you have a ruble?' Chaldonov reeled and caught the edge of a table with his white fingers: this stroke of joy turned out to hold such power that everything took off right before his eyes, floating past, slowly gathering speed, and clickety-clacking over the joints on the rails.

'Why do you look so pale, anyway? Are you hungry?'

Chaldonov shook his head like an old horse. He still couldn't speak. He still couldn't believe it.

'And what is it, are you really not happy at all?' said Marusya, still insistent. 'And you don't even want to kiss me? We probably can now, you know.'

She raised herself on tiptoes and put her smooth lips in position, just like that, as if she'd already done this a thousand times. Chaldonov closed his worthless eyes just as Grisha, Marusya's younger brother, burst into the room, furrowing the rugs.

'Just can't get enough Easter kisses?' he asked maliciously. 'All those locusts in there will finish off the whole piglet without you!' he said, jerking his head toward a door. The hungry post-Lent Pitovranov family was making a racket behind that door, forcing their way into the dining room.

'Scat, go on!' Marusya said, laughing. She took Chaldonov by the arm and they went to the table, gracefully, splendidly, and in step, as if they'd walk and walk and walk their whole life. Grishka, in the grip of early hormones, triumphantly ran ahead of them, shrieking, 'And they were kissing, I saw it myself! Kissing!' Everyone had already taken their seats around a festively and thoughtfully decorated dining room table where a suckling pig really did lie on a plate as a centerpiece. It looked small, very child-like, and frightened, squeezing together eyelids swelled like a newborn's. A bad premonition came over Marusya for a second, but only for one second because this year was a great blessing for the whole planet: the year of the discovery of the Shroud of Turin, a miracle not of human hands and also the source of much heated debate among the Pitovranovs and, well, of course nothing bad could happen in a year like that. Couldn't and wouldn't. And also because in late spring Chaldonov graduated from Moscow University with distinction and was kept on at the department to be groomed for a professorship, per order of his teacher, the great Zhukovsky.

He and Marusya married in early summer.

Right after the wedding ceremony the young couple left for a honeymoon voyage along the Volga: this was Marusya's idea and later turned out, like all her ideas, to be the only possible and favorable option because nobody could have thought up anything better. Amidst all the wedding fuss and then travelling by rail to Nizhny Novgorod, the important thing Chaldonov had feared so much and wanted with such naïveté and agitation was delayed. Only on the very first evening, when he and Marusya were finally alone in their creaky cabin on the steamship, did he feel the full gravity of his undeserved and unbearable happiness. There was a scent of delicate river dampness and long, flowing, lulling shadows floated along the ceiling, and then the whole world around them entered that same flowing, lulling rhythm: the swaying lamp light, the gentle, weak lapping of the Volga's waves, and Marusya's responsive movements, which made Chaldonov's besotted heart alternately stop short and then strain commandingly.

It was the most honeyed of all possible honeymoons, long and unhurried, just like their steamship, the Tsesarevich Nikolay, rebuilt by the Caucasus and Mercury Steamship Line especially for navigating the year 1890. The Tsesarevich hadn't lost its provincial leisureliness now that it was two-decked and equipped with a brand-new Compound American engine. As was customary, the slow breakfasts on deck under a canvas tent included grayish caviar that was supposed to be spread with a special little ivory spoon on the porous flesh of hot white *kalach* bread, and there was a never-ending tea party hosted by a small, round-bellied little samovar: Marusya said on the first morning that it looked as important and puffing as a bishop. Chaldonov looked out over the stern at the rapid sunny water with eyes wet from uninvited tears: he saw Marusya's noticeably puffy lips and the tender, nearly invisible bruise on her young neck, slightly golden from the sun, and squealing seagulls to whom the esteemed public tossed generous pieces of still-warm bread rolls. What did you say, my love? Pardon me, I didn't hear you. I said you look like a Saint Bernard in the Alps. Just as shaggy and sentimental. But I had no idea I was marrying a crybaby.

Marusya got up from the table, deftly straightened her first truly grown-up lady's dress (with an uncomfortable bustle she just couldn't get used to) and went to stroll around the deck after quickly sticking her tongue out at Chaldonov. He watched her through the blurry rainbows still on his lashes: she walked along boards washed to whiteness and she was quick, smiling, and all composed of flowing lines and silken shadows. He feared only one thing, that he would die of happiness without living until the next evening.

During their long port stops, shrieking, dressed-up country women sold scruffy lilac branches and early wild strawberries. From the deck, Marusya observed the crush on the wooden docks and the many-layered attire of the provincial ladies and happily explained to Chaldonov why the Peredvizhniki artists' work wasn't art but simply a pathetic imitation of what's sinful to imitate. Do you understand? It's a sin! Just take a look, see that woman over there with the little pies, quite a charmer, isn't she? Strong as an ox! And those eyes, what eyes! A marvel! Could it really be possible to convey something like that with paint or even words? Marusya was pensive for a second. Could it be played? As a fugue? I think that woman over there is even more grandiose than a fugue! And Marusya, who was musical, like all the Pitovranovs, began quietly humming something thick and titanic that really did resemble the merchant on the dock who held, effortlessly suspended, a huge basket of little pies, new-born, piping hot, and wrapped in rags. The pies were plump, satisfying, and stuffed with offal, onion, and buckwheat kasha, horrible things, Marusya laughed, crouching and sharing a common person's treat with a heavy-breasted stray mutt that circled and wove around Marusya's feet in flattery, here you go, take it mommy, treat yourself. Admit it, you have a lot of little puppies, don't you?

The mutt snapped greedily at the aromatic dough, not forgetting to use her entire hindquarters to signal her most ardent attachment to the newly minted Mrs. Chaldonov. The mutt had seven puppies but a shopkeeper had drowned all of them in a cesspool a couple hours earlier. He wasn't a mean person or even greedy, he was just rational and sensible, as a true Samaritan should be. He could easily feed the bitch and her litter but he just didn't need eight dogs, and the mutt had yet to learn this. But for now, well, everything was good for now: the sun, the filling fried up with onions, the affectionate hand in a white glove that scratched behind an ear then the nape of the neck, and each breath blessed the Lord, and He didn't even seem to be indifferent.

The dog nearly melted with happiness when Marusya ruffled her shoulder one last time. Then Marusya brought her husband for a stroll around Plyos, a lovely little doll-like place resembling a pearl that had escaped into the grass from someone's pin: the pearl is genuine, even if it might be a little dusty and not perfectly even. People in the market stalls shouted, energetically played the accordion, and shoved fragrant textiles, ring-shaped rolls, and famous local yarn into gaping faces: it was clear to both Chaldonov and Marusya that neither of them had erred and this was just the beginning of a long, wonderful journey where everything would truly be as promised. Awaiting them were a peaceable life, many years together, and love for one another in worldly unity. And they would be granted enough of heaven's dew, earth's richness, bread, wine, holy oil, and benefaction to fill their home and share the abundance with the needy. If that's how it would be, it wouldn't be scary to die at some point, on the same day. And all those promises came true on, literally, each count. Except one.

After a year of the very happiest married life, Marusya was somehow still able to laugh off questions from kin who wanted to bounce grandchildren on their knees, come what may. A year later she, too, began to worry. Several years—certainly the worst in the Chaldonovs' life together—were spent in a desperate struggle others didn't see. Marusya was unusually sensitive and thus especially virtuous, and so found doctors particularly difficult to bear. Go behind the screen and undress, please; confident male hands, torturing instruments, a sweaty fist crumpling a hankie that doesn't utter a sound, humiliation, horror, humiliating hope, time after time, time after time, the same, always the same, always the same. Each circle of Hell was certainly travelled: trips to the waters and mud baths, university luminaries with diplomas, expensive private doctors, obscure healers who'd 'performed a real miracle with that Anna Nikeyevna,' even though that Anna Nikeyevna, the friend of friends of some friends, was by now as completely anonymous and impersonal as a banknote. What distinguished Anna Nikeyevna from a banknote was that Anna Nikeyevna couldn't buy you even a few grams of happiness. Even the homeopaths, who were quickly becoming fashionable, entered into all this, and only an innate spiritual squeamishness saved Marusya from trips to see wise women, charlatans, and wizards. This wasn't so much a matter of sin as the promises of shrewd metaphysical hangers-on (many of whom, as it happened, charged so much for a visit that even the most voracious Aesculapian would be ashamed) to change the will of God himself with their hurried incantations, towels cross-stitched on the hems, and broken candles. Deep-down, Marusya felt more than anyone that God's will was not to grant children to her and Seryozha. There was no point in opposing that will: you might only make a request, as you might request your parents give you a doll from the Simon & Halbig factory for your name day though you always risked receiving yet another little one-kopeck book about a bear or a slap in the face from your father instead of the beautiful poured wax doll in a stylish silk outfit. Marusya wasn't afraid of slaps in the face, though: she simply wanted to know why she was being denied. And why her?

For Marusya, the trips to doctors (which Chaldonov insisted on) were akin to fetters for holy fools: just another ordeal that brutally tortured the flesh, though there was an equally brutal tempering of the spirit in return. Something else was more important: the icon of the Mother of Jesus called 'Seeker of the Perished'; the icon of Joachim and Anne, the upright parents of the Virgin; the icon of the upright Elizabeth, mother of John the Baptist; the relics of the holy martyr of John the Infant at the Kiev Monastery of the Caves; the miracle-making Tolga icon at the Tolga monastery and, right next to it on a railing, the icon of Our Lady of the Sign, under which one must crawl three times, tearfully praying to the Most Holy Mother of Jesus. Marusya crawled and cried so much that she was taken by the arms and helped out of the cathedral.

There was also the Convent of the Conception and the miracle-working icon of the Gracious, and the relics of Saint Sofia of Suzdal. Marusya's confessor, Father Vladimir—a withered, sly-bearded, gray old man who seemed to have baptized and given guidance to the entire Pitovranov clan—advised writing to the Hilandar Monastery on Mount Athos. After three months of waiting that nobody noticed, Marusya received a little package from the Athos monks containing a small piece of the vine of Saint Simeon the Myrrh-Streaming, which had already borne fruit for a thousand years. The package also contained a small icon of Saint Simeon and three little raisins. The raisins were to be eaten by the infertile spouses—two for the wife, one for the husband—after spending forty days on a strict fast without wine, jam, or olive oil. In practice, this meant bread, water, and raw vegetables. Father Vladimir said Simeon's vine was the surest of sure methods. Chaldonov didn't maintain the fast, though, breaking it after a week when he followed the aroma of cabbage soup like a starving dog, only coming to his senses in a tavern amid smelly coach drivers and the shabbiest of folk. When he'd cleaned the bowl in front of him to a shine, the waiter, deftly holding his arm behind his back, was already lugging a tray with boiled beef, tear-inducing horseradish, and salted cucumbers. Burning from shame, Chaldonov gave up on himself and demanded some vodka to go with the beef and intensify the horror of his fall.

Marusya didn't give in and didn't retreat, though she was so weak she nearly stopped seeing people, and thus Pitovranov Senior dropped in himself to see the young couple because he missed his daughter. The Chaldonovs were then renting half a house on Povarskaya Street: Sergey Alexandrovich had a good reputation and earned a very, very decent income, if you counted private tutoring. Pitovranov silently looked at Marusya's face, bony from torment and hunger, and led Chaldonov by the sleeve into another room.

'Sergey Alexandrovich, I didn't entrust my daughter to you so she'd go off her head,' he said quietly but so frightfully that Chaldonov hid his suddenly sweaty hands behind his back like a boy who'd played a nasty trick. He loved his father-in-law and they had become even closer friends after the wedding, all without inhibitions, without obligations. Neither, of course, would have his friendships any other way.

'I tried to dissuade her, Nikita Spiridonovich, but Father Vladimir gave his blessing for a fast and said only abstinence and a feat of prayer would work.'

Pitovranov senior squeezed his luxuriant beard with his fist and then tugged as if he wanted to tear it out.

'That old fool Father Vladimir will get it in the face,' he promised. 'But you, Seryozha! You're a mathematician and a learned person, how could you allow these absurd, primitive superstitions into your home?'

Chaldonov fell helplessly silent: hearing something like this from a professor of theology was incredible and even terrifying, but Marusya was even more terrifying: on the outside, her coloring was as cheery and steady as before but she was contorted, all for naught, on the inside.

An anxious Father Vladimir came to see them that same evening—to reason with a spiritual child who had wandered too far—and when Chaldonov treated the old priest to tea and preserves, he unwittingly searched for traces of beatings on a face wrinkled from a lifetime of proffering affection. Despite his churchly learnedness, Pitovranov senior's fists would be the envy of any merchant. Marusya, however, wouldn't listen to anyone and continued observing a lonely fast no one needed. Chaldonov knelt and wept as he begged his wife not to destroy herself and not to destroy them both, but he also understood his tears and entreaties were all in vain, all for nothing, and wouldn't change a thing. Marusya was stubborn, both in her heritage and in her own way, and there was nothing inert, wild, or pained in that stubbornness. She simply wanted to know. Simply wanted to know why and for what reason.

Forty days later, the raisins from Athos were eaten with a prayer, with trembling, and with an improbable and visible hope. All for nothing. The door didn't open. And no doorman even came out to convey the message that there wouldn't be an answer. Marusya waited a bit longer and then quietly returned to herself.

To Chaldonov's timid joy, everything seemed to return to where it had been; the pastors and doctors ceased, as did the unending vigils in front of icons that resulted in nothing but aching kneecaps. The Chaldonovs were sitting at the table on a Sunday: it was summer and morning once again, the white curtains in the dining room billowed and subsided, green and gold outside billowed and subsided, and Marusya's batiste dress was cool on the outside but fiery-smooth on the inside.

'This will be embarrassing when Agasha comes in,' Marusya said, reproaching Chaldonov and affectionately slapping at his forehead with a teaspoon that was also hot and smooth.

'She won't come in,' Chaldonov mumbled, struggling with tiny, smooth little buttons and a silky ribbon. 'I sent her off for the samovar, she won't be back for a couple hours.'

Marusya still gently deflected his hands but he could hear and feel her breathing change, and he knew everything would be different in a moment—flavor, heat, aroma—she was surprisingly, unbelievably responsive. One could only dream of a beloved like her, if Chaldonov could, of course, have dared dream of anything like that...

'Seryozha, wait,' Marusya said. Her upper lip always swelled instantly from kisses, a special charm of hers that made Chaldonov's hands shake and head spin even more. 'I need to go to Kostroma, to the Theodorovsk icon of the Mother of God.'

Chaldonov backed off, dazed and unable to understand how she, so tactful, could ruin everything so suddenly: the morning, the sunny spots outside the window, the translucent dribbles of honey on the table knife, and the taste of her own lips.

'This will be the last time, Seryozha,' Marusya said, lightly stroking him on the cheek. 'The last time. I give you my word, I promise.'

They went to Kostroma together but it ended up feeling like an unhappy shadow of their wonderful honeymoon, despite their all-out attempt to be their usual selves. The miracle-working Theodorovsk icon of the Mother of God, painted by the evangelist Luke himself, resided in the Holy Trinity Ipatievsky Monastery, which was defiantly rich, white-stoned, and reminiscent of a stale crème torte. Chaldonov's delicate peasant fear of getting in the way or ruining something with his clumsy presence prevented him from going to the Trinity Cathedral, so he stayed outside instead. Marusya—still very thin and humbly wrapped in a simple grayish scarf with dots—glanced at her husband from the threshold as if she were afraid, or couldn't bring herself to take the final, truly final, step. Her lips moved soundlessly and ceaselessly, and

Chaldonov knew Marusya was praying to Anna, the mother of the Mother of God, 'Give fruit to the womb of those who call to you, releasing them from the darkness of their infertility, through the release from infertility make childless ones fertile, they praise you and eulogize the Son of God, your Grandson, and Creator and God.' The world is a mind-boggling place if even God has a grandmother and you can complain to that grandmother about an aching heart as well as an aching knee.

Chaldonov sighed and sat on a secluded little bench hidden in the very heart of some fluffy shrubbery. The monastery was cared-for, green, and distinguished, a repository of Romanov tradition. Its external flashiness was unfailingly maintained even though everyone had long grown accustomed to regular visits from the tsar's family. The monastery's gardens and soldier-like tidiness were enviable. Chaldonov sat, patting his pockets out of habit: he so wanted to smoke that his saliva was bitter, but he couldn't bring himself to get his cigarettes. There was a scent of sunny, lush, recently watered foliage and rich, satiated black earth, and a bird chattered deafeningly in tangled branches, scolding Chaldonov for disturbing her nest.

Pilgrims scurried around the monastery: wiry black monks agilely rounded them up into their proper places like sheep and smartly dressed laypeople sedately went to prayers, but the majority of those swarming about were unattractive, broken, beaten down by life, and humiliated, people who'd dragged themselves here looking for final refuge and the hopes they no longer harbored, even within. Chaldonov knit his brows, secretly disdaining the wounded birds the Russian Orthodox Church eternally collected around itself. It was painful to think that his Marusya—so lively, wonderful, and genuine through and through—had ended up among the desperate, orphaned, and wretched who crawled toward the entrance of the promised heavenly kingdom. He respected any faith and Marusya's, too, in particular, though for goodness' sake, what did the institution of the church have to do with anything? It was a monster as unwieldy as a government, capable of pulverizing even the very best human material to dust.

A monk appeared on the square in front of the Trinity Cathedral as if in answer to Chaldonov's thoughts. He was not some gold-leafed monk from a Nesterov painting but a genuine warrior of Christ, the Lord's dog, but with an orthodox appearance. He was tall, broad-shouldered and unbelievably, almost scarily, handsome: otherworldly, inhuman and, of course, with a beauty that wasn't Godly. And he walked, broadly inflating the black wings of his robes and looking over human heads with furious disdain, as if afraid of being soiled. The crowd parted before the monk, standing back in reverence and crossing themselves, struck dumb by a being of such an otherworldly, singular breed. 'Oh, he's so fine,' said one young hussy, enraptured and ahhing, a fine specimen herself, like a peeled onion. The monk's face instantly contorted out of hatred, as if a bright, black flame had blazed up inside, but then it tightened again into a disgusted grimace.

Chaldonov began to feel uncomfortable, as if he'd stumbled in some high place and caught his hand on an unsteady railing at the very last minute. God didn't care one iota about people, that much was clear. He indiscriminately and ineffectively filled vessels extended to him without noticing tears or listening to prayers. Why was this home-grown Lucifer from Kostroma granted so much bodily beauty and power? Why was Marusya kneeling once again in front of yet another icon—in the dark, in fear, and in desperation—and seeing nothing but oily ochre splotches of light on a huge old board? Why had the Lord not found them worthy of seeing the children of their own children? Was that really just?

The bird decided to change tactics after despairing of ever frightening Chaldonov by chirping. She came down from the branches and began hobbling around on the grass, dragging a wing and naively limping first on one foot, then the other, pretending to be injured and vulnerable. She was saving her children.

'Don't be afraid, you ninny,' Chaldonov mumbled, wiping his wet eyes. 'Marusya's right, I am a real crybaby and a sniveler. And no, I won't touch your nestlings.' The bird stopped and looked at Chaldonov with a round, impenetrable eye: he loved starlings for their intelligence, cheer, and industriousness; they had plenty of starlings in the country. 'I'm leaving, do you hear? I'm already leaving. How much can a person take, huh? For so long! How much longer do I need to wander? Will this torment go on long? Until death itself, mother! Until death itself...'

He wanted so much for Marusya to come out of the cathedral that of course he missed it when the huge door opened. Then the air around him simply changed, all at once, and it turned out Marusya was already walking through the yard, head bent low, walking very slowly as if yet another cross—instead of a consoling hand—had been lowered on her shoulders inside the cathedral. And it was completely overwhelming this time. That's it, Chaldonov grasped, that's it, nothing helped. Not even this last thing. They've broken her. Mutilated her. Finished her off. My Marusya. He wanted to shout or even yelp: it was as if someone was tormenting a child or a cat right in front of him and there was absolutely no way to prevent the pointless, long torture of a completely innocent and uncomprehending being. Marusya kept walking and walking as if she were plowing through heavy water in her sleep, and with each step Chaldonov hated God even more. The hatred was swelling up inside him, growing larger and larger within his dark, empty rib cage, first making it impossible to breath, then to believe, and finally, to live.

Marusya walked over and lightly placed a warm palm on her husband's sleeve.

'How was it, sweetie? How are you?' The fidgety Chaldonov kissed Marusya's temple, straightened her jacket, and tidied her hair for some reason, as if his awkward, petty bother was an attempt to distract God from his own nest. The hatred was gone and there was only fear that an unavoidable fiery pillar might now collapse on Marusya's head, too. He'd ruined everything again, brought tremendous harm to everyone. A blunderer. A clod. A damned fool. He wanted to look his wife in the eye but was desperately cowardly. She was so strong, his Marusya, but even she could be crushed. Anyone can be crushed, especially if you're God.

'Let's go, Seryozha,' Marusya quietly said. 'Let's finally go home now.'

'But what about…' Chaldonov stumbled on his words, not knowing how to finish the question. What about faith? What about children? What will happen now? What's the next station? The madhouse? Church divorce? A noose hastily attached to a chandelier?

'Let's go home, Seryozha,' Marusya softly repeated. 'I came to an agreement about everything.'

Chaldonov finally dared look at her face. Marusya's eyes

perfectly matched her scarf—light and speckled—and very calm. They held neither pain nor wrath nor hope. Nothing at all. Complete silence.

She truly had come to an agreement.

Neither she nor God told Chaldonov the terms of the agreement, but they both firmly kept their word. Chaldonov was as happy in his marriage as only a mortal man can be with a mortal woman. There was never another question about children, just as there were no children. This apparently never again worried Marusya at all.

She willingly and even gladly took on tasks for her husband: his rapidly growing career, scholarly work, and university squabbles. Chaldonov was finding his way in the world, confidently and steadily, and his blend of peasant stubbornness with a tremendous gift for mathematics allowed him to combine all sorts of activity that are usually extremely unwilling to combine. Chaldonov simultaneously proved himself an outstanding scholar and a sensible administrator. He was valued, promoted, and invited: in short, everything took its proper, happy course and in the evenings Marusya knelt on a chair that squeaked under her weight and made a clean copy of her husband's future dissertation, diligently sticking out her tongue and not understanding a single thing. She wrote in a precise hand that leaned strongly to the left, something uncommon that graphologists claim speaks of reason having full control over feeling. '…Thus the solution of the corresponding problem regarding the flow of gas may be written with the help of a series in which all members contain certain equalizing coefficients expressed through Gaussian hypergeometric series…' Chaldonov came up behind Marusya and lightly blew right into the fluffy, ticklish little curls on her neck.

'Don't pant on me!' Marusya said, angry. 'Can't you see I'm working? You said yourself you need this soon!'

Chaldonov submissively stepped aside and she ordered, without turning, don't ravage the sideboard, dinner's coming soon. Not me, no I wouldn't do that, Chaldonov vowed, trying to keep the treacherous little door from squeaking.

'Gaussian hypergeometric series…' Marusya repeated in a singsong voice. 'Very beautiful. Though incomprehensible. Does this happen to mean anything?'

Chaldonov mumbled eagerly, attempting to swallow the piece of meat he'd just stolen.

'Shameless,' Marusya said, indignant. 'We'll be sitting down to eat in an hour and you're snacking… Veal! And it's even cold! And you finished it all! You didn't even leave me one little piece!'

When the round-hipped cook came in to set the table, she found a married couple peaceably eating preserves right out of the jar, moreover Chaldonov was animatedly expounding to Marusya on the basics of gas dynamics, not noticing his young wife was wielding the spoon and unconscionably eating out of turn. 'On Gas Streams,' which he presented as a doctoral dissertation to the Physics and Mathematics Department of Moscow University, was brilliantly defended in February 1894, the very same year the Chaldonovs celebrated their fifth wedding anniversary.

Contrary to the logic of happy marriages, Marusya didn't turn into an enraptured shadow of her own husband. That might have been because Chaldonov understood perfectly that the house his wife kept—which was sometimes as stubborn and capricious as a living being—was also work, something creative that the world needed no less than his scientific investigations or, say, the purring of a cat licking sleepy, sated kittens. Beyond that, Chaldonov sincerely believed there was far more meaning in Marusya's everyday life than in his own. In the pattern for a new dress laid out on the big table, in arranging personal happiness for the maid (for some reason the Chaldonovs' servants were particularly susceptible to romantic passions and Marusya gave away girl after weepy girl for marriage), even in how Marusya scratched her delicate neck with a pencil as she thought up tomorrow's lunch, economizing by using the same piece of beef for a sauté, cabbage soup, and filling for turnovers. All of this had its own astonishing, touching, and immediately understandable logic of small events, the only things that can possibly add up to major happiness. At night the Chaldonovs slept together, embracing, and neither woke up when they both turned onto the other side as soon as someone's arm went to sleep and become all fiery, needly, and disobedient.

The Pitovranovs—who'd grown even noisier and friendlier during this time—often visited the Chaldonovs. Nieces and nephews were born each year in a frightening, almost geometric progression and they adored Auntie Marusya, who possessed an innate feminine gift for bouncing, swaddling, nourishing with thin porridge, taking to task for a shattered dish (while expertly hiding the shards from other adults), frightening with scary stories, and explaining geography. She did all this in such a way that even the most capricious child didn't feel for a second that he was being coerced into something he didn't want to do or couldn't do himself. Chaldonov was even jealous of the young horde that constantly hung on Marusya's skirts even though she never fussed over them and could leave a superb, burning imprint on a guilty rear end when necessary.

Her parents once raised the idea of getting an orphan from an almshouse but Marusya just raised her eyebrows in surprise.

'Why?' she said. 'I'll have a child. I know it. There will be a child. I believe that, do you understand?'

Her mother lost her composure and burst into tears: she'd given birth fourteen times herself, raised six, and the Almighty had taken the other eight so there was someone to romp at the feet of His gleaming throne.

'What are you talking about, Marusya? Is there some way around it if the Lord doesn't allow it?'

'But I'm not getting around anything, Mama,' Marusya stubbornly repeated. 'I just know.'

That was in 1899: it was the beginning of a new century and a new era, and Russia drowned each evening in bloody half-crushed sunsets that were written about by everyone able to write, and that alarmed even those who had nothing to worry about. Marusya turned thirty, something that was already discernible: her bosom had softened a little, her cheekbones had sharpened a little, and in the morning she didn't respond to her husband so gladly, though she knew he loved those moments more than anything, when she was half-asleep, warm, and slightly hazy from a long, blissful non-existence that wasn't the teensiest bit frightening. Life passed through Marusya and by Marusya, though she still knew God would fulfill the promise He'd made, just as she'd kept the word she gave to Him. And God turned out to be just.

Marusya's child appeared when she was forty-nine years old.

And it was fine that he turned out to be a frail little Jewish boy with warm and happy—contrary to the nation's dictates—eyes. It was fine that he was eighteen and brought terribly nasty scabies into the house along with his lice. This was her child. Marusya's. Her only boy. Her treasure. Her Lesik.

She knew that as soon as she opened the door.

Chapter Three: Lazar

Lazar Lindt had a convenient birth year—nineteen hundred—that pre-emptively made calculations simple for leisurely gawkers at cemeteries. Others among the deceased seemed to offer—both for themselves and witnesses—a certain opportunity for fortune: the less round numerals on their gravestones appeared to hold the promise of especially long and unpredictably interesting lives or even immortality that, of course, lasted exactly as long as it took the passer-by to mentally subtract one four-figure numeral from another. With Lindt, however, there was no mental exertion or silent lip motion: his entire fate fit smoothly and neatly into one elementary arithmetical operation. Minus one hundred. Let's go, why're you still at that grave? Yes, yes, dear, sure, here I am.

Lindt himself didn't care the slightest bit about silliness like his own death: he was an unequivocal atheist and staunch devotee of Bazarov's burdock. Strange though it was, that very sense of the definiteness of mortality and the finiteness of earthly existence gave him the gift of the same steady and joyful fearlessness that burned in early Christian martyrs who were devoured in arenas by ever so slightly cartoonish lions. As he aged, however, Lindt's atheism slowly began acquiring a bitter flavor and losing its strength, as if some kind of rubber gaskets that sit against the stopper in a bottle—like the bottle with the strong iodine—had dried out and cracked. Lindt didn't exactly become a believer; most likely he simply tired of doubting. From any perspective, though, he lived an unbelievably long and very successful life because so much happened to anyone else but him: failures, arrests, shootings, ideological opponents, and common enviers. Friends idolized Lindt, opponents respected and feared him a bit, and women adored him. With the exception of one woman. That wasn't even an error, it was something less. Simply a defect at the thousandths place after the decimal point.

'Lazar, it's as if you don't live in our time: neither the devil nor Soviet power takes you,' Chaldonov muttered, stuffing an icy Validol tablet under his parched tongue.

'It's because they don't exist, Sergey Alexandrovich. That's why they don't take me.'

'Who doesn't exist? What are you talking about?'

'There's nobody, no devils, no Soviet power, Sergey Alexandrovich. People have always been the same, ever since the creation of Adam. I just know how to come to terms with them.'

Lindt shifted around as he settled his gaunt, caustic rear end into a chair and enjoyed a look around. He loved Chaldonov's home office: bookshelves, huge desk, tempting lodes of brainy paper debris, and semi-darkness. Honestly, he would have stayed here forever.

Chaldonov shook his head. The most cannibalistic of times were setting in, whether you could come to terms or not. It was 1937 and the Trotskyites in the Physics Department at Moscow State University had been zealously routed—the scholarly minds may have avoided a major disaster but feathers did fly. The infighting, however, was exclusively internal and we can give the Motherland credit for barely harassing physicists at all and, apparently, understanding what's what: who their womenfolk would continue birthing and that certain people were best left untouched because messing with them would certainly have been more trouble than it was worth. You'd have to wait another hundred and fifty years for the right combination of genes and engage in petty thievery of your neighbors' obsolete technology in the meantime. Chaldonov, though, was a clinically decent and honest person who perceived every verbal squabble during academic council meetings as a real battle with a thoroughly Dostoyevskian spirit: God was wrestling with the devil, and peoples' hearts were the battlefield.

Lindt made a point of sitting as close as possible to the speaker during those council covens and quickly began scribbling something in a notebook. He might have been taking minutes or might have been working but hardly anyone could decipher his horrendously hooked, absolutely spidery handwriting. Admittedly, hardly anyone understood the essence of the notes, either, though perhaps a couple dozen scholars on the whole planet would roll their eyes in reverence at just the name Lazar Lindt. The banality of that statement doesn't make it any less significant. Lindt worked at the nexus of physics, chemistry, and, probably, mathematics, at those unbelievably high levels where final human doubts disappear and the real flesh of One God begins shining through the worn fabric of Big Science. Lindt was the most ordinary genius: even those who didn't understand anything at all understood that. Especially those in science.

Despite all the genius that was obvious to everyone, Lindt was still regarded as a wunderkind at thirty-seven: that title is as silly and narrow as short pants on an over-aged halfwit but what else could Lindt be called in a world where the seventieth birthday was considered the average age for recognition? The youngest professor, the youngest author of the most discussed monograph, the most prolific researcher who'd gathered the tightest covey of the most audacious youths. He certainly annoyed many people. Very many. In terms of logic, Lindt should have been heading up an entire department long ago, and in terms of intelligence, he should have had his own institute, because he himself was neither able to implement nor even truly remember all the ideas he generated, often at odd moments or on the go. Like any human upstart blessed by a higher power thanks to chance, Lazar preferred working only on what interested him personally. What 'interested' him, moreover, covered not just science but also, for example, the fair sex, for whom Lindt (a charming man, like all hideous freaks of nature) was a great gourmand and enthusiast. He also loved good books, the goodness of which was determined not only by author and content but year of publication. Out of principle, Lindt didn't acknowledge printed materials published after 1917, and Moscow's second-hand booksellers adored him for his marvelous snobbery, sense of humor, generosity, and striking intuition, though they adored him most for the tenderness with which he took each tattered volume in his hands. It was as if he were reaching for the knees of a beautiful half-naked woman shuddering from impatience. He was a magnificent lover—meaning, of course, a magnificent reader—who was generous, skilful, grateful, and bold. No woman and no book ever felt offended when she left him: it's pleasant and advantageous to be friends with women and books. Lindt only taunted and mocked men. With men it was pleasant and advantageous to have nothing to do with them at all. Unfortunately, things couldn't often work out that way.

It stands to reason that the Motherland very quickly retooled Lindt for war, just as it retooled everything else considered even the slightest bit useful. Lindt wasn't against that:

it didn't matter to him how his findings were applied, be that for strengthening the country's defense or increasing milk yields. This was Lindt's firm and deliberate calculation rather than a lack of scrupulousness or an inner deafness. For one thing, Lindt thoroughly lacked illogical human sentiments, for another, the process of solving yet another scientific problem interested him far more than the final result, and beyond that, he was an adult and very intelligent person, unlike many who came after him, who first recklessly invented the hydrogen bomb, then repented, just as recklessly. In Lindt's opinion, physics was the most inappropriate occupation for weenies. Either you're a physicist and take everything to its conclusion or you're just cowardly, deceitful, and undereducated. Lindt couldn't tolerate Pharisees.

It's tough to say why he wasn't finished off or at least imprisoned. Perhaps because he was unbelievably, almost humorously, impractical and unambitious. Then again, in all the Stalin-era cases—you can plow through them yourself— what always comes to light is a trite, petty human passion for money, honor, and glory, things there's never enough of to go around. Or maybe it was because of his sense of humor: tussling with a person who laughs all the time is pointless as well as demeaning for the aggressor. Or maybe the secret was hidden in his notorious genius: Lindt was just like everyone else in terms of appearance, but in terms of barely perceptible characteristics, of how he went so strongly against the usual grain, he differed not only from his biological species but also, possibly, from all protein-based life forms in general. The speed with which he thought. The distinct, slightly mechanical laugh. The magnificent neglect of all norms of deliberate human morality. A habit of quickly scratching his prominent genitals like a monkey. The terrifying, primitive, and material chaos he produced. Lindt was clearly composed of a different, otherworldly material, quite possibly even on the cellular, biochemical level. This was completely clear and very frightening. Truly frightening. For those, of course, who were capable of understanding.

Chaldonov's protection certainly had tremendous significance: Chaldonov pulled Lindt behind him with a cast-iron, locomotive-like persistence, his wheezing, white-hot sides shielding Lindt from even the slightest stray, unfriendly breath. Lindt would undoubtedly have made it on his own, maybe a decade later or maybe at another price, but he would have made it. But the Chaldonovs…

Lindt lived at the Chaldonovs' for almost three months in 1918, two months longer than necessary because everything—ration cards, supplementary rations, authorizations, a room—was ready almost immediately, thanks, of course, to Chaldonov's efforts. The lice disappeared almost immediately, too, just as the arguments began almost immediately. Lindt and Chaldonov hollered at one another, inflating the veins on their throats and arguing with particular zeal about the theory of motion of a body subjected to nonintegrable constraints.

'You're a little boy,' Sergey Alexandrovich shouted, 'an ignoramus and a milksop, and I even won a gold medal from the Academy of Sciences for those findings!'

'From the tsarist Academy of Sciences,' Lindt said with a spiteful smile. 'And that, you must agree, completely changes things in the current situation. If the Academy were truly interested in science, it would certainly have brought this charming illogic to your attention…'

Lindt began writing right on the back of some decree or

order. The government meticulously furnished Sergey Alexandrovich with endless encyclicals and circulars; absent this generosity with printed and clerical materials, Chaldonov probably would have had to quit smoking.

'Some tea, boys?' Marusya asked, looking curiously over Lindt's shoulder. The brooding Chaldonov huffed, mumbling unintelligible but obvious curses, over his other shoulder. Lindt jumped up without finishing his writing.

'Some tea, of course, Maria Nikitichna. Here, I'll help you.'

'But you didn't finish writing!' Chaldonov cried out. 'You didn't finish! Because there's nothing to finish writing and there's nothing illogical there!' Chaldonov was secretly very terribly satisfied with their knock-down, drag-out arguments (Oh, it had once been just like this with Zhukovsky!) as well as Lindt's cheerful impertinence and even with the wild, bitter, and distinct smell of fur he brought into the house. It was as if Chaldonov and his wife had domesticated a young weasel that wouldn't allow anyone to pick him up.

'Be quiet, Seryozha,' Marusya said. 'Lesik, don't listen to him: they gave that gold medal to me, not him, and it was for my excellent penmanship. How many times did I copy your theory of the movement of bodies nobody whatsoever needs? That's right, six times! By the way, Lesik, you won't believe this but today I traded six little silver spoons for ten eggs! Just think, in 1914 those very same little spoons cost ten rubles and ten eggs cost twenty-five kopecks!'

'But you could never stand them, Marusya,' Chaldonov said, consoling her.

'The spoons?' Maria Nikitichna laughed. 'Or eggs? Here, let's go celebrate this grandiose deal. I was able to procure a little flour along with the eggs so I baked some absolutely pre-

Revolutionary little pies, without sugar or butter, of course, but they look completely delicious. By the way, they're asking three pounds of inferior tobacco for forty pounds of rye flour now, can you imagine! Forty whole pounds!'

Lindt and Chaldonov expressed harmonious indignation: How could Marusya even think about dragging forty whole pounds of flour on her person from Khitrovka when there were two strong, able-bodied men in the house! The strongest and most able-bodied, Marusya cheerfully agreed as she set the table, using her elbow to block the plate of pies from her husband's encroachment. But you're silly men, too: think about it, where am I going to get three pounds of tobacco if certain people never take their hand-rolled cigarettes out of their mouths! Don't ever smoke, Lesik. It's a disgusting habit! You won't start smoking will you? Promise!

Lindt nodded with a seriousness nobody noticed or appreciated. He quit smoking that same evening: he went out into the icy-cold Moscow courtyard and turned his pocket inside out, though he didn't even have real tobacco, only tobacco dust, the trash of tobacco, acquired God knows where and at what price and so stinky that Lindt—who'd been devotedly tarring himself with tobacco from the age of ten—had never even dared roll a cigarette in the Chaldonov home. He never took another puff in his life and if Marusya had wanted to wrap him around her little finger, she would have wound up with enough wrapping to cover all Russia, perhaps even the whole inhabited and uninhabited world. But she didn't want that. She didn't want to torment her boy. She was so sensitive yet didn't see or notice a thing. Groaning, Lindt inhaled constricted air permeated with frost and went back inside. Into the warmth. He didn't care a bit about the tobacco. You can renounce anything at all if you truly have somewhere to go.

Even after he'd moved into his room and then his own apartment—Lindt's prosperity grew in direct proportion with the favor of the government and in inverse proportion with his own demands—he never stopped spending time at the Chaldonovs'. Nearly every day at first, then every week, a torturous period of unnecessary tactfulness that Marusya completely and quickly cut short when she grasped what had happened, and then every day again. This meant Lesik soon had his own cup at the Chaldonovs', his favorite place at the table, and a sofa where he slept if it was late and he stayed the night, a privilege truly used only under exceptional circumstances. When Marusya nearly died from typhus in twenty-three. I don't even want to think about that. I don't even want to remember it. I'm not going to. It's too frightening. Or in twenty-nine, when the Chaldonovs celebrated their fortieth wedding anniversary and Sergey Alexandrovich nearly died from joyfully overimbibing in 'Rykovka,' which was sixty proof and foul, but quick to fill the young Soviet government's coffers.

One must admit that of all the deeds implemented by the Council of People's Commissars, the decree issued in late 1924 allowing the sale of vodka deserves recognition as the most successful and significant. Drink-related revenue grew many-fold, from 15.6 million rubles in 1922-1923 to a thrilling 130 million in 1924-1925. Not bad considering a bottle cost about a ruble and seventy-five kopecks. The ungrateful little people, however, went out of their way to call the vodka 'half-Rykovka,' enviously claiming the real 'Rykovka,' at a full hundred and twenty proof, was apparently consumed by Rykov himself, chairman of the Council of People's Commissars. All of it presumably going into just his snout. How could he not burst, the bastard!

'Half-Rykovka,' however, was plenty for Sergey Alexandrovich, a light drinker who felt sentimental at his wedding anniversary and consumed it tactlessly, lacking restraint. And so Marusya, cursing and laughing, asked Lindt to stay because, I can't handle it alone, Lesik, and then he's always getting ill. No, no, don't clean up! Do not, under any circumstances, clean up! Let him wake up in the morning and see the mess he made! Chaldonov, who'd been pacified and driven to bed with considerable collaborative effort, slumbered peacefully after laying his halo of noble and slightly barfy gray hair on a pillow. As a real member of the Chaldonov household, Lindt suddenly realized he was in the master bedroom for the first time: it was small, upholstered with nocturnal shadows, and looked like an immodest jewelry box slammed shut from inside. It was almost unbearably stuffy from scarlet drapes, vomitous aromas, a red down quilt that hadn't been put away for the summer, and the venous blush wandering Chaldonov's cheeks. Even the June poplar fluff that shifted in the half-shadowed corners, weightlessly and almost unnoticed, seemed as stifling and eerie as the stuff of nightmares. And only Marusya was cool, wearing a cool dress, and the smooth pearl buttons on her back were cool, too, and bare, like vertebrae.

Eleven years of nearly daily meetings. Never an incautious word. An age difference of thirty-one years. She'd noticed crows' feet around her eyes for the first time the year Lindt was born; they didn't go away, no matter how much Marusya moved the lamp that attempted to deceive her sly reflection. She found herself unexpectedly distressed, particularly as a woman who considered herself sensible and always preferred healthy practicality over pointless fashion when choosing new boots. After finding her in tears with unintelligible complaints, Chaldonov rushed off to the pharmacy, carrying home in his loving beak a package whose contents, according to his simple-hearted belief, would magically transform Marusya into the fairytale princess she unquestionably already was, but, just don't cry, Marusenka, why are you crying, just look what I bought you!

Marusya really did stop crying instantly when she discovered what was on her dressing table: Pharmacist A.M. Ostroumov's Head Dandruff Soap (thirty kopecks a cake, sold everywhere, or a double cake for fifty kopecks, and the prudent Chaldonov, of course, bought double because it was cheaper and would last longer) and Dr. Thomson's Depilatory Powder (completely safe, the best method for removing hair from undesirable places, price for one box: one ruble, fifty kopecks). Marusya conducted a most magnificent, refreshing, and youthful dressing-down for Chaldonov: she fully intended to file for divorce immediately thereafter, but then she laughed so long and hard that she wore herself out when she heard her mortally frightened husband's awkward explanations about how he'd done what was best and how they'd sworn at the pharmacy that these were patent preparations, the very best and absolutely safe for the skin, too.

At the very next holiday, the absolutely safe-for-the-skin depilatory and dandruff soap were ceremoniously presented to a yard worker, an indecent fop and lady-killer who, judging from his satisfied appearance, had already used these patented and very best preparations to certain advantage for himself, even if the results weren't visible to others. Marusya zealously made a bet with Chaldonov that the yard worker would be left without his magnificent moustache, but she lost a stroll at Neskuchny Garden and four kisses to Chaldonov. After that, she stopped worrying, once and for all, about such simple and obvious things as life, fading away, and death.

Of course Lindt didn't know—couldn't have known—any of that. Most of Marusya's life didn't just pass by him: it existed before and outside his life. Within his memory, she only aged: easily, cheerfully, selflessly, and without suffering. Her age suited her well and so did her husband, who was old and in love with her forever; stuffy twilights flowing with vomit, milk, and honey suited her, too. The lamp, thoughtfully covered with a shawl, glowed dimly as if it were a firebird burning out, and its light—soft and coppery, with silky tassels—played off Marusya's lively face, muting her gray hair and gently smoothing her wrinkles. *Animula, vagula, blandula...* My unexpected joy.

Go on, you good-for-nothing, get ready. It's now or never.

'I love you, Maria Nikitichna,' Lindt quietly said, looking away, into a noiselessly sighing corner, into another real world.

'I love you very much, too, Lesik,' Marusya said, easily and inattentively, as she straightened a pillow so her husband could lie more comfortably. 'And Sergey Alexandrovich also loves you. The Lord didn't give us children, you know, but...'

Just then Lindt began hoarsely coughing as if he were barking; he quickly left the room, almost at a run.

'Lesik, did you choke?' Marusya took off after him, frightened. 'You need some water, drink some water right now.' Just then, Chaldonov loudly snorted, in peals nothing short of a manor lord's, and began tossing and turning in bed. After wavering for a second, Marusya chose her husband. She chose her husband.

'Shhh, sweetie, I'm here. Lie down more comfortably. There you go.'

When she hurried into the kitchen, literally a minute later, absolutely everything was fine. Lindt had fully regained his breath and was washing a glass under a twisty stream of water. This wasn't the glass he'd been drinking from but someone else's, blotched along the rim with bright greasy lipstick. The guests had left entire Babylons of dirty dishes.

'Are you all right, Lesik?' Marusya asked, worried.

'Completely, Maria Nikitichna,' Lindt said politely. 'Something went down the wrong way, pardon me.' His eyes were red and wet but completely calm. 'Go in with Sergey Alexandrovich, I'll tidy up in here for now.'

'Thank you, sweetie!' said Marusya, as Lindt took the back of his head, deftly and unnoticed, out from underneath her affectionate fingers. He'd hoped in vain, dreamed in vain, of snapping up something that did not and could not belong to him. Her very existence was more than enough. Just that she simply existed. Simply existed: others didn't even have that. Wise men, Lazar, are content with small things: apparently it's now time to become a wise man. Lindt took another dirty dish, sprinkled baking soda on it from a carton, and the plate squeaked, yelped, and answered under his fingers.

Yes, he was twenty-nine and in love with a sixty-year-old woman. No, not in love: he loved a woman who was sixty and he'd loved her when she was forty-nine. And fifty-five. And he would love her when she was eighty and (as was already completely clear) when he was eighty. Let he who considered this feeling abnormal throw the first stone: Lindt would enjoy ripping out the swine's Adam's apple in return. Nothing on earth was more normal, clear, or simple than his love, and that love was all lightness, and loyalty, and the desire to protect and care for her. To simply be there. To admire. Listen. Follow with amazed eyes. Get angry. Argue. Adore. Fall asleep, pressing her close with all his might. Wake up together. And not let anyone else have her, ever. Why was this possible for Chaldonov but impossible for Lindt? What did age have to do with it? What difference did those wretched thirty years make?

Yes, Lazar Lindt had countless concubines and wives—King Solomon had nothing on him—and though women excited him and he excited women, he loved only Marusya. The others were just empty, dark, echoing vessels where he attempted to hide because he loved Marusya but she didn't love him. He and his lovers met and parted easily, and he barely distinguished one from another, not remembering smells, not considering what they said, not paying attention to gestures. In Lindt's case, there was no point whatsoever in Lent: celibacy didn't change anything so there was no point in torturing the flesh for nothing, and besides, his poor flesh was certainly not guilty of anything. He received tremendously animated, animal, and avid enjoyment from women, and gave even more to them, but Marusya... Marusya. Maria Nikitichna, I love you. What an idiot. Pathetic nobody. If those thirty years are all so irreparable, Lord, please make me born a half-century earlier, even as a cretin, halfwit, or tattered beggar who can't read or count. I'd find a way to find her. She'd love me anyway. Lord, make it so that You exist...

The dish cheeped pathetically under Lindt's fingers again and broke into sharp, uneven pieces. An excellent sign, Lord. I never doubted You didn't care that You don't exist. And there's no need to mention Freud, you can keep the funny gender theories of that masturbating Jew, desperate smoker, and possessor of the most bourgeois of little apartments in the center of unhurried, respectable Vienna. Calm down, my mother has absolutely nothing to do with this, she was merely a fertile fool, a wordless machine stamping out Jewish babies nobody needed, and she quite possibly might have been a saint but my father most certainly wasn't much of a carpenter. At least I was lucky about that. It was quiet in the Chaldonovs' bedroom; Marusya had probably fallen asleep, curled up alongside her great husband. If he weren't my teacher and her husband, I'd kill him. No, that's not it. I'd kill him no matter what, if it would change anything.

Lindt ran his eyes across the bastion of washed dishes. The garbage pail reeked of soured table scraps. The goose Marusya had prepared was beyond all praise. All was sated and lazy in 1929 Moscow, and it was only at sunrise, which spilled in through the window like a pale, slow-moving, fruit-flavored pudding, that there was any sense of some sort of vague, future worry. More new times were coming, and they were again frightening. Lindt went to the entryway, took his jacket off the hook, and quietly closed the door behind him. A huge indifferent sun was rising at the end of the empty street. A long life was ahead. Very long.

And Lazar Lindt earnestly set off, heading toward its last page.

He was originally from a shabby, sleepy little place—maybe in the south of Kherson Province, maybe somewhere else—and in the beginning nobody took the trouble of clarifying anything, either with Lindt or with a map. But when the time came for relentless, painstaking applications, Lindt was already in demand, oh yes, so in demand that they had to satisfy themselves with just a difficult-to-pronounce toponym—Malaya Seydemenukha—and the very quickest of checks. You're saying your whole family died in the Civil War, Lazar Iosifovich? Shot by the White Guard? A telegram from the comrades in Malaya Seydemenukha laconically confirmed that Lindt's family truly had been shot in such-and-such year. Of course in that very same year, the unfortunate little town was being routed by Reds, Whites, Greens, and God knows what other monstrous men, unclassifiable by either party or political lines, but still very capable of burning, hanging, raping, and killing. In any case, they didn't bother clarifying exactly who had wiped Lindt's kin off the face of the earth, since knowing could create an embarrassing, and completely unnecessary, situation. Lindt himself never talked with anyone about either his childhood or his adolescence. It's not that he hid it, he just joked it off, agilely splashing his tail like a fish and diving to some depth unfathomable to his conversation partner. It was as if some unhealed abscess remained in the past, so horrible and swollen that it couldn't possibly be touched, even mentally.

Out of curiosity, Chaldonov rummaged around in pre-Revolutionary statistics that were absolutely unhelpful for Lindt: Chaldonov found that in 1897, three years before Lindt was born, 520 people lived in Malaya Seydemenukha, of whom 96.5 percent were Jews. The majority eked out a living on the land, with each family having an average of eleven or so acres of land, one and a half cows, and thirty-eight chickens. Many indulged themselves as craftsmen to keep the strain from sending them to their death; there was a particular concentration of glaziers. Glasswork, as it happens, was popular among Jews. Beyond all the local indulgences already noted, there was a house of worship (though the residents of Seydemenukha only came to have their own synagogue in the beginning of the twentieth century), a heder, and Abram-Traitel Leibovich Shaikin's private primary school—Shaikin was a loony Jewish saint who'd diligently sown much that was rational, good, and everlasting in Malaya Seydemenukha: if there's one thing Jews have always had plenty of, it's the eternal.

Shaikin, who'd came from a very poor and itinerant family, didn't just learn to read and write by his thirties: he'd also extorted an education degree out of the Russian Ministry of Education (a ministry just as dense-headed and inert as other ministries), a heroic deed in and of itself. That wasn't enough saintliness for Shaikin, though, so he insisted on martyrdom. Oh, my crown of thorns! Instead of calming down after finally becoming a teacher, Abram Leibovich opened his own father's home as a school—and attention! it was private and secular!—where forty or fifty runny-nosed, large-eyed peasant children, wonderful little Jewish kids, studied in three shifts each year. And Shaikin (who also happened to be papa to seven of his own eternally hungry offspring) taught them arithmetic and geography as well as other bits of wisdom that were extraordinarily necessary in that backward, rocky ass of the world. Of course absolutely everyone in Malaya Seydemenukha considered Shaikin a consummate idiot and of course more than seventy percent of them were illiterate or semi-literate in that little place, despite all his titanic efforts. It's not that easy to disrupt global harmony, even if you're a saint as well as a Jew. Especially if you're a Jew. And a saint besides.

'Lesik, were you a student of Shaikin's, too?'

'I didn't go to school at all, Maria Nikitichna,' Lindt said, very serious. 'There just wasn't time.'

'But you had parents, didn't you? Why don't you ever talk about your mother or father?' Marusya continued trying to get answers, paying no attention to beseeching grimaces from Chaldonov, whose tact writhed from any intrusion into another person's life, something especially precious because it belongs to another.

'Of course I did. Although I'd prefer to have been found in the cabbage patch, preferably so you could cook me up in one of your pies,' Lindt said. He smiled and drew a plate with puffy, browned little pies toward himself in a way that made it absolutely clear the conversation was finished. Marusya always added a hardboiled egg, ground black pepper, and mushrooms to her cabbage filling. 'These are white mushrooms, aren't they, Maria Nikitichna? It's wonderfully delicious.'

For several months after his memorable pre-dawn declaration, Lindt spoke to Marusya with the unsteady, evasive caution of an accomplice or a tightrope walker, as if something really did depend on every word or gesture, as if Marusya truly had heard or understood him. That game later bored him, too, since it was pathetic self-delusion yet again: walking on feet with open sores along a nonexistent rope (What mockery!) stretched over fairgrounds crammed full of gawkers who had nothing to do with him because they themselves didn't even exist. That wasn't bad as some kind of brainteaser game, but it was ill-suited to life. And so for a long time Lindt reconciled himself to the existing way things were, just as you reconcile yourself to gravity, which doesn't allow you to fly, though it's difficult to imagine anything more natural for the human body than flight.

Everything had gone back to how it had been, maybe even better. Lindt, after all, had a job he appreciated. Not the employment itself, which tore a piece out of his life every day from nine to seven, leaving only a few hours for the joys of a free existence—and the majority of that time was necessarily spent on sleep and food—but the work itself, which was well-organized in every respect. For the sake of fairness, it should be noted that Lindt was indebted to Chaldonov for his job and, really, practically everything else.

Chaldonov, truth be told, didn't torture himself long in his job setting up Moscow State University: by the end of 1918 he'd already had it up to here with young Bolshevik bureaucracy and so he went, hat in hand, to Zhukovsky, yes, yes, the very same one, his university teacher, his protector, practically his father.

Zhukovsky, who had once noticed a perceptive young man from the village amongst his students, didn't just bring Chaldonov into Big Science: in many ways he also took pains for Big Science to be favorable to Chaldonov. He was extraordinarily approving of his foster-child's marriage to Marusya and he honorably performed all the tiresome best man duties at their wedding, including holding (on tiptoe) the wedding crown over the huge Chaldonov and listening when their scholarly colleagues burst into terribly long and tedious speeches, one after another, wishing health to a groom who was beside himself with happiness. Zhukovsky completely charmed Marusya when, with a horrible absent-mindedness that inspired anecdotes, he took Father Seraphim, an old friend of the Pitovranovs', for a lady: Father Seraphim's mighty red beard didn't perturb Zhukovsky in the slightest. Father Seraphim's festive white and blue vestments and plump rear end, however, could mislead anyone, so Marusya, bubbling over with laughter, barely managed to save the monastic personage, whom Zhukovsky wanted to invite for a paso doble as if nothing had happened, despite not really understanding what a paso doble was, or even how it was danced.

After many years of tremendous friendship, Zhukovsky and Chaldonov suddenly had a harsh falling out in 1910 because of something trivial and appallingly unscholarly. Worst of all, the reason evaporated from each man's memory almost immediately, just as powder disappears with a flash, allowing a missile to sail off on its lethal journey. Even so, all the efforts of Marusya and Zhukovsky's daughter to reconcile the two willful men were in vain. Zhukovsky and Chaldonov not only stopped meeting, they stopped talking, too, which went on for, hold on, hold on… Lord have mercy! For over eight years!

And so Chaldonov—his ears blushing and his nose, too, for some reason—stood once again before his old teacher, who was now old in the most literal, Methuselahan sense of the word. Of course they both teared up in the pre-Revolutionary way and firmly embraced, also in the pre-Revolutionary way. Chaldonov extracted alcohol (thoughtfully obtained by Marusya) out of nowhere and the vodka contained in that cloudy, evil, microscopic little vial melted his teacher's already-softened heart for good. After discussing the new politics and power, as well as old friends, to their hearts' content, and then taking potshots at appalling prices and the similarly appalling ignorance of their common scientific opponents, Chaldonov and Zhukovsky once again regained both their peace of mind and each other. Neither could remember what had caused them to take offense: they found in that a truly Gogolian humor that could have ended up as Hoffmannesque sorrow had they not reconciled. Just think, Seryozha, I'm an old man after all, I could have died without telling you how dear you are to me!

All that would have been unbearably trite if not for Zhukovsky's quivering head or the gaping wounds on his bookshelves. He had nothing to heat or barter with and of course Zhukovsky, a widower for many years, didn't happen to have a sly Marusya who could trade a pair of excellent gold earrings for a pair of equally excellent logs and never feel any regret about the earrings. My daughter is just like me, Seryozha, just as foolish and unable to adapt to anything… beyond all that, she doesn't even know mathematics. I have no idea how to live. But do I need to, anyway? Maybe we aren't any use?

Chaldonov waved his arms in indignation, oh, what are you saying, Nikolay Yegorovich, what are you talking about, just listen to my idea and see why I permitted myself to visit you. Remember how you and I talked about the wave resistance of artillery missiles? Zhukovsky began smiling, his head still quivering. He remembered, how could he not!

'And so,' Chaldonov said, speaking quickly, 'just imagine we could put all this on a purely scholarly and even industrial basis rather than just discussing it, and we could receive, let's say, a distinct field to work in, our very own, with separate financing, though that's not the point of it. The primary thing is to have something to work on other than that…' Chaldonov winced, remembering his tedious sufferings at the university.

'But why don't you take it on yourself, Seryozha?' Zhukovsky asked.

'They wouldn't give it to me, Nikolay Yegorovich,' said Chaldonov. 'I lack the authority. As they see things, I'm good enough to be allowed to nurse the semiliterate, but they might not let me at the war industry. You're the one that has to go: they'd certainly trust you, you're the only specialist who...'

Chaldonov stopped and Zhukovsky crisply finished for him, 'Who hasn't died off yet or left the country.'

They both went sullenly silent, mentally trying on all the possibilities. The winter hadn't been easy and the choice wasn't easy. In the icy air, Zhukovsky's breath looked like faint gray hieroglyphics that melted faster than anyone could read them. He was old, completely old, and that was agonizingly painful. But Chaldonov had Marusya and Lindt on his hands and didn't intend to give up.

The next morning, Chaldonov himself escorted Zhukovsky to the Kremlin. Getting there was difficult for the old man: he was tiny, shriveled, and completely lost in a huge overcoat covered with hoarfrost and he slipped so much Chaldonov could hardly keep up, catching a light body that already belonged almost entirely to another world. His audience lasted a long time and Sergey Alexandrovich completely froze as he strolled around near the Borovitsky Gates. Zhukovsky was with higher-ups Chaldonov wasn't yet permitted to see, despite his unconditional acceptance of the revolution. If only they knew Marusya's stubbornness was the sole basis of that very same unconditional acceptance, Marusya who didn't want to abandon her parents' graves or salted cucumbers, barrel-brined cucumbers with big pimples and crunchy white little butt ends.

'Where are you planning to go? England? Where do you think I'll get horseradish in England? Or currant leaves? Or oak bark, not to mention an actual oak barrel! No, no, and no!' Marusya angrily paged through *A Gift to Young Housewives; or a Means of Reducing Household Expenses* (author,

Elena Molokhovets, 22nd edition, corrected and appended, St. P., 1901, N.N. Klobukov Press, Pryazhka Emb., no. 3) and displayed the relevant page for her husband. 'See, it's right here: salted cucumbers, the fifth way, they're made exclusively with oak bark.'

Chaldonov tried to object that if nature offered a minimum of four other ways to salt cucumbers, it probably wasn't worth getting too stuck on the fifth, and that there was probably more than enough horseradish in England and very possibly currants, too, and that Elena Molokhovets was most certainly a poor adviser on questions of life and death.

'What does Molokhovets have to do with it!' Marusya indignantly said. 'Salted cucumbers are a matter of life and death for me!'

So of course they didn't go anywhere.

Two hours later, Chaldonov had already resigned himself to the thought that Zhukovsky had most likely been arrested or even shot right there in the Kremlin—horrible things, things completely in the spirit of Afanasyev's most terrifying folktales, were said about shootings. These listeners, however, weren't five-year-olds and nothing would change if they tried to squeeze their eyes shut or wake up. Another quarter-hour later, however, Zhukovsky suddenly appeared, accompanied by a young, well-mannered little soldier. Zhukovsky was alive, well, and terribly satisfied, and even his split beard glistened like silver, like an honest-to-goodness beaver collar that had been torn off and bartered long ago for oil that turned out to be rancid.

Several months later, in early 1919, a small institute with the clunky abbreviation TsAGI, instead of its actual name, Central Aerohydrodynamic Institute, was opened specially for Zhukovsky: it was a particularly small little institute but it had a very extraordinary charge. Over time, the entire group who'd gathered there under Zhukovsky's leadership made their way into encyclopedias and reference books, and not just Soviet books but books read 'round the world, meaning, gentlemen, that brains of a planetary scale had gathered there and the results themselves were, necessarily, planetary. As deputy director and the one who'd come up with the idea, Chaldonov sat to his teacher's right. He'd prudently held onto his department at Moscow State but given all his energy, of course, to Zhukovsky, who possessed a singular, almost preternatural reserve of strength, despite his apparent decrepitude. Under his leadership the little institute puffed along like a boiling teapot, actively building itself up as it burst with brilliant ideas, fulfilled government orders, discovered glistening peaks, disregarded certain personages, and furiously dethroned others.

Zhukovsky caught pneumonia in February 1920. This could have been more than enough to send him to his grave, but he recovered. His daughter, however, succumbed to consumption while he was burning up in an elderly fever, don't even dare sympathize with me, he'd cut people off, and nobody dared. To be honest, no sympathy would have helped anyway. In June, Zhukovsky suffered a stroke from which he also contrived to recover, as if he truly had sold his soul to the proletarian devil during that intimate audience at the Kremlin. Otherwise there could be no explanation for how even a partially paralyzed old man could dictate a course on theoretical mechanics to a small herd of lively but completely uncomprehending stenographers. He compiled his own autobiography, which was as dry, modest, and small as he was, and he willed the remnants of a once-splendid library to the young Soviet republic, after which he quickly contracted typhus and suffered a second stroke that didn't kill him, either, though it prevented him from a wild celebration of his fiftieth anniversary of scholarly and pedagogical work. Even the devil didn't have the power to pull this one off forever, though. Zhukovsky didn't wind down until the dank March of 1921, when he was buried in Donskoy Monastery and Chaldonov inherited TsAGI. Of course Lazar Lindt had worked at the institute from the day it opened.

Zhukovsky, as it happened, didn't like Lindt one bit.

'I understand, Seryozha, that he's a talented autodidact, a diamond in the rough, and that's always devilishly charming…'

'A genius, Nikolay Yegorovich,' Chaldonov said, quietly clarifying, 'Not a diamond in the rough but a genius.'

Like any teacher, Zhukovsky couldn't tolerate being interrupted—even if there was a reason—and he angrily rattled his fingers on the lunch table. The office allocated to him at TsAGI was even huger and colder than Chaldonov's abode at Moscow State, so Zhukovsky preferred working at home. As they say, at home even the walls will assist you.

'Fine, let's say he's a genius, though even that's very debatable. But, for goodness' sake, he's completely soulless. He's broken, prickly, and inverted, but outside-in, not inside-out. He hasn't the slightest deference to anything and he respects no one's authority, to the point of outright boorishness.'

'Nikolay Yegorovich,' Chaldonov said, once again permitting himself to interrupt, 'the boy's barely turned nineteen. He came here on foot from God knows where, from some horrible settlement, all his family were shot, and he was saved by some miracle. Have you heard about the Jewish colonists? There was hunger and the Stone Age there even in the tame times before, so can you imagine what's happening there now? By all the laws of God and statistics, Lazar should really be illiterate but well, take a look, he manages to befuddle not just me but you, too. And you know yourself that deference in science only leads to stagnation and even petty servility...'

'I don't know, Seryozha, I don't know. But I do remember you at nineteen: you weren't born in any palace, either, but you made a completely different impression, so there's no need to blame age or surroundings. There's just no need!'

'I was never a genius, Nikolay Yegorovich.' Chaldonov fell silent after this admission, giving Zhukovsky an opportunity to assess the admission for himself, too. It was a pure and sad truth, so nothing hurt. 'So I ask you, humbly, humbly, most submissively...'

'Enough of the silly ceremony, Seryozha,' Zhukovsky said, finally angry, which was always a sign of definite capitulation. 'If you want to look after your wandering Jew, for God's sake go ahead. But what do you want from me? To promote him to academician?'

'Just one single signature,' Chaldonov said, speaking faster out of gladness. 'Lazar will become an academician on his own, you'll see, but for starters he needs some kind of paperwork to straighten out his education. He doesn't have anything to his name but a birth certificate, and that's probably forged, too. By all the official rules, he'd still be nothing even if he took charge of a department at the institute right now. But your signature will procure him a full diploma of higher education!'

'Fine,' Zhukovsky muttered. 'Bring in your wunderkind

next week. But I'm warning you now: no allowances will be made!'

And no allowances were made. It was as if Lazar Lindt sensed Zhukovsky's enmity and thus behaved with a wonderful modesty that suited him well, as did Chaldonov's old frock coat, which Marusya had cleverly altered to his build (Lesik, look at this splendid camlet, angora with silk, I always knew it would never wear out!). His hair had already grown back after his initial delousing but he hadn't grown out his wild curls, instead showing off his large head with short, smooth curls like astrakhan fur: basically, he didn't look like a homeless ragamuffin any longer. He answered his venerable examiners' questions—which really were quite difficult—so quickly, correctly, and surprisingly dully that Chaldonov caught Zhukovsky derisively glancing at him a couple times. Quite a genius, to be sure. Memorized three textbooks and brags about it.

Chaldonov felt bewildered, like the unsuccessful entrepreneur who's amassed an entire circus to show off a learned dog that knows four basic arithmetical operations but then comes to realize it's a very lovely but completely dim-witted mutt sitting in the ring, looking important.

'Would you care to speak a bit about Maxwell's equation for electromagnetic fields, Lazar Iosifovich?' Chaldonov said, attempting to save the day, if only a bit. 'You and I had a very interesting discussion about that recently.'

'No,' Lazar said, refusing politely but firmly. 'I don't want to.'

'Don't have your own opinion, colleague?' Zhukovsky asked, venomous and very satisfied with the ruined performance.

'I have one, Nikolay Yegorovich,' Lindt admitted. 'But you'd likely find my opinion unsatisfying.'

'And how's that?' Zhukovsky asked, not sensing any dirty tricks.

'Because,' Lindt said, articulating each word, 'it's impossible to solve any of the electromagnetic field problems, particularly the ones related to the speed of light, on the basis of classical mechanics and Maxwell's equations you referred to. But you claim the opposite. Why should I argue with an incompetent opponent?'

Chaldonov gasped and squeezed his eyes shut, as if a tram had just run over a carefree, red-blooded provincial right in front of him. Zhukovsky silently gaped, suddenly resembling Father Frost in a children's book, albeit a disheartened Father Frost who'd just been unmasked. Lindt lightly bowed to both, a gesture that could be taken as either apology or mockery.

'But, ex-excuse me, dear sir,' Zhukovsky mumbled, regaining his composure, 'Meaning you want to say… It stands to reason that no sensible person would begin to argue with the idea that when velocity increases and nears the speed of light, the value β nears zero and the mass of the body subsequently grows to infinity. All that is highly interesting for radiology but why lapse into Einsteinian metaphysics if it's possible to make do perfectly well with ordinary mechanics? Max Abraham compiled equations for the movement of electrons long ago, using Maxwell's equations…'

Lindt cut him off. 'Your Max Abraham is just an ignoramus!' he said. Chaldonov now began loudly laughing, finally unable to contain himself, whooping and panting like simple folk. Zhukovsky looked at him in amazement for a time then suddenly began laughing, too, in a wonderful staccato, an old man's laughter as cozy and dry as crumbly crackers.

'Why, you little shit!' Zhukovsky squeaked in admiration, poking at Lindt with a yellowish hand that, to be honest, looked a lot like a chicken foot. 'What an amazing little shit! What garbage dump did you find him on, Seryozha? You can barely see him behind the table but there he is, ready to bite off someone's nose!'

All three argued voluptuously for another hour until they'd finally exhausted each other completely. Zhukovsky took the unfortunate petition and waved a sharp quill pen tarnished with multicolored iridescence.

'But pardon me,' he suddenly drawled, dissatisfied. 'There are other subjects on the diploma beyond physics and mathematics. Geography, for example. Or that… what is it called now… philology!'

'That's all Marusya, Nikolay Yegorovich,' said Chaldonov, who had clearly prepared this answer in advance.

'What do you mean, Marusya? She's going to take the exam for your genius?'

'No, come now, God help you! Marusya has been working with the boy personally and you can believe me…'

'I don't doubt she's been working with him,' Zhukovsky said. 'She probably read fairy tales to the numskull. Afanasy Nikitin. *Journey Beyond Three Seas*. Most likely they both went wild from the pleasure.'

He quickly affixed the ostentatious signature of an old pedagogue in the proper place: the signature looked deceptively simple and round, but was wisely equipped with a twisty little tail that eliminated any possibility of forgery.

'And don't stick your nose in the air, you little shit,' he said to Lindt, as if preaching. 'This signature is a respectful tribute to Sergey Alexandrovich and a big advance payment to you.

The gaps in your education are comparable to the gaps in your upbringing. You'll need to study a lot. Quite a lot. Foreign languages, for example. I'm sure you don't know either English or German. And everything's impossible without German! It's the language of Big Science!'

Lindt nodded. German truly was a useful instrument, if only because German colonists lived in misery near Malaya Seydemenukha: things were just as bad for them as for Jews but, unlike Germans, they were happy to use their hands as well as their heads. Yiddish and German become especially similar when discussing the joint conquest of the hard Kherson earth. The blood and sweat of various nations taste the same. Their tears, too. Most likely. Yes, tears, too. This meant Lindt had no intention of arguing about German and, when in early August of 1941 he stood in an interminable line at the military recruitment office, he mentally repeated, booming, his very favorite part of *Faust*:

Ja, was man so erkennen heißt!
Wer darf das Kind beim Namen nennen?
Die wenigen, die was davon erkannt,
Die töricht g'nug ihr volles Herz nicht wahrten,
Dem Pöbel ihr Gefühl, ihr Schauen offenbarten,
Hat man von je gekreuzigt und verbrannt.*

---

* The things that people claim to know!/ Who dares to call the child by its true name?/ The few that saw something like this and, starry-eyed/ But foolishly, with glowing hearts averred/ Their feelings and their visions before the common herd/ Have at all times been burned and crucified.
Faust, Johann Wolfgang von Goethe, tr. Walter Kaufmann, Anchor Books, Doubleday & Company, 1961.

Of course it was impossible to say it out loud: you could get slammed in the snout these days for German, though they probably would have appreciated his pronunciation at the recruiting office. After all, the people there were no fools. And even if they were fools, knowledge of the enemy's language is considered an advantage under any wartime laws. They had to take him. They were simply obligated to. He was, after all, only forty-one!

Lindt looked around: there weren't that many obvious young boys around him. That one over there, for instance, in the checked shirt, with the thin face gnawed by misfortune, couldn't be less than forty-five. The man turned when he felt someone's glance on him and looked at Lindt with despairing eyes that had sunk into darkness. What life are you escaping at the front, you sad case? What makes you think you'll get lucky this time? A strong, broad-faced guy pushed the man, slamming him in the face with a stuffed duffle bag and shoving him to the side without even noticing.

The line shifted uneasily, twisting, stretching into a taut string, then chaotically blocking part of the street. And here, there, and everywhere, an accordion yelped and someone took to dancing, desperately, as if hammering their fear into the cobblestone roadway. A woman unable to contain herself yelped back at the accordion and took to keening, mourning her Vovka or Kolka, all of them, all of them, while they were still whole, while they were still strong, sweaty, and shifting from one foot to the other, making a racket. They were near and dear. They shut her up right away and she fell, sobbing, onto a shoulder, her husband's or her son's, desperately trying to inhale enough familiar scents to last the whole war. I won't let you go anywhere, won't let you go, I'm telling you, who are you leaving me for, oooh my dear, oooh, my dear-ie! Shush, you fool! Don't disgrace me in front of the guys, I'm telling you.

Lindt was alone, as always, as it's supposed to be. Nobody could have imagined him in that line and that made him happy and cheerful, like just before… Lindt stopped. He couldn't remember the last time he was cheerful, or why. Maybe if they'd celebrated something at home when he was a child and decorated a tree for the holidays, all while someone invitingly rustled bags filled with presents behind a closed door. He grinned. We'll consider him happy and cheerful, as it should be before war.

Lindt deeply inhaled the warm, cinnamony, almost spicy air of the Moscow roadway. Moscow recalls its village heritage toward autumn and begins smelling of apples, bread rolls, crisp new cotton fabric, and sturdy foliage, slowly cooling. There's nothing finer than Moscow in September and there wasn't even the slightest hope the war would be over by November, though that was all anyone talked about in line. Lindt understood that everything would just be getting started in November: it only took a third of his brains to grasp that, but he didn't interfere with the hysterical animated general chatter. Let them think it. They were mere people. Poor people. An example of tautology. The main thing was that the recruiting office not send him away.

A smart, bug-eyed automobile pulled around the corner and braked at the sidewalk, blinding the future soldiers with its varnished glint. 'My word, it's a 1935 Horch 853,' a young man behind Lindt nearly groaned as if he'd clambered up a dozen crates, barely keeping his balance, and finally gotten to a hidden crack in the wall where he could see a naked girl. A real naked girl. Velvety-soft, vaguely lunar, barely discernible in the dimness of the steam bath.

A striking young ignoramus got out of the Horch and gracefully slammed the black-and-white car door. He was tall, round-headed, and smiling, and he wore a foreign tweed suit. The stupefied crowd, unable to believe their eyes, observed his dandified little case of genuine leather, short pants, and molded calves gracefully embraced by—but no, that just can't be!—dense, taut socks. Bourgeois, I fucking swear! said some foul-mouthed person behind Lindt. And look at that! Just bourgeois! Just so you know, they corrected him, dissatisfied, he's a foreigner, not a bourgeois. A foreign correspondent. He'll write an article about us.

Meanwhile, the foreign correspondent dismissed his incredible car with a stately gesture and headed to the very thick of the line, all with the same exultant, dopey smile of a very young and very healthy person who eats white bread with butter and pink, slightly dewy ham every morning. Plus, of course, warm milk. In the thinnest of light-blue glasses, maybe his grandmother's. So well-fed, a regular hog! said the envious in the line, from the bottom of their hearts.

The young ignoramus vacillated indecisively for a second, searched the crowd, and walked up to Lindt, displaying uncanny precision in identifying someone of his own sort. 'Hello,' he said affably, in the purest, most wonderful and juicy Russian. 'Pardon me for approaching you, but I'd like to sign up for the front and don't know how to start…' Lindt wanted to answer but didn't get a chance because the exceptional young man was immediately swept away by a sea of the people's love. He was literally passed from hand to hand: slapped on his round tweed shoulders, welcomed with curses, squeezed like a sweet puppy, and yelled at, all at once, as they tried to determine where this absurd wonder had come from. But how can, how can you, fuck, are you really one of us? Where'd you come from like that? A general's son, has to be! Nope, guys, we'll win for sure, just look, you can't get around a face like that in a tank! That's it, he should be a tank driver. No, a pilot. You could bomb them with him: not one Fritz would be left, they'd all crap themselves from fear. Come on don't yell like that, what's your name, handsome? And where'd you lose your pants? He didn't lose them, he grew out of them! And Mama didn't have money to buy him long ones!

This all resembled an explosion, an explosion of general relief. The crowd had been like a painful boil for a few hours: bluish-crimson, numb from fear, and painfully tense. It was as if the appearance of this ludicrous young man, whose villainously bourgeois clothing belied his otherwise heroic Soviet being, had released everyone's agonizingly accumulated tension: pus, fear, and sticky lymph all burst out, along with a hysterical jollity. It hadn't even been this frightening in 1918. Lindt remembered that with certainty. Things had been happy in their own way in 1918.

After acquiring a name—My name's Sashka, Sashka Berenson!—the young chump beamed like a bare rosy buttock out in the cold and answered all the questions at once, simultaneously trying to open his foppish case. The case turned out to hold an imported Solingen shaving kit and two packages of peanut brittle. Have some! It's my very favorite! You can't get this for anything, not even in Berlin! Why would I put you on? I lived in Berlin for five years.

And thus was solved the mystery of the Horch, the socks, and the short pants.

It turned out Sashka—also known as Alexander Davidovich Berenson—was just the son of a diplomatic worker: he was a young, decent dunce filled with patriotic impulses of the most naïve persuasion. While his dear papa handled government matters somewhere in the Kremlin after being recalled home because of wartime, Sashka decided to go to the front as a volunteer, something he accomplished without delay. The men, mouths agape, listened to his stories about Berlin streets and coffee shops, which emphasized ice cream a great deal because of his youth, though the simple-minded public demanded stories about women. Is it true they go around without drawers and the dresses are see-through?

'I don't know anything about drawers,' admitted the embarrassed Sashka. Everyone started buzzing with disappointment. 'But! But! But I saw Hitler,' he blurted, attempting to save his tottering position. Everyone went silent. Hitler, that was serious.

'So what's he like?' asked a thickset man of about thirty-five who looked like he came from a family of factory hands.

'Nothing special!' Sashka said. 'Shabby, with a little moustache under his nose. I could take him with just my left.'

'Shabby, you're saying?' asked the same man. 'And with one left? But that same shabby man is driving us away from the border like puppies...'

'Instigator!' some woman quickly shrieked. 'Comrades! There's an instigator among us! We won't let the enemy break our fighting spirit!'

The crowd forgot about Sashka and closed in around the factory hand, everyone screaming and proving to one other—and to themselves, too—that we can take the fascists with one left, it's as good as done!

It got shrilly frightening again.

The bewildered Sashka kept offering what remained of his peanut brittle, but nobody noticed him anymore.

'What do you think?' he shyly asked Lindt, 'Will they take me? I know what you're thinking—I'm very strong! I do exercises every morning.'

Lindt shrugged noncommittally: if it were up to him, he wouldn't even let this splendid milksop near toy guns.

Two hours later they were both on the recruiting office's front stoop. Lindt, white-hot with humiliation, didn't know where to look. A recruiter—mean, narrow, and looking like a lancet that had been rubbed with alcohol—had cursed him out with quiet, tedious, and thus particularly unpleasant abuse. You took it into your head to play silly games, comrade scientist? You felt like suffering? Fighting for the Motherland? Do you have any idea what kind of exemptions you have, professor? They're as solid as a KV-2 tank! You're not going to the front, you should be under guard yourself! Thought you'd send me to the tribunal, did you, you fucking hero? You don't feel like living yourself and decided to take someone else down with you? Listen to my command: About face and march the fuck out of here! Now!

Sashka was as exultant and crackly as a holiday firecracker after receiving his assignment for junior officers' training. Lindt firmly shook his hand, feeling for the first time in his life that he was old and unneeded by anyone. Neither Marusya nor the Motherland required his voluntary sacrifices. Nobody. The volunteers around him buzzed, pushed, waved their arms, and shouted. Ninety percent of them would die in the first days and months of fighting after they reached the front. But Sashka—Alexander Davidovich Berenson—would remain.

(Professor, doctor of legal sciences, head of the department of criminal law at the International Legal Institute, ladies' man, gourmand, and man about town. He just died last year. And even at the age of eighty-eight, he still looked like a tall, puffy-cheeked, spoiled landowner's son.

(If you don't believe it, search it on Yandex.)

Lindt, dispirited and looking drawn, went from the recruitment office to the Chaldonovs': his feet automatically took him to Marusya, just as his hands automatically laid money on the counter at the ornate Yeliseyevsky Food Store. I'd like cream puffs, meringues, tartlets, two of each please, no, let's make that five each. A pretty little ruddy-cheeked saleswoman, herself reminiscent of a warm, tasty, glazed baba au rhum, extended a plump little finger as she neatly placed the pastries in a large box. 'Would you like some chocolate balls? We have them glazed or with sprinkles,' she warbled, sounding like a gentle plotter, as if she were offering God knows what spicy, forbidden services to Lindt. The client was interesting: pale, small, and nervous. A Jew, of course, but it was immediately obvious he had a respectable position and money. Beautifully dressed. Not young but, well, he wasn't going to be boiled up for dinner! With mechanical enjoyment Lindt assessed the touching dimples on the saleswoman's elbows and the taut, gentle strength that stretched her well-starched white uniform. She was probably clumsy but she was also hot and hungry, enough for ten. Not now, my dear, I'm sorry. No, no, no cream horns, thank you. Marusya couldn't stand cream horns.

Lindt couldn't remember such havoc ever reigning at the Chaldonovs', it was like a sandstorm. Marusya was simultaneously packing three suitcases and the sight of the box from the Yeliseyevsky made her toss up her hands and drop Chaldonov's knitted vest, which she was unsuccessfully attempting to cram between her own shoes and her husband's archive. You're crazy, Lesik! Pastries! At a time like this! Lindt picked up the vest and neatly rolled it into a tight tube. It'll fit that way. What do you mean, a time like this, Maria Nikitichna? There won't be starvation until winter, why restrain ourselves now? Are you getting ready to move? Or just nervous?

Marusya looked Lindt in the eye, incredulous: he was a master of trickery, pranks, and mockery. A paradoxical mindset, paradoxical sense of humor, and utter fearlessness. Verging on idiocy. Lindt's little jokes at TsAGI and at Moscow State were legendary: he took no heed of position or rank. As a twenty-five-year-old boy, he nearly drove Lidia Borisovna Iliyenko, the academic council's secretary, to a stroke, and she was a lady renowned for her monumentalness in all realms, human stupidity included. It was said she ruled over dissertations, academic luminaries, and even comets. That the quivering of her second chin was an auspicious sign. That she slept with someone so high up in the Party that there was an assumption of a certain automatic, as it were, professional asexuality. Few people, however, believed there existed a seeker of Iliyenko's stale allure, even within the highest echelons of the Party, but then again, it's common knowledge that true Communists are capable of all sorts of heroics.

Legend or not, however, Iliyenko truly did shake academicians around like twig brooms: even the most venerable, gray-haired high priests of science groveled before her like mischievous puppies. All but Lindt, who simply preferred not to notice Lidia Borisovna. Once, however, she stopped him on the doorstep of the auditorium where yet another academic coven was getting underway.

'And you, where're you going, young man?' She sang this out in a tone that didn't bode well for anyone. 'It seems to me you aren't even a member of the academic council.'

'Absolutely correct, Lidia Borisovna,' Lindt said in amiable agreement. 'I'm not the council's member. I'm its brain.'

And what do you think? Absolutely nothing terrible happened to Lindt if, that is, you don't count the fact that the totally demoralized Iliyenko finally learned Lindt's name once and for all after drinking herself silly on valerian. Once and for all.

But no, this time Lindt most certainly did not laugh; someone else might have been mistaken, but not Marusya. What, you really didn't know they're evacuating us all? They posted the order at the institute first thing this morning. Sergey Alexandrovich phoned and told me to pack right away. What, they didn't call you in to the institute? Why aren't you saying anything, Lesik? Where were you gallivanting around half the day? Lindt shrugged noncommittally as he placed fragile, slightly crackly meringues on a plate. Marusya didn't have to get him ready for the front so she might as well pack her husband's things calmly.

'Lesik, confess, are you involved with someone again?' Marusya asked, interpreting his silence her own way. 'What, is it finally serious this time?

Lindt remained silent again and Marusya instantly forgot about evacuation and even the war so she could hurry off along a magical yellow brick road to meet up with someone else's delightful happiness. Like any childless woman, she adored matchmaking, christening, betrothing, leading someone into marriage, and carefully taking hefty grunting babies in her arms: in short, she adored furtively overlaying her own unfulfilled dreams onto the unattractive conventionalities of real life. It was one of several methods for turning the most everyday little cotton cloth into a festive brocade, and Marusya certainly knew her way around quality fabrics.

'And you didn't even invite her for tea! You are shameless! Sergey Alexandrovich and I do seem to have a certain right,' she said, reproaching Lindt as she quickly took the empty box away from him and brushed invisible crumbs off the table because they were unworthy of keeping company with the most mediocre porcelain Soviet teacups, which looked like precious bone china in her hands.

Marusya was soft, light, and silky-smooth in her joints as she moved, lovely—that was it, lovely, and time had no power over that loveliness, over those tender lips, over the gray hair that seemed to rhyme with the lace cuffs on her dress and the bluish pearls on her earlobes. He had given her those earrings himself, paid for them out of his first serious honorarium for his first serious monograph. What did Goethe say?

Ihn treibt die Gärung in die Ferne,
Er ist sich seiner Tollheit halb bewußt;
Vom Himmel fordert er die schönsten Sterne
Und von der Erde jede höchste Lust,
Und alle Näh und alle Ferne
Befriedigt nicht die tiefbewegte Brust.*

---

* His spirit's ferment drives him far,/ And he half knows how foolish is his quest:/ From heaven he demands the fairest star,/ And from the earth all joys that he thinks best;/ And all that's near and all that's far/ Cannot soothe the upheaval in his breast.
Faust, Johann Wolfgang von Goethe, tr. Walter Kaufmann, Anchor Books, Doubleday & Company, 1961.

'You're not listening to me at all, Lesik!' Marusya said. 'And here I am dreaming about grandchildren. When will you finally deign to marry? I don't want to die without seeing your children.'

'You won't die, Maria Nikitichna,' Lindt calmly said. 'Anyone but you. I promise.'

He lightly caught her small, hot hand and pressed it to his lips, stunned again by its aroma: midday filled with sunny hay and ripe apples; a sleepy, blazing hot, and rather stuffy attic; ripe kisses furtively plucked. Everything would work out. Everything would work out in this life, because there's no other life.

Chaldonov found his wife and Lindt peacefully drinking tea together when he came home two hours later, all in a lather after endless ball-chewing from the higher-ups. A neat heap of packed crates and suitcases towered in the corner and Marusya was persuading Lindt that her cream puffs compared favorably with the Yeliseyevsky's and that hers were even rather superior. Lindt cheerfully disagreed as the pastries they'd set aside for Chaldonov slowly dried out on a plate at the very edge of the table. There were no cream puffs among them because Marusya had eaten all five in her search for suitable lines of reasoning.

In late August 1941, nearly the entire staff of TsAGI left for evacuation in Ensk. Even Lindt—rocking in a train compartment, dozing off, pressing his temple to the throbbing glass, and mechanically counting Russia's endless versts—didn't suspect the journey was for forever.

It took nearly a month to reach their destination, unprecedented speed at a time when dozens of trains amassed at every junction and were forced to wait for hours, even days. Hundreds of cargo cars refitted for human habitation dozed on dead-end sidings, and they looked more like houses than trains after sprouting roots and washed undies. Evacuees wandered the platforms, babies howled, women brutalized by this overwhelming way of life argued, and older boys played intense war games, while men worn out from waiting smoked and spat bitter slobber onto crushed rock. And the railroad men—sweaty, fierce, and having forgotten about rest, sleep, family, and pies for a long time—continually ran around, cursing. There was no use pestering them with questions or complaints: Lazar Moiseyevich Kaganovich's clutch of fledglings knew the harsh temper of the people's commissar for railways perfectly well. The iron commissar didn't like joking and often repeated that every catastrophe has a first name, a surname, and a patronymic. That was before the war and now there was no need at all to count on good humor. Everyone understood that nobody would be imprisoned for negligence now: they'd shoot you on the spot instead, in an unmowed ditch just under the roadbed. Right behind the special train that didn't leave for the front on time.

Every possible exception, however, was made for the train carrying TsAGI to evacuation. In those days, Soviet power brought its plans to life harshly, and there were plans for establishing a large-scale military-industrial complex in Ensk to supply the army with whatever it needed. A large and very businesslike delegation met this train filled with select brains from the capital at a cramped little rural train station: Ensk had just became a regional center in 1937, so they'd held festive events that year, despite what contemporary history books might say. The confused scholarly folk were quickly shoved into trucks and sent to their new places of registered residence, though Chaldonov and the rest of the institute's management were taken for meetings with city authorities. Chaldonov grabbed Lindt at the last minute, whispering something in the ear of the head Party member who was hosting them and putting the poor fat man in a sweat; he even sank to a crouch in a sudden gush of respect. Lindt dug his heels in like a child who's carried off to bed just when all the guests are gathering at the table, but his attempt was in vain, and he was courteously pushed into an automobile. Marusya's face flashed through the little oval back window; she'd been left on the platform in a crowd of bewildered women, screaming children, and scruffy bundles. As always, nobody went out of their way to take care of families until the very end.

'Come now, Lazar, don't fret like that, for God's sake,' Chaldonov said, teeth rattling as he made his tired request. The car shook mercilessly; the roads in Ensk had always been worse than atrocious. 'In the first place, I'm sure this won't be for long. In the second, believe me, Marusya will get by just fine on her own.'

'And don't you doubt it!' said the fat Party man, leaning over the front seat to butt in. 'Everyone will be accommodated and settled within the next twenty-four hours. In complete accordance. According to all the norms. By order of the people's commissar!'

And so it was: the TsAGI wives barely had a chance to worry in earnest before they were taken in hand by a flying column of cheery servicemen with frantic dreams of the front but forced, hell, to do some damned work on the home front. They dashingly divided into pairs and began jostling the ladies from the capital (some of whom happened to be exceptionally good-looking) into vehicles. Marusya was assisted by a ruddy, round-faced little officer whose belts wrapped him up tight, like a holiday bouquet. The talkative little lieutenant managed to tell Marusya twice about his uncomplicated but valiant life, all while a private placed the Chaldonovs' belongings in a personal truck (Academicians are always esteemed here!) and brought their dear guest to her new place of residence. Despite sharing the unity of time, listener, and place, the two versions of the story differed strikingly, though the main character in both completely overcame all obstacles and acquired half a kingdom (his own eight-square-meter room) and a beautiful king's daughter (If only you could see my Natalya, wow! She can lift me with one hand!) and Lord knows what other fairytale dividends.

As a result, the charmed Marusya missed all of Ensk as it floated by, remembering only the truck stopping at a gloomy three-storey building. The little officer nimbly helped her out of the truck after receiving a sack of little sugar pillow candies as a reward (I'll bring them to Natalya, oh, she'll be so happy, what a sweet tooth!). So this here is where you'll live. Likhonin, haul it up to the second floor. No, don't drag it, you fiend, you'll bang up the goods! Marusya climbed a marble staircase that had obviously once gleamed with merchant grandeur and curiously entered the apartment.

A long dim corridor. One room on the left, two on the right, there should be a kitchen over there. Yes, a kitchen!

'You've been given housing fit for a tsar, Maria Nikitichna!' the little officer reported, opening one door after another, obviously proud of Ensk hospitality. 'All the facilities are in the nook around the corner, there's even a little pantry in case you decide to hire someone for housekeeping… Careful, don't trip, there are little children's sleds here, at first we thought we'd take them away but then decided who knows, maybe comrade Chaldonov has grandchildren and, anyway, they're nice things, why throw them out if you've arrived from Moscow almost empty-handed. It's better to have things set from the get-go, so you can sit right down to work, give it all you've got instead of being too distracted by everyday things. For the front! For victory! Isn't that right?'

Marusya nodded, strangely quieted as she looked around a home that had clearly been dear, loved, and abandoned in a hurry, under some sort of horrible circumstances about which—this was obvious—asking was not just impossible, but also useless, because then she'd have to admit to herself that this wonderful, clear-eyed boy with the lieutenant shoulderboards was also to blame for all these orphaned curtains sewn by someone's affectionate, dexterous hands, for cabinets forever frightened and filled with dishes pining from loneliness, for these… But why list them all? And she, Marusya, was guilty, too. Of course she was guilty. Who else could be to blame for all this?

Marusya walked up to a table covered by an embroidered tablecloth and ran her fingers over it as if she were blind. Bulging little roses alternated with large-eyed daisies: satin stitch, chain stitch, open work on the edge, an entire winter of painstaking, cozy, evening work. Marusya embroidered beautifully herself—there was the quiet crunch of piercing the fabric, the colorful fiddling with threads, a callous on a hard-working index finger. Thimbles were for the lazy and this homemaker was obviously not lazy. How old was she? Where was she now? Where were her children? Could they survive? Or at least forgive?

'You aren't feeling ill are you, Maria Nikitichna? Shall I go for a doctor? In a jiffy!' the little officer said. Marusya, all blue-gray and suddenly empty, shook her head no.

'You go ahead, Kolya. Everything's fine. Thank you. Go, you have plenty to do, I'll get along just fine by myself, all right? Be sure to convey my greetings to Natalya.'

Lieutenant Kolya saluted obediently. 'I'll convey your greetings. Are you sure you're all right?'

Marusya used her last strength to smile.

'Fine then,' the officer said, hurrying off with relief. 'You settle in comfortably and we ask you to excuse us if anything's not right. Likhonin, to the door!'

And so Likhonin, who hadn't uttered a sound, stopped his ant-like fussing with the suitcase and dragged himself to the door behind his commander. The door banged. And then another bang, the front door downstairs. Marusya surveyed the room again and realized, yes, that was exactly it: the little shelf in the corner was certainly for icons, but now a silent loudspeaker had settled in. The dish-like speaker might fool some people but not Marusya, no, she immediately recognized a deserted icon shelf, a perch for angels, a quiet little bench where the Lord could sit down, catch His breath, and look around after making his rounds to all the homes. It must have been left by the very first residents, the merchants, who'd, yes, that was it, also been taken away from here in a hurry, in the pre-morning darkness, with tears, cursing, and oaths. And the mistress of the house, that same one, the first one, kept turning and wailing, and was probably sorry about something very trivial, maybe an unfinished little pillow or some silver tea glass holders that were set aside for guests thus never used, meaning they stayed in the cabinet their whole life, waiting in vain for their festive hour... Marusya could clearly imagine how she herself, disheveled, frightening, and nocturnal, would have been torn away from her husband: she could even see how he'd find the strength to smile in parting and how his poorly shaved gray chin would quiver like an old man's.

Oh Lord, when will all this be over? When will this endless chain of horrors finally break?

The Lord was silent, as if he were hiding behind the dusty radio speaker, not that there'd have been a place inside, even for him: Levitan's war reporting voice was too vast and the news digests from the Soviet Informbureau were too frightening. And then Marusya sank to her knees, labored, and began praying to the silent radio speaker, furiously and feverishly, as she'd never prayed to anyone in her life.

By the time dimmish Ensk began to turn dark blue outside the window—it got dark earlier here than in Moscow, and it was cold in a non-Moscow way, this was after all, only the end of September—Marusya's knees had begun to ache and the small of her back cramped in hot pain from her prostrations. It was time to get up, fix something for dinner, and search the bundles and suitcases for the grains she'd managed to come across at some station along the way: she'd never in her life left her husband hungry, not even during the Civil War, and she wouldn't leave him hungry now so Lord, forgive me for cutting this short, You have others to listen to anyway, and You haven't been noticing me for a long time anyway.

So forgive me, dear, for nattering on.

Forgive me. Do You hear?

Forgive me.

Marusya stood and wandered, shivering, to the kitchen. She flicked the light switch: there was no blackout here, though there'd been a full blackout when they left Moscow, where Marusya had kept turning until the car went around the corner, searching out the beloved windows she'd x-ed out herself with paper crosses. She'd said goodbye.

It was empty, quiet, and frightening in the kitchen. Marusya feared all the alien things in the kitchen as much as they feared her unfamiliar hands: they shuddered, shunned her, and went out of their way to crawl off to far corners, into a shadowy refuge, as if they were human. She had to speak with every teacup, taming and stroking it on its quivering side as if it were a long-suffering abandoned puppy, and so, while Marusya cooked, she stirred, moved things around, and, mumbling, grasped with a towel and covered with a cautious lid. These weren't prayers at all, but pure sorcery familiar to any woman: the roots go back to impossibly ancient times when there wasn't even God and there wasn't the Word, only pure love nothing had sullied. And so Marusya sorcered with all her might, listening for the door to click open: it felt as if only her husband's presence would return meaning and order to everything, chase away the fears, and pacify a dense darkness that was almost cubic. The apartment needed a master, even if he was as muddleheaded as Seryozha, but he wasn't coming and wasn't coming and so in the end Marusya decided to give up, turn off the stove, and sit all night at an impenetrable window in the age-old pose of the waiting woman. It was always exactly the same, no matter how many centuries passed.

The apartment withdrew into itself, too, though it quietly sighed every now and then, as if it were adapting to Marusya. Something occasionally landed outside on the window sill, scratching on deafening nocturnal tin, distinctly clawing. Marusya convinced herself it was pigeons, ordinary pigeons, but of course it wasn't pigeons at all. When a big nonexistent cat streaked through the entryway like a quiet shadow, Marusya couldn't contain herself and burst into tears.

Because she had no more strength.

Neither Chaldonov, who didn't come home until dawn, unshaven and nearly drunk with exhaustion, nor even Lindt noticed anything. Sometimes Marusya thought they were so absorbed in their little scientific toys that they didn't even notice the war, meaning four years of fears, news digests, and endless waiting in lines fell exclusively on her shoulders. Lindt was allotted an excellent room nearby and no matter how much Marusya tried to convince him to move in with them, he obstinately refused. Marusya thought, with sadness, that Lesik was all grown up now and didn't need her any longer, though it would have been so easy to have him around. Not easy, of course, but a lot easier because he would have calmed any ghosts: he didn't give a damn about ghosts because her Lesik didn't believe in anything and that happy, fearless disbelief that usually distressed Marusya so much would have been just the thing right now.

Sometimes Lindt did spend the night with them, though, and then everything was almost like before: happy evenings at a happy table, Marusya didn't see any cats, and the apartment felt warm, peaceful, and bathed in light, exactly the same as it was before for everyone except her. Except her. But then Lindt would leave in the mornings, quickly kissing Marusya's hand and finishing an argument about something with Chaldonov on the way out: a hundred twenty million missiles and mines, fifteen thousand seven hundred ninety-seven airplanes, and innumerable deaths were on their conscience. There was nothing on Marusya's conscience, but it was they who hurried off down the stairs laughing like little boys as she stood on the threshold watching them go while a huge, frightening, lonely day impossible to fill with household chores stood silently and warily behind her back.

Meanwhile, Ensk swelled threateningly, taking in wave after wave of evacuees who arrived by the trainload, by the factoryload, even by the industryload. Fifty large enterprises were transferred to Ensk just between July and November of 1941, and a total of around nine million people were evacuated throughout the country. Around nine million, just think! The city grew crowded with tens of thousands of evacuees who were frightened, ripped from their homes, and crazy from exhaustion and that wild, desperate, absolutely unnecessary freedom the war brought. The housing shortage was catastrophic and everyone was squeezed in tighter: where four once lived, space was suddenly found for another ten.

Marusya hurried off to the city council: Comrade first secretary, don't you think four rooms for two people isn't very fair? The comrade wouldn't even hear her out, waving her away with his only hand. The second had been rotting somewhere near Verkhneudinsk since the Civil War, well probably not rotting any longer, only the white bones would be left. So get the hell out of here with your whims, sweetheart, there's a war going on and you don't know yourself what you want. She has a lot of rooms, you understand. It might be a lot for you but it's just right for an academician. Basically, I'm not going to even begin to trouble comrade Chaldonov with this, and I advise you to do the same, I don't care that you're his wife, oh, what we would have done to have wives like that in our time!...

The end of the sentence, however, penetrated an already-closed door. And what about me, Marusya mumbled, walking onto the city council building's front stoop, which was equipped with two frosty sentries instead of pillars, and what's happening with me, I never asked anyone's advice or permission in my life and now here I am, take that, and I jumped right up, oh, my father, my master, allow me to do a kind deed and kiss your tender shoulder. Or maybe I really have gotten old? But not if I have any say in the matter!

Quick and nimble as always, Marusya wrapped herself up in a scarf of such gentle gray it wasn't obvious where the scarf's fluffiness ended and the sky began. She hurried down the street, lightly and hastily, her resoled heels leaving starlike tracks. You just wait, I'll show you… she thought to herself feverishly, without understanding who they—those 'yous'—were and what she could do. What, oh Lord?

Marusya turned, then turned again, suddenly realizing she had no idea where she was. This was yet another part of Ensk she hadn't mastered or gotten to know. She was on a long, totally empty and dazed street with a bloody, almost viscous-looking sun, slowly floating overhead. And there was no smoke, no clatter, not the slightest movement. For a second it seemed as if everyone had already died, leaving only Marusya, and now she'd have to eternally wander this mute, bloodless city without the slightest hope of help or salvation.

It was piercingly cold and quiet, but the purest of snow, unblemished by anyone, screeched underfoot and Marusya didn't initially realize the snow wasn't crying out exactly in time with her steps, like a child continues to cry even after he's already been left alone, after nothing hurts anymore… She stopped and the snow immediately went silent but a small childlike voice became more distinct. I've lost my mind, thought Marusya, feeling a certain cheerful relief. She took off a mitten and pinched herself as hard as she could near her wrist, in that sensitive place where the delicate, resilient bead of the pulse lives.

The crying wouldn't go away: the howling continued somewhere around her feet, and it was weak, clingy, and nauseating, like a worn-out, stray little animal that you can't abandon but are too disgusted to take in your arms. There was no doubt it was a crying child, a live child out doing something on an Ensk street dazed from the cold in February 1942. Marusya looked around again and hurried off toward the quiet squeaking, bending for some reason as if she were sniffing but not noticing she'd dropped a mitten on the snow, a little red mitten that looked like either a half-open flower or a dead bullfinch.

Those who say soldiers and people in love don't get sick are most certainly lying. As proof, Lazar Lindt spent at least half of February 1942 with a humiliatingly bothersome head cold that neither love nor war diminished in the slightest. That would have been perfectly understandable if he'd been standing alongside a bunch of women and teenagers at a lathe: the newly assembled machine shops weren't heated until forty-three so people had to work for hours at a time in a huge, echoing coldness that was beyond the control of simple humans. No, the coldness was even beyond anything of this world, meaning that by the end of a shift it felt like you had nothing left, not life, not exhaustion, not even air itself, only a completely empty and icy expanse extending back to the first day of creation or a big bang or maybe even God Himself. And you also really wanted to eat. Really wanted to. The whole front had to be fed so it was hard to think straight, even about victory.

But no, Lindt wasn't freezing, he only had to walk from his building's front door to a car, and he could eat until he was sated, albeit without delicacies—they got wonderful rations almost like the ones for the front, nobody economized on them for a minute; thank God there was someone's pocket to pick so the best scholars could be fed. Essentially, the whole country behaved austerely and surprisingly rationally, as if it were a huge dying organism: in order to preserve the main things—the heart and the brain—they shut down one body system after another, starting with what you could do without but still hold on a little longer, all the while obeying the laws of biology. The brain, by the way, was the penultimate frontier: it's surprising, of course, but even the brain had to be sacrificed to save the heart. Surprising, frightening, and very harmonious. Especially if you take into account that many, many people wanted to consider themselves hearts.

It's a shame the head cold wouldn't abate, even after philosophical inferences like that: the head cold was having a fine time in the secluded corners and echoing emptiness of Lindt's spacious nose, such a fine time that Lindt, groaning from humiliation, first used up all his existing handkerchiefs, then assessed the scale of the disaster and put an entire sheet into service, tearing it apart with a cool crispness, rag by rag. And he would likely have to attack another soon. His head was just indecently achy but neither tea nor aspirin helped, so the lady doctor with the panicky fear of pneumonia who'd been appointed to treat Lindt even went to the trouble of procuring the most difficult-to-come-by bacteriophage to prevent reason's renowned light from dimming. It took some effort but Lindt calmed the doctor and even forbade her to come by more than once a day, because, Nina Sergeyevna, I understand your desire to mourn at a dying man's deathbed but I intend to live a while longer, please do forgive me.

The doctor rattled on and resigned herself to that but still strove to look in on Lindt in the mornings and evenings. She was, as it happens, very pretty, thin with a deft little nose and delicate, slightly puffy circles under her eyes. A Petersburg girl. Lindt liked her, especially her unexpectedly strong, almost masculine, hands that were never flustered, unlike the doctor herself. Now let's have another look at you, Lazar Iosifovich. Lindt obediently lifted up his underclothes, baring a hollow stomach with a black curly plume that ran to his groin; he felt especially warm and alive under this woman's intelligent, searching fingers. It was too bad the accursed influenza had completely deprived him of the sense of olfaction because she probably smelled glorious. Especially coming in from the cold. She most likely smelled of something cool, pink, and smooth. Like Marusya's lips.

And that's why he wasn't getting better: Marusya wasn't there. She didn't come to see him. Not once, the entire two weeks he was sick.

This was so strange there wasn't even any point of looking for explanations, at least not logical explanations, the only explanations that even existed for Lindt. Any of Lindt's ailments in the past—and, to be totally honest, not just his—gave Marusya genuine spasms of tenderness and compassion. Not that she fussed, sympathized, started wringing her hands, or even sat for endless hours at a bed burning with fever. She simply entered the room quickly, got up on tiptoes and opened the ventilation window, and then, how's this for news, Lesik? There's no reason to lie around so sit up, we're going to have some bouillon and gossip now because you just can't imagine, Kurnakov acquired himself a new flame, and what a flame! A magical blond with a bust that could hold place settings for twenty.

'A graduate student?' Lindt asked, noticeably livelier.

'Think higher, a waitress!' Marusya happily said as she generously added ground black pepper to the bouillon as if it were sugar, energetically jingling a spoon. 'Landau's so jealous he's ready to scoff up his necktie from envy.'

"Dau doesn't wear neckties, Maria Nikitichna.'

'His sandals, then,' Marusya said, obligingly. 'His horrendous worn-out sandals. How can he do that to himself, Lesik? You're a genius, too, but you always wear perfectly clean boots anyway. And don't look at me with those eyes like some wounded fawn a bullet went through. Drink your bouillon before it gets cold.'

Lindt smiled and swallowed bouillon fiery hot with pepper and as fatty as glycerin. He could physically feel the mercury in the thermometer return to normal in bouncy jolts. He could endure anything alongside Marusya: amputation, torture, or death. This time, though, when he was genuinely sick for the first time in ages, for some reason she didn't come. She'd only telephoned once in two weeks—two weeks!—though she knew perfectly well he'd caught a cold. She'd sighed and asked if he needed anything, but that was only in passing and in such a quick, happy voice it was as though Lindt were some admirer she'd grown tired of and had to get rid of as quickly as possible so she could run off to her guests, where there was music, animated hubbub, and the traditional mandarin orange smell around a holiday tree.

Lindt phoned Chaldonov at work, but Chaldonov just bleated out something incomprehensible through the crackling and rustling of an undependable military line. How could anyone get well under circumstances like that? Nohow!

Nevertheless, by early March—the peak of the furious cold snaps—Lindt got a grip on himself and got well. More specifically, he tired of his own fickle behavior, malingering, and scaring the pretty doctor with symptoms he'd extracted at random from *A Guide to Pathologies and Therapies for Illnesses of the Nose, Mouth, Throat, Larynx, and Windpipe*, which he'd bought from a local second-hand bookseller when the opportunity presented itself. (Dr. Maximilian Bresgen, Saint Petersburg, publication of the journal *Practical Medicine*, 44 Kazanskaya Street, 1897. With numerous illustrations in the text.) Despite the war, his passion for old books hadn't gone anywhere, just as his love for Marusya hadn't gone anywhere.

Lindt had realized long ago, with sadness, that he was a one-woman man.

He could no longer lie around on the sofa and fill himself to the eyebrows with tea. Besides, Lindt possessed excellent health and had already made it through the crucible of natural selection as an infant: statistics were respected in Malaya Seydemenukha, which is why in the best case scenario only one in two babies lived a full year. Lindt also had plenty of work to do so he dropped the influenza through sheer will. Marusya, apparently, didn't notice.

He bided his time for another week, out of principle, and that was difficult. Very difficult. Then he went to see the Chaldonovs himself.

Nobody answered, either when he rang or when he knocked, and Lindt thought he and Marusya had somehow missed each other, which made him fleetingly and very youthfully sorry everything would be for naught: his freshly cut hair, sharply creased pants, and the surprise hidden under his overcoat, fresh flowers in February of 1942. They were impossible to procure in wintry Ensk even during peacetime but the lab assistants kept an excellent geranium on the windowsill and he'd pinched off a lush microscopic little bouquet, almost a boutonniere. But it was flowers, genuine fresh flowers. Now they'd die with no glory.

After Lindt put all his hopes in the theory of probability and knocked again, the door suddenly and obediently swung open, hitting the guest with a communal din and stench so impossible in Marusya's home that Lindt decided he'd either gone to the wrong apartment or the wrong floor.

A frail and disgusting little boy of around nine stood on the threshold. He was shaved bald, evidently for hygienic concerns that were completely beside the point because the boy was still dirty. More specifically, he was unwashably grubby, and even the woman's sweater he was got up in had a mirror-like greasy sheen on the elbows and belly, but this was Marusya's sweater, Marusya's thin, pale blue jersey, which Lindt immediately recognized. Unlike millions of men, Lindt knew his way around women's clothing, particularly Marusya's. He could easily have listed everything she'd worn since the first day they met, even back in November of 1918. This was Marusya's sweater and it had no business being on this mangy, large-eared boy who looked at the unexpected guest with the insolent transparent eyes of a notorious hooligan. Boys like this were known as fatherless bastards in the south and flogged every Saturday as a preventative measure, though they should have gotten it on Mondays, too.

'What d'you want?' the boy asked. His lazy, disdainful

grimace so precisely copied someone adult, dangerous, and mean that for one wild moment Lindt imagined goodness knows what: arrest, exile, Marusya trudging along a waterlogged road in a convict's overshoes, the scrape of bolt locks being drawn, jumping German shepherds steaming with happy fury, and impudent plebeian natives moving into the wonderful nest of a home Marusya had built.

Lindt's rage pulled first at his scrotum, and next at the skin covering his cheekbones and temples, but then he shook himself by the scruff. What nonsense. A woman's ravings. I'd probably have known, they would have told me right away and who would have dared. To touch Marusya. To touch HIM personally! That was absolutely impossible. Of course there were plenty of blockheads at the top—just as many as there were below—and, honestly, Lindt very rarely met intelligent people, and opportunities to simply have a chat with someone as an equal without bending over backwards or adapting, were, well, few and far between. But nobody ever bothered him. Nobody would ever dare bother him, this was an axiom that was absolutely clear for Lindt and just as clear for any clinical idiot as the difference between Lindt himself and any clinical idiot.

Everyone understood that.

Lindt was one-of-a-kind.

There were plenty of talented people and plenty who were capable, bright, and brainy. Up and coming, promising to hatch into something good. But not geniuses. No.

There were no more geniuses.

At all.

Lindt, who'd lived with this since his earliest years, suddenly sensed the huge dusky shadow of his own gift as if it were something distinct, monstrously heavy, and lifeless. Apparently he hadn't gotten used to it, no. He simply had no choice.

'Where's Maria Nikitichna Chaldonova?' he harshly asked the brat, as if he were an adult. The boy's face immediately fell and he stepped back a bit then opened his mouth like a wallet and suddenly yelled out, with juicy Ukrainian pronunciation for the whole apartment to hear, 'Granny Musya! Granny Musya! Some guy's here to see you!'

And then a happy young voice echoed from somewhere in the depths of the apartment. Marusya's voice.

'Lesik, is that you? I knew it was you. For God's sake, Pavlusha, bring Lazar Iosifovich back to the kitchen and close the door, there's a draft!'

Lindt quickly released his silently squirming victim and headed toward Marusya's call as if bewitched, stumbling over some bundles and wooden items, what the hell had happened around here anyway?

Marusya stood in a kitchen filled with ringlets of an almost edible cloud of blue steam: Marusya herself was pink, disheveled, and wet, washing, in a huge zinc tub, a quiet baby whose gender was indiscernible to Lindt. Yet another child, who looked a bit older, sat in the corner on an enameled pot, gripping the handles and looking straight ahead with such focused persistence that even Lindt could see the process was complicated and demanded complete control.

'Hello, Lesik!' Marusya said. 'I'm so glad you're finally better! No, no, don't come too close, you came in from the cold, and Katyusha has weak lungs.'

Lindt—who wouldn't have agreed, for love or money, to approach that animated, naked, but also human little larva—stopped in the doorway. After surveying all the bathhouse and laundry chaos, he asked 'Did you rob a kindergarten, Maria Nikitichna?'

At that moment, the tot enthroned on the pot darkened threateningly, strained, and suddenly shouted with victory. Marusya shoved a sponge at the indifferent girl, who looked like a naked little Buddha, and rushed, with a clucking unknown to Lindt, to the little pooper's rescue. After lifting his ample bottom she confirmed—with a glowing gladness that had also, incidentally, been unfamiliar to Lindt—that everything was in order (Lindt squeamishly wrinkled his nose after sensing a small cloud of fresh stench) and then started in on her sanitary fussing, using newspapers and persuasion. And why are you crying, Kolyushka, look what a good boy you are, now we're going to wipe everything off, finish bathing Katyusha, and then wash off your bottom. And you'll have a nice pink bottom, all clean and fresh-smelling, it'll breathe and be happy...

Kolyushka obediently shut up, apparently enticed by the impending metamorphoses of his bottom, but then the forgotten Katyusha began screaming: she didn't just begin screaming, however, she hurled the wet sponge and started pounding on the washtub as if she were having some sort of fit, hitting everything around her with a pungent, whitish spray of soap.

Marusya straightened and threw up her hands in distress, lacking the power to tear herself in two but desperately wishing she could. 'Lesik, will you get Katyusha? There's a towel over there on the chair.'

'Please spare me,' Lindt firmly said. 'I won't get her and I advise you not to. She's clearly out of her mind and probably contagious, too. I can't seem to grasp what's happening here.

Did some idiot move other people in with you? How could Sergey Alexandrovich allow it? I'll call right now...'

Marusya cut him off, 'Nobody moved anybody in with us. I'm the one who moved them in with us. There are people living in dugouts, practically giving birth on the streets, all while we... And you...' She cast a furious glance at Lindt. 'I wouldn't have expected this from you. On top of that, Katyusha isn't contagious but you most certainly could be. Meaning get out of here. I don't want to see you here until you learn to behave yourself properly.'

Lindt somehow smirked with the very edge of his grinning mouth. 'I'm afraid that will be too long to wait, Maria Nikitichna. But as you wish. I hope you're finally happy now. It's a pity, though, that saintliness is the one thing that doesn't flatter you a bit.'

He left, shaking from fury and humiliation, even kicking a silent, dashing, shaggy cat along the way. Disgusting, they'd even found a way to bring in a cat, too! And Marusya, young and unkempt with red splotches on her cheeks, energetically began soaping up the screaming Katyusha, who was already completely clean, and who had very definite sights on the porridge moldering away on a burner, wrapped in newspapers and a flannelette blanket.

'What a wretch,' Marusya muttered, swallowing tears that were either her own or from the soap. 'Just think, Katyusha, what a wretch he is! Of all people he calls you and me contagious... He should just have a look at himself!'

Marusya found a little bouquet of barely live geraniums in the hallway a couple hours later and spent a long time resuscitating them, finally bringing them back to life and putting them in a glass on a shelf. High enough so the children couldn't reach. And on the third day, a defeated Lindt came to ask forgiveness.

This was pretty much their first—and most definitely their only—fight.

The sway held by all those children—who were of varying ages and varying degrees of wretchedness—was already clear before Lindt and Marusya made up. Chaldonov, a hostage in his own home, was fairly shaken by this new family situation, and quickly admitted to Lindt that Marusya had first literally dragged an evacuated woman and her two children in off the street, then another one and, you won't believe this but she has two little offspring, too, and to top it all off, Marusya had finally organized something like an at-home kindergarten and was now gathering up an entire bunch of tots from the whole street every day and fussing around with them while their mamas supplied the front with necessities. The factories were tirelessly toiling in three shifts, so the head count of children at the Chaldonov apartment never wavered, and it's just like an insane asylum, Lazar. Bedlam, Sodom, and Gomorrah. Diapers, screaming, and shit around the clock. But it's impossible to out-stubborn Marusya on anything.

Lindt nodded, experiencing something resembling sympathy for Chaldonov for the first time in his life: they were both finally in the same boat, both had finally been abandoned and both were jealous in unison, which gave Lindt a strange and almost unfamiliar sense of familial warmth. It was warmth despite being woolen, stifling, and very slightly reeking of goat. Lindt even casually patted Chaldonov on his lightly frayed jacket, also from before the war, but then immediately regretted it. The academician, who had suddenly and undeservedly been deprived of wife, peace, and fresh shirts, sobbed and then Lindt was forced to listen again to his raspy, completely elderly complaints.

'Don't do anyone any favors, Lazar, or you'll end up stepping in it yourself,' Chaldonov said.

But Marusya truly was happy. She'd been happy her whole life, happy even at the most terrible times because she'd been lucky to be born that way. Being happy for her had always meant loving, but only now—at seventy-three, as a wartime evacuee—had she finally realized loving someone didn't mean making the person her own. It's possible to love those who don't belong to you, too, meaning you should love only them because only then will they become yours.

It all began on that unfamiliar snowy Ensk street and later Marusya often said, laughing, that all it took for her to find what she'd been looking for her whole life was to lose her way. She didn't look back on what she'd been thinking when she hurried past the lifeless houses, bent over, and firmly grasped the thread of a child's hacking cry. Who did she expect to find? An abandoned child? A dying human puppy? Yet another unborn child? Lindt, after all, had grown up long ago, Lord, how fast, how frantically everything had flashed by, a whole life, and it was already impossible to discern anything or bring back the most interesting details.

It wasn't until the fifth side street that day that Marusya found the definitive meaning of her life. Sure, there turned out to be three foundlings all in that one place—it's just that two of them were quiet, evidently unwilling or unable to complain or beg any longer. Only one, a ragged little bundle, was fighting for life: she was an unseen doll who categorically did not want to die, and she was lying on the knees of a woman who sat very straight, as if she'd turned to stone on the front steps of a boarded-up, freezing granary. A child wrapped in a tattered shawl stood just as straight and unbending next to the woman, and Marusya immediately knew from his eyes and from how firmly he held his mother by a red hand puffy from the cold that it was a boy. He wasn't protecting himself. No, he was protecting her.

'What are you doing here?' Marusya asked, amazed herself at the stupidity of the question because in this war everyone was either surviving or dying. Nobody did anything else and these two clearly intended to die, despite the objections of the third. And that third one, wrapped to the head in rags, was undoubtedly the smartest, because that child wanted to live. That child also went silent immediately after sensing Marusya's presence, as if the rescue mission had been fulfilled and the goal had finally been reached.

Marusya herself couldn't remember how she dragged all three of them home. She only remembered that she'd wailed the whole way, horribly, at the top of her lungs, like she'd never wailed in her life even when she buried her parents, even when she'd realized she'd never have children, even when she was a child and lost a fiery-smooth marble so bright it was even a little liquidy inside and all the children had marbles, everyone but her, because her mother said if she couldn't take care of it, well, it served her right.

Anele most likely remembered all the details of that trip but she barely spoke Russian and was so quiet by nature as to be nearly inanimate. This may, however, have been because of her fate rather than her nature: even Marusya couldn't understand if her Old Testament God was testing the unspeaking Anele or just toying with this small Jewish Bessarabian woman the way bored children torture a live, suffering, warm-blooded cat.

Anele had been through a thousand misfortunes, maybe even more. She was born in Faleshty, a Jewish-Moldavian place in Bessarabia with a funny name, a place successively considered a territory by everyone who felt like it, and just about everyone felt like it. Anele's parents were docile, prosperous, and not particularly religious people, so they sent their bright little girl off to study at a local school. Anele spoke Romanian beautifully, easily switching to Yiddish at home, but the total amount of time she actually spoke—she'd even chattered and laughed!—wasn't very long, because God quickly gathered that this wasn't good. And then Anele's parents died, one after the other: first some Moldavians killed her father for some unknown sins, then her mother died, either from illness or because she'd truly loved her husband so much she couldn't see the point in parting with him because of some divide.

An uncle took in Anele: Jews just don't abandon their own, either in joy or in sorrow, and even if they're not loved for that, truth be told, they're not loved for a lot of things, and the list is so long debit would never balance with credit because the invoices are written up so fast there's really not much point in paying. And people will still chase, burn, or shoot anyway. The uncle was the proprietor of a guesthouse and tavern and got the local population drunk, that Jewish jerk, so there was work up to here and Anele had to leave school because that particular genocide needed helping hands: someone had to sweep, wash dishes, and feed vocal chickens and turkeys. All in all, it was a good family—her own family—and Anele never went to bed hungry, thank God, and every child in the house was dressed and fed and they were prosperous enough that an old dress wasn't worn to holes but given to the ragman to fetch a little extra money for the synagogue.

It's hard to say how Yankel, the ragman and an orphan, and Anele, the niece of the tavern owner and a former schoolgirl, managed to see eye-to-eye but they did see eye-to-eye, and they reached an agreement without even saying ten words, understanding that they loved each other and that the time had come to send for the matchmakers, for that is how the Torah orders it, and it was written, 'O Lord God of my master Abraham, please give me success this day, and show kindness to my master Abraham. Behold, here I stand by the well of water, and the daughters of the men of the city are coming out to draw water. Now let it be that the young woman to whom I say, "Please let down your pitcher that I may drink," and she says, "Drink, and I will also give your camels a drink"—let her be the one You have appointed for Your servant Isaak. And by this I will know that You have shown kindness to my master.'

But Abraham's God had his reasons once again: in the long run, it's possible to understand Him because it's all pure theater, a small-town Romeo and Juliet only without the family animosity because there was no point in the family of the most respected restaurateur in Faleshty going to war with a mere ragman who had no family. They were from two nonintersecting universes, from different castes, oh yes, Jews have their own castes, their own untouchables, everything's just like it is for regular people because Jews—you won't believe this—are people, too.

Anele and Yankel were forbidden to meet, though they hadn't been meeting, except with their eyes, as was customary for nice young Jewish people because non-Jewish young people would have remembered long ago that they lived in a very real twentieth century and wouldn't have cared about all those silly prejudices and backward kin. They would have scampered as far away as possible, at least to merry Odessa or, at the very worst, cozy Kishenev, all sugary-white. But Anele and Yankel stayed and she went into the yard every day at noon to rinse unwieldy mugs at the same time he came up to the gate and watched, just watched with his huge, stupid, helpless, and wonderful eyes. And so that went on for ten years in a row, every blessed day, without holidays or weekends—rebellions come in many shapes—and then ten years later God and the tavern owner were finally tired of all the silent movies because Anele had turned twenty-five and nobody wanted that skinny fool for a wife. Nobody, that is, but Yankel.

And so they were allowed to marry.

They were completely destitute—it was horrible how destitute they were—but they were just as happy as they were destitute because Yankel was inept with the household and a ragman, too, though Anele had a bun in the oven right away and the first-born, Isaak, came into the world at the appointed time, *bubele*, my *kepele*, I wouldn't have taken you from my breast for a whole century. Anele was laughing again and talking again but that was, of course, just downright unacceptable.

And thus, on June 28, 1940, as the result of a peaceful resolution to the Soviet-Romanian conflict, Bessarabia was returned to the Soviet Union and the Law on the Formation of the Moldavian Soviet Socialist Republic emerged from the seventh session of the Supreme Soviet on August 2. This wasn't really so bad except that if you look at the dates it wasn't the right time—arithmetic is an exact science that knows no sentimentality—and so Anele hadn't yet managed to be as happy as she should have been that they, the great unwashed, were now respectable people simply because they were the great unwashed (Anele's world was just filled with paradoxes) when June 22, 1941, rolled around. And it wasn't two days before they began bombing Bessarabia and Yankel was drafted and Anele hung on his neck crying bitter tears and trying to press against her husband as tightly as she could with her huge belly because she was carrying their second under her heart and wanted the unborn baby and the father to be able to embrace before they parted. Kiss your father, Isaak, give him a big kiss.

Another three days later, Anele loaded herself onto a heated freight train with other evacuees, pressing her son to herself with one arm and embracing her unwieldy belly with the other. The Soviet government did everything quickly, punishing quickly and pardoning quickly. Innumerable kin—and in a small town, everyone's somehow kin to everyone—waved to the departing passengers from the platform, oh and that fool Anele, a real *schlimazel* and her husband's just like her but at least he was forced off to war while she's voluntarily letting herself be taken to Siberia!

Anele weakly waved back, the train car jerked and shook on the rails' joints, and the baby jerked and shook in her belly but she was so frightened she didn't even cry. And on July 26 of that same 1941, Bessarabia was occupied by Romanian troops who, by force of habit, nobody even attempted to resist. Quite the contrary: everyone was happy, which is how the Romanians methodically, town by town, cleansed the land defiled by the Soviets. All the Jews who'd stayed in Faleshty were rounded up to Bălți where they were cleansed, too, shot in a ravine, carelessly, without malice, and in a hurry. Including Anele's uncle the tavern owner, crooked Rivka with her children, and the fat holy fool Shmulik. Three hundred and eleven people. Everyone. Everyone. Nobody was left.

Along the way, somewhere near Chelyabinsk, Anele gave birth to a tiny, angry little girl and then stopped talking again so it was seven-year-old Isaak, the only adult male in the family, who named his little sister Klara and took care of her and his mother because they were both helpless and might forget they needed to eat; well, his mother might forget but Klara cried quite soundly when she wanted to eat. Loudly. He would never have gotten lost in Ensk either, her Isaak, except that it was Mama who forgot at first where they were supposed to go and then they completely lost their way. It's good you found us, Mama Masha. That's what he called Marusya: Mama Masha. And she called him Isochka or Isa. He was a bright little boy, quick on the uptake, just very, very serious. And then Anele didn't talk at all. But what, honestly, did she really have to talk about?

Valya appeared at the Chaldonovs' a few days after Anele, brought in by Isaak, who'd voluntarily begun taking on lots of responsibilities right away, even though he'd barely settled into the household. This might have been a question of survival or he might really have needed something to do to be useful, otherwise he could have lost not only the stimulus but also his reason to exist. Little Klara needed to eat but the silent, starving Anele was a terrible milker—her milk was thin, bluish, and bitter, even to the eye—so the desperate Marusya sent Isaak to the market after she'd cut the sleeves off Chaldonov's fur coat and made her new son some excellent fur boots. She praised herself that they were warm and would never wear out, and tucked money in Isaak's mitten. The mittens were hers and so, of course, was the money. Isaak understood that, he actually understood money a whole lot better than any adult, a whole lot better than Marusya herself: poor people are generally the best financiers on earth because they always have to count, very often in negative terms.

Isaak came home an hour later and carefully placed two icy discs on the table—milk was sold frozen and round in Ensk—and he sniffled as he pulled off his mittens and held a clump of bills out for Marusya: her change, though she'd given the exact amount of money, just right for a liter of milk. 'I didn't steal, I bargained,' he said quietly but firmly, though Marusya hadn't even thought to suspect him or even ask anything. She herself would have stolen if she'd had to, Lord, she'd probably have even killed without so much as thinking about it if anyone had tested her or her life like that. But her life had been tested in a completely different way.

So she just took the money from Isaak and put it in a little box that used to stand on the top shelf of the sideboard but now, look, I'll put it here because you can't reach the top so next time you go to the market, just take what you need. Just don't carry around anything very heavy, all right? Why? Isaak didn't understand. And Marusya very seriously explained, your bellybutton could come untied and I don't know how to tie it back up.

They both laughed. Foraging now rested permanently on Isaak's shoulders, but he never messed up: he not only knew the current situation beautifully, he knew all the salesladies by name and bargained with such gusto and spirit that even the most stubborn peasant women yielded, and they gave in, stunned, because well, just think about it, Auntie Olya, if milk's two hundred seventy a liter and I need a liter and a half, that means you divide two hundred seventy in two and add another two hundred seventy but I have to get potatoes, too, oh no, how can they be a hundred sixty a kilo if Agasha over there is practically giving them away at a hundred fifty for a little more weight but her milk doesn't taste good and yours is the very best, no, no, I told you I need a liter and a half of milk and that's two and a half discs. But give me three.

He spoke Russian beautifully, by the way, without the slightest bit of an accent for anyone to make fun of: they'd travelled so long, and kids just have an ability for languages anyway. Wouldn't you like to work with the boy, Lesik? He obviously has talent—I do calculations slower on paper than he does in his head and I'm sure you're slower, too. But, oh no, Lindt didn't want to and he didn't want to speak Yiddish with Anele, either. Why do you think I know that barbaric language anyway, Maria Nikitichna? What do you mean, how did I speak as a child? I really didn't talk at all as a child, for your information, because there wasn't anything to talk about and nobody to talk with. So you don't need to shove your Isochka at me, damn it, he doesn't have any abilities at all and he never will, he'll be a shopkeeper when he grows up, just as he's preordained to be, and that's the end of that.

(Lindt was wrong, though: Isochka grew up to became a major in the Soviet Army, an excellent missile launch control officer, because it had been preordained for him to die so many different times that God himself got confused about what to do next and so let Isochka's life take its own course, which is why his life shaped up so particularly well.)

And so on his fourth day with the Chaldonovs, Isaak brought Valya home from the market. Actually, Valya came on her own, following her daughter, whose hand Isaak held firmly. He was very serious, very responsible, very adult.

'Mama Masha,' he said when Marusya opened the door.

'This is Elya Tulyaeva, she doesn't believe we have a piano. She says I'm lying and there can't be a piano. But I'm not lying. Can I show her?'

Marusya looked over a six-year-old girl dressed in a beautifully sewn coat with big, adult buttons. The girl had a doll's lovely, round, and very capricious face. Which portended nothing good for Isaak.

Behind the children stood a woman so tormented you couldn't tell how old she was; in this war they all looked like forty-year-old old ladies.

'Please excuse us,' she said to Marusya, 'For God's sake, excuse us, but let the little boy show what he wants because otherwise,' and now she nodded in the little girl's direction, 'she won't let up for anything. She's stubborn, the worst. I'd give her a thrashing but I know there's no point.'

'Why thrash her?' Marusya said. 'It's easier to just show her. Come in.' She stepped aside, letting them in. 'And I don't want to hear any "just for a minute" or "I'll wait on the stairs." It's cold on the stairs and there's tea in the kitchen. And a piano's never for just a minute. It's always a long story. So you're welcome to come in!'

The woman smiled gratefully and then unexpectedly looked very young, no older than twenty-three. The end of her nose turned up like a duck's and there was a very sweet, funny little gap between her front teeth.

'My name's Valya,' she said, flustered. 'Valentina Tulyaeva. And that's my daughter, Elvira. We're from Voronezh, evacuees. We're staying across the river.'

Marusya nodded, noticing how Isaak was genuflecting and helping his little guest take off her shoes. The crystalline and unusual name Elvira fit the girl extraordinarily well: it was an apt name, matching perfectly with her ample bright mouth, tiny pale eyebrows, and, especially, the happy indifference with which she allowed Isaak to look after her. But who had taught him to be so genteel, sensitive, and adult? Nobody. Chaldonov still couldn't help a woman cope with her coat but this small-town boy, how about that, was already helping this six-year-old doll of a girl off with her coat as if he were unwrapping a bouquet: nimbly, carefully, and tenderly, without damaging a single petal. Where did he get that? It wasn't clear.

Valya caught Marusya's glance and straightened her daughter's woolen dress. Like the coat, it was surprisingly adult, with pockets, a little belt, and what even looked like a yoke. 'I sewed it myself,' Valya said. 'I graduated from the forestry technical school before the war but I sew for fun, for myself and the children. I have a little son, too, Slavik. And I sew a little to sell, of course I have to, otherwise it's too hard to buy food, you know all about that yourself. Do you need me to sew anything? I don't charge much.'

'Maybe something for Isochka,' said Marusya. 'I'll think about it, all right?'

Isaak took Elya by the hand again and led her off to show her the piano, which had been silently waiting for its former owners in one of the rooms, but Marusya still didn't know if she could speak with her new acquaintance about that or not. Life would let her know.

Life let her know, literally a few days later, when it was clear Elechka only left the Chaldonovs' at night and Valya had to make a hefty detour on the terrible night streets. The main thing, though, was Isaak's eyes when they took Elechka away.

And so Chaldonov discovered when he came home from work that life hadn't yet demonstrated all its tricks and now, thank God, he didn't have an office any longer though he had three more orphans in addition to Anele, Isaak, and Klara: Valya, Elechka, and one-year-old Slavik, plus the five or six other pests who came by at the same time during the day, many even staying the night if their mothers were on the second and third shifts…

One might think life had worked out just fine. Right, yes. Worked out fine.

Oddly enough, though, literally a few days later all the residents of the Chaldonov home already felt as if they'd been living together forever. It was as if the overall problem—that damned war, when would it ever, finally, end?—had cemented their fates, instantly mixing them together with a quick-setting, super-reliable mortar. It was as if Elechka and Isaak had always played blocks together in the long hallway cluttered with junk, heads touching, gingham and felt, light and dark, oily-smooth and wavy like a fleece.

'Where are you putting it, can't you see it'll fall down?' Elechka said, indignant. She was agile, sneaky, and not at all the crosspatch or brat Marusya had initially thought she was. She was just very willful, with a personality that couldn't be any stronger. The block tower fell down, deferring to Elechka's sense of engineering, and Isaak guiltily sighed but his hands, clumsy from Elechka's presence, began raising the Tower of Babel again: his patience could last a million years if only this little girl with the angry, colorless little eyebrows, and thin braid interwoven with a scrap of a blue-dyed bandage instead of a ribbon could be sitting on the floor with him all those years. (And he did have enough of that patience for a million years because Elechka and Isaak are my mother and father, and they're still together, and he still takes her by the hand when they come home, and she's still dissatisfied with how he handles the household...)

It seemed as if the dissatisfied Valya was eternally arguing with Anele or that, well, Anele was eternally lying in her own little spot behind a wall, withered, disembodied, and immersed in a deafening but soundless monologue known to and intended only for God, as Valya furiously banged firewood around the kitchen, muttering that Anele'd certainly been able to birth two children, so she could wipe their asses after them, I have just as many of my own so why the hell should I shovel away someone else's shit? Here, Elya bring the little babies in, Klara's already bawling up a storm, she wants to eat, and it's time for Slavik to eat, too.

Isaak and Elechka appeared in the doorway: he had her brother in his arms and she had his sister. They didn't even divide their burden into mine and yours, and neither, honestly did Valya, it's just that there was a war and Valya resisted it out loud but Anele preferred to lament in silence.

Marusya would watch closely as Valya poured warm milk for the children: there was no doubt her own son didn't get a drop more than Anele's screaming little girl and she cut each potato for Elechka and Isaak in half so each received exactly as much as the other. Valya's god was justice—supreme justice—and fury, strength, and rage served as its archangels. She's not sick, Maria Nikitichna, that's your Anele, so now you know, she just doesn't want to work. And what of it? Just lie around. My husband says there will always be fools to do the work...

Valya fogged over for an instant, mentally searching among lice-ridden foxhole mates for her man, her dear, but then she got a grip on herself: Marusya had never in her life met anyone so uncompromising and so lacking even the smallest notions of faith. But if goodness had fists, they were Valya's reddened, scratched-up fists, and her dexterous hands could do anything at all better than anyone else's hands, whether that was sewing a soldier's footwrap into a holiday dress, baking plump, round little rolls out of acorns, or boxing the ears of a gaping child. The problem was that Valya absolutely demanded the same mastery and honesty from everyone else… but 'everyone else,' as we all know, meant uncentered, mortal simpletons who weren't quick enough, dropped everything, and refused to see with their behinds or, to be honest, even with their fronts, meaning they didn't notice half of what, in Valya's opinion, they should have noticed immediately. Notice and then reach appropriate conclusions.

Valya, however, always managed to get everything done—everything and for everyone—whether she was working at the factory, cooking, sewing, or tatting little 'whimsies' to sell: lace for the camisoles that women, young things who felt hungry without their husbands, stubbornly continued to wear underneath hideous raggedy clothing that was aging along with them. To Marusya's horror, Valya paid like clockwork for her room, which she called her 'billeting,' but when Valya realized everything she paid was spent on her and her children, she also took to making clothes and laundering for the whole Chaldonov family, including the newly arrived members. This meant Marusya came close to becoming a real layabout in her old age since Isaak took care of foraging and provisions, Elechka played with the babies, Chaldonov invented bombs and brought home ration cards and foodstuffs, and quiet Anele silently prayed for everyone or, perhaps, suffered alone on everyone's behalf.

And then in the evenings a minimum of seven people—not

including the infant Klara who peacefully snuffled in her basket right there with them—sat down at the table and reported on their days. Valya vigilantly watched to be sure the children got equal portions of food. Marusya, her eyes damp from emotion, saw Isochka sneak the best morsels from his own plate to Elechka's. A gentle steam curled over the teapot. Chaldonov read the newspaper and mechanically patted sleepy Slavik, languid after eating his fill, on the head. This was happiness, happiness nobody would want to dream about because nobody would believe it could be so kitcheny and simple.

Sometimes Lesik came to visit and then the happiness was complete, almost perfectly spherical, and then everyone listened only to Lesik, even little Klara, who didn't shriek in his presence. He was so entertaining, Marusya's eldest, and it was so good they'd all come together, though it was too bad he came by so rarely, too bad he only looked at her, always only at her.

Chaldonov would get up from the table, hand Slavik, all bulky, sleepy, and sated, to Marusya and ceremoniously invite Lindt to the 'smoking room,' meaning the stairwell because, how could you smoke in a house with so many children… Marusya didn't even have to continue, since it was clear from her eyebrows that anyone who disagreed with that postulate would be kicked out like a punished cat so Chaldonov didn't even try to object. Quite the contrary, he even touchingly tried to find as many advantages as possible in his new situation. No, Lazar, now I see there's a fair bit of sense in having a harem. Just think: now there are masses of wonderful women in the house so there's no reason to worry about dishwashing or firewood because the girls do everything and all very handily, too!

In reality, though, Chaldonov, the poor old man, was desperately missing certain things, particularly the firewood, which had to be carried in so Marusya didn't ruin her hands, and the dishes, which he'd so enjoyed drying with a towel while standing alongside his wife: that had all been so glorious that even the clean dishes moaned from pleasure in his hands. Could it possibly happen that he and Marusya might never again spend their evenings together, just the two of them, quietly, with cozy conversations and memories that were only dear and comprehensible to the two of them? 'We'll sit down at one and rise at three, I with book, you with embroidery, and when dawn does break we won't foresee that no more kissing was now to be.' Lindt thought in time with Chaldonov and then set the words—someone else's, Pasternak's, in fact—free because 'Autumn' wasn't written until 1949 and it was only in 1949 that everything he'd tried not to think about since 1918, when he was eighteen, would happen, what he couldn't stop thinking about every day, closing his eyes, slipping into slumber, no, no, that can never be, never, not that, never... Marusya won't die, everything will stay the same as usual, both now and always, and unto the ages of ages, forever.

July of 1944 came around first, though. That summer happened to be unprecedentedly hot, overripe, and berried, and hundreds of evacuees seemed to leave the city for home each day, thank God. Those who stayed behind wandered the lively, decorated streets in the evenings as if they were drunk from the unusual heat, the scent of dust, and nearby victory; because there was plenty of bread, even more than before; and because a legendary velvety baritone reported in a chesty voice from every wide-open window that the city of Minsk had been completely liberated on July 3 as the result of a victorious offensive by troops from the Third and First Belarusian Fronts, and then it was the city of Vilnius on July 13. 'Rita-Rio, Rio-Rita, the foxtrot's sounding again, oh, how I want this evening to last a whole year!' drowned out waves of noisy government news bulletins. Couples pined as they danced a well-known paso doble, under the direction of Marek Weber, that passed itself off as a foxtrot: of course the couples were all cheries and ma cheries, but if you squinted it was easy to imagine you weren't dancing with your girlfriend but with your one and only, your dear, beloved, long-awaited man. And they spun and spun, not opening their eyes: they were older, exhausted, and happy.

Instead of death notices, there were now more letters and telegrams saying, Meet on fourth, love, kisses, stop, though there weren't actually fewer funeral notices: there just hadn't been any good news at all before but now there was, and people came in droves to see and touch the lucky ones, as if they were miracle-working icons seeping joy. The big thing, though, was Anele. Anele had also received some paper and Yankel—seriously injured and completely decommissioned but whole, thank the Lord, with his arms and legs—promised to come for her and the children in late July. He was alive.

Marusya, Valya, and Anele, who'd woken up and surfaced from her mute non-existence, first wailed on and on over the long-awaited letter and then, just as harmoniously and amicably, threw themselves into preparing for the big day with an energy no imperial triumph had ever matched. Everything in the house, including the children, was scrubbed and polished. Marusya thought up an unprecedented meal with five loaves and two fishes, and Valya procured a piece of light blue prewar panne velvet from her secret silos and sewed up a new dress with a waist and a yoke for Anele right away, don't turn, I'm telling you, she said through an angry and incomprehensible mouthful of pins. I'm going to put a pleat on the bust, we have to do something in the front otherwise your man will say we starved you here. Valya quietly sobbed and Anele, whose huge, blue-gray, perfectly panne velvet eyes had suddenly been revealed, lightly stroked her shoulder, which made both women suddenly embrace and begin howling again, mentally forgiving each other for everything that wasn't their fault.

Those were good tears, the last good tears for the next many days.

Little Slavik died on July 20. They were expecting Yankel on the twenty-seventh and Marusya was planning on preserves and then the pie that would logically follow, which is why they sent Elechka and Isaak to the woods, where the edges were overgrown with impenetrable bushes rapidly dropping raspberries. Three-year-old Slavik was foisted off on them at the very last moment so he wouldn't get underfoot with the adults at home: Elechka and Isaak were ordered to watch him at all times, and they did an honest job of it because Slavik only managed to pick one single berry from a bush and stuff it in his mouth. Just one. But that was enough.

He got feverish in the morning and Valya never forgave herself for being so mean: she'd scolded her whining, capricious son, you bonehead, you always find the wrong time and never do anything right. Slavik got much worse toward evening and five days later Marusya was already kneeling beside a hospital cot, sharply and mechanically tucking a blanket under a small, clay-like body that was slowly cooling. Valya sat in the corner, swaying like a dervish and letting out a piercing, seagull-like cry each time she exhaled. The cry was not a woman's and most certainly not a human's but she cried, O Lord, she cried. She felt better.

A nursing assistant appeared from somewhere: she wasn't a young woman, and she'd already seen a lot, been through a lot in her years, oh no-oh no, as if it weren't enough that so many men folk had been killed, now children have to be buried, too. She embraced Marusya's shoulders, let's go see the doctor, honey, papers need to be signed, don't let it get you, he won't freeze anymore, the little love, he's done suffering now, look, the dysentery ate him away, dried him right up, poor boy. The nurse pronounced the word 'dysentery' with the showy carelessness of a semiliterate person who's spent enough time among smart, educated people to borrow all their unnecessary superficial gestures.

Let's go, I'm telling you. Let his ma say goodbye to him.

Marusya obediently got up, not realizing she kept clasping and unclasping her fingers as she tried to cover Slavik, tried to at least keep his warmth in a little while longer. Good Lord, he was so small, so silly with those dimply cheeks, so lively. Even through foamy, bloody vomit and diarrhea, he smelled like fresh bread, pinkish simmered milk, and even slightly of flowers, very familiar ones, such small ones, barely purplish, on the roadside, but Marusya just couldn't remember what they were called, just couldn't remember, couldn't remember. Couldn't.

'*Baruch Atah Adonai Eloheinu Melech ha-olam, dayan, ha-emet**,' said someone in the ward in a beautiful low voice that

---

* Blessed are You, Adonai our God, Ruler of the universe, the true Judge (Hebrew).

contained a mysterious breathy burst of air that seemed to carry ancient kingdoms and scorching sand. Marusya looked around. Anele had been sitting in the corner of the ward staring frantically at nothing for five whole days as Slavik died, but on hearing the news she suddenly squared her shoulders, stood, and loudly ripped the bust of her new panne velvet dress, the same dress she'd twirled in, carefree, before the mirror. '*Baruch Atah Adonai Eloheinu Melech ha-olam, dayan, ha-emet*,' she repeated firmly. Marusya, Valya, who'd stopped crying, and even the nurse understood that Anele was speaking with God.

Then King David stood.

And rent his garments.

And this was of no use whatsoever to anyone.

Yankel the soldier, who'd returned home without anyone noticing, took his family away in early August. Anele still wore the same dress, torn at the bust and suddenly old, not to be mended until thirty days after the funeral, and then mended badly, with purposefully uneven stitches. She firmly embraced Marusya and Valya, and touched her lips to the howling Elechka's forehead. Isaak, stupefied with grief, pressed a set of drafting instruments, a gift from Lindt, to his chest: it was a regal gift, and Isaak only realized its full luxury in military school many, many years later.

'Now you write to me, Anele, and you, Isochka, for God's sake, you write to me, too,' Marusya said, choking on painful dry tears. And until her own death in 1975, Anele wrote long, detailed letters filled with unbelievable grammatical errors. The postman brought them regularly, once a month, to the Chaldonov home until 1949, then he began bringing them to Lindt, who just as regularly brought them to the cemetery and placed them, unopened, by Marusya's gray stone cross, which cast a winged shadow spacious enough to hold little Slavik's gravestone and a ridiculous bust of Chaldonov that didn't look like him.

Nobody touched the letters, not even the guileless cemetery paupers who gathered spice cookies and candies at the graves of people they didn't know: excellent chasers, by the way, and not a sin at all, since they're in remembrance of the soul. And so Anele's missives first gradually yellowed, then soaked up the Ensk rain and snow, swelled, and melted away, turning into earth, into dust, returning to dust and through that dust there grew grass on which new letters were laid, and the conversation still didn't cease—a soft, unheard conversation between two women, one who'd kept silent nearly all her life, the other long dead.

A week after Yankel took his family away, Valya received a funeral notice, though it wasn't really even a funeral notice but a notice that her Mikhail Tulyaev went missing while heroically liberating something out there. Valya's eyes skimmed over it but she didn't remember or grasp anything so handed the sheet to Marusya who gasped and pressed her hands to her mouth in fright.

'But what is this, Valya? How can this be? Don't let it kill you just yet, maybe they've mixed something up. Anyway, missing, that's some kind of hope, don't you think?'

'Why would I let it kill me, Maria Nikitichna?' asked Valya, who'd hardened up so much inside over the last few days, for now and for forever, that it never left her: having grandchildren didn't help, nor did another son, born from another husband, nor the husband himself (and he, after all, loved her terribly, so, so much, only he loved drinking just as terribly, but that's—well, it can happen to anyone). It was fate. Why kill yourself if you've already been killed? She needed to get ready to leave: Voronezh had been liberated nearly a year ago and the newspapers said the economy was recovering. Plus Misha's folks had stayed behind, hadn't evacuated. I'm thinking maybe they're alive. It'll be easier for them if I'm there, I can help, even if it's only a bit.

And Marusya suddenly grasped everything and didn't even begin to talk her out of it or invite her to stay. She just said, right there on the platform at the train station, 'You go, don't worry, I'll look after Slavik.'

It was as if he was playing right there, all small, warm, and real, covered in ghostly train station dust. And Marusya hadn't lied: to Chaldonov's horror, she went to the cemetery nearly every day, without hysteria, tears, or even the toys that look so out-of-place on children's graves. She was just there as often as possible, so Slavik wouldn't be scared.

Knowing his wife's character, Chaldonov tolerated this sympathetically, cursing himself with all his might for his secret, shameless joy: the war had rapidly rolled along to a conclusion, their in-home kindergarten had dispersed, and he and Marusya were together again, inseparable again, and alone again. Marusya categorically refused to pack her things when the fraternity of scientific stars slowly began returning to Moscow. 'I'm not going anywhere so don't even hope for it,' she announced with the same youthful ardor with which she'd refused to go to England in 1917. 'You can go if you want but I'm staying here.'

Of course Chaldonov stayed, so—hat in hand and groaning with humiliation—he visited academician Skochinsky, helmsman of the newborn Western Siberian division of the

Academy of Sciences of the USSR. After his audience with Skochinsky, Chaldonov received everything befitting a venerable scholar of his rank who'd lost his mind in his old age and voluntarily decided to live out his days in the devil's ass on the very edge of charted territory. 'Don't grumble,' Marusya warned. 'What have you gotten into your head? We'll work things out wonderfully here, you'll see.'

They bought an old house on the nearly rural outskirts of Ensk. It was big and unwieldy, with stoves that were always smoking, but it lacked ghosts and bitter memories, either theirs or anyone else's. Marusya expertly built a nest—yet again—and Lazar Lindt, who'd naturally also stayed in Ensk, came over in the evenings. There'd been squawking about that in Moscow, but nobody even thought to object, since these two were working on something painfully serious. Rather, Lindt worked on it, of course, but Big Science has its own rules and you only retire feet first, meaning in a coffin, and the teacher's name always comes before the student's name, even though that defies logic, the alphabet, and ordinary human conscience. Lindt, however, really couldn't care less. He knew his own value as well as Chaldonov's and Big Science's. And it was perfectly clear who was worth more in the end.

Somehow the war ended, unnoticed: Marusya didn't even consider making a celebratory dinner, she just changed the tablecloth and set out a small carafe of vodka. Three shot glasses clinked quietly and a bit sadly over plates, Marusya furtively wiped her eyes, and the men grunted as they reached for bread, and then it was over. Four years of sorrow, just think, four years! And just as much still lay ahead.

Everything flowed along quietly and cozily after the war.

Marusya cooked, Chaldonov finished writing a big book nobody needed, understanding with sadness that he was rehashing his own feeble ideas from long ago, and Lindt unexpectedly took an interest in the material embodiment of his own theoretical perceptions of the world. He took a liking to proving ground tests, long business trips, papers with official rubber stamps, access clearance, and quiet peons. It suddenly turned out that his impeccable paper-based conclusions had acquired, in practice, a cheerful, multicolored materiality. It was downright festive, with the brown steppe, little soldiers digging expertly, and a cramped command post steeped with a particular barrack-like feel that had a delicious blend of the stale reek of last night's alcohol, hot sweat, and the worn leather of shoulder belts, which themselves smelled of all the accoutrements of military life: tobacco, gun powder, and that particularly idiotic courage possessed by anyone prepared to give his one and only concrete life for such an abstract, nebulous notion as 'motherland.'

Lindt liked everything at the tests: kasha with canned meat so hot it completely lost its flavor and was thus unbelievably filling, alcohol drunk from half-liter mugs (an 'officer's lemon' was offered as a chaser: a freshly peeled onion, sugary on the cut), and the little officers themselves, those small gray horses of war who were hardy, outgoing, and cheerful, all with the reddish necks of the sanguine, as if they'd been selected for that. Everything was easy, eager, and with a smile, whether you wanted to kill or drink. They loved Lindt at the testing ground, just as they loved all the 'craftsmen,' the inventors who came here to personally monitor how their beloved children boomed: supplemental alcohol was allocated, meaning everyone associated with the tests could get stinking drunk with unfeigned fervor, and only after that would they get down to the booming.

In short: little boys. Little boys and fools.

The 'craftsmen' were all different: some showed off, some steered clear of the plank outhouses, some puked on the first shot like teenagers or tried hard to weasel out of the whole celebration by referencing an ulcer. But Lindt didn't show off and didn't put on airs because he was a doctor of science. He cheerfully chuckled at the collective table and never forgot to set out—for everyone—a few bottles of something rare and expensive he'd brought with him, like Armenian cognac or something completely unheard of, like war trophy schnapps.

The overall friendliness, which warmed intensely with the alcohol, was so great that a lieutenant who'd once identified Lazar Lindt as a 'Yid,' completely correctly and without the slightest intent of offending anyone, got a thrashing. All so the shithead would learn to be a better judge of character. Lazar Lindt never found out about that precedent, which is too bad because he loved amusing situations and loved to be convinced yet again that the system recognized 'us and them,' something that goes beyond ethnicity and denomination. He'd seen more than once that a sense of humor, a moral mentality, the way one drinks, or even one's natural scent had far more fundamental meaning than common citizenship or even a common set of chromosomes. This was logical, correct, and just. According to this logic and this justice, there also were not and could not be lonely people in the world. There were only people who hadn't identified their familiars and were, thus, forced to wander with strangers.

For some reason, that warmed Lindt's heart.

He liked the war more and more: this was particularly

strange considering it had just ended, though it never hurts to get ready for the next one, now does it? On top of that, there was something exceptionally truthful in the fact that he'd finally taken on something that was genuinely real and now found himself among genuinely real people. Lindt began coming home more rarely and less readily, and he no longer chose his shirts and cleaned his shoes in the morning with his former pensive pleasure and a mental glance at Marusya's opinion. He even picked up a lively way of swearing that spiced up every command and sentence at the proving ground the way a caring mother sweetens an unpleasant medicine to convince a feverish crying child to take one tiny spoonful, little one. Just one little spoonful. Just one.

'You even smell like a sergeant-major now, Lazar,' said Lara, one of his many no-strings-attached lovers.

'How's that?' Lindt lazily asked. He was skinny, his loins biblically covered with a crumpled sheet that looked especially white against his dark, almost olive, complexion, which sometimes seemed almost solemnly bronze.

'It's obvious: a belt and a dick.' Lara got out of bed and felt around with a perfect pink hand for a pink shirt thrown off in a sexual frenzy.

Lindt began laughing. God alone knows how lonely he was. Why was it the people who considered him their familiar weren't the ones he considered his own familiars?

Lindt had a particularly fascinating business trip to Semipalatinsk during the second half of July and all of August 1949: a whole lot was going on then with the first Soviet atomic bomb. Chaldonov stayed in Ensk because of his age and other completely understandable reasons and was so desperately nervous and jealous he didn't even try to hide it.

'Why are you letting it get to you?' Marusya gently reproached him. 'They wouldn't have brought you anyway. Unless maybe to sprinkle sand in front of the bomb. And it would have been your very own sand, that shakes out of you. There's no need to sulk, and we're not having any of that "If only I were twenty years younger." Your outstanding hemorrhoids had no place in the trenches even twenty years ago. And throw away that cigarette right now: you just smoked a minute ago! Perhaps the Bolsheviks will get by without you! Let's go, you can help me tie up the wolfsbane.'

Chaldonov obediently stuck his juicy cigarette, barely started, in the ashtray and plodded after Marusya to the small front garden, what the hell, so that's called wolfsbane? I thought these were those, what are they, lilies! Marusya laughed, lilies in Ensk, Seryozha? Have you even noticed we're in Siberia? And this planet, I'll tell you just in case, is Earth. Who knows what other illusions you're still living under. Chaldonov shook his head, untrusting. He was practically certain about Earth but the wolfsbane… were they really not lilies? Marusya laughed even louder, she probably could have even grown lilies, too, everything bloomed for her and the lush, luxuriant mass of flowers sticking out of the garden was enough to turn the heads of passers-by and for the neighbors to jealously ask, just one little cutting, Maria Nikitichna, please. But would you plant it yourself, you have such a light hand. And Marusya planted, tied, and crumbled the impoverished Ensk soil with her fingers, quietly repeating something as if she were giving the scraggly shoots additional strength.

Everybody loved her, absolutely everybody, even the plants.

She woke up early on August 26, as if a sudden, painful jab had awakened her; Chaldonov slept soundlessly beside her like a child and his face was so offended and dear that Marusya's heart sank, then began beating unevenly, out of tenderness and love. The sky outside looked like dewy, predawn milk and everything was unbelievably quiet, as it can only be in the morning and only outside the city, so Marusya had no trouble at all hearing when little bare feet began loudly tromping across the front steps. She remembered it had been five years since Slavik died. Five years. He'd have already started school. The child's staccato stamping quieted as if someone stood outside by the door and couldn't decide whether to knock.

'Go ahead, sweetie, I'll be there soon,' Marusya silently promised. The little feet obeyed her and left. Just then the awakening birds began singing energetically, all at once, and Chaldonov began tossing and turning in blanketed torpor, and the day gathered speed, its wheels turning faster and faster as it clacked along on its glorious set itinerary: breakfast, milk, fiddling with sighing elastic dough, the cemetery, the garden, a cup of strong tea that seemed to appear all by itself at her husband's elbow as he bent over a manuscript. Thank you, sweetie, no need… I could have made some just fine myself. Marusya pressed her tender mouth to the top of his old, completely bald head. With so much sorrow around all my life, it's shameful to live my whole life as a happy woman. Thank you, Lord. For this cup, for my husband, for not abandoning me, for holding me all those years under your long-suffering wing, like a hen.

They ate dinner together on the squeaky rough little porch Chaldonov had been meaning to have insulated all summer, but he couldn't catch the workman sober, why don't you talk with him, Marusya, he'll listen to you, it's already getting toward fall, already getting cold, no I don't want to hear it, I don't want you catching cold. He brought his wife a fluffy shawl that was elderly, too: it had lived through so much with them it was nearly alive. Marusya gratefully wrapped herself up, pressing her cheek to her husband's shoulder, and they sat for a long, long time and talked about nothing, about how sorry they were Lesik hadn't been around all summer, and about how the pie had risen so much better this time than last and all because there's no reason to get creative—if it says two eggs put in two, not four—and that they could start pickling the cabbage in September, just think, they're still wearing sandals in Moscow in September, but here, it's just about winter.

You don't miss Moscow?

No, I never miss anything when I'm with you.

Shaggy, soundless moths flew onto the porch, attracted by the delicious light of the rose lampshade and falling on the tablecloth with the quiet thud of a petal, singed, happy, and having lost all reason from love and pain, and the conversation kept flowing, never stopping, cozy as a cat's purr, until the hot water ran out in the little samovar and Ensk's purplish dusk thickened into an impenetrable, cool darkness filled with rural sounds.

They felt their way to the bedroom instead of disturbing the evening's precious charm with electricity and they went to bed, embracing, as they'd gone to bed all sixty years of their marriage, and there hadn't been a day—not even a minute—when Marusya regretted that this particular person was alongside her.

'I love you,' Chaldonov mumbled, slowly sinking into sleep, opening its stiff doors and awkwardly balancing on the threshold of half-drowsiness because it was impossible to go to sleep without hearing the second part of the spell, the secret answer to the password he'd given, and so Marusya obediently answered, 'I love you.'

And that's what they'd heard from each other every evening and every morning for sixty years, since their first honeyed night on the steamship Tsesarevich Nikolay, when the water had lapped just as gently every night and airy, lacy, living shadows had floated along the ceiling…

Chaldonov woke in the middle of the night just as Marusya had woken that morning—as if he'd been jolted—and he knew instantly what had happened. It was pitch black and an unseen alarm clock on the nightstand ticked resonantly under its big-eared metal hat, and Chaldonov's arm was still lying on Marusya's chest, and he still sensed the velvety aroma of her nightgown with his cheek but Marusya herself was no longer there.

At all.

Chaldonov didn't make a sound, he couldn't, he simply lay there until morning, until it got light, afraid to stir, lest he disturb his wife, all small and curled in a little ball, still warm, she'd be warm for a long, long time because for the first time in his life it was he feeding her his own warmth. He not her. And only at dawn did Chaldonov allow himself to stir, when his arm began to hurt unbearably from falling asleep. 'I love, you,' he said quietly. 'I love you, do you hear?'

Marusya was silent and Chaldonov buried his forehead in her motionless back and finally began to weep.

Chapter Four: Galochka

Galina Petrovna was luxuriously, shamefully, and ravishingly happy until she was seventeen. Rosy-cheeked sprites wearing crimson neckties around their scratched young necks had laid all the accoutrements of a golden Soviet childhood alongside her cradle: they were brightly colored, a teeny-tiny bit garish, and made of celluloid, like the toys watchful parents set afloat in funny little baby bathtubs to ease a child's tear-stained struggles with learning personal hygiene.

Galochka's father, Petr Alekseyevich Batalov, was pursuing a career as a petty Party demon in the city's regional government: he was an amusing, pot-bellied little man with a touching patch of fluff on the cozy, pudgy nape of his neck and a well-groomed long lock of hair that outlined a mirror-like bald spot running from one round ear to the other. He was too stupid and good-natured to accomplish even the simplest administrative exploits and fight his way into the fiery ranks of true communist archangels. He thus spent entire days patiently moping in a cramped little office, amassing piles of pointless papers on the corner of his desk and sitting down to dinner at home at exactly six-fifteen: brainless, pink, fresh, innocuous, and wearing an ironed pajama top.

Beet-red steam floated over a bowl of borscht as Petr Alekseyevich brought a brightly glistening lead crystal shot glass to his soft little mouth, holding at the ready a fork crowned by a fat, juicy morsel of sardine. Vodka so cold it was viscous guggled in his Adam's apple and Galochka said with a melodious laugh, another one, Papa, another one! Petr Alekseyevich delicately sniffed the spicy fish flesh, swallowed a second shot just as smoothly and stunningly as the first, and then thrust a spoon into the depths of his hot borscht, winking at his satisfied daughter. Galochka's mother, Yelizaveta Vasilevna Batalova, shook her smoothly coiffed head with affected reproach and removed the little round pitcher from the table for effect; Petr Alekseyevich never drank a third shot. Their life was, essentially, wonderful.

Being an undistinguished parasite on the swollen body of the great (and one and only) Party brought Petr Alekseyevich neither honor nor valor nor glory, not that his household truly needed any of that anyway. To make up for it, he qualified for satiating extra rations, an exemption from army service, and a very decent little apartment in a brick building. The apartment was sufficiently spacious for Galochka to blossom and develop properly in her very own room with a branchy aloe plant on the windowsill, a fragile étagère, and a brown-eyed teddy bear who patiently sat on her bed all day, wide-open for plush animal embraces. He pressed on Galochka's warm cheek at night, blowing lightly on her disheveled, damp curls: he chased away the quiet, red-lipped, incorporeal monsters that flew in after midnight, rattling invisible black wings and settling on the headboard to feast on children's dreams that were as opaque, joyful, and sticky as the cheap lollipops pugnacious gypsy women, all bundled-up and variegated, sell near bakeries.

Galochka grew into a strong, bright girl who wasn't bratty between classes at school and brought home report cards containing tables densely filled by large, bold numerals denoting the highest grades. Taken together, all that—along with a mother who headed up the pedagogy department at a neighboring school—secured her solid status as the prettiest girl in her class, a position that, up to a certain age, had nothing to do with leg length or epidermis quality. By sixteen, however, Galochka had shaken off her silly baby fat and obtained herself a slender, curvaceous figure as if a lathe had turned her from some wondrous dense golden alloy. She had a reddish braid with the slightest little glint of honey (Galochka's impeccable, absolutely un-Soviet incisors constantly nibbled on its twisted lion-like end), stormy transparent blue-gray eyes, a neat little stub of a snub nose, and dimples on dark cheeks slightly rough from youth and the sun... The bewildered little boys with big ears who'd begun swarming around the entryway to the Batalovs' apartment building dreamt about more than just sneaky ways of copying Galochka's math homework.

Beyond all that, Galochka, who'd been chirping away at some school concert or other since she was little, inhaled a new voice for herself along with her curvy young breasts: the lower notes of her heavy, thrilling, and passionate voice shimmered with a precious and dangerous ruby warmth. She was immediately made a soloist. When she went on stage for end-of-term holiday concerts dressed in a rather tight wool skirt naively stretching over her splendid hips and then extended her neck with childish diligence as her anguished, husky alto began drawing out idiotic little songs about a speeding locomotive and 'Bravely, comrades, keep the pace,' there arose in that most politically tested concert hall a completely indecent exultation that would have been more appropriate in a dive bar.

Galochka's true crowning moment, however, was the song 'Hostile Whirlwinds.' Immediately after hearing the very first notes of this revolutionary recitative—with Galochka's decisive 'r' rolling and roiling around like fiery orbs at the song's very depths—important personages on the presidium felt the front of their pants harden and didn't recover from their criminally sweet haze until near the end of the concert, meaning their excited, blinded hearts missed out on a poetry montage and sailor dances and gymnastics exercises from skinny little Pioneers stretching their future indestructible muscles to fight for Lenin's cause.

Whispers about the promising girl rustled their way to the regional committee of the Komsomol and it was from there that some obliging young clod quickly placed a call, wishing (for his own benefit) to offer the exhausted leadership a treat. The damned idiot called her at home to make an offer wisest not to refuse but fortunately Galochka's father took the call. He was taking an opportune sick day in the pleasant company of some raggedy ancient *Ogonyok* magazines and strong tea with raspberry preserves. After carefully hearing out the novice Komsomol leader, Petr Alekseyevich offered the neophyte a few lines that were completely empty and innocuous but a sort of password, an invisible verbal sign with which one undercover secret agent recognizes another who's even more secret.

When the young man figured out he'd unexpectedly stumbled upon one of his own (and from the regional Party committee, and someone senior on the organization chart at that!) he quickly bleated out something incomprehensible and abruptly put down a sweaty telephone receiver that suddenly smelled to him of some awful, animated, animal hatred. It was as if neither the Party nor the Soviet Union nor vodka for twenty-five rubles and twenty kopecks was left in the world, leaving only the infernal sky on the fifth day of creation, a supercontinent overgrown with rustling snake grass, and a sable-toothed male dangerously baring his teeth over a lair containing a naked and slippery new-born.

Petr Alekseyevich carefully returned the telephone to its rickety three-legged table and gazed for several minutes with furious empty eyes at Kramskoy's *Portrait of an Unknown Woman* thumbtacked to the wall until he'd mentally sorted through the full arsenal of horrendous tortures for the brazen defiler. After the scoundrel—castrated, mutilated, limbs broken, bellowing from a mouth torn diagonally—had writhed and croaked for the last time, Petr Alekseyevich went to the kitchen, drank the rest of his tea (now cooled and coated with an oily film) and sat there, hunched and tapping a fierce little beat on a clean cotton tablecloth until Ensk's chilly dusk crept through a slightly open window and his wife came home from work, scratching with her key in the entryway.

When Galochka hurried home from chorus that evening—with a tapping clatter of shoes tossed off, her round sheepskin fur coat, a contraband puff of elegant air turned pink by the cold, and I'm home, Ma and Pa—she found her parents in that very same kitchen. They were sitting next to one another at the table, quiet and as glum as if they were at a wake when everyone still remembers why they've gathered and the widow, swelled with distress, is dripping her first cloudy swirling valerian into her vodka. What scared Galochka most, though, wasn't the quiet or the parental faces crumpled with a mysterious grief but the air in the kitchen: this was the dinner hour but the usual warm sprites weren't hovering over a domestic hearth cloaked in hot, starchy potato steam and the aroma of braised meat bubbling away in a pot. The air was as empty and sterile as an operating room humming with a chirring antibacterial lamp. There was only a silent plate on the table holding apples that were unimaginable for Ensk even in summer: bright red, abnormally shiny, and grown in a faraway imported world without caterpillars, black rot, or horrendous frosts that tear at tortured, groaning tree trunks.

'Did something happen?' Galochka didn't quite say or ask this. She felt as if a soft, unfamiliar paw was pressing her heart, squeezing it in its furry fist and pulling down toward the solar plexus, to the place where the soul—tiny, rumpled, and as cloudy as a breath on cold glass but nevertheless alive—hides in reddish darkness.

'Galina,' Yelizaveta Vasilevna began, rattling her vocal chords in her usual teacherly way. 'You're a grown-up girl already, you're in the Komsomol…'

Galochka batted her heavy eyelashes, uncomprehending, and Petr Alekseyevich winced with dissatisfaction.

'Hold on, Mother, you're not saying the right thing. Look here, hon…'

He took an apple off the plate and bit off one of its cultivated sides, firmly crunching with his jaws and spraying his wife and daughter with the fragrant juice that had foamed instantly. Then he placed the apple—disfigured and covered in spittle, its mutilated greenish-golden insides exposed—on the tablecloth. Next to it he immediately placed another apple—whole, polished, and crimson, obediently casting a round, rosy patch of light on the table. 'Which one would you choose, hon?'

Galochka's smooth forehead gathered in a soft pleat (the trace of a future adult wrinkle and a hint of an impending mortal life lacking joy) as she strained to guess, and then she mechanically stretched for the whole apple. When she suddenly got the point, she gasped, burst into graceless full-volume crying, and rushed to her room to a teddy bear who'd aged and lost a soft ear in his skirmishes with demons but was still serious and still ready to do anything at all for Galochka.

About twenty minutes later, a faint smell cautiously wended its way into the former nursery: it was the smell of tiny homemade pelmeni that had been chilled to the hardness of glass in the freezer but were now slowly and torturously boiling, acquiring a doughy, nearly translucent flesh that enveloped succulent seasoned meat. Yelizaveta Vasilevna followed the pelmeni and looked into the wintry-blue, almost nocturnal room, where she sat beside Galochka, who'd fallen face down on the bed. She stroked Galochka's warm, maidenly back, which still shook from tectonically deep sobs. Let's go eat dinner, Galochka.

With her whole face buried in the teddy bear's consoling stomach, Galochka shook her head for no and snuffled once more, confirming her suffering. Let's go, Galochka, Papa's already tired of waiting, Yelizaveta Vasilevna said affectionately. And Galochka crawled from the wet teddy bear's stomach to her mother's knees as if she'd been magnetized by the affection. She began crying again, this time with the most weightless of tears, crystalline, maidenly, and unable to redden the nose or puff the eyelids: these tears had the opposite effect, magically transforming the entire face, igniting it from inside with that slightly sad, soft, and surprisingly feminine light for which men around the world essentially live, slavishly going out of their minds, losing fortunes, and unleashing hundred-year wars.

Yelizaveta Vasilevna kissed the round, trusting top of Galochka's head, which had a natural aroma that couldn't be ruined by either Family-brand soap or the wild animal-like scent of the fluffy Orenburg shawl Galochka wore in winter instead of a hat. Then both of them, mother and daughter, headed for the kitchen, completely at peace with the world and one other. And the lamp in the kitchen burned for a long, long time, nearly until midnight, the teapot hissed through its teeth as it came to a boil again and again, and little ramekins clinked, filled to the brim with sugary raspberry preserves. The Batalovs kept talking, kept discussing, interrupting each other and feeling glad about what was coming up, what hung right there over the table like big, translucent, airy curls that naively pretended they were the strong, homey steam of tea.

Only the teddy bear, still lying all alone in the dark nursery, his fat paws spread as he eavesdropped on the unintelligible babble of the kitchen conversation, sensed that Galochka's childhood was slowly leaving him behind, drop by drop. The tears on his soft stomach dried, unhurried, leaving barely noticeable salty splotches on plush old fur worn to a sheen. The bear was still alive when Galochka came to her room around midnight and began undressing, happy, excited, and purring (but with carefully brushed teeth before bed—discipline and hygiene are oh-so important!).

He lasted almost until morning, gathering his final strength and waiting to see if the demons would arrive. He was ready for his last battle. But the demons never came and the bear lay on his back for a long, long time, afraid to stir lest he disturb Galochka's arm, which was unbearably heavy, fiery hot, and a little damp on the inside. It was familiar, too. When two rectangular ceilings slowly began to lighten in his glassy eyes and Galochka rolled over, knocking him to the floor with a restless elbow, the bear was still able to produce a short, strange, and almost sobbing sound that was completely human.

It was all over by seven in the morning when the alarm clock began shrieking at top volume. 'Galochka, you up?' Yelizaveta Vasilevna asked from the doorway. And Galochka swung her smooth young feet to the floor, knocking a heel into the motionless little sawdust-filled body. 'I'm up, I'm up!' she said in a happy, velvety half-awake voice before stepping over the dead bear and heading off with a bounce to wash up.

Singing in the chorus was, unanimously, all over and done with after the great apple conclave, as was other school and social ado, and peace reigned once again in the sacred Batalov family unit. There was still plenty to take care of even without final concerts and hostile whirlwinds: Galochka was, after all, set to finish high school in the spring and transform from a little doll into a magnificent graduate after shedding her chitinous shells and segments. They weighed all Ensk's institutes of higher learning, one by one, on invisible scales. On one side lay a bright future with a sturdy career ladder scrubbed immaculate white, a salary advance on the fifth of the month and the rest on the twentieth, and—Oh, dear Lord of creation!—a guaranteed local trade committee trip to Gagra in the summer! (Gagra in summer!) On the other side sat Galochka herself, swinging slender legs that even rough ribbed cotton tights couldn't make ugly. The scale's needle pierced at a parent's very heart: What were the struggles of textbook literary characters sacrificing their lives compared to the bloody struggles of the Batalovs, who were sending their one and only progeny off to meet her future happiness?

Galochka hinted at the old maids' pedagogical institute, but the indignant Yelizaveta Vasilevna just flapped wings that were slightly tattered from teachers' battles but fully swanlike nevertheless. Wreck your nerves for the sake of someone else's idiots!? I won't allow it! After Petr Alekseyevich consulted with some of his older comrades regarding serious prospects, they decided to send Galochka to the local technical institute, though for peace-loving water supply and sewage instead of defense-related subjects, lest she sit all her life in some secret 'post office box' place and never be allowed to travel abroad, not even to Bulgaria! Besides, if there's a lot of something in this country, hon, it's shit, enough for you to live twice. And don't you make that face, the work's actually clean, you'll sit in a design institute in a little white lab coat or San Sanych will hire you at the water treatment plant. He promised. You, my little dove, just need to get in, then the rest will happen on its own, smooth sailing.

Galochka dreamily lowered her gray-winged eyelids and saw, through the heavy ends of tangled lashes, a dim, mirage-like room with a giant window that was filled to its very horizon with a glowing aquatic smoothness on which a lone and unusually charming sail melted like a microscopically bright dot, pretending to be a little white lab coat. Extraordinary people—brave and honest with inspired smooth foreheads like figures on posters—bent over drafting tables that looked, honestly, more like artists' easels in Galochka's fantasies. That wasn't important, though, not important at all, because just then—Oh!—the most crucial, most inspired, most high-foreheaded person rushed in. He had the young Strizhenov's devilishly bent brows and the bouncing gait of the fiery revolutionary Arthur Rivares, nickname Gadfly, who was successfully shot only on the second attempt. Galochka's fuzzy aspirations now switched to the purely cinematic: Kriuchkov, Merkuryev, Kadochnikov. Galochka never missed a premiere and the tender ardor with which she adored every gray shadow on the screen threatened to turn into a real-life human love story in the very nearest future.

So far, of course, Galochka had only seen that love in the abstract, almost cubic, symbols of a young virgin who was simultaneously a Soviet Komsomol girl: whispers, timid breaths, passionate glances, collaborative creative labor, and the asexual and thus particularly solemn blending of two highly moral personalities and communist builders. Galochka's lower, animal, feminine essence, however, was already completely prepared for moist battles on a groaning metal cot, zealous fights about salary, and the happy horrors of multiple live births. In short, she was ready for everything that makes women of all epochs and social systems genuinely immortal.

Mathematics, physics, and Russian language, however, stood in her path to a happy future and a full-fledged family unit: they were a gloomy bunch, as bristling and somber as petty thugs standing in a breezy passageway, so bored they're ready to stick a Finnish knife into a venerable family man wearing an astrakhan hat, or even into their own half-neglected buddy who's mistakenly wandered in from a warring region they don't control. Even if the chances were slim for coming to terms with Russian and math—appealing for sympathy and managing to at least somehow scrape by, collecting spider webs and whitewash on your quivering back as you slink away, pressing against buildings and hurrying off down the next street—well, physics was mute, unbending, incomprehensible, and, therefore, particularly horrifying.

Once the Batalovs clarified the full horrendous degree of Galochka's naïveté in the field of gravitational force and rotating bodies, they quickly hired a physics tutor, a graduate student from Ensk University, a distinguished and well-known university that boldly and successfully competed with Moscow's best institutions. The Batalovs, of course, couldn't even dream of the university, satisfying themselves with the gentle saying of all cautious, simple-minded people about the hen who pecks at just one piece of grain. Indeed, all the pre-graduation and pre-college hubbub had made Galochka even more charming and she even resembled a hen with her gentle pointless bustling and the especially quick motions she made when she bent her pretty little head (with its silky reddish glint) over her textbook.

The graduate student, a lanky guy with the tragic eyes of a hungry Judaic demon, came to the Batalovs' twice a week, on Mondays and Thursdays, to coach (under Yelizaveta Vasilevna's invisible monitoring, as she reigned in the kitchen) the future engineer for impending feats of sewerage. Yelizaveta Vasilevna feared a flash of inopportune and unforeseen passion between teacher and student and thus frequently used invented and awkward pretenses to look into Galochka's room. Yelizaveta Vasilevna's concern was groundless: the graduate student detested poor Galochka despite the ten pre-reform rubles due for each hour of their joint academic sufferings and the round breasts the student obediently lowered on the edge of the desk in an attempt to use some form of physical effort to force Hooke's disobedient law to progress from a standstill.

Beyond all that, Galochka was so completely lost in the presence of this young man she barely knew that she even forgot everything she'd dutifully learned by rote, out loud, at school. The graduate student grasped at his head, his legs measuring the nursery with quick, mean strides, like a drafting compass: the room had long been a tight fit for the appetizingly ripened Galochka, both in the armholes and in the chest. But how can you not get it? It's completely elementary! The amount of absolute deformation is proportional to the value of the deforming force with the coefficient of proportionality, which is equal to the rigidity of the deformed object! Galochka hurriedly noted down his pointless and terrifying words as she secretly, out of the corner of her eye, looked at the strong hands sticking out of her furious teacher's coarse hand-knit sweater. The sweater was unquestionably in need of immediate laundering but the veins swelling on his strong masculine forearms didn't just prevent Galochka from concentrating: she couldn't breathe properly, either. She tugged worriedly at the throat of her stifling flannelette top, often raising her eyelashes—beseeching, huge, and damp from effort—at the student. The desperate student grasped at a head in need of a wash and inhaled on a Belomor until it crackled: he smoked with the desperation of a convicted man and took the cigarette from his bitten-up lips only when the cigarette's cardboard shell was thoroughly soaked in bitter spittle. His fingers were covered with yellow tobacco spots that also excited Galochka tremendously.

The miracle took only an instant. After granting the young teacher yet another cash sum and a sour smile, Yelizaveta Vasilevna shut the door behind him and quickly ordered Galochka to air out her room, this is abominable, we're living in Soviet times after all, and he has a higher education but he reeks like a wandering menagerie. Galochka flinched squeamishly, opened the tight little ventilation window with a scrape, and jumped down off the stool, completely cured. The grad student simply ceased to exist for her, first as a representative of the disquieting opposite sex, then in general, as a person.

Convinced that Galochka had memorized her physics textbook by heart with the strictness of a seminarian, the relieved graduate student returned to his university and entertained his colleagues for another forty years with stories of the utter fool incapable of distinguishing a body's weight from its mass. And Galochka… Well, a day later Galochka had already callously forgotten everything: m-v-squared-by-two, her tutor's not-so-simple name (German Kirillovich), and the complex, vague feelings she'd had for him.

She truly was ready: most definitely for love, if not for college.

It's hard to say exactly how the Batalovs' offspring infuriated the Creator, but the toilet department didn't accept Galochka. Nothing helped, absolutely nothing. Everything was for naught: obsequious, Jesuitical phone calls from Papa Batalov, who went through all his considerable connections, and the moral and spiritual efforts of Yelizaveta Vasilevna, who was crazed from concern and—combining the mystical with the pedagogical—either woke her sleepy daughter up at dawn to go through test questions again or knelt for hours in their bathroom at midnight, offering torturous and wordless prayers to a dusty ventilation grate. It didn't even save the day that Galochka was fairly well-prepared: the grad student had achieved almost unprecedented, albeit circus-like, results after harshly schooling her for several months in a row. Despite not understanding anything about physics, Galochka could still quickly, cleverly, and completely mindlessly solve any problem from the high school curriculum, just as a circus rabbit can pound out a set beat with identically mechanical effort on a toy drum, an overturned bucket, or even the last volume of *War and Peace*.

Everything seemed to have been taken care of. Galochka went to the entrance exams dressed in the most modest of her modest Soviet dresses, concealing even the slightest hint of her carnal existence under speckled cotton; she was the very embodiment of diligent and energetic innocence. A smooth braid coiled on the back of her head (never wash your hair the night before an exam!) with even the lightest little curls on her temples and near her forehead mercilessly pinned by coarse, hidden black hairpins; lowered lashes; palms sweaty from fear; and a sweaty round yellow five-kopeck piece placed under her left heel for luck. Five kopecks worth of luck wasn't enough, though.

Galochka didn't fail any subject, and she made it through all the exams at an unostentatious, even, pace but she still didn't total enough points, coming up one short. Only one, just think! When she didn't find her name on the list of those accepted (Maybe it was a typo? Don't shove, I'm telling you!) she experienced, for the first time in her life, the complex and humiliating feeling of her own inferiority, something familiar to professional athletes who sometimes miss out on a record by some pathetic centimeter, turning all their endless, torturous training to dust. What was most painful and offensive of all was that this wasn't a matter of lack of effort but rather that her opponent's limbs were simply that one fateful centimeter longer, something he'd been given for no reason at all—just like that—a total gift. A gift from God. A divine gift. The harshest and most unjust thing in the world.

The Batalovs' desperation was totally out of proportion with what had caused it: Galochka, after all, wasn't sick, hadn't died, and wasn't unmarried and in the family way. She didn't even have to serve in the army, so the lost year couldn't be considered lost, even theoretically. Still, Petr Alekseyevich had a most genuine attack of angina pectoris, with arrhythmia, icy sweat, and the deathly horror that's for some reason directly connected with mild heart disease, as if the soul really does live somewhere near the aorta. A tear-stained, puffy Yelizaveta Vasilevna saw the ambulance doctors to the door and a sobbing Galochka sat on the edge of her bed holding her father's hand just after he'd gotten his shots: it was as if she were five years old again, only now it was even scarier to let go of Papa's hand. It's fine, hon, don't cry, it'll all be okay, Petr Alekseyevich whispered, though he himself was ready to begin howling out of sweet, lulling self-pity. Your daddy will think of something, you'll see. Galochka nodded and believed him; her father had never deceived her. These were the last months they were all together, as a family, when they could just be themselves.

Fifteen years later Batalov was a pensioner wasting away from rectal cancer and dying all alone in a huge, dull oncology institute; Yelizaveta Vasilevna had passed away a year earlier. They might not have been an ideal pair but they couldn't get by without one another, either in this life or the next. Petr Alekseyevich grabbed at the sleeves of Soviet medical personnel who were as unhurried and indifferent as pagan gods, nurse, I'm begging you, call my daughter, my Galochka, I just want to say goodbye. The nurses put Batalov's pathetic rubles in their pockets, nodded their agreement, and maybe changed the linens for the tiresome old man in ward three an extra time. But nobody was game for calling his daughter Galochka: she'd drowned the head of the department, a venerable, plump proctologist, in such an icy stream of curses that the poor professor'd had to be treated in the residents' room with equal portions of tea and alcohol. And you just remember, I don't have any father and never did. And if you call again, I'll let you rot alive, you old dick. I do hope you understand what I'm saying.

The proctologist understood, as did everyone else because Batalov died in his room in quiet, dreadful pain and quiet, dreadful loneliness. Of course nobody came to claim the corpse, which meant the mortal flesh of the former regional Party committee instructor was cut into shreds and used for specimens, to the joy of young and inquisitive students, mere embryos in the medical field who dreamt of vanquishing cancer and heart attacks and giving humanity a hale, hardy, communist immortality.

Lord only knows where Petr Alekseyevich's soul ended up. Maybe he perched, whimpering, in a corner of his daughter's huge apartment so he could sneak up to her bed in the deep, dark night every now and then and look into her beloved, placid face. She was always cute, Galochka, and she'd become a real beauty at thirty-two, a little languorous, buxom, and magnificent. They'd had her, Galochka, their only daughter, late in life. Petr Alekseyevich was thirty-two when he went to the maternity hospital to get his wife, who was pressing a precious, tightly swaddled little bundle to her breast. Yelizaveta Vasilevna was also thirty-two, of advanced maternal age for a first child, and she'd struggled during labor, it was scary to even talk about. Thank God nothing happened to Galochka. Sleep, little girl, sleep, my sweetie. Sleep. Your daddy will think of something, you'll see.

'The salt spilled all by itself in the kitchen again,' the housekeeper complained in the morning, handily digging around with a broom. 'I'm telling you, a house spirit really did move in. We should get some holy water and sprinkle it around.' 'What house spirit, you clumsy fool,' Galina Petrovna lazily said, testing her coffee with her lips, like a child, to see if it was hot. 'And was it a house spirit that broke the Kuznetsov china plate last week, too?' The offended housekeeper went silent. What could you say, Galina Petrovna was nasty—nasty and a bitch—but she paid well. Everyone said she didn't cry one single tear when her parents died, didn't even go to their funerals. Not a heart but a stone. Galina Petrovna moved the cup aside, wrinkled her brow, and went to her bedroom, where she touched her beautiful face with warm fingers and lightly rubbed a delicate, melting cream into her skin. She felt no guilt and had no intention of feeling any. Nobody in her position would have forgiven their parents. Nobody, ever.

Luckily, the Batalovs recovered fairly quickly from their daughter's disgraceful failure. After his sick leave, Petr Alekseyevich once again called all the necessary people and, after hearing and vocalizing tons of unneeded verbal rubbish—Just think, buddy, only one point!—he secured Galochka's acceptance to the technical institute after all. Not as a student, of course, but as a lab assistant in the Chemistry Department, within the department she needed for her much-desired water supply and sewage. If you do a good job, Galochka, you'll get familiar with things and start to belong and then you'll definitely get in next year. Just be sure you know who to be useful for and don't waste your time… Yelizaveta Vasilevna straightened her daughter's white collar, which still smelled of recent school days. It was Galochka's first day of work and they were both nervous—this was no joking matter—and Galochka couldn't even really eat breakfast so a stack of golden *bliny* with lacy edges remained on the table, cooling. Her mother had gotten up an hour early and stood at the stove toiling over two iron skillets for nothing. At least drink some tea, Galyunya. I can't, Ma, or I'll be late. Galochka quickly pecked Yelizaveta Vasilevna on the cheek and hurried off, her softly pleated skirt billowing.

It was a warm August, unusual for Ensk, but by October Galochka already belonged so much at the department that she allowed herself to shout at upperclassmen, who'd quickly sized up all the brand-new little lab assistant's smooth merits. You can go to your movie by yourself, Svetlov, I'm three flasks short again after your group and don't make that face like you don't think I know you're all making homebrew in the dorm. Watch out I don't report it to Nikolay Ivanovich! Svetlov left, humiliated by the undeserved refusal (and deserved suspicion), taking with him the now-disgraced reputation of an experienced lady-killer. Galochka watched him inattentively as he left and her lips—warm, smooth, and as bright as barberry candies—still preserved the form of a wonderful name. Nikolay Ivanovich. Nikolenka. Kolyusha. Kosha. Galochka sighed from the completeness of her happiness as a gentle, apple-scented breeze spread through the institute's despondent corridors.

She was in love, finally.

Finally happy.

And her great happiness had been issued a term of four months and three days.

Nikolay Ivanovich Mashkov was just a lanky, bashful assistant in the Chemistry Department, where his place in the hierarchy was, honestly, only a tiny bit higher than Galochka Batalova's, and she'd only been entrusted with preparing reagents for classes and washing lab ware after the students. But Mashkov was like a god for Galochka: infinitely adult (his twenty-five to her seventeen) and infinitely intelligent. Nikolay Ivanovich led lab sessions and was sometimes even a substitute lecturer for his research advisor, pudgy professor Leshchinsky, who suffered from shortness of breath. The mouthy students were interested and listened to Mashkov carefully, something Galochka knew for sure because she'd enviously followed the proceedings through a keyhole. And there's nothing shameful about that if it's for work, it's even completely allowable, so there!

Nikolay Ivanovich was also unusually handsome, just unbelievably handsome: bright-eyed, golden-haired, and smiling. Galochka thought he was like some sort of festive Lel, the God of Love, and a one-person incarnation of all Russian folktales, stories she fell asleep to as a child, surrounded by woods spirits' troubling dances, Zmei Gorynychs, hardworking Vasilisas, and wonderful, heroic Ivan Tsareviches. Tsareviches, no less.

In reality, however, Mashkov was never within striking distance of any tsareviches and what Galochka's besotted eyes took for gold and azure was really a banal Central Russian light brownness that could be taken on occasion for an altogether mousy color. Nikolay Mashkov came from a family of the dullest craftsmen, wore cheap, eternally wrinkled suits and traces of youthful blackheads on his sunken cheeks, and was going to start losing his hair within about five years and finally become a lecturer in ten. Even the oily sheen on his nose, though, seemed like a divine sign to Galochka, a symbol of the higher, mysterious power with which Mashkov had so quickly and wonderfully won over her inexperienced, unarmed heart. Galochka smiled, flustered as she twisted the end of her braid around a thin finger. Mashkov smiled in reply: he had a marvelous smile, really marvelous, it was wide, cheerful, and a little mischievous, like a ten-year-old boy's, and his teeth were whiter than white and a front tooth was a tiny bit crooked, and Galochka especially loved that funny, slightly childlike tooth.

Of course Mashkov loved her, too, though they hadn't even spoken twenty sentences to each other about anything but work. Galochka didn't just know he loved her, she sensed it, just as people sense the unseen sun's affectionate, silky touch when they're at the beach with their eyes closed. And so when Galochka was arranging her chemical inventory, she could feel—exactly like the sun, not having to turn—when Mashkov had entered the department: the air around her just suddenly felt different, all fragile and quivering from a glowing crystalline tenderness.

At first they only exchanged cautious smiles from afar, with barely any contact. Then Mashkov somehow helped Galochka gather up some tumbling books (she'd rehearsed the subtlest of gestures at home for more than an hour: a barely perceptible hip motion that instantly sent an entire stack of big, heavy Talmud-like books to the floor), then he was delayed for an extra half-hour after his lab work, the very same half-hour Galochka used to tidy up the tables and glass retorts. And then it seemed natural for him (so adult and strong) to suggest to her (so young and vulnerable) that they walk together to the bus stop, Who cares which one?

It was the most wonderful of dates—and of course it was, since two guardian angels literally flew their wings off trying to make sure everything, absolutely everything, was arranged properly, just right. All the buses magically disappeared from Ensk's sleepy, empty streets, and the autumn evening crunched from the lightest of frosts, like a sheet of smooth, bluish vellum paper folded into fourths. Galochka smiled at Mashkov through her eyelashes, through bare branches, and through radiant streetlights. Oh, no, allow me, I'll carry your satchel for you, no and no again, it's not right for young women to carry so much weight. Mashkov's fingers were reddish, chapped, and rough. With just one second and one touch, the captured satchel was once again floating over the asphalt, looking downright toy-like in his hands. Even iced-up gobs of phlegm on the sidewalk looked semiprecious, like lunar opal, greenish onyx, or tubercular brown hematite. Mashkov courted her with such abandon the whole way that he himself nearly lost the thread of his chatty monologue about his academic life, and Galochka didn't understand even half of it but... But, oh, how she remained responsively silent, brushing aside her falling tresses at just the right time, and brimming with a gentle reddish luminosity!

Well, this is my building, Nikolay Ivanovich. Thank you for walking me home. Mashkov stopped short, memorizing the three entryways and five storeys that should become the center of his world from now on. That was so fast! I mean, very nice, he mumbled. Galochka smiled again and took her satchel from Mashkov. Inside the building she hurriedly took a little mirror out of her pocket and happily confirmed that the cold had been kind, pinching her cheeks but sparing her nose, which wasn't at all red. Her lips were tender instead of chapped and her beret very successfully covered the nasty little pimple on her forehead. Galochka put the mirror away, giggled with satisfaction, and quickly ran up the stairs, up, up, up.

Mashkov walked Galochka home the next day and then the next and then again the next week. They found new, ever more intricate and complex routes each time, never discussing them and always wandering further from their final destination as if they were tossing airy, lacy, invisible loops over a map of Ensk. Fifteen minutes of leisurely walking first turned into a half-hour and then an hour: Ensk's infrequent streetlights came on one after the other, marking their blissful evening walks with a trembling dotted line. Mashkov lost weight from all these out-of-the-ordinary pedestrian endeavors and his voice often cracked with a boyish happiness in classes. And Galochka… Galochka glowed with such a naïve midday light that she was as embarrassing to look at as a new bride.

The ubiquitous ladies of the department started whispering a little about this outrageous romance and impermissible relationships but they quickly bit their jealous stinger-like tongues. There was nothing outrageous or impermissible about these two looking at each other, besides it was completely obvious that things were moving in the direction of a wedding and a legal—even socialist—marriage, so impeding these love-crazy young clods would have been the same as telling a clueless little child that it was the roaring drunk neighbor, Misha, a plumber with minimal qualifications and incorrigible bachelor, who'd brought the gifts in the sack, not Father Frost, who doesn't exist anyway. The ladies grumbled a little more for the sake of appearances, remembered their own youth—which had flown by in such a hurry—and then the whole flock of them zealously switched over to a lively divorcée from the union who was trying to wreck yet another home. Mashkov and Galochka were alone again without having even noticed the public storms that had been thickening around them. Everything between them was proper and genuine, despite all the gossip and concerns, and they hadn't even kissed once.

It was a delightful feeling, both awkward and touching, like a two-week-old puppy with fat paws and a naked pink tummy. Neither Galochka nor Mashkov knew what to do next: Galochka because she really didn't know and Mashkov because he was in no rush. He was an unshakably decent adult with, as they say, serious intentions, meaning he was in no hurry and wanted the walk down the road to the wedding registration office with his beloved to be methodical, without missing turns, glances, secluded little corners, or anything else. This naïve Mashkov hoped to live a long and happy life with Galochka so, like any good spouse, he got started early stocking up on memories and events to help him overcome the unavoidable boredom of everyday existence later and provide endless topics for endless conversation with children and even grandchildren, It was right here that Grandma and I first kissed, and that's the maternity hospital you came home from, oh how you cried that first week, let me tell you, your mother and I couldn't figure out what to do with you! She wailed herself out, poor thing… And then it got easier but it wasn't until little Masha was born that your mother played with her like a doll, just for sheer enjoyment. You know how it is, you learn everything by the third child…

Mashkov wanted everything, absolutely everything, to be the way it should be, even better: the wedding, Galochka's veil, a noisy feast, and kisses when the guests demanded to see something sweet. There'd be embarrassed kisses scented with happiness, beet salad, and jellied meat. Mashkov wanted children, lots of them, as many as possible, so he could get up for them in the night, carry them on piggyback, and sing them songs about a locomotive. He wanted to lie down under the same blanket as Galochka and then eat breakfast with her in the morning, to entertain friends and make borscht together. Mashkov was selflessly prepared to take on the job of peeling onions and potatoes and Galochka would never, ever, take out the trash, and he'd handle the dishes himself, too, no problem, especially since after the army it didn't matter if there were five dishes to wash or five hundred. That was how much he loved Galochka: so much he'd already begun a quiet but fierce siege of the local housing committee without saying anything to anyone, declaring his love, or meeting her parents. He'd simultaneously started collecting recommendations for joining the ranks of the Communist Party of the Soviet Union. That Mashkov was a good Soviet man, and he honestly believed the motherland and Party would do everything so he and Galochka had their own apartment. Not right away, of course, but maybe in about ten years. But their own. They'd figure something out for now: maybe rent a little corner somewhere, who knows. Or live with someone's parents. The main thing was to be together.

Of course Mashkov wanted Galochka beyond belief: how could he not when she was so lithe, curvaceous, and golden, brimming with lush, sunny life? But that was exactly why he didn't hurry, instead allowing himself to anticipate and sit politely at a table set for the holidays, as well-bred, cultured people do. Besides, the Soviet morals that inoculated little boys in earliest childhood dictated completely set rules on how to behave with the woman you love: it was strict and wonderful in its nearly chivalrous asceticism. Until the wedding, you were only allowed to respect your future wife. This was a test, the most important phase of initiation, and only after enduring all the temptations could a winner receive rewards like a horse, half a kingdom, and the sacred right to unhook the tsar's daughter's brassiere, something simple, a little ugly, and made of cotton, thus abnormally and almost painfully sexual.

Though Galochka had no inkling of this young Soviet Werther's sexual sorrows, she still sensed deep down that Mashkov was hovering on the doorstep of something very important. She'd even shared her uncertainties with her more experienced girlfriends, who were actually just as remarkably naïve and foolish as she. According to them, all men—no exceptions—dream about how to feel up a girl in a dark corner and basically think about only one thing, like lechers. Galochka shrugged: this was one more incontestable argument that her Nikolenka was better than the rest.

That same evening, Yelizaveta Vasilevna came to look in on Galochka before bed. Galochka was standing in just her nightgown in front of the vanity mirror, trying to fashion something like a bridal veil out of a lacy pillow cover. The pillow cover wasn't cooperating and didn't want to pleat properly and Galochka pressed it on this way and that, her cheeks aglow. Yelizaveta Vasilevna sighed like a peasant woman, went over to her daughter, and helped her gather up her heavy, messy braid. See, we'll catch it with hairpins and it'll be just how you want it, she quietly suggested. Galochka nodded, flustered, then she and her mother stood in front of the mirror for a few seconds: the three mirrors reflected the two of them, making six of them, multiplied perhaps by optical illusion, evolution, or fate. But did it matter? The coarse white lace on the pillow cover gave Galochka's beauty an elusive Spanish flavor that was a tiny bit tragic and completely from another place, making Yelizaveta Vasilevna marvel yet again: Who had her daughter taken after, to be so fine? She did look like her parents—the brows were her father's, and her nose was exactly like a grandmother's, rest her soul—but it was still obvious they were all just genetic garbage, mass-produced nothings. But Galochka, Galochka was truly one of a kind, hand-crafted, something to be wrapped in silky tissue paper, put away in a cool little box, and only taken out for important holidays. Not to be touched without washing your hands. To admire, holding your breath. And rapturously adore.

'Is he at least a good person, Galochka?' Yelizaveta Vasilevna softly asked. Galochka bit her lip and nodded with such furious conviction that the improvised veil floated off her head and quietly landed on the floor like an angel. 'I hope to God,' Yelizaveta Vasilevna mumbled and returned to the kitchen and her husband, who was having his evening tea sweetened with the latest issue of *Pravda*. 'So, Petya,' she sadly said, 'How much do we have on the bank book? Is there enough for a wedding?'

'What are you talking about? What wedding!?' Petr Alekseyevich asked, flabbergasted and trying to let his emotions overflow a bit, but Yelizaveta Vasilevna just waved him off.

'For a regular wedding. With an accordion and witnesses. Like it should be. Our little girl's grown up, Father, and we didn't even notice.'

They decided to meet their future son-in-law a week later, and those were seven days that shook the world. The Batalovs' world at any rate, for sure. As zero hour neared, Yelizaveta Vasilevna got it into her head to rearrange the furniture, whitewash the ceilings in the whole apartment again, cook enough food for an extremely hungry motorized rifle company, and even get herself the ridiculous hair waves called a 'permanent' on the beauty salon's price list. (To do this she had to sit forever under a gigantic construct, her head so heavily armed with curlers—each connected to its own electrical wire!—that she could barely hold it on her shoulders.) They ordered a new dress for Galochka from the seamstress, not a refashioned dress but a completely new one of dark blue polka-dot crepe-de chine with a waistband, full skirt, and cap sleeves. The seamstress vowed a solemn vow that it would be ready by Saturday and she kept her vow, as stipulated, after looking Yelizaveta Vasilevna in the eyes.

Petr Alekseyevich attempted for some time to resist the overall hysteria but by Wednesday he'd broken down: not only did he come home three hours late for the first time in his life, but he was also seriously under the influence.

'Just the thing, go off on a bender and shame your only daughter!' Yelizaveta Vasilevna rumbled as a Batalov she barely knew turned himself inside out over the toilet.

'It was for the cause, Mother,' said a limp Petr Alekseyevich, justifying himself. 'I went to see Grigorich, you know what I mean. To make some inquiries.'

Grigorich, an old friend of Batalov's, was a veteran Chekist but he was also an inveterate drunk and morose, lonely man. Yelizaveta Vasilevna immediately shifted into reverse and dragged her weakened husband into the kitchen for confessions. She was nervous for nothing, though: according to reliable sources at the KGB (formerly known by other abbreviations—MGB, NKVD, OGPU, ChK, and so on—with all sorts of various *oprychnik* stops, too), Galochka's intended, Nikolay Ivanovich Mashkov, was a most excellent model of the Soviet human species. Fit for breed, fit for seed, even fit for the Communist Party of the Soviet Union. Yelizaveta Vasilevna wept with relief and reached into the sideboard for the vodka carafe. Petr Alekseyevich hurried off to the lavatory in convulsive hiccups to finish his purging procedures as Yelizaveta Vasilevna poured some of the bracing liquid into a shot glass with shaking hands as if it were valerian, then drank it and sniffed a kitchen towel.

As a result, Saturday concluded favorably, despite all the worry from absolutely everyone. And on Monday Galochka headed for work as a real, true fiancée. Hurrah, comrades! And it really was hurrah. Of course the Batalovs didn't intend to push their under-aged daughter into marriage and of course (thank God) there weren't any shameful reasons to hurry things. They decided to hold the wedding the next autumn, first celebrating Galochka's eighteenth birthday in March and then in early summer… Petr Alekseyevich raised an authoritative parental finger that pointed and cautioned. Mashkov nodded fervently. Of course Galochka would have to be accepted at an institute first. Of course higher education was absolutely necessary. He would personally take it upon himself to speak with the right people and of course he'd tutor Galochka, though there wasn't the tiniest doubt about her acceptance, no doubt at all. Yelizaveta Vasilevna pursed her lips at the word 'tutor' and Galochka blushed. The restless ghost of the Judaic graduate student appeared for a second in the corner and quickly vanished into his infernal physics abysses. Nobody, by the way, even noticed him—such is the lot of all predecessors, all plowmen whose destiny is simply to prepare a field for the coming harvest so someone else can be sure to eat something delicious.

It was wonderfully cold in December—not an Ensk cold, not a mean cold—so after the loving couple had received parental blessings they again roamed squeaky dark-blue streets in the evenings. And my God, who could have known how much Mashkov adored even Galochka's white mittens, especially the left one, with the little hole where a little finger poked out, all pink and new-born, a finger Mashkov could finally kiss as much as he wished. The stubborn Mashkov never moved further than that little finger, though, as if the status of official fiancée made Galochka even purer and more inaccessible.

All was for naught: raised eyelashes, light breathing, and trill of the nightingale. Galochka even swiped her mother's Red Moscow perfume in the naïve hope that Brokar's scents, 'the empress's favorite bouquet,' which was now slyly passing itself off as an honest Soviet item, would definitively knock her fiancé off the communist builder's worn path. Alas. The heavy aroma, as dusty as a curtain, just made Mashkov sneeze three times and then guiltily excuse himself three times. When Petr Alekseyevich caught a whiff of the unbearable notes of carnation, iris, and ylang-ylang on his daughter, he conducted a high-quality scolding for the juvenile offender, Oh you, what have you thought up, you little brat? Taking it out of your own mother's purse! It's not yours, so stop gawking. You'll get married, your husband will earn enough for Red Moscow, and then you can splash it on by the bucket if you want. Galochka burst out in nervous tears, slammed the door, and then completely reconciled with her father an hour later.

Basically, she was unbelievably happy. Everyone was happy in those days.

A new year, 1959, was hurtling toward them. In classes Mashkov kept forgetting how he'd started sentences and he mixed up elementary explanations, causing the students to exchange envious, good-natured glances. Everyone knew the beautiful touch-me-not Galochka was spoken for. The Batalovs put their heads together in the evenings and rapturously discussed the dowry: towels (kitchen), sheets (linen, hemmed and dated), fabric (woolen), plus construction of a new between-season coat for Galochka. And that's where the horrible arguments began because Galochka insisted on a hood and plaid, but Petr Alekseyevich thought that was anti-Soviet. Meanwhile, Yelizaveta Vasilevna mentally totaled up snifters and shot glasses, estimating how many of their kin to honor with wedding invitations and who'd just come and make trouble.

In short, they were all immersed in a thick, warm pudding of horribly outrageous, anti-Soviet philistinism and requirements that had no relation whatsoever to productive labor. Long holidays, guests, New Year trees, dance parties in cultural centers, and an endless life together filled with endless and very human joys were all on the way. Galochka was even amused that some very famous academician (Galochka just couldn't remember his name) would be giving a public lecture at the institute on December 25, and Nikolenka insisted they both most definitely had to go because this was a great mind, a genuine genius, It's just mind-boggling that he's our contemporary. Wouldn't you want to go to a lecture by Einstein?

'What, he didn't die yet?' Galochka asked, frightened. 'I thought they told us in school... Or was that not Einstein?'

'Oh, my joy,' Mashkov said, burying his lips in Galochka's hair. 'If only you knew what a joy you are!'

'Shh!' Galochka cheerfully scared him off. 'You're crazy! They'll see! Fine, we'll go hear your Einstein. We'll definitely go. But one condition: you have to sit next to me and interpret everything your academician says into Russian. Otherwise I'll fall asleep. And you'll be embarrassed.'

'No, I won't,' said the earnest Mashkov.

'But what if I start snoring?'

'I still won't.'

'Then go,' Galochka ordered, 'Or you'll be late and the students will all run off.'

'And thank God,' Mashkov said. 'Let them run off. Then you and I can run off. We can escape to the movies. Do you want to go to the movies?'

'I do,' Galochka said. 'I want to go everywhere with you. Even to Einstein's lecture.'

Mashkov nodded, finding it difficult to restrain the dancing, dizzying, happy world on his shoulders, then he hurried off to his lecture. Galochka stayed in her storage room to rearrange fragile chemistry equipment that was always going out of its way to slip from dreamy fingers and shatter with a divine sound into rainbow-colored crystal shards. Galochka sighed and nimbly brushed the crystal ghost of yet another murdered flask onto a dustpan. So much glassware had been broken during these last days, and all for happiness. For happiness, for happiness, for happiness.

But everything began to unravel strangely on the morning of December 25, 1958. First off, Galochka overslept and was horribly, shamefully late to work. Secondly, the academician's long-awaited lecture was moved from one o'clock to two-thirty, meaning Galochka couldn't possibly go because she had to get the lab ready for the night students, which, of course, raised the question of who holds lab sessions just before New Year's, anyway? So now, rather than sitting in the assembly hall with her fiancé, feeling his shoulder, knee, and elbow—and here's an interesting question, would they dim the lights during the lecture, like at the movies? And so instead of sitting next to each other, and Nikolenka, what a smart guy, had stood more than two hours in line for tickets and gotten great seats for opening night of *My Dear Man*, in the very last row, so if he couldn't bring himself to do it this time she would do it herself, for sure. Absolutely for sure, right away, as soon as he took her hand, she could turn as if by chance to ask something, as if it were about the movie, what's the difference if it's dark, anyway, the main thing would just be to turn…

And what was this?! Not again! Galochka said a grief-stricken 'Oy' and crouched over more completely innocent glass. Someone knocked lightly at the door and she angrily said, 'I'm preparing an experiment,' without raising her head.

'Will there be difficult mistakes?' Mashkov asked, laughing as he played on Pushkin. He sat beside Galochka and added, 'Careful you don't prick your finger.'

Galochka shook her head and some long strands of hair that never found the right place tickled her downy, dark cheek. When she was crouching, she and Mashkov suddenly turned out to be the same height and Galochka saw his lips right next to her for the first time. The sound immediately went off for some reason so she missed his lecture about methods for careful handling of glass shards. All Galochka's courageous plans for conquest had quickly flown out of her head, too. Plus it had gotten very hot.

'You sure you didn't hurt yourself?' Mashkov asked, concerned. He tried to take her by the hand but lost his balance and fell, his clumsy hand knocking into her breasts.

They both stood without saying anything, red with confusion, and then immediately knocked against each other with their shoulders so heavily and clumsily that Galochka gasped from agitation and bit her lower lip: it was puffy, smooth, and looked a lot like a lozenge. A second later, it was obvious it tasted like one, too. And everything around them immediately began moving in quick, hot jolts, as if someone was joyfully and unevenly tearing the world apart, and Galochka simultaneously saw a dusty light over her head and a wall with a framed Lavoisier who, she remembered with absolute certainty, had just been looking bored behind her, and then she saw a few bristles on Mashkov's cheekbones that had miraculously escaped the razor, and it was only then that she remembered you're supposed to close your eyes when you kiss because you only kiss with your eyes open if you don't love someone. She squeezed her eyes shut, frightened, but the world kept noisily tearing itself to pieces, twitching and pulsing in time with her heart, which for some reason had fallen way down to the pit of her belly, no, it wasn't exactly in time, a little faster, even faster, strong and hot so Galochka sensed she'd lose consciousness now and right then she keenly felt something hard under her and opened her eyes, roughly pushing Mashkov. The storage room obediently stopped its unlawful spinning. The hard thing turned out to be the table she was sitting on (How? When? Why?) and Mashkov, red and nearly unrecognizable, was buttoning up her lab coat with shaking hands. A spot of phenolphthalein blazed on the pocket like a squashed berry. It would most definitely not wash out. Mama would let her have it.

'Galya,' Mashkov said guiltily, looking in all directions at once, as if he'd been caught doing something horrible and truly shameful. 'Forgive me. I shouldn't have but…' Galochka thought he was about to cry. 'I just stopped in for a second to be sure you wouldn't leave, so you'd wait for me after the lecture.' He reached to fasten the buttons on her chest but then withdrew his hand and blushed even more.

Galochka jumped off the table and quickly adjusted her lab coat. She turned away and glanced at Lavoisier, who looked a little animated for the first time she could remember.

'Will that academician be here soon?' she asked matter-of-factly.

'In about fifteen minutes,' Mashkov said. 'You're mad at me, aren't you? Really, I didn't mean to, I just… I love you, you can't even imagine how much. I love you so much. I know myself we don't need to hurry…'

'What do you mean?' Galochka asked, as matter-of-factly as before. 'We actually do need to hurry. You said yourself there's only fifteen minutes…'

She couldn't contain herself and burst out laughing, doubled over, and Mashkov, not understanding anything, began laughing, too, first uncertainly then louder, as if he'd plugged into Galochka through some invisible electrical outlet. Everything was clear and simple and good after they'd both finally laughed themselves out, and there was still tons of time until the bell, meaning they could kiss. Now they were cautious, with all the careful, complex, and tender details that are only for first-time kissing.

And so they kissed. The whole fifteen minutes. And a little longer.

When Mashkov finally left—on the third try, who could have torn himself away the first time, anyway?—justifying himself that it was only for a little while, really, just don't leave, this lecture can go to hell, but I can't skip out, I'm the one who volunteered to meet Lazar Iosifovich downstairs, if only I'd known, I would never in my life...'

'Just go, go ahead,' Galochka said, laughing. 'Go, I won't disappear, honest.'

The door closed behind Mashkov. Galochka quickly straightened her messy braid, took her brush again to finally clean up that broken... flask, was it? Or a retort? What difference did it make now, anyway? The brush slipped away as if it were alive but Galochka didn't even notice: she was feeling the imprints of kisses that slowly melted on her lips and neck, and all she heard was a round, wooden knocking that sounded far-off, as if it were through cotton batting. And again. And then again. She didn't immediately grasp that the brush had long been lying motionless on the floor and someone was knocking at the door.

'He is funny,' she mumbled. 'He came back again. What a silly!'

And Galochka happily yelled, 'It's open, come right in, sweetie!' at the top of her precious voice.

Chapter Five: Galina Petrovna

Galina Petrovna—she was now and forever no longer a little girl, Galochka, or Galyunya—went through her entire pregnancy listless and swollen from imminent tears that filled her right up to the softest dimple between her collarbones. For some reason, the tears never rose any higher, as if they'd gotten stuck in an unseen but durable membrane, and so Galina Petrovna always seemed to be attempting to either clear her throat or burst out sobbing, which scared the doctors of the Fourth Main Division, charged with observing and guarding the maturation of the brilliant Lindt's precious semen.

As it happened, the medical fears all proved unfounded: nineteen-year-old Galina Petrovna was wonderfully, outrageously healthy and couldn't indulge the doctors with either the vomitous ordeals of early morning sickness or high blood pressure or uncontrollable urges to treat herself to raw plaster or the smelly contents of an overripe rubbish bin. Her lungs were virginally clean and her larynx was so flawlessly pink and cathedral-like in its arches that it could be shown to students as a model. They thus decided to disregard her strange, worrisome cough but prescribed radish juice with sugar (one teaspoon, three times a day) for Galina Petrovna, just in case.

And it never occurred to anyone—anyone—that she simply couldn't burst into tears.

Then again, it didn't occur to Galina Petrovna herself, either, even as she carried her inflated belly with obedient horror: it was terrifying, silky, and golden brown. Alive. Galina Petrovna was afraid to touch it with her hands—and not just to touch it!—she even squeezed her eyes shut when she changed her clothes, lest her glance fall on the swollen belly that hid (and Galina Petrovna had no doubts about this) something even more horrendous, shaggy, and articulated than Lindt himself.

About three weeks before giving birth, Galina Petrovna even dreamt that an endless paper strip (Lindt would have called it a Möbius strip) all covered with Lindt's twisted, impossibly squiggly handwriting was stretching out of her belly. When the squiggles, quietly chirring, began crawling off the paper onto her bare and terrifyingly wide-splayed legs, Galina Petrovna awoke with such a scream that she threw almost the entire esteemed building for elite government workers into a panic. Even half-awake, Lindt could still figure things out better than most slow-witted mortals, so he stealthily checked the sheets under the hiccupping, laughing Galina Petrovna. Then he felt her pregnant stomach quickly, cautiously, and carefully, as if it weren't a stomach at all but an injured little wild animal that was frightened and desperate, hence capable of taking a big bite.

Nothing was wet or painful anywhere, and besides—despite being hiccuppy, despite being sleepy, and despite being nearly ready to pop after an unthinkable eight months—Galina Petrovna looked outrageously healthy and seductive sitting there on the bed in heaps of fluffed, crumpled pillows and blankets: curvy breasts in the curvy neck opening of a wrinkled shift, milky young knees glistening in the glow of the nightlight, and a mouth swollen and a little parched from heat and horror. Even her huge bulging belly fit harmoniously with a celebration of fertility, generously scented with fresh sweat, apples, and future milk. Having heard from Galina Petrovna about Lindt's appetite for love, however, the lady doctor had already strictly forbidden any and all sexual high jinks a couple months ago so Lindt just grunted, put the brakes on hands that were already openly stroking rather than exploring, and dragged himself out to call that same lady doctor, yes, Olga Ivanna, pardon me that it's so late, no I don't think it's started, it's just… what's that you're saying? Well, as you wish, as you wish, it's your diocese, your decision, so do what you think you have to.

Olga Ivanna saddled up the nearest ambulance, rushed over a half-hour later, and whirled into the academician's apartment, and why are we so sad here? And where's our bag for going to the maternity hospital? And how's our blood pressure? Oh, our blood pressure's like a fighter pilot's! And within an instant she'd dragged Galina Petrovna, who hadn't even stopped laughing and hiccupping, off to the nethermost reaches of birthing, reserved for gods—Party and otherwise—who benefited the Motherland.

Lindt looked small, withered, and alternately like a stuffed old lion cub standing on its hind legs and a minor Egyptian idol trying to appear younger. He stayed to pace at an icy night window, seeing his wife off with sad eyes (she didn't turn, no, and she didn't turn this time, either). As the ambulance's fat, red-eyed rear end circled the courtyard and finally left, Lindt mechanically calculated an algorithm for the alternation of snow-covered tops of spruce trees and fence pickets crowned with cast iron spikes. Then he returned to the bedroom, the only lived-in place in the gigantic apartment other than his office. It was obvious there was really no reason for concern but his heart was still troubled, perhaps because during the past year Lindt had gotten used to falling asleep after filling his palm to the brim with a young female breast, or perhaps because by morning Galina Petrovna always contrived to slip out of those unwilling embraces and crawl far, far away, to the very edge of the bed, which meant Lindt nevertheless woke up alone, his empty hand stretched out in vain as if he were an urban beggar or deranged old man trying to grab life by skirts that were, inevitably, slipping away.

It was painful every morning, for a whole minute. As an honest and adult person, though, Lindt knew his pain was valid—not to mention adult and honest—because how else could he pay for the keen happiness of falling asleep every night, lying with his desired woman, merged like two bowls, smoothly and handily stacked one inside the other? And so the morning pain balanced out the evening joys, even making them sharper so the world's overall harmony remained unchanged: this was Old Testament mathematics with divinely clear-cut rules for retribution and justice, a coherent and truthful calculation, and it was only the hundredth digit after the decimal point that sometimes made Lindt doubt. He hadn't even pronounced the word 'love' in his mind since Marusya died. Never. The word 'love' was no longer from the tablets with the commandments: it was now an imprecise definition, something Lindt didn't like.

He buried his face in the ravaged bed. The pillow smelled delicately but strongly of something tender and golden, moist and reddish-pink, of Galina Petrovna's flesh and her essence, all of which had become his own scent in the last ten months or so, as if it were a continuation of his own essence. No, it was his own essence, for a man leaves his mother and father and cleaves to his wife and they become one flesh. For some reason a disturbing swampy tinge of an odor—decaying, oily, and a little muddy—blended in with that youthful, familiar, dear scent, but this was a trace of Galina Petrovna's nightmare and the smell of adrenaline. It was for that smell, along with development of beta blockers for adrenergic and histamine receptors, that James Whyte Black would win the Nobel Prize. Relieved, humanity would now understand its genetic horror of swamps: swamps simply smell of our concentrated fear. None of that was happening soon, though, not until 1988. As Lindt tried to go to sleep and perhaps chase off his horrible animalistic longing for his wife, he pondered all the things left undone during the day: fragments of formulas, problems, and cursory marginalia.

It's natural and biological that mammals are accustomed to sleeping in heaps, Lindt explained to himself as he dozed off, quietly releasing his immortal, agitated soul, something he himself, a militant and brilliantly armed half-agnostic/half-atheist, had never acknowledged. And his soul—all soft, smooth, and unseen, but gleaming clearly in the dark—was in a hurry, storming off toward the point that so painfully attracted it. It unerringly found Galina Petrovna's room after whirling through hospital corridors: Galina Petrovna, drugged up on harmless motherwort and valerian but still so frightened she could no longer even hiccup, simply lay on her back, staring at the ceiling with huge, dry eyes and using her last strength to banish the chirring letters.

Lindt's soul quickly perched right at Galina Petrovna's heart like a therapeutic feline ball and purred so inaudibly and soothingly that all the confusion and fears hurried off and the letters crawled away into the corners, powerlessly hissing and baring their needly little teeth. The hospital bed was ultra-stylish, bristling with levers and handles that could instantly transform that bier of suffering into, for example, a comfortable armchair or an operating table. The bed began gently swaying and the ceiling, formerly hostile, dry, and white, was now damp, spinning, and close. Galina Petrovna began slowly immersing herself in it, layer after layer, step by step, getting closer and closer to an earthly, lullaby-like light that held nothing but peace and love, nothing but love and peace…

The palm of someone's warm hand caressed her forehead and stroked her damp hair. It was a maternal, nonsexual, endlessly sympathetic gesture and as soon as the devastated Galina Petrovna finally fell quietly into a dreamless, horrorless sleep, Lazar Lindt silently began weeping in his sleep on the other side of Ensk, where he wept until dawn, until Galina Petrovna's unwept tears finally stopped.

In the morning, a frantic alarm clock brought everything back to normal, including Galina Petrovna, Lindt, and his soul, which smelled of the hospital and was slowly melting from exhaustion and night vigils. And then everything began flowing along its usual dull course, except that, for the first time, it didn't feel so futile for Lindt's hand to stretch across the bed. The pillowcase was soaked, too, so the flustered Lindt even brooded as he shaved his wrinkly blue cheeks in front of the mirror, wondering if maybe he'd started drooling in his sleep as an old man.

In the morning, of course, he went to the hospital instead of the department, grabbing half the central market on the way: apples; homemade farmer's cheese; pimply, porous lemons; solemn, unhurried honey that transformed a trite sticky liter jar into a palace light fixture flickering from within; and (most important!) fresh hothouse cucumbers, unheard of in December.

'What is this, Lazar Iosifovich, you're hurting our feelings! Do you think we starve our patients or something?!' asked the head of the pathology department, deeply indignant as she ran around the tiny, focused Lindt first from one side, then the other. 'Take a right here, please.'

Lindt just waved her off, though: it was as if he knew the way himself, a turn, a turn, an irregular heartbeat, then an immediate left to the cherished door.

Galina Petrovna was sitting on the bed, rested, bright, and brimming with a peaceful, rosy color.

'And here's our beauty!' the department head said, ingratiatingly singing it out as if she herself had shaped Lindt's young wife out of the softest, freshest, finest butter. Lindt unloaded the bags on the nightstand and pecked Galina Petrovna in the soft dip between her neck and shoulder; he'd actually wanted to kiss her on the lips but fine, that doesn't matter, the main thing is, how are you, my fair one, the Aesculapians all swear in unison everything's absolutely and completely good. Galina Petrovna didn't even nod in response, immediately fixing her wooden gaze to stare straight ahead. It was as if she'd instantly slammed shut when Lindt entered the room: Lindt even thought he'd heard the quiet but distinct little click of an invisible lid falling shut, meaning once again he hadn't managed to discern what was inside other than stiflingly bright fabric scraps and the quivery scattering of mismatched, dispersing beads.

A weakened, diluted, dusty December sun crept through the window, barely alive. Its listless paw touched Galina Petrovna's hair and rolled along cucumbers that had spilled out of the bag onto the nightstand: they were unnaturally long, somehow even plastic, but they were delicately, strongly scented with a spring that hadn't yet arrived. Lindt looked around in search of medical help and support, but the department head had tactfully made herself scarce, leaving the high-ranking visitor one-on-one with his nineteen-year-old pregnant wife and life's insoluble problems.

'Are you really okay?' Lindt asked again of the hospital pillow, of the sun, of life, and of himself, too. The babble of answers lacked only Galina Petrovna's voice. Lindt awkwardly tried to smooth her hair; there was a curl out of place around her ear, something they'd called a heartbreaker in his youth. In his youth, in her youth. An age difference of nearly a half-century. How could he have dared? What could he hope for? Who was he trying to fool?

Galina Petrovna jerked her head as if she were chasing away a big, fat, persistent outhouse fly.

Hopeless. Oh, yes, it was hope-less.

'Don't you worry so much, comrade Lindt, really, I'm telling you,' his driver said, sympathizing. He was a kind young guy just getting started in the complex career of a personal driver and so hadn't yet broken himself of the habit of human speech. 'Women, they lose their last wits when they're carrying kids. Your spouse will birth a little son for you and it'll all go back to normal, you'll see.'

Lindt shook his head in doubt. 'You think it'll be a son?'

'What else?' the guy said so simply, with such amazement, that even as Lindt went into the department a half-hour later, he was still snorting from tectonic laughter, wiping his damp eyes, and mumbling, 'You bugger, what a bugger, of course, what else, huh, my dear Mikhail Nikitich, hello, yes, hold on a minute with your signatures, I'm just going to tell you this brand-new joke now...'

There was a sort of inadvertent joy in that laughter, in the usual institute hubbub, and in the ozony smell of equipment and papers, as if the birth of a son (what else!?) really could miraculously change everything at once, immediately fix everything, and find the sought-after tone that—and Lindt understood this beautifully—he'd failed to capture for the first time in his life. Women had always loved and coddled him, even Marusya, who'd loved him, loved him very much even if it wasn't the way he'd wanted her to, but he'd never had to do much for that, and now here he was trying with Galina Petrovna but it was all for naught. Maybe he had to stop running after her, groveling and fawning? Maybe it really was just pregnant, hormonal, deep-seated, and thus especially meaningless whims? Maybe she'd have the baby and finally start to see him differently... with Marusya's happy, joyful eyes?

But he couldn't fool himself for long—only for as long as a cup of tea—and so by the time all that was left at the bottom of the cup was a thick, sugary goop that's not good for anything (a foolish habit, putting in five spoons of sugar without stirring), Lindt already understood that everything was for naught and that he was in love for the second time in his life, but the second time was unhappy, like a mockery. No, the light was the very same, Lindt couldn't be mistaken there: it was Marusya's purest light but it lacked Marusya herself because Galina Petrovna—and there was no mistake here, either—had turned out to be an empty and worthless creature. Unfortunately, that, too, didn't change anything.

Galina Petrovna spent three whole weeks in the hospital before giving birth. She had no pathologies whatsoever but they decided to keep her in pathology. Just in case. Lindt stopped by each morning before work, laden with delicacies, sweets, and small, lovely, but completely unnecessary little things that weren't even so much little things as meager grunts of deaf-mute human tenderness. Mornings were the most difficult time. But Galina Petrovna knew that if she could endure those five or ten minutes, torturous for both of them, the day would then roll along easily, gather intensity, and even gallop a little in particularly significant places: doctors' rounds, lunch, swimming in a blue pool steaming with chlorine and heat, and physical therapy, when absurd pregnant ladies as taut as blown-up balls proudly and deliberately raised their hands toward the ceiling and cautiously bent over until the physical therapy nurse, a quick and sharp-nosed individual who resembled a shepherd dog in charge of a flock of wayward sheep, finally allowed them to disperse and go to their rooms. Some of the expecting, however, stayed in their rooms at all times, on constant bed rest so as not to disturb, heaven forbid, a capricious and coddled fetus.

Galina Petrovna initially hung back from everything, timid because of her youth. For many reasons, some of which Galina Petrovna herself didn't fully understand, everyone at the hospital treated her with identically awkward and curious caution. In the first place, she was the youngest and prettiest of the first-time mothers and with the oldest husband, too. In the second place, that husband resided at such unbelievable hierarchical heights and had such staggering influence that nobody was even envious of Galina Petrovna, well, no, that wasn't it: they were just spitefully surprised at how some people toil away their whole lives and get nothing while others don't do a damn thing and seem to understand even less, but get a magic carpet and some magical instrument that plays music all by itself plus who the hell knows what else, all slathered in fancy chocolate, too, chocolate you couldn't even buy through special order. And everyone at that elite Soviet maternity hospital was a specialist in special orders.

Of course there were plenty of wealthy and famous people: daughters, wives, and sisters-in-law of party nomenklatura, big economic planners, and venerable management big shots. They were the Soviet cream—the very freshest, fatty yellow right out of the cow, and so thick a spoon would stand in it—but even if you put all those high fliers together, all their connections, opportunities, and influence were a far cry from Lazar Lindt's. Any Party boss could be schemed against and removed, and any red director could be unmasked for embezzlement and imprisoned, and of course they could all be shoved into retirement: the pension package might have been a special 'personal' package but it still meant a definite drop in all the customary amenities. But you couldn't do anything to Lindt: he was a one and only, unique with his small steps, unpleasant smirk, unkempt graying Jewish curls, academician title, and three government awards. And nobody at all, particularly Lindt himself, even bothered to count the smaller, more numerous, more linear, and more liftable awards.

You hear? the big-bellied ladies murmured in the corridors, dazed by boredom and gluttony, he's forty-one years older, or so they say, took her out of school, the old lecher, he was practically watching her from first grade on and could hardly hold out until her woman's bleeding started. How 'bout that! What are you talking about? She's the one that did it, came to his house and pulled up her skirt and of course he, a man getting on in years, single, couldn't resist and then right after that she slapped together some papers for the right people and even brought a statement to the police, the little underage bitch, and so then LazarIosich had to cover up the sin and get married but I'm telling you, this one, Lord forgive me, was already with child when she came to him, and it's unclear who the father is and you don't have to believe me but, I, unlike you, know all this first-hand because my husband works with LazarIosich and he said Lindt was literally sobbing on his shoulder when all this happened. Literally sobbing!

Galina Petrovna would come out of her room, a tiny bit frightened, her cheeks blazing with agitation and youth, and the pregnant women would immediately crawl back to their corners, hissing, well, he might be an academician but he didn't even toss together any clothes for his wife so she drags herself around like that in hospital clothes! What an idiot! Galina Petrovna followed them with sad eyes and pulled her bleached white flannel hospital gown harder over her swollen breasts. The packages Lindt brought her, lovingly wrapped in cambric and silk, were still piling up, unopened and unnecessary, around the nightstand. His daily treats—a devout thanks to our Lord God and the dear Academy of Sciences—were dragged home by the hospital aides, underhanded and eternally hungry, no matter how much you might give them. Galina Petrovna would have shared with roommates but she was entitled to a personal room, a personal torment, and a personal fate.

A week later, though, they'd gotten used to Galina Petrovna and she felt fully at home in the maternity hospital and even began carrying out cautious, inquisitive sorties beyond the boundaries of her own ward. The most interesting place turned out to be the smoking area, a stair landing fitted out with a couple spittoons around which there swarmed cheery, rowdy ladies from the abortion clinic: ever since 1955, five or six times a year, they'd vigorously supported, with you-know-what-body-part, the reversal of the resolution of the Central Executive Committee and Council of People's Commissars (dated June 27, 1936) prohibiting abortion. These abortionists—lovers of strong expressions and strong, expensive cigarettes—quickly introduced Galina Petrovna to their simple pleasures and within a few days she'd not only stopped frantically blushing at their ornate, pointless cursing, she'd overcome coughing and disgust to internalize the smoky differences between various cigarette brands: Moscow, Troika and—oh, miracle of miracles—that special Duchess Pear brand, with cotton filters, for the ladies.

'You shouldn't be puffing it up with a belly like that, hon,' one of the ladies said in passing to Galina Petrovna. Right then and there she regaled the group with the spine-tingling story of how one girl had smoked when she was pregnant, too, and then she went on, piling on the most outlandish and wild details, from which Galina Petrovna grasped only that a baby could suffocate right inside from tobacco smoke and have to be plucked out with hooks. After that she started smoking with conscious discipline, on the hour, as if she were taking the only medicine capable of saving her life, something still precious even if nobody really needed it any longer. The hooks didn't scare her, let them do it. So long as the baby died. Suffocated, whatever it took, just so long as it wasn't born. Anything but Lindt's baby. It was too unjust.

It was wrong to keep bumming cigarettes, so Galina Petrovna found a way to buy smokes from nurses who'd have even been willing to supply their highly placed lady patients with cyanic potassium or a carefully soaped rope for a hundred pre-reform rubles. In terms of killing potential, however, cyanic potassium had little on throat-destroying Pamir cigarettes (aptly nicknamed 'Poor Man of the Mountains') and Galina Petrovna took an especial liking to smoking them at night, standing in a rumbly, empty smoking area filled with icy drafts and moaning hospital ghosts. To be on the safe side, she left her robe in her room and quickly tossed off her slippers in the smoking area. Then she would stand for a long time, shivering beside a window that leaked air through all its crevices, deeply inhaling the reeking smoke, and feeling Ensk's soulless cold through the bare soles of her feet; it rose languidly and imperiously, ever higher, toward the baby. The very same dead cold stood, unmoving, in her heart. An errant wind quietly whined in the window, alternately flinging a handful of snowy stinging grains at Galina Petrovna and attempting to snuggle up to a warm human being, but Galina Petrovna didn't notice a thing. Just as Pavlov's mutilated dog had gotten lost in the expanse after its occipital lobes were removed, depriving it of vision and hearing for the sake of someone's sadistic curiosity, Galina Petrovna stubbornly crawled along some invisible circle, returning time after time to the point where her happy, normal, human life had ended.

She and Nikolenka had planned to marry.

No.

She couldn't think about Nikolenka.

It was just impossible.

There were really too many things not to think about: the end of last year (it was just last New Year) and the smells of floor polish, dust, and slowly thawing felt boots at the institute, which was teeming despite the upcoming holidays.

Everyone was making a racket like they were deranged and they were hurrying to the public lecture by that academician whose name Galina Petrovna giddily didn't remember. And now that name was written in her passport for the ages to improve her memory, you couldn't think up a more excellent lesson for a pretty little empty-headed fool, now, could you? She didn't go to the lecture then because she had to clean up the lab room and it seems she broke a flask. Or was it a retort? She was endlessly smashing state-owned glassware back then, believing that it would lead to happiness—she just didn't know the happiness wasn't for her at all.

And then Nikolenka came in and they kissed for the first time…

No, just not Nikolenka, no, please, I'm begging you!

Thinking about her parents was impossible, too, as was thinking about the cherished piece of white crêpe de chine, dense and silky, and looking like a cake of soap: all she'd had to do was unwind a couple weightless meters of that cake and press it to her chest for the enchanted ghost of a future wedding dress to appear in the room. The fabric was probably still lying somewhere in her parents' cabinets, dying a slow, tortured death. Galina Petrovna jerked her head and lit another Pamir to keep from thinking about that and a thousand other little things as painful and itchy as a rash. One night, one pack. She would have smoked two a night but she'd begun vomiting bitter bilious foam; still, the baby didn't even consider suffocating—it would arrange itself comfortably, little hands under a cheek, little eyes closed, or else merrily romp around inside. Apparently it hadn't even frozen, though Galina Petrovna's icy bluish feet were numb when she left the smoking area in the mornings.

And what do you think? The monster inside her was happier than ever, and she herself didn't even catch a cold.

Even when she was sneaking past the shamelessly snoozing duty nurse and awkwardly clambering back into her hospital berth, Galina Petrovna never stopped her unceasing mental movement, stumbling again and again on some unseen obstacle, catching her breath and whimpering, and trying to crawl further. In essence all she had left were the final moments of her former life, which had left such an indelible impression on her memory it was as if she'd actually died: happy, disheveled, crouching over rainbow-colored shards of lab glass, lips swollen from first kisses. Then someone knocked at the storage room door and she'd shouted, 'It's open, come right in, sweetie!' She'd yelled it herself. And it was she who'd lightly jumped up and thrown open the door, certain it was Nikolenka, and he'd escaped from the odious lecture so they'd never, ever be apart again. To stay with her, together, until death itself. No, even longer, for always.

Lindt, who'd been standing at that very same door during those same imagined long hours, albeit on the other side, was thinking with quiet sadness that matter was unquestionably rational but also very unjust because not one sign had been given to him that day, not the slightest hint, not the slightest jerk of the divine leash, nothing saying anything like, get ready, you sad sack, pull yourself together, the big moment, maybe the biggest moment in your whole life, is about to happen. Maybe not just in your life. But no, the Universe kept quiet and, beyond that, Lindt had attempted until the very end to get out of the boring lecture, first thinking up ailments, then pretexts. Though he spoke beautifully and could effortlessly hold the attention of any audience, he'd always hated public appearances. His was a form of brilliance that could communicate with anyone, even a five-year-old child. Only, damn it, why must I spend time on a five-year-old child? They wouldn't understand dick even if I played the lecture on the accordion. And danced, too. Oh, please, Lazar Iosifovich, we're begging you, it's only forty-five minutes and the students will remember it their whole lives. Your shitheads have quite the wonderful lives planned for themselves if this dull, pain-in-the-ass stuff—and they won't understand the first thing about it—turns out to be the most exciting event in their lives. I'll do it, though, I'll do it, just leave me alone. And make sure there's none of that idiotic 'Let's have a collegial little drink after.' I have work up to here, so don't empty the department coffers for nothing. And nobody needs to meet me at the entrance, I beg of you. I still haven't lost my mind so I certainly won't get lost.

And what do you think? He got lost.

Despite all Lindt's requests, a courier was appointed and sent in good time to meet the illustrious academician, to stand guard for the great mind at the entrance so he could then be led to the proper auditorium with full honors. But Mashkov, of course, simultaneously lost his sense of time and his mind, too, after he'd finally and greedily fallen on Galochka's lips. And so Lindt awkwardly stamped around on the institute's empty front stoop, shrugged, and entered an echoing, granite vestibule resembling a burial vault. He decisively turned right, then right again, and found himself in a forest dark. Endless corridors, endless doors, endless absence of logic in numeration: next to auditorium number fifteen was an unnamed room, and right after that was a door with the mysterious plaque '442-M.'

'What dumbasses,' Lindt mumbled, dissatisfied. 'They can't organize anything, not even a corridor.'

And then something crashed behind the unnamed door as if in answer, as if fate had placed a deafening full stop at the end of a sentence. Heartened by the possibility of finding a way to make someone talk and get a line on finding his way through this maze-like institute, he politely drummed on the peeling panel of a door.

'It's open, come right in, sweetie,' answered a velvety female voice that resonated, preciously quivering, on the letter 'r,' just as the door swung open, exactly like back in 1918. And exactly like back in 1918, Lindt nearly lost consciousness from exhaustion, from happiness, and from the light, that very same compact cube of light where Marusya had stood: young, laughing, immortal, her two hands straightening her hair, and glowing with joy.

After discovering her chemical inventory didn't contain smelling salts, the kind-hearted Galochka just sat the ashen, pale old man on a chair and flung the window wide open. The Ensk cold hit Lindt flatly and heavily in the face like some cad itching for a duel, and, what can you say, dreaming of murder. Spiky, glinting grains of snow danced in the air, cooling Galochka's glowing cheeks and covering Mashkov's hair with a strange, uneasy grayness as he rushed around in front of the institute, vainly searching for the lost academician. An icy pathway insidiously hidden under the snow threw itself at his feet and then threw him down so his rear end sonorously settled on something frozen and hard. Like anyone who's fallen, Mashkov struggled absurdly to get up, then suddenly saw everything at once, as if he were looking up from the very bottom of his own happiness, something almost physically unbearable: a motionless tar-colored sky with a tiny lopsided moon; the institute looking like a fairytale castle all covered with lit windows that resembled long, fiery embrasures; and an old frost-fuzzed streetlight, its milky, nocturnal rays swimming with snowflakes as melty and tender as Galochka's lips. All this came together for a second in a picture of fantastic precision and beauty that boded well for discovering some sort of grand and thus particularly useless secrets, but then it all suddenly blurred, trembled, and filled with hot, salty liquid—and Mashkov realized to his shame that he was sitting right on the icy asphalt and crying like a little boy, like a fool, snuffling his runny nose and smiling a huge, stupid, totally child-like smile.

'Maybe call for an ambulance after all?' Galochka asked again, concerned. Of course the old man was pretty disgusting—gaunt, wrinkled, and all covered with unkempt blue-gray stubble—but a Soviet girl was expected to respect even lesser specimens. The elderly are always honored here.

'I do thank you, but no,' Lindt courteously said, straightening his jacket so his medal ribbons were visible, but then despising himself so dreadfully that his cheekbones creaked. 'Could you please tell me instead where auditorium 204 is?'

'Oh, so you're going to the lecture, too!' said Galochka, and smiled. Lindt quickly averted his eyes, fearful of going blind or bursting into tears: those delicate cheeks, those lips with their defined, curved, milky, baby-like stripe. Your lips, my bride, drip honey; honey and milk are under your tongue! Drink it for an entire eternity moaning from pleasure at times, and don't believe in your happiness until death. And don't think about the next verse about how, A garden locked is my sister, my bride, a garden locked, a fount sealed. What one person has closed, another always opens. O Lord, how she looks like her! No she doesn't. She's better.

'Everybody's just lost their minds over that academician,' Galochka went on, not noticing anything, but very satisfied that at least someone was easing the dullness of preparing for the lab. 'The only thing missing is standing in line. It's as if the Moscow Art Theater came or something.'

Lindt nodded in agreement—it was usually appallingly ignorant (thus especially unpleasant) people who created a commotion around his name.

'It'll probably be stuffy at that lecture, you shouldn't go,' Galochka said, still painstakingly courteous in looking after Lindt and mentally reproaching herself for a squeamishness that came at her from points unknown—and me a Komsomol girl, is it really his fault he's old and ugly?

'I'm afraid they won't start without me, so I'll have to go,' Lindt said regretfully, and stood. Galochka, completely missing the reference to Andersen that was as light and elegant as a butterfly, decided she'd made a mistake. It was quite possible the old man hadn't come to escort a granddaughter (first guess) or supplement his sparse intellectual baggage (second guess, cultivated in a Soviet girl's firm conviction that people born before the Revolution were illiterate, brainless idiots whom Soviet power had given glass beads, Lenin's lamp, and a primer).

'You must be the academician's assistant, right?' Galochka said, cheerfully guessing. 'Do you help him with experiments?'

She imagined a circus ring, a nimble twirling wizard in a roomy cloak covered with stars, and the withered Lindt with his mincing gait, pouring some hellish potion into a mysterious device with two crystal globes and a dangerously jagged electric arc humming between them. Lindt imagined almost the exact same thing and for an entire second they were—for the first and last time in their lives—thinking in unison. Then Lindt began laughing, exposing large teeth, and it was as if someone had quickly rotated a squeaky, bony cogwheel. Galochka felt a keen unpleasantness again. As if she were in the same room with some giant, loathsome insect.

'Here, I'll take you there,' she said coldly, and a tight young lab coat floated smoothly before Lindt's eyes: a half-belt with a silly round button, small fists tucked in pockets, coarse bleached fabric, and a deep, light-blue crease that fell first to the right, then to the left, wherever an unbelievably pure line fell from her slender, strong waist toward her hips. That line was bewitchingly pure, the motion of life itself, and Lindt could see nothing but that life: not the dim hallway lamps, not the anxious auditorium filled to overflowing, not the quivering crimson cheeks of the fawning institute director who kept pulling Lindt by the sleeve in the direction of a banquet they'd organized anyway, as if he were a small child trying to convince a grownup to look at foolish toys nobody needs. It never let him go, not even twenty-three years later, when the eighty-one-year-old Lindt was dying and saw before him not his mother, not God, not his whole huge life in reverse, not even Marusya, but that ideal little white lab coat floating along the hallway, a reddish braid carelessly pinned to the back of a head, and the quick gesture with which Galochka straightened her hem as if she were flicking away some clinging, unpleasant debris: it was Lindt's enamored, bewitched glance, his life, Lindt himself.

She didn't look back once.

And he never, ever caught up to her.

Nikolayich looked in on Lindt that evening, as always, and it was, as always, allegedly for a reason, one that had been delicately prepared in advance, though, God forbid, there was nothing urgent, nobody wanted to disturb the great mind or roil his calm, it's just they sent over this little contract from the publisher about the reissue, they want to sign it again, I already checked everything, you just have to scribble your autograph. And then he stopped short, cutting off his cozy mumbling: Lindt had pulled his knees up to his chin and was sitting in the corner of the couch like a tiny wizened mummy, staring straight ahead with bitter, unmoving eyes. It was the first time Nikolayich had seen his boss away from his desk or so unlively. Jesus, he probably hadn't even noticed that damned couch before!

'Something happen, LazarIosich?' Nikolayich himself was surprised at how disobedient his voice immediately became: work was under control and everything was definitely in proper shape, meaning he'd overlooked his health, oh, what a dickish dickhead he was, he should have sent Lindt off with a kick for yet another medical screening and not listened to any excuses, but just you try not to listen to that stubborn mule if he can still jump straight up on the desk and just laugh up there saying there's only two people in Russia who can do that: him, of course, and Pushkin, that son of a bitch. Dare to try, Nikolayich? Perfectly obvious I don't dare, I have to eat less potatoes with melted butter, and anyway I wasn't assigned here to jump around on tables like a macaque. Not for that. So let him amuse himself alone however he wants in his own high places, and we'll just keep trying to plod along here on earth without stumbling.

Lindt didn't answer, as if he hadn't heard or didn't understand the question or maybe didn't even notice Nikolayich come in—he'd treated him like family from the start, sat him down with himself, never a word out of place, and he'd get up and see him out and give him a gift for any holiday and oh, they'd downed so, so much vodka together and conversed in so many conversations, and he never disdained anything, despite being an academician.

'LazarIosich, what is it, dear friend? Your heart?'

That was his invention, a personal one, the nickname LazarIosich, he could say the man's name as beautifully as anyone but he didn't want to, just like he didn't want to use the informal 'you,' even though Lindt had invited him to a hundred times, no, he needed something else, something like Menshikov being 'Mein Hertz,' just for the two of them and so everyone else would understand the degree of closeness, the warmth, and the respect whose back-breaking weight Nikolayich feared, yet again, might smother him. He'd thought up that 'LazarIosich' and mumbled it the first time rather than saying it, ready for a reprimand or even a beating, but Lindt had just laughed, and Nikolayich loved it so much when Lindt laughed that he'd do absolutely anything, like crawl around on his belly or dance in squatting steps, but that little word took on a life of its own, wouldn't you know it, and it was so agile and lively it spread like fleas, so they started calling the academician LazarIosich at the institute, at the Academy of Sciences, and in the servants' quarters but only, of course, out of earshot. Only Nikolayich dared say it to Lindt's face and he preserved that privilege with all the grand, jealous fury of a best friend and third-generation lackey.

Nikolayich wanted to feel Lindt's forehead as if he were a little child but decided against it at the last minute, taking the academician by the shoulder instead and gently squeezing with a hand clumsy from tenderness, as if to verify that Lindt was in one piece. Lindt emerged from his strange stupor and smiled, almost guiltily, 'Ah, Nikolayich, hello, you old sot.' That was another of their words. Theirs alone, they had a lot that was just theirs. 'No, no, I'm not dying, don't sweat it. Though maybe you almost guessed, about the heart.'

'Stabbing pain? Pressing?' Nikolayich asked, straining to be businesslike as he felt the fear he'd begun to release squeeze everything inside him into a humiliating icy knot again.

'Stabbing and pressing and aching, you old sot. And it won't leave me alone. I'm in love, or so it seems, Nikolayich. Can you imagine? And at my ripe old age!'

Nikolayich silently went into the kitchen, a huge, unlived-in manor kitchen where nobody but he had ever cooked or taken charge. He came back a couple quiet minutes later holding a painted tray, as hideous as all mass-produced Russian crafts and given to Lindt by heaven knows who. Gracing the plump painted flowers on the tray were a little carafe of vodka, shot glasses wiped by a man's inexpert hand, and a roughly opened can of dark sprats that Nikolayich himself had socked away just in case because Lindt might get up in the night and feel like eating and, well, you never know. Nikolayich put the tray on the couch, sat next to it, and deftly poured the vodka, almost forcefully putting a little glass in Lindt's indifferent fingers.

'So now tell me,' he nearly ordered, using the informal 'you' with his boss for the first time in his life. Now he could. Now, in particular.

The next day, toward the end of work, Galochka was hurriedly putting her chemistry supplies into the cabinet (Nikolenka was certainly already waiting for her out front, hiding his large, reddened hands in the pockets of his worn coat, he was always forgetting his mittens but that's fine, we'll take care of that and get him a new coat right away. And mittens, too!) when a visitor stole in. He was a heavyset little man with the thick sides of a peasant who'd moved to the city and the tenacious, smart, furious look of a stray dog who'd been kicked in the ribs as a puppy by cheap boots for no reason. The dog didn't forget.

'Galina Petrovna Batalova?' the little man quietly confirmed, dexterously grasping the starched elbow of her lab coat. Galochka nodded; she sensed her legs suddenly weaken for no reason and perspiration as thick and clear as dew begin to form on her forehead. 'Follow me, please.'

And Galochka Batalova's life ended.

Despite the cold, it was stuffy as a coffin in the black Volga and just as deafeningly quiet, too, but Galina Petrovna, so dazed she couldn't even cry, suddenly stopped pathetically melting in her own humiliating sweat and began shallowly chattering her disobedient teeth like a rodent. Horror literally pounded at her, the very same mortal biological horror known to any living being on the brink of its own destruction: confused perception, fever, chills, perspiration, and the involuntary loosening of all the sphincters. Even burly bears and full-grown human males instantly and rapidly unload in their pants in situations like these, not because they're cowards, but because the body desperately attempts to release everything that could impede it from battling to the death or bolting from death in a panic. Galina Petrovna didn't even pee herself, but only because, on the very edge of a consciousness that was trying to save itself, she desperately believed that this was all a dream, all foolishness, that page from the children's book where the horrid cannibal drags cute, curly-haired Hop-o'-My-Thumb into his lair. She'd feared that picture so much as a child that she just couldn't examine it in all its horrendous details and buried her head in her father's merciful knees with a squeal.

But how could this happen? Papa himself had said there'd be no return to the old days, meaning there'd been some kind of mistake, a misunderstanding. Galina Petrovna was a completely young fool—born in 1941—and all she knew about those old days was snippets of overheard conversations and that everything got less scary after the war, though her father grumbled at times that there was no point giving so much freedom to the little people, oh, no point, and then Stalin went and died and everybody cried so much. Even Papa. Galina Petrovna attempted to say all that, to explain things and ask where they were taking her, but all that came out was a feeble 'Av-va-va.' The little man sitting next to her on the back seat tossed a quick impenetrable glance at Galina Petrovna and commanded, go ahead, warm it up a little more. The silent driver clicked something without changing the expression on the back of his wrinkled red neck, and another wave of artificial heat floated through the car.

They stopped at a huge leaden building with ostentatious towers and flourishes, and Galina Petrovna, who was already prepared for anything, realized with astonishment that it was a residential building: behind the filigreed wrought-iron spikes on the fence were women out playing with funny round tots diligently making a pudgy snowman. Children's voices rang out brittly in the cold and streetlights were slowly filling with a turbid, placid light. They were elegant in a non-Ensk way and they, like everything in this building and this courtyard, were made soundly and lovingly, not in the usual flashy Soviet way. The little man grunted as he helped Galina Petrovna out of the Volga and they crossed the courtyard with the driver, who was laden with bags. The little man bowed so nimbly and affably to everyone that Galina Petrovna suddenly calmed, completely and very inopportunely, despite having decided to call for help or run—whatever worked—whenever the situation was right. This really must all be a misunderstanding. Or maybe they wanted her to be in a movie, and why not? There were rumors Sergey Gerasimov was planning to come to Ensk to talk about his *Quiet Flows the Don*, maybe he saw me on the street or at the institute? Or at some concert? Galina Petrovna imagined herself singing her signature song about hostile whirlwinds for the great director, then immediately saw her face on an advertising poster with her vampish mouth all rapaciously lipsticked; she even smiled at how simply and harmlessly everything had resolved itself. The little man looked at her again and snorted, probably forming, for now and forever, an opinion about the mental abilities of young Komsomol member Batalova. Galina Petrovna could barely contain herself from sticking out her tongue, and she was right to contain herself, because a cozy elevator brought them to the fourth floor with a scrape and then the truly scary part began.

The little man unlocked the door to one of the apartments, let the unburdened driver go, and escorted Galina Petrovna into a huge, absolutely empty room that was apparently intended as a dining room, though it was obvious from the start that nobody had ever, ever eaten at this spacious table for about twelve and it was doubtful anyone had even been in the room except, perhaps, to dump a load of some kind of messy files and books in the corner. A rapidly thickening and darkening evening cautiously peered inside tall, thin windows—even they were naked, desolate, and curtainless. Galina Petrovna obediently settled on a chair that she admittedly had trouble moving, screeching its legs along the dark parquet; that short, mechanical, lifeless screech stayed in her ears for a long time, as if it belonged to her.

Meanwhile, the little man extracted a stiff grayish table cloth from somewhere and kept diving into bags and a dusky sideboard, then he smartly, but without fuss, set a dinner table for two, twisting napkins and arranging treats Galina Petrovna had never heard of on plates. He spoke the whole time, patiently, very quietly, incessantly, and nearly in a monotone, as if he were explaining a difficult problem to a clueless child. Fearful of even stirring, Galina Petrovna grew paler and paler with each word until she finally took on a very beautiful, even, almost olive shade.

By the time the table was all ready—champagne hidden in a sweating bucket and fruit placed in a bowl—she'd completely understood what, exactly, would happen to her, her parents, and, most important, a certain citizen named Nikolay Ivanovich Mashkov, yes, yes, meaning Nikolenka, if she so much as allowed herself a peep in protest, or spoke out of turn, or displayed even a shadow of disrespect, and just you try saying one word to anyone about our conversation, nobody will help, don't even think about it, not God, not the devil, not the chairman of the Presidium of the Central Committee of the Communist Party of the Soviet Union because he personally—are you listening?—PERSONALLY wishes Lazar Iosifovich Lindt a happy birthday every year, and he doesn't make do with a telegram, oh no, he telephones, dials the telephone with his own little royal hand to express his greetings and wishes.

'You got that, you foul bitch?' the little man asked when he finished. He thought for a bit then subjected Galina Petrovna to such ugly, rough, and filthy verbal abuse that she didn't even understand half of it, though it wouldn't have mattered if she had. There was one thing she just couldn't grasp—who this Lazar Iosifovich Lindt was—but Galina Petrovna instinctively felt, in her animal gut, which was quivering again, that she couldn't ask because nothing was left in her, nothing non-animal and nothing human. Nothing at all.

'Very good then,' the little man said with unexpected cheer, as he selected a large orange from the bowl and nimbly pocketed it. 'Be sure to eat your vitamins and behave yourself,' he advised her, almost affectionately. Then he quickly disappeared with silent speed reminiscent of a petty and thus almost criminally dangerous bogeyman, leaving Galina Petrovna alone in the huge dining room at the fancily decorated table. And she sat for almost two hours, afraid to stir or even lean her tense wooden back against the back of the chair. During that entire two hours she desperately dreamt, through her fear and an overwhelming nausea, of twisting off just one translucent pink grape, as round as a maiden's nipple. But she didn't dare. Though she'd never tried grapes before in her life. Not once. Ever.

By the time the front door loudly clicked, Galina Petrovna almost didn't care who she'd see or what, exactly, would happen next. The only thing she had strength to do was sit even straighter, which is how Lindt saw her the second time: frightened, pale, sitting uncomfortably on an uncomfortable chair, the toes of her small felt boots turned a little in and her fluffy old shawl, like Marusya's, sliding down the back of her head—the little man hadn't suggested she take off her coat— and Galina Petrovna hadn't even noticed she'd sat the whole time in her fur coat with only the buttons undone. For a few long seconds Lindt—stupefied and not at all expecting to find the embodiment of his nocturnal and not-so-proper aspirations—didn't notice anything but the open fur coat and the fists Galina Petrovna firmly clenched to her chest. Lord, and then she suddenly just glowed with such tender, lively joy it was as if she'd been waiting for this meeting as much as he, as if Marusya really had returned, as if everything had finally come true.

Lindt strode over to her, spreading his arms, and Galina Petrovna readily fell into those disbelieving, unhurried embraces, and pressed against him, burying her nose somewhere in his shoulder, shuddering from both laughter and tears so Lindt, who'd nearly fainted from her aromatic, warm weight, even reeled. She mumbled something, he didn't hear, and only when he raised her lovely, tear-stained face to finally kiss those unbelievable, half-translucent, lush lips did he suddenly understand that she was hurriedly gasping, swallowing whole words instead of just syllables, and saying, Take me away, save me, I beg you, please, I beg you, help me, Lord, it's so good you're here!

They didn't bring Galina Petrovna home for another hour: she was very quiet and squeaky clean, her hair smoothed by Lindt's comb, which he'd washed off in the bathroom, embarrassed and hurrying. Damn it, I'm an old goat, mangy, and covered in dandruff, okay fine, it'll all work out, but Nikolay-ich, it's beyond me how he convinced her to come, that old sot, we'll have to make an effort to get him a medal or something, for laughs.

Galina Petrovna categorically refused to eat or drink, so the fancy table stood untouched in the middle of the room, obviously ashamed of its own indecorous grandeur. Lindt attempted to explain everything, interspersing compliments and apologies, and Galina Petrovna apologized, too, not raising the long, still-damp arrows of her clumped lashes. No, no, nobody had dragged her here or forced anything, to the contrary, she was very glad that… And Galina Petrovna fell silent, racing around inside her own skull and feverishly grasping with blind hands at icy-cold stone walls that even felt slightly dewy: No, no, that's not a way out, don't even think about going that way, HE said they'd arrest Nikolenka, torture him, torment him, he'd said it as he layered sturgeon with amber fat on a plate, describing with gusto exactly *what* they'd do.

Galina Petrovna swallowed and raised her impossibly blue-gray eyes to Lindt, 'I was just tired of waiting and happened to doze off and when you suddenly came in, I was half-awake, you know… I could imagine anything. I'm sorry I didn't recognize you yesterday, I'm very ashamed, truly. That's what I came for, to apologize. You probably thought I was a foolish girl, didn't you?'

Lindt flailed like a crazed windmill, his blades thrashing in all directions. He launched into such wild talk that he himself got all mixed up, well, how could you, Galina Petrovna, how could you think and this and that and the other. And there it was, now she was Galina Petrovna. Even though Nikolenka called her the same as Mama did, Galyunya, and his lips moved as if to quietly, gently whistle or, just as quietly and gently, kiss. Mama! Galina Petrovna suddenly grasped onto this merciful thought. But of course! Mama! She'd give Galina Petrovna advice, think something up, Mama would save her! An idle hope but then again, have you seen many non-idle hopes?

After starting to feel completely at home within the nightmare she'd fallen into, Galina Petrovna was so happy she nearly fainted when the old man from the institute—the wizard's helper—came into the dining room instead of the monster she'd expected. Here was a familiar person she'd spoken with, if only for a couple minutes, but he had to help her and come to her aid, as one Soviet person helps another Soviet person. After all, in Galina Petrovna's former world, evil had always been absolutely anonymous, but people who'd spoken with one another, even just once in their lives, automatically became comrades, and so die if it's your fate, but come to the aid of your comrades, those people you have tamed. Besides, the old man was AN ADULT, an elder, and he couldn't cause her any harm, not under any laws, either Soviet or human or biological, and he was obligated to bring her out of this enchanted castle, call the police, stir up the public, and sound the alarm! Instead of that, however, the old man suddenly began kissing her with his huge, hot, slobbery mouth and when she began tearing herself away, scared, screaming, and mumbling about some sort of misunderstanding, he released her and again gave the same scary password the little man had already uttered: Lazar Iosifovich Lindt. The old man repeated it twice before Galina Petrovna realized he was just introducing himself.

She came to her senses, assessed the situation, and found the only possible solution in literally a few seconds, and that speed was like a flattering compliment to Lindt himself, who suddenly discovered he didn't have a sobbing, frightened little girl in his apartment but a slightly slow though unusually friendly beauty who was, of course, a little confused but obviously interested in continuing this acquaintanceship. This was a genuine miracle. Fear for Nikolenka shifted Galina Petrovna's brain into overdrive for the first time, giving her enough ingratiating circling patterns and cautious, absolutely bird-like deception to last several months—we've already seen another bird like this somewhere, taken out of her nest—though Galina Petrovna, unlike that sneaky starling, had been wounded for real and was ready, for real, to do whatever it took so Nikolenka, her Nikolenka, wouldn't suffer. Lord, she didn't care at all what happened to her now, just don't let anything happen to him, don't let anything happen.

Nobody guessed anything, not one person, not even Lindt, not even Mama. Her parents essentially renounced her immediately, abandoning her to die, helpless and broken. Galina Petrovna knew this the second she returned from Lindt's. She read it in their subdued, furtive glances, in the way nobody really asked why she was so late or where she'd been; she knew it because when she stepped out of the black car she'd seen so clearly how her mother pulled aside the kitchen curtain, red and white checks, very cheery, though a little crooked because she and her mother made those curtains a few years ago when her mother taught her to sew on the Singer, a scarce war trophy with a treadle. Galochka's lovely little head just couldn't grasp and remember all the complex motions: the feet smoothly pumping the pedal and the hands moving the fabric in a completely different, independent, direction, and the quick, blinding needle deliciously and dangerously chattering as it perforated the fabric. And then everything suddenly made sense and found its place, including on the gleaming round spool, and Mama happily said, nice job, hon, you'll sew for your whole family when you get married, you wait, I'll show you how to crochet, too, and you'll make little napkins for your home and maybe even a tablecloth if you have enough patience. And Galochka believed she'd have enough patience because Mama never lied to her. Adults just don't lie. Especially to their own children. And they never betray them. Unfortunately that, like the crocheted tablecloth, turned out to be an untruth, too.

Galina Petrovna hurried up the stairs, opened the door with her own key, and could immediately feel she'd hoped and hurried for no reason. The little man had already been here—that was obvious by how her parents hid their eyes, by the vivid scent of valerian drops that still hovered, frightened, in the corner of the kitchen where someone, most likely her father, had counted the drops in the shot glass, lips moving, thirty-one, thirty-two, thirty-three, here, Mother, drink it and don't sob. Nothing bad's happened. He's an esteemed person, after all, distinguished, and even if he's getting on in years, well, it's not like we have to boil him up for soup… Galina Petrovna pulled off her fur coat and went to her room without saying a word. She never had another conversation with her parents, never.

Galina Petrovna didn't go to work the next day and she never worked again, by the way, and goodness knows what place this took on the list of 'nevers' in her new life. Lindt came over in the evening, all withered, dressed up, and scented, with a bouquet of tea roses almost as tall as he for his future mother-in-law and a whole arsenal of alcohol for his future father-in-law, and so the flustered Petr Alekseyevich Batalov discovered pour spouts for liquor bottles and the sterile, lifeless flavor of imported vodka. His head wasn't splitting from it in the morning despite having also tried—shameful to admit it—not only excellent, well-aged Scottish whiskey with a scent and flavor indistinguishable from horse urine, but also a liqueur in a round, very unusual bottle that tasted like beloved Soviet condensed milk diluted with alcohol, come on, don't be shy, Mother, put back another shot, it's sweet. Giggling from embarrassment, Yelizaveta Vasilevna put it back and then ran into the kitchen, fanning her burning mouth with her hand, to keep an eye on the pie she'd hastily whipped up and shoved in the oven.

Galina Petrovna sat at the table, not raising her eyes and only occasionally smiling ever so slightly; nobody suspected that smile was the result of a completely mechanical, almost involuntary tensing of muscles, like a pinned frog on a lab bench that lets electric shocks run through itself time after time. Lindt presented her with a small velvet box whose impenetrable depths yielded a lovely little gold ring, very simple, very small, with one single sapphire, not large but so ancient and pure and fine that it was immediately clear the ring cost an entire fortune. Galina Petrovna tried it on her middle finger, where it was a bit tight and then her mother whispered to her, hinting, the ring finger. Galina Petrovna sobbed and jumped up from the table. Lindt followed her with hungry, pathetic eyes and then, clearing his throat, said everything customary one says to the parents of a future wife, about hand, about heart, and about the happiness of your daughter.

Given the groom's age and position, they decided to avoid a stir. And so, with universal tacit approval, Galina Petrovna simply moved in with Lindt exactly one week later. Nikolayich carried a small wooden suitcase with a silly girl's junky clothes for her, instantly becoming as indispensable in her parents' home as he was in Lindt's own home.

Galina Petrovna saw her passport on the table when she came out of the bedroom in the morning, tousled and with vacant eyes: the passport was new, creaky, and red, with a slightly smudged stamp regarding a legally registered marriage and a fresh new last name. 'Galina Petrovna Lindt' she read on the first page and burst out laughing. They'd taken everything away from her. Name, wedding, bridal veil, celebratory beet salad, her firstborn's first little step, and her beloved's last breath, which would have corresponded with her own. Everything. Her whole life. Galina Petrovna no longer had anything.

Galina Petrovna spent the first several weeks of her unexpected and involuntary marriage in a strange, painful stupor and though her entire subsequent life with Lindt differed little from those first days—in terms of quantity of spousal caresses, in terms of his tenderness, and in terms of her disgust—it was that month, that honeymoon, that turned out to be the most unbearable time. She spent hours uncombed, in a wrinkled nightgown, hanging around the echoing and nearly empty apartment (Lindt was too busy to actually inhabit the five unneeded rooms and she was too busy, too, even more so) and gaping from time to time at a window or a pile of books or a table, as if she were a mechanical toy that needed winding. Any rustle made her quiver like a genuine clinical neurotic. She was waiting.

Lindt grew more and more attached to his young wife: he openly neglected both his job and his scientific research and went out of his way to leave later for the institute, pop home during his lunch break, and come home as early in the evening as possible, meaning Galina Petrovna's primary occupation was listening for the front door, did the bolt in the lock click, no, thank God, it only sounded like it. The danger had passed this time. No matter how much she hoped, Lindt always came back anyway and he was immediately everywhere, happy, horrible, and alive, setting delicacies on the table, rustling packages, grunting, taking off tiny, hideous little boots that looked like a gnome's and then grunting the same way, creeping in under her shirt straightaway with both hands, touching, first slowly and focused, then going into more and more of a passionate fit. Galina Petrovna immediately broke out in a sweat from disgust and he went even wilder from the smooth aroma of her perspiration. Lindt could rarely make it to the bedroom, so it felt as if the apartment was covered in spots of foul slime. Galina Petrovna couldn't feel comfortable among all those invisible traces even when she was left alone: he did me here and here and here, too. And, of course, in the bedroom. A huge bed. Every day. Morning and evening. Sometimes even at night, and that was worst of all because she didn't have a chance to prepare herself and get ready before falling into a series of nightmares that moved from one to the next and she couldn't wake up, let alone scream. Galina Petrovna froze for an instant, like a caterpillar, under any of Lindt's touches, and then she went limp, also like a caterpillar, but she became particularly complacent, silky, and soft instead of dying, and Lindt simplemindedly took that as an ashamed agreement, making him even more zealous. He had never tried so hard for a woman. Not in life, not in bed. Not for anyone, ever. He thought this was more than enough for both of them to be happy. Galina Petrovna never once said a word, never once attempted to push him away. A pathetic excuse, of course. By the time Lindt grasped that, nothing could be changed. Or nearly nothing.

His brilliance, alas, didn't extend to the simple, barely noticeable laws of daily human life. He'd lived alone too long and observed only the visible side of the Chaldonovs' most happy of marriages for too long to be able to duplicate a miracle like theirs in his own home. Beyond that, Galina Petrovna didn't just simply fear her husband, nor did she simply hate him. She couldn't stand him in the same way some people can't stand snakes, cockroaches, or even some completely innocent things like naked, translucent baby birds who stick their squeaky, gaping mouths out of a nest. This was Lindtophobia, pure and simple: lingering headaches, loss of appetite, nausea, excessive sweating, and a twitching the jubilant Lindt took as spasms of a completely other type. Fear. No, it was FEAR.

Lindt didn't notice anything. My *feygele*, he'd mumble waking up, surprised himself at the Yiddish that floated out of who knew where. Apparently a supply of the most frenzied tenderness is nevertheless stored within us from infancy and the language of that tenderness is always the mother's. *Feygele*. My little bird. Galina Petrovna noiselessly got out of bed, plodded into the bathroom and washed, washed, washed until the skin on her fingers grew chalky and shriveled, like a drowned woman's. The hot water throbbed and her curly reddish hair floated around in the water, covering her tortured, tormented nipples and her privates, her shame, painfully swollen from the academician's ardor. That's what it was: shame. You couldn't choose a more precise word.

Lindt brought his young wife to Marusya's grave when the Ensk winter began to break, weaken, and moisten along the edges in anticipation of spring. It was piercingly cold outside the city and a razor-sharp wind that whistled like thugs talking through hideous front teeth lashed at Galina Petrovna's face. Bundled up in her old pre-marriage fur coat (she'd never put on the new one from her husband, hadn't even looked inside his packages), she watched Lindt fuss around a small mound invisible under the snow banks, stamping at the snow and not even noticing he was stepping on two other graves: some gloomy old man and a little child who didn't even have a photograph, just a frost-covered gray stone where Galina Petrovna could only read the name Slavik and two dates that sternly cut two ends for a small life. Probably kin, Galina Petrovna thought indifferently and her eyes were also gray and frost-covered. Lindt warmed Marusya's porcelain face with his palms and mumbled, ashamed and trying so nobody would hear, here, sweetie, I finally brought my wife to you. You always dreamed of this, remember? Marusya smiled with just her eyes and then there were her light brows, light hair styled simply and high, and tiny pearls in her ears. His pearls. Chaldonov said she'd been buried in them.

Lindt stroked the oval picture on the gravestone again. Galina Petrovna sniffled and glanced back at the Volga grumbling in the distance, where the driver was grabbing a nap, languid in the warmth and capable, like any experienced personal driver, of falling asleep instantly even at the epicenter of an atomic explosion, so long as the boss was out of the car. Let's go, Lindt hurried her, you're completely frozen. He tried to reach her cheek but Galina Petrovna involuntarily started and hastily turned away. Fine, Lindt mumbled, following his wife along the cemetery path and trying not to step in her small, round tracks that were charming to the point of tears. Fine, it'll all work out, the sun will rise, life will go on. Marusya always said that. But nothing worked out. And Galina Petrovna's cheek under his fingers was colder than the porcelain on dead Marusya's photograph.

The daymare dispersed slightly a few months later and Galina Petrovna began, little by little, to adapt, just as people adapt even to concentration camps and barracks, to daily torture (from eight to eleven), to getting up at the whistle, to miserly advance payments, to old age, and to the fact that everything, truly everything, ends as it must, in death. Of course that was a habitat, not a life. But people do live in prisons, too. And at least Galina Petrovna was well-fed, clothed, and shod. For the most part she was still skittish, kept quiet, and didn't leave the house. She didn't even speak with her parents by telephone, quietly stepping aside and shoving the receiver at the perplexed Lindt, who conscientiously performed all the simple duties of a son-in-law until Galina Petrovna finally gathered up all her strength and shut off even the tiny revitalizing trickle to her parents. But that was later, much later. For now, Galina Petrovna was, like a typhus patient, slowly and weakly relearning things that had been simple and even habitual before: combing her hair, brushing her teeth every day, eating on time, or turning on the radio occasionally to listen to something pacifying about milking cows or haying. She even somehow ironed a blouse and was surprised when the ivory buttons barely fastened over her breasts.

Outside the window there jumped dark-blue, very spring-like raindrops and sparrows skinny from winter but plumped up from an uproarious racket. The April sky could barely fit in a small window flung wide open, and out in the courtyard a sluggish nanny hurried after the chubby offspring of a government worker: the boy had taken it upon himself to measure a brand new puddle with his own feet. Boom! The nanny stretched to her entire substantial length and the tot, malevolently laughing, ran right into his puddle, raising icy waves as if he were a stubby little barge loaded with kilograms of joy, fresh sirloin from the bazaar, and warm milk. The door clattered and for the first time Galina Petrovna didn't flinch or clench up but turned, still feeling a small, buttery-tasting smile melt on lips that had fallen out of the habit. But it wasn't Lindt. It was worse: Nikolayich stood in the doorway, pressing some sort of folder to his chest. Like an experienced courtier, Nikolayich hadn't permitted himself to be alone with Galina Petrovna since that memorable meeting so long ago. Neither said a word about what they might have, though they didn't want to speak anyway.

Galina Petrovna stopped smiling and quickly left the room, followed by Nikolayich's gloomy gaze. It only took him, an old bachelor, a second to understand what it had taken Galina Petrovna long weeks to realize, and Lindt was, as is traditional, the very last to know. Her light, which used to be delicate, had now thickened to a visible, almost honey-like consistency. Those dark, sweet shadows under the eyes and in the corners of slightly turned-up lips. Breasts barely covered by a simple little blouse bursting open from the strength of an obvious but unseen force that resembled the force that broke through even thick, thick asphalt in the summer to send silky, resilient, round, mushroom caps into the world.

Galina Petrovna was pregnant.

Lindt spent the whole summer of 1949 in the Semipalatinsk region, in a dusty cocoon of heightened nervousness, secrecy, and heat. A host of people gathered and they were expecting Beria, He Himself, the end of the world, Egyptian plagues, and executions on the spot. Nobody, including Kurchatov, believed the damned RDS-1 would detonate: the Americans had struggled quite a bit with theirs, so they were preparing for the worst, just in case, though in Lindt's opinion, the worst case was the atomic explosion itself. As it happened, he was one hundred percent certain there would be an explosion: It's pure mathematics, colleagues, you needn't doubt. It's physics that's full of surprises but everything's precise in mathematics, it's the only thing you can thoroughly depend on.

Nobody slept after August 27. They just couldn't. He Himself didn't come, though Beria did. Beria was very stout, but with the unexpectedly effortless, almost elegant, manners characteristic of certain particularly successful fat people. Lindt liked him, which was thoroughly predictable: Beria was an excellent listener, businesslike, intelligent, and charming, as any good executive should be. He even behaved like an executive, not acting superior, generally solving rather than creating problems, and even trying to pretend he was tangential there, just in the shadows, You're the main ones here, comrade scientists.

Lindt corrected him, 'The main people here are our comrade engineers. Everything's correct on paper so everything will go as well as possible if they didn't make a mess of it.'

'You think so, Lazar Iosifovich?' Beria asked politely, wiping his forehead and neck with a handkerchief for the hundredth time. He suffered terribly from Kazakhstan's heat.

'I don't think so, I know so, it's a crucial difference,' Lindt muttered. 'Let's go for a walk, huh, comrade minister? None of this will be here tomorrow, which is too bad,' Lindt nodded at the huge test site, about 300 square kilometers and painstakingly built with railroad bridges, homes, and roads. A city built only to die. Like any other city, though. It was getting dark, doomed camels were roaring, and some other unlucky cattle sensed, even without any mathematics, that this night would be their last. People called out to one another in the distance, marching soldiers sang briskly, and a deliciously meaty aroma wafted out of the field kitchens.

'So why did you turn down the job heading up the testing?' Beria abruptly asked.

'Oh, please, Lavrenty Pavlovich! Running around, signing papers, trying to find supplies of copper wires at warehouses? It's awfully dull. Even Kapitsa, though he's a fool, refused it, too. It's a better job for Kurchatov, he's young and ambitious.'

'You're only two years older, Lazar Iosifovich,' Beria said. He was panting desperately, trying to keep up with the light Lindt. 'Phooey, don't run like that or my heart will jump right out.'

'It won't jump out,' Lindt promised, slowing his pace and adapting for the amusing fat man. He was very touching. But how could it be that everyone trembled in his presence? 'Don't tell me two years isn't a big difference. I was sweating over Kraevich's textbook when he was still sucking on his mother's tit. Let him catch up.'

They both laughed a little more jovially than fit the situation, company, and place.

The next morning, on August 29, 1949, at seven in the morning, the first Soviet atomic bomb test successfully took place. Marusya had already been dead for three days, Lindt just hadn't been informed because they didn't want to risk distracting him. And so he jumped around with everyone else in the bunker, hugged them, and was glad everything boomed so beautifully. He might have even shouted. But he didn't feel anything. Nothing. Not one single thought, not even the slightest premonition. He was an adding machine. A thick-headed calculating brute.

Lindt didn't return to Ensk until toward the end of September. The flowers on Marusya's grave had already almost completely descended into juicy rot and decay, and a fine sleet kept mixing with snowy grains that dryly slashed at the cheeks. Chaldonov, who'd instantly aged a thousand years, hunched, his head quivering as he kept trying to repair the collapsing clay side of the grave; his hands shook just as finely and pitifully as his head.

'Don't, Sergey Alexandrovich,' Lindt said, unable to hold back. 'I'll do it.'

Slippery, greasy clay had filled Marusya's lovely mouth for the ages.

'Mine should be right here, Lazar, alongside hers,' Chaldonov managed to say, then he began sobbing again, unable to hold back; it stretched his stubbly old gray cheeks horribly. He didn't die until four years later, in 1952, and Lindt could never even admit to himself that he despised and hated Chaldonov for that, though he never left the old man until his last minute, after his slow slide into dementia. Chaldonov had an obligation to die right after her, together with her, instead of her. They both had an obligation.

Lindt, however, had a chance—an excellent chance, nearly one-hundred percent—and, God is my witness, he didn't intend to refuse it. His conversation with Beria on the eve of the Big Bang might have seemed insignificant but it turned out not to be the usual social chat of a nervous dignitary and a mad scientist. That much became clear after the first call from Moscow, in November, a few months after Marusya's death. Some professor or other from the Academy of Sciences was calling, allegedly an acquaintance but such a distant one that Lindt couldn't connect his bleating little voice with anything resembling a face. It was a warning call, and the officious numskull had been ordered to convey that they were dissatisfied with Lindt. Lindt wasn't an idiot so he already knew this perfectly well. Nobody was dissatisfied with Lindt himself, of course—who would have dared—though his stubborn refusal to return to Moscow, by the way… Lindt rudely hung up.

Ioffe was the second to call. Lindt would always be a skinny orphan at heart so, as rule, he respected very few people—in science, just as in life—though he made an exception to the rules for Ioffe that was, really, more like a grammatical error. Ioffe was a Teacher, not in a divine sense but in the simplest pedagogical sense of the word, which is the only reason to write the word with a capital letter. Ioffe didn't mind fussing around with the small and weak or the lonely and wretched, and there was something very Jewish about that. Very Marusya-like, too. Beyond that, Ioffe was a splendid theoretician and Lindt beautifully remembered a few very, very happy minutes he'd spent back in 1922 over Ioffe's work regarding the real stability of crystals. And so, instead of hurling the receiver, he enjoyed speaking at length with the old man, around whom clouds of the new anti-cosmopolitanism campaign were also thickening, clouds that would very soon pour out real sulfurous fire. Ioffe was removed from his post as director of the Physical-Technical Institute of the Academy of Sciences of the USSR, an institute he'd cultivated with his own hands from a small department in 1921. Again, Lindt wasn't touched, as always. I obviously need to attend a couple of academic council meetings with my pants down since nobody recognizes my face, he quipped, seemingly even a tad offended, once again, by yet more biased inattention from the powers-that-be.

But then, in early winter of 1949, Ioffe called, not to complain, quite the opposite, Lazar Iosifovich, I beg you, I emphatically beg you to come back to Moscow, and I do have reasons! Lindt attentively heard out both a proclaimed list of positions and remunerations (completely uninteresting) and a highly tempting program of research plans for the near future. All that is very, very seductive, Abram Fyodorovich, and I'm flattered you even took it upon yourself to lie, as if you couldn't get by without me. Honestly, though, why do I need to drag myself to Moscow for all that? I can work on it perfectly well here, too, the postal service, thank God, still works here. It's not like it was under the tsar, of course, but it copes. And if there's something unbelievably urgent, a courier could be appointed.

Ioffe grunted but didn't risk warning Lindt about dangers since he didn't trust the phone lines. Only when saying goodbye did he say, take care of yourself, Lazar Iosifovich, and Lindt obeyed, pensively spending the evening packing an old canvas duffel bag: two pairs of underwear, mug, spoon, woolen socks, notebooks, and Marusya's photograph. The selection was the usual, the same junk he packed in the same duffel bag when he headed off to Semipalatinsk for tests. Lindt pulled the very worst pants from the wardrobe, weighed them on his arm, and suddenly burst out laughing. Well, fuck you! In your dreams! He quickly changed into his best tailored suit, the special one for meetings and awards, enjoying the perfect, cool fit of the snow-white shirt embracing his shoulders, and the feel of his dressy necktie's knot resting so smoothly on the proper spot. He moved Marusya's photo to the inner pocket of his jacket along with his documents and then kicked the unnecessary duffel bag under the bed.

When they rang the doorbell at three in the morning, he opened the door already dressed, wearing an excellent custom-tailored coat with a graying astrakhan fur collar that was nearly indistinguishable from his own smooth curls, which were also a bit touched by frost. The stern scent of the war trophy cologne, Kölnisch Juchten (geometric green glass vial, red cap, white label), stood in the entryway along with Lindt as if it were an adjutant for his eminence, and the smells of damp suede, lightly smoked meat, sweet talcum powder, and something else elusive, foppish, and officer-like were all in tune with the visitors, their squeaking shoulder belts, Lindt's own perfectly shaved cheeks and fresh underwear, and the situation itself. It wasn't for nothing that Luftwaffe pilots so adored Kölnisch Juchten and it wasn't for nothing that Lindt kept the vial, which had come to him through heaven knew what bloody means.

A gloomy major who looked like a log outhouse saluted from surprise when he saw this dressed-up nobleman, though he'd actually just been intending to ring again and then pound on the door with the usual fists, the ones accustomed to the hammer and the sickle. Some sleep-deprived soldiers milled around behind him.

'Search?' Lindt asked, bowing slightly in invitation.

'Nothing of the sort,' said the major, as dissatisfied as a child who's suddenly been told the wrong version of a fairytale that's a particular favorite because he's learned it by heart. 'We have orders to transport you.'

'Then transport me,' Lindt commanded, pulling on soft leather gloves sent to him from London before the war by Sir James Chadwick, the 1935 Nobel laureate in physics. And Lindt was the first to hurry lightly down the stairs, almost as if he were skipping.

Lindt didn't utter a word during the entire long night journey, why bother? The interrogation called itself off as soon the black maria left the city after wending its way through the streets, and the execution without trial and inquest faded, too, when the military airport's tower lights flashed in front of them. The thought of execution hadn't gladdened Lindt, if only because it was impossible to find a ravine drowning in Nabokovian bird cherry trees in early December: without those, an execution by firing squad just isn't an execution by firing squad for a Russian person, even if he's triply Jewish. There wasn't anything to talk about in the ice-cold, snarling, shaking airplane, either, not that there was anyone to talk with anyway. If we're flying, that means Moscow. Simple logic. Reason makes a person fearless. But feelings are excellent killers.

Lindt remembered Marusya and the motion she'd used to pull her light hair off her neck as she cheerfully managed to reproach him—incomprehensibly, with hairpins clenched in her teeth—for being late and bringing yet more gifts. Now what is this, Lesik, you're loaded down with packages again, you really are a marauder, I swear. Somehow I never heard they had ration cards for smoked salmon. This is 1922 after all! Smoked salmon was officially recognized as a remnant of the tsarist regime long ago! Where did you get it? I stole it, Maria Nikitichna. Don't slander yourself now, Lesik, you're a good boy, it's written on your face. Lindt threw up his hands, flustered, What can you do, I really did steal it.

In reality, he'd gotten the salmon in a trade, palming off a hastily drawn sketch of a perpetual motion machine on a fool of a Nepman, a fat nervous shopkeeper. Look, you can assemble it from any primus stove. Even a child could do it. And it'll make electricity even without fuel? Without stopping? The shopkeeper was doubtful and vaguely guessed he was being cruelly deceived but he didn't understand exactly how. It won't stop until Judgment Day, and then it'll do as God allows, Lindt promised, placing the fatty fish in a bag. The shopkeeper, still doubtful, followed the salmon out with despondent eyes. I wrote my address down in case it breaks, just stop by and I'll fix it, Lindt reassured him as he left. He did leave an address and it was a home address but it wasn't his own but that of Tikhon Ivanovich Yudin, professor of psychiatry at the Moscow Institute for Disturbed Children. A very sweet person, by the way, and an old friend of the Chaldonovs, a smart man, from the intelligentsia. It's too bad they don't make them like that anymore.

Marusya subdued one last curl with a hairpin and laughed. 'Come here, Lesik, I'll kiss you,' she said tenderly, and Lindt, forty-nine years old, twenty-two years old, felt his huge heart wildly beating in his throat, not fitting anywhere. 'She died,' Chaldonov suddenly said, loudly and reproachfully, and Lindt jerked and woke up. The airplane whined and came in for a landing. City lights were already gleaming, drifting, and growing in the pitch dark on the horizon. Lindt wiped away his tears with a dry, deadened palm. It was Moscow.

Awaiting them at the airport was a war trophy Mercedes, a new source of amusement for the drivers from SAG, the Special Assignment Garage. A wordless orderly turned Lindt over to an equally silent golem. They slammed car doors and the impenetrably dark, deserted streets began to gleam. It was barely four in the morning, though they'd also left Ensk at four, spending a minimum of five hours in the air, an elegant physics joke, the result of time differences multiplied by the modest speed of flying machines at that time. Lindt heavily wiped cheeks overgrown with stubble—everything was closed, he couldn't get a shave, and he'd arranged this whole clothes-changing carnival for nothing. He suddenly realized he hadn't missed Moscow at all, even though he hadn't been here since 1941. Everything lost its meaning without Marusya.

The Mercedes stopped in Vspolny Lane at an elegant mansion that was obviously the work of a very decent architect. Lindt dug around in his memory and, unfortunately, rejected the name Erikhson, which floated up from somewhere. A well-groomed young man in a beautiful civilian suit with a beautiful deportment, almost like a lancer's, saw him into an office with a lamp, desk, bookcases, sofa, and heavy drapes. Lindt sank into a chair, only then realizing how tired he was.

The door quietly opened and someone entered.

'Hello, Lavrenty Pavlovich,' Lindt said without opening his eyes. 'If you count the fuel you spent on me and all these...' Lindt circled his hand in the air, choosing a word. 'And all these armed and silent man-hours that are really ass-sitting hours, it totals more than a thousand government rubles. Beyond that, Alexander Bell was granted a patent for inventing the telephone back in 1876 and the very idea of transmitting the human voice through space...'

Beria interrupted him, 'Lots of people have told me you're crazy, Lazar Iosifovich. But even crazy people fear something, and believe me, I know what I'm talking about.'

Lindt opened one eye, then the other, and yawned. 'I want so much to sleep,' Lindt complained. Beria, as fresh in his untucked but ironed white shirt as if it were noon in July instead of dawn in December, looked at Lindt, biding his time. Chagrined, Lindt thought his own shirt was, unfortunately, already far beyond such blinding perfection. A shower would be nice, too.

'Of course I have fears, too, Lavrenty Pavlovich,' he admitted. 'And of course I'm not crazy.'

'Then why are you refusing to come back to Moscow? It's just plain stupidity. We're prepared to arrange everything, this is the capital after all, the leading region for science, as it were.'

Lindt shrugged. 'Science isn't a geographical concept,' he said. 'There aren't any leading regions. Or nonleading, either. Everything's constrained by the limits of the skull.' He knocked himself on the forehead with a finger and began laughing because it resonated so much. Like a half-moronic child who'd been held back in school.

'But why?'

'The woman I love is in Ensk,' Lindt said, in simple explanation.

'That's a lie!' Beria turned red with rage. Suddenly he wasn't so cozy. That's a lie! You have a bunch of pointless broads in Ensk and I put half of them under you myself!'

'I'm very grateful,' Lindt said. 'You have excellent taste,

though I admit I'm not the pickiest customer. I eat what I'm given and don't complain. But I'm not talking about pointless broads. I'm talking about the woman I love. She's in Ensk. And I won't leave her.'

'Then bring her to Moscow, what's the problem!' Beria calmed just as instantly as he'd exploded.

'I can't,' Lindt said quietly.

'She's married?' Beria asked, businesslike. 'That's fixable.'

'It's not fixable, Lavrenty Pavlovich,' Lindt said, even quieter. 'She's unfixably married, do you understand? Beyond that, she's dead.'

Lindt stood and feverishly looked around the office.

'Where's your lav?' he asked abruptly, sensing with horror that he was about to burst into tears, begin howling, shrieking, and beating the rug with his fists, because it was unjust, damn it, unjust, he'd given these bastards his whole life, squeezed his brain dry, thought up a damned bomb for them, not just one, but a million bombs, missiles, and ammunition, he'd done in a fucking cloud of people for the sake of their wretched communism. And they couldn't resurrect Marusya. They couldn't, the bitches. If they simply hadn't wanted to, he'd have forced them. But they couldn't. Nobody could. Nobody. Why didn't I become a doctor? Or a biologist? I probably could have come up with something. Anyway, if cell apoptosis is biologically programmed, there should be ways to reset the process or...

'Down the hall, on the left,' Beria quickly said. 'And don't worry so much, Lazar Iosifovich. We'll come up with something, you'll see.'

Of course they didn't come up with anything, but they did have an excellent breakfast with good coffee and hot rolls that Beria refused, slapping his imposing stomach with obvious sadness. 'The doctors forbid it,' he said, discontented. 'Now that's who the real wreckers and executioners are in our country!'

Lindt laughed, not suspecting that wasn't a joke, not at all, not at all.

Toward evening Lindt returned to Ensk on the same airplane; nobody had even managed to notice he was gone. Nobody bothered Lindt anymore after that, with either calls or persuasion: instead he felt with all his being, for the first time, how easy and enjoyable it is to ride in a comfortable train car pulled by a machine as ravishingly powerful as the government, even if the machine is soulless and thick-headed. He was allotted an entire institute and—after swallowing his rude declaration that idiots should handle administrative jobs—was given that very idiot, a professional Soviet director pathologically and almost nervously furtive but brilliantly capable of conjuring out of thin air anything the institute needed, whether it was toilet paper or the most complex equipment recently introduced somewhere in New York or Munich. Toilet paper was, of course, far, far more difficult.

Life was improving and unexpectedly becoming more and more bourgeois, as if Lindt lived not in the USSR but somewhere outside Stockholm in a quiet little house as the king's personal friend. Publications, republications, new developments, prizes: Lindt received one of the very last Stalin Prizes and was presented a five-room apartment practically by force, though he asked to be given the Chaldonovs' little house, why do I need an abode like this anyway, when I rush out to see the old man twice a day? Heels clicked at the highest levels and Chaldonov was instantly given a round-the-clock practical nurse, a gorilla-like woman who set about her benevolent duties with the touch and warmth of a plugged-in machine. Chaldonov was so immersed in a quiet grief that he'd lost his senses and didn't care, but Lindt almost openly sighed with relief: Chaldonov was helpless, slobbering, and unkempt without Marusya, and he'd become totally unbearable for Lindt.

The new high-ranking position came with its own surprises. Nikolayich appeared along with the gigantic apartment that miffed Lindt so much. And Nikolayich didn't so much appear, like some house spirit, as spontaneously generate, like the mice in Leeuwenhoek's old rags. One fine day Lindt came home from his institute to discover that all the ceilings in his apartment had been whitewashed and a thickset guy in old soldier's cotton was working hard amidst the fresh, damp aroma of lime, gathering splotched newspapers off the floor: he was barefoot, round-headed, and very sturdy.

'Now don't you worry,' he said, as if he were reporting to Lindt instead of greeting him, 'I took everything with Iosif Vissarionovich's photograph and put it all in a little pile before getting started so as not to dirty anything. So's there won't be any incidents.' He pronounced the word 'incidents' with the painstaking importance of a child who'd only recently memorized a very long and complicated poem. Lindt smirked.

'What, could there be incidents?' he asked, interested.

'People are shot for less, comrade Lindt,' the guy admitted in a way that made it immediately clear he'd had to take direct part in the ugliness, but what could you do? Work is work! He wiped his hands on his ample rear, stood at attention, clicked his rough, bare heels, and reported for duty as guard sergeant Samokhov, Vasily Nikolayevich. His eyes were as firm as Marusya's salted cucumbers and of the very same appetizing bottle-green color. Lindt liked him from the start.

There was, in fact, only a little of the guard in Vasily Nikolayevich Samokhov, other than perhaps the audacity and thickheadedness required for even the most worthless of army feats. Beyond that, Nikolayich hadn't served in the regular army and hadn't even really fought, if you didn't count the years he'd plodded along at SMERSh, Beria's SMERSh, of course, not Abakumov's: lots of people mixed them up, especially since there was also Kuznetsov's SMERSh, the one attached to the Administration for Counterintelligence of the People's Commissar of the Navy, but Nikolayich would never, ever have gone into the Navy. The bell-bottomed pants wouldn't have tempted him, nor would the daggers or the satisfying rations that could make you burst. And this was all because Samokhov was so afraid of water he got sweaty balls. Besides—and this was even worse than water—he was afraid of not rising above the crowd.

Nikolayich was originally from a village called Elban and everything you might imagine just hearing that resonant toponym pales by comparison with the reality into which our hero was fated to be born: he lacked intelligence, talent, conscience, and shame, and even a mama, because she died giving Nikolayich the gift of a life he had no need of whatsoever and she didn't even leave him any memories of herself. She didn't die of illness, oh no, but of unrestrained drinking. Everyone drank in Elban and those who couldn't sat tight in their yards. The grim village was of decent size, with vicious women, vicious dogs, and vicious winds that combed the streets, wailing year-round, shaking gaping pedestrians, and flinging a fine dusty chaff into the sky. Even in a place like Elban, the large and obtuse Samokhov family had a reputation for being alkies and outcasts, and Nikolayich gulped down enough in the first fifteen years of his life that Dickens and Dostoyevsky would have had plenty of material for whole series of novels with beastly faces on their thin, cheap covers.

The Samokhovs had likely known better times at some point—maybe before Nikolayich's mama's death, maybe even earlier—but those times left them only a rough cottage some unknown person had solidly hewn. Someone among the grandfathers must have gone all out but nobody had kept a family chronicle for years, and in their home-brew haze the Samokhovs barely recognized the present time or even themselves. Nikolayich's father drank for years on end, rarely regaining consciousness. His liver most likely would have astonished any doctor but Elban had no fans of astonishment, just as Elban had no doctors. Of the twelve children produced by Samokhov the elder, (and they were a thoroughly pure breed, all sons), only seven managed to survive infancy, and the older ones were already worthy of competing with their dear father for the bottle. Nikolayich was younger. The youngest. Born in 1926.

Nikolayich grew up in destitution, but not in that honest Protestant poverty where everyone strains so hard to earn a kopeck, all while still finding the pluck and time to plane the kitchen floor till it's white and clean the copper coffee pot with brick dust. No, Nikolayich grew up in the horrible, muddy, tenacious, hopeless Russian destitution that so loves to shrilly complain about God and just as shrilly trust in Him, displaying, of course, raggedy elbows and a soul just as raggedy and worthless. He had to fight his brothers to the blood for a boiled potato or pair of felt boots, just like in Darwin, and with Darwinesque success. Nikolayich turned out to be a mutant of such surprising strength that he survived, despite coming down with every trashy disease a child living in hell could come down with and being scrofulous and emaciated, a perpetual line of snot running onto his upper lip. Sure, the Soviet regime helped a bit, fine. There was a reason Nikolayich respected the Soviet regime. It was warm and there was free food at the school where he'd been brought and registered by a Elban teacher who still fulfilled her civic duty, if only through inertia, despite having long ago lost the habit of sympathizing and experiencing surprise. If you chopped wood or washed floors with a sour reddish rag, you could spend the night at school after receiving permission from a guard swollen from homebrewed beer but meeker than Nikolayich's father, who pummeled the children with the senseless rage of a natural disaster whenever he was sober for a while.

There was a photograph of comrade Stalin at school, too, and when that goner Nikolayich looked at Stalin's fluffy moustache, clear forehead, and affectionate eyes with the happy little beams inside, he felt the very same thing exhausted pilgrims experience when they finally reach a longed-for holy place. Comrade Stalin emitted the light and strength and affection and love Nikolayich had never known in his life, but love hadn't gone anywhere, so Nikolayich reached out for it, shuddering all over like a needle in a compass that, like him, probably hadn't ever heard of a magnetic pole either. Nikolayich believed in that love and it essentially kept him alive: he had no doubt comrade Stalin knew everything, including about him, a little shit from Elban, and rooted for Nikolayich with all his heart. Nikolayich felt that concern and pain over thousands of kilometers and was even sometimes ashamed that Iosif Vissarionich wasn't sleeping again because he was thinking about him, but he couldn't call because there was nowhere to call in Elban; there'd never been any connection and nobody even brought telegrams here, besides, who was there to telegraph anyway? Who remembered them? Who needed them besides comrade Stalin?

For the sake of comrade Stalin, Nikolayich refused even a drop of alcohol, for his sake he drenched himself in well water every morning with a grunt, for his sake he thought hard at school using the weak, forgetful head of the son and grandson of the village alkies, and for his sake he worked hard at the collective farm: he saved up his share of the farm's income and made himself some kopecks, hoping one day he'd be able to escape wretched Elban and go to Moscow so comrade Stalin could see that his giant, kind heart hadn't been worrying in vain and that everything was great with Vaska Samokhov. Including his pants, galoshes, jacket, and the diploma in his pocket.

This was, of course, love in its highest and purest manifestation, a son's love for his father; no, it was a Son's love for his Father, and a human being's love for God, a love that's God itself, light, and hope. If Nikolayich had been born five hundred years earlier, the world would have received a great man of fervent prayer, perhaps even a martyr or a saint, but nobody asks a person which cross is most convenient to bear. And so the youngest Samokhov lived in his native Elban until he was fifteen: he was passportless, powerless, underage, destitute, lonely, and unloved by anyone except Comrade Stalin.

And then his desperate, wordless prayers were finally heard and the war started.

Nikolayich obviously wasn't an acceptable volunteer: he was considered an underage human cast-off unfit even to die for the Motherland or Stalin, and he carefully, without spite or offense, placed this in a piggybank of the humiliations he'd borne so that one day he could break it open, leisurely but with gusto, and repay absolutely everyone in full. Sly and accustomed to primitive survival, Nikolayich was first able to force his way onto a heated freight car for soldiers, then into a boxcar filled with warm cows; a few months later, after endless stations, delays, and transfers—he had to move against the current, a flow of many millions gushing into evacuation—he stepped onto a platform at Kazan Station in Moscow, lousy and more mature after learning quite well how to live by begging and (even better) stealing, but still burning with his same unquenchable, self-sacrificing fire. He'd arrived to defend Comrade Stalin and he announced that to the very first patrol he met. They glanced at each other and sent the passportless little guy with the wild eyes right to the NKVD.

That was the first big piece of luck in Nikolayich's life.

He was lucky the second time when he met academician Lindt.

It's safe to say the people of the district NKVD department weren't particularly thrilled about the vagabond from Elban. The department head, comrade Kovalchuk—a handsome, strapping Ukrainian with round shoulders and a round butt, who resembled a statue of a Greek youth got up for some reason in dark blue NKVD breeches and a twill custom-tailored tunic—was already literally running his legs off even without Nikolayich and his high ambitions. An indescribably slovenly chaos reigned at the NKVD, due not to the war but the customary administrative reshuffling. On July 20, 1941, by Order of the Presidium of the Supreme Soviet of the USSR, the NKVD and the NKGB were merged into the NKVD USSR, which happened even though on February 3 of that very same

1941, the very same Presidium of the very same Supreme Soviet had enacted an Order of the very same rebar-like strength about dividing the NKVD USSR into the NKVD USSR and the NKGB USSR. After ceding about half his kingdom to Merkulov, Beria became the main man once again; along with this came a paranoid reorganization throughout the entire department, all reinforced by reports from the front and many, many new encyclicals from the overwrought leadership.

An order regarding accountability for dissemination of false rumors that alarm the public during wartime. A resolution on organizing local anti-air defense in cities and settlements in the Russian Soviet Federative Socialist Republic. An order about disrupting the German army's rear, etc., etc. This infernal paper-based red tape was infernal in the real sense of the word, too, so comrade Kovalchuk was always turning himself inside out, trying to oblige all the bosses at once. It would have been better to be sent to the front, the sons of bitches, than be worked to death one drop at a time. But of course they wouldn't let Kovalchuk go to the front.

He cracked Nikolayich in forty seconds; thankfully, it was immediately obvious there was nothing dangerous or bad in him. Just a weakling village boy who'd suffered enough at the edge of the earth, maybe even a little touched, though probably just very hungry. He couldn't be sent into the army, though the boy swore at length he was already eighteen (lying, hopelessly lying) and a resolution from the Board of the People's Commissariat, 'On Placing Children Left Without Parents,' was still wandering the depths of the government apparatus, waiting for January 23, 1942.

The easiest thing, of course, would have been to apply another order, a brand-new one dated November 17, 1941, under which a Special Session of the NKVD USSR was granted license number one to kill, the right to hand down punishment for matters related to counterrevolutionary crimes and particularly dangerous crimes against management policy of the USSR. Of course this went as far as shooting. Comrade Kovalchuk mentally placed Nikolayich, so skinny he nearly rattled, on Nemesis's scales and took a newspaper-covered parcel out of his desk with a grunt. Here you go, sonny, take it, have something to eat, he sang out in a velvety tenor with a melodious tenderness neither Moscow nor his damned job could destroy. Nikolayich grunted and sank his teeth into a rust-colored heel of bread covered with a finger-thick slab of homemade salted pork fat. It's from Zhitomirsk, my mother salted it, Kovalchuk said. Do you have a mother? Nikolayich shook his head without tearing himself away from the food: he didn't have a mother, just torn pants and gnawed, hungry cheekbones with the shadow of eyelashes long enough to be a girl's. Kovalchuk sighed like a woman: his son, a tiny, easily amused little lad, had had the same eyelashes before scarlet fever ate him away in a week in 1936. Right after the funeral Kovalchuk's wife returned to her parents in Ukraine, saying, I can't bear the sight of you, Petro, or your damned Moscow. As if someone had asked him whether he liked Moscow. As if he had any choice in the matter.

Nikolayich swallowed the last shred of salted pork, licked his fingers, and quickly looked around like a wild animal. 'Here, I'll wash the floors for you,' he offered. 'And the window.' Nikolayich didn't know any other way to say thank you. Hadn't learned any. Comrade Kovalchuk's face lit up when he looked at the trampled, scuffed floor.

'Go ahead, wash them!' he said. 'Go ahead. I'm off to the

warehouse. Just don't make a run for it, kid, or I'll shoot.'

Nikolayich didn't make a run for it. And he became a son to an NKVD district department in the city of Moscow. With full rations and uniform, for free. He was a real person by the time he greeted Victory Day with the rank of sergeant in the Main Division of Troops for Rear Security of the Red Army in the Field, within the NKVD's Main Division for Internal Security. Nikolayich still didn't shine in terms of education, but he wasn't running with fools, either, so he no longer aspired to love and protect comrade Stalin. His divine love for the father of all peoples had vanished without a trace, along with his youthful pimples and hungry skinniness. Nikolayich put on weight, matured, earned an excellent salary, and learned all the dangerous and crafty behind-the-scenes games necessary for existing within any large, hierarchical structure. Despite his nineteen years, he had a reputation as an excellent investigator: sneaky, tenacious, and completely lacking even a hint of sentimentality. Comrade Kovalchuk, however, had been shot three years earlier, unable to dodge one of those resolutions.

Nikolayich hardly ever thought about him.

Lindt understood, of course, that Vasily Nikolayevich Samokhov hadn't been appointed to work as his valet, but for God's sake, why not? This sensible and efficient spook was a hundred times better than some bungling but inspired comrade-in-arms. In Nikolayich's skilled hands, Lindt's household moved forward without squeaks or pushes, just like a well-oiled and maintained cart owned by some industrious peasant proprietor. Beyond that, Nikolayich was hilarious and even touching in his own way. Lindt sensed a strange kinship with Nikolayich that he didn't completely understand, but that might be explained by the superficial resemblance of lives they hadn't told each other about, or perhaps even some sort of biochemical nonsense like a certain combination of pheromones or coincidental oxytocin levels. If you think about it, all the feelings we have for one other are just activations of guanine nucleotide-binding proteins, a form of chemical goodwill between signal molecules. Nothing more.

The only thing that distressed Lindt a little was Nikolayich's attitude toward Galina Petrovna. No, really, sakes alive, Nikolayich, what did she do to you? He would coax Nikolayich, not noticing he was speaking in the same tone he'd use to admonish a big, mischievous dog. And Nikolayich would turn his frowning muzzle away, just like a dog, not favoring Lindt with a response. He was jealous. Come on, don't scowl, you old sot, come on, tell me what's going on. Did you get a crib? Lindt ruffled the wolfhound-like nape of his neck with a light hand and Nikolayich nodded, softening, of course I got one. The very best, larch, you could nurse ten kids in it and it still wouldn't wear out.

What do I need ten for, I don't even know what I'm going to do with this one. You think it's going to be a son, too, huh, you old sot? A son, Nikolayich said, certain. Her belly's up so high, like she swallowed a globe, and her skin's clear. It's only the girls what drink up the mother's beauty, women always look prettier when they're carrying boys. Lindt, barely able to contain a wolfish smirk that was distorting his face, remembered the hot, lightly salted skin on his wife's pregnant belly, how she closed her eyes as she submitted to his pressure, and the live, strong, damp warmth inside her and—as if by contrast—her pale-pink nipples, always cool, thin-skinned and so tender he wanted to gather them up, lips barely touching them, as if they were weak, early raspberries almost, just almost, ready to fall.

The all-understanding Nikolayich sighed. Be patient, she'll be home soon. The doctors said she'd birth right exactly at the end of January.

And so it was: Galina Petrovna gave birth on January 31, 1959. Despite the general worries, she gave birth easily, like a cat. Only thirty minutes—of which ten were spent waddling from the smoking area—elapsed from the first gentle labor pains to the moment when the obstetrician deftly held a baby as purple as a prune under its wrinkled, flat little rear end and sang out, 'A son!' in a thick voice. The child looked a bit horrifying to her but, thank God, not as loathsome as Lindt. Still, Galina Petrovna went into full-fledged hysterics for the medical staff a day later when the little baby boy was first brought in for feeding: her son's slightest attempt to latch on to her breast sent her into true convulsions. The doctors darted back and forth, attempting to rule out the possibility of epilepsy coming from who knew where, but the truth of the matter was that Galina Petrovna simply found it disgusting. She calmed down just as suddenly as she'd gone into her fit but she categorically refused to feed the child and even hurled a jar of very lovely clotted cream at a nurse. This was a harbinger of extreme outbursts of rage: they inspired legends that spread around Ensk and were just as frightening and colorful as Bazhov's tales. Galina Petrovna, however, kindly agreed to express her milk, so they conferred and decided the baby would be fed from a bottle. She turned out to have so much milk there was enough to feed two undernourished babies, too: the grandson of the director of a huge defense factory (the director's daughter turned out to be a tight-breasted crying fool) and the late-born, precious, hard-won young of some celestial Party being who'd begged his gods for forgiveness for long decades because, by their own order, he'd shot unlucky people in dungeons. He finally received the desired offspring, a tiny moon-faced little daughter with Chinese eyes and a huge tongue that didn't fit in her mouth. Everyone at the maternity hospital pitied the little baby with Down's, even urging them to turn her the hell in to the government as damaged goods, but the little girl's mother (neither young nor pretty, and cruelly deprived of both a future and even a single drop of milk) rocked her mentally retarded little one for hours with such frenzied tenderness that it was obvious she'd fight tooth and nail for her if she had to. And wouldn't abandon her.

Nobody approached Lindt's son except the expeditious nurses. It was even Nikolayich who named the baby, this after Lindt, burning from impatience (no tearing! no stitches! it's allowed! it's allowed!) brought Galina Petrovna home and pretty much wouldn't let her out of the bedroom for nearly a day except to have a drink of water and express yet more milk. Then let him be Borik, why not, decided Nikolayich, awkwardly rocking the bulky, bawling baby and vaguely recollecting that the highest-quality, best-bred goats in Elban were named Borik.

And so Galina Petrovna and Lazar Lindt's son became Boris, Borik.

It would be hard to imagine a child so utterly unwanted by everyone.

Lindt turned out to have a ludicrously low involvement in fatherhood. The gene for Judaic fondness for children had apparently weakened like worthless old perfume by the time it found itself in Lindt's blood after making its way from Abraham, who sired Isaak, who sired Jacob, who sired Judah and so on through all the tiresome stops in all the innumerable lines of thirteen Israelite generations. Or maybe all Lindt's zeal was spent on Galina Petrovna: if viewed from the heights of his sixtieth birthday, after all, she was just as much of a child at nineteen, though she was far more fragile and vulnerable than the roly-poly newborn who crapped his diapers a hundred times a day and demanded to be fed with such a forced, purple howl that it was clear the little shit was absolutely indestructible, you couldn't break him with a crowbar. There was no sense even trying.

Galina Petrovna didn't love her son, which was completely understandable and even excusable, but he was alive and helpless and she needed to tend him, just as she would have tended the repulsive rats in the school activity room. And that was because she was a Soviet, meaning moral, person, and not some damned fascist or American. And so Galina Petrovna did an honest job picking up little Boris, swaddling him, and rubbing his little back to burp him, but she experienced nothing beyond dull, tired surprise. She was as awkward as any young first-time mother and she hadn't completely gotten used to everyday existence in her new situation: bottles had to be boiled, milk expressed, and the sour diapers and swaddling cloths in a basin had to be laundered, rinsed, and ironed on both sides. Galina Petrovna lost weight, looked drawn, and grew plain. At night she escaped to the nursery and sat for hours tensely listening to Borik's quiet snuffling, just like any normal mother, though she didn't dream the baby would sleep longer: she dreamt he wouldn't wake up at all. Lindt would come in like a silent, tiny ghost, blue in the pre-dawn darkness and deceptively unreal. You can't go on like this, you'll do yourself in. Let's go ahead and get a nanny. Nikolayich has already offered a hundred times, he said he had some woman in mind. Come on, why are you being temperamental? Galina Petrovna stubbornly shook her head: she didn't need Nikolayich's spy women, it was enough that he came by a hundred times a day, as quiet and horrifying as a bloodsucking ghoul, businesslike as he handled things, fussed around, and periodically caught Galina Petrovna's eye, thinly smiling with the very edge of his mouth as in, Remember our agreement, you little bitch? Galina Petrovna remembered.

There, there, don't cry, *feygele*. Lindt came closer, drew his withered, wrinkled fingers along her neck, then her cheek, as if he'd somehow heard, in some unfathomable way, heavy tears rising inside his wife. It'll get easier soon, you'll see. Let's go nighty-night before that little glutton starts hollering again. Galina Petrovna nodded obediently but didn't move from her place, feeling her husband's fingers sliding along her collarbone, crawling lower and lower to breasts as heavy and full as a pitcher. He could never limit himself to just consolations. Or it wasn't nighty-night, was it? Since we're both not asleep and the moment has presented itself? Lindt mumbled more forcefully and meanderingly, and his hands moved more forcefully and more meanderingly, and the sleeping Borik grunted as if he were teasing his father. Galina Petrovna felt a baby rattle she herself must have dropped; it jabbed hungrily into her hip as she watched the slowly brightening ceiling twitch and jerk, and she thought about how she probably shouldn't wish death on her child and husband, child and husband, child and husband—those two beings so alien and unpleasant for her—no, it wasn't her child and husband who had to disappear from her life so everything could finally work out for her. She was the one who had to disappear.

Zoya, the visiting nurse, saved her from suicide, a completely real suicide: Galina Petrovna had thought it over with the cold composure of a housewife figuring out the cleverest way to chop the head off a chicken for soup. Zoya came weekly, per order of the Ministry of Health, visiting the fruit of Lindt's passion as well as the mommy of that same fruit. Zoya was jolly, snub-nosed, fat, and a complete fool but she was also an unusually energetic fool. She wound her thin, pale braids on top of a head that was stuffed full of all sorts of superstitious nonsense and she meddled in absolutely everything, especially when nobody asked her to. However, Zoya knew her job extremely well and even the most spoiled babies didn't scream during her inspections: they just kicked chubby little legs with rolls of fat and googooed touchingly. Zoya was satisfied with Borik Lindt's condition because he'd put on weight and height according to the Ministry's instructions, hadn't gone out of his way to close off his fontanel too early, and even pooped out meconium with a textbook aroma and consistency. No, what worried Zoya was Galina Petrovna Lindt.

Galina Petrovna kept more and more to herself, looked at the floor with bright empty eyes, and moved with a lingering delay, as if she were ten seconds behind the rest of the world, like a diver in a heavy, tightly sealed suit striding along the bottom of a thick, peaty pond. It would undoubtedly have been logical to suspect postpartum depression, but that wouldn't have been half as interesting as the evil eye or the celibacy wreath, both of which mixed all too well in Zoya's head with symptoms of infant jaundice and basic developmental defects. And so Zoya seized the moment and brought Galina Petrovna to the kitchen, where she began energetically convincing the academician's nineteen-year-old spouse that someone had put a 'wither away' curse on her family tree. It's obvious someone hexed you, said Zoya, like a passionate campaigner. Her round, dark-blue eyes bulged like porcelain globes as she grasped Galina Petrovna, first by the shoulder, then by the hand. People are envious, they don't forgive anything, neither beauty, nor wealth, and they could place a candle *upside down* or even *pray for eternal rest*. But for a living person!

Zoya raised her brows so expressively they almost reached the nape of her neck, but Galina Petrovna was as out-of-it as a big, sleepy fish just reeled in from the water. Zoya was even a little distressed: even the most incorrigible Communists reacted quickly to the upside-down candle. Galina Petrovna was just as indifferent to Zoya's appeal to shake out pillows in search of the spell and to her threatening stories about how shards of mirror furtively placed in people's old junk brought on the eeriest cataclysms of spiritual energy in those trusting citizens' vulnerable lives. She didn't even care about christening the little baby so he'd sleep better and not have fits.

Then the affronted Zoya pulled her most cherished trump card out of her sleeve. Galina Petrovna abruptly stood, sending the stool clattering. Her lips trembled and turned as pink as a heart patient's after finally receiving a life-giving breath from a brown, rubberized oxygen bag powdered with the finest stinking talc.

'Are you telling the truth?' she asked, grasping Zoya with both hands.

'Why would I lie?' Zoya asked, indignant since she truly

didn't receive any dividends, other than moral satisfaction, for her pointless activity.

'Swear to me, give your word, your honest Lenin word,' Galina Petrovna said, demanding the scariest oath she knew: it was sworn, childish, and sinister, with origins in claustrophobic, walled-in schoolyards, intricate games, and Young Pioneer chants.

'Honest Lenin word,' Zoya said, articulating each word, and crossing herself to be on the safe side.

Galina Petrovna slowly nodded. Borik, bored, had set up a loud, hacking wail in the nursery and right then Nikolayich—a true custodian of the boss's property who considered Lindt's child a sort of fragile new possession that one grows tired of, despite obviously being dear to the bosses—started buzzing around like a bumblebee. Galina Petrovna listened to the buzzing and smiled for the first time Zoya could remember. It was a childish, clear, very trusting smile. 'All I need is for nobody to know. Could that be arranged?'

Zoya nodded her head, understanding, This is so simple, just lean over... And Galina Petrovna obediently put her ear next to Zoya's whispering, which was ticklish and a little frothy from hurrying spittle.

'Nobody will suspect a thing, don't worry about it,' Zoya said, very satisfied her reputation as a mystic hadn't suffered.

Nobody suspected anything. The tricky operation was carried out with a precision that would have brought honor to any Chekist spy. A week later the driver—who'd brought Galina Petrovna and Borik to the clinic for a planned exam with the neuropathologist—dozed off at the entrance because his boss said the drawn-out proceedings would take at least an hour. Galina Petrovna quickly went into the lobby, gave her bulky son to Zoya, who looked around as if she were a spy, then walked the length of the entire clinic and exited through the back door where a taxi Zoya herself had already ordered was waiting. She returned exactly an hour later in the very same taxi and picked up the child, who had actually been examined by the neuropathologist, and then rapped her knuckles on the front window of Lindt's personal Volga. The snoozing driver snapped his jaw shut and wiped eyes soured from sleep. Home, Galina Petrovna ordered, with such an unexpectedly imperious tone that the driver finally woke up completely and kept looking at his young boss in the rearview mirror the whole way home. A beautiful woman nevertheless, what could you say. And a nice ass, just like a mare's. The academician's no fool, even if he is a dirty Jew. But her? She's a fool. Blows her whole life on the old man and no money will help. Galina Petrovna winced as if she'd been able to feel those thoughts: they were as sticky as an abandoned cobweb strewn with debris. Watch the road, she coldly ordered, and the driver obediently looked away, vaguely guessing his passenger in the back seat was some new person he didn't know at all.

And that's how it really was. In April 1959, Galochka Batalova passed away forever and Galina Petrovna Lindt took her place.

Years later, Galina Petrovna could only snicker to herself when she remembered the horror she'd lived through in the first year of her marriage: how afraid she'd been, how dumbfounded she'd felt thinking she was under observation, and how firmly she'd believed in the omnipotence of Nikolayich, who seemed like her personal demon, almost the earthly embodiment of Satan. And to think that during the long months she spent in his presence she was even afraid to think about anything important, assuming in all seriousness that this subservient, semiliterate person, essentially a toady, was somehow capable of infiltrating her thoughts.

Back then, though, she nearly fainted from fear in the taxi because she was certain the plot would be discovered any minute, Zoya and Borik would be snatched away, they'd all be exposed, and the black marias waiting around the corner were about to emerge and take them away. Beyond that, Zoya had apparently mixed something up with the address and Galina Petrovna was almost ready to turn back because the aging, slow taxi driver circled the outskirts of Ensk so long, grumbling, I've been driving twenty years, damn, and never in my life heard of these buttfuck places. But then the city suddenly ended. Completely. The car bounced along a country road, the road took a turn, and then again, and the taxi driver braked by a small house. Looks like it, said the uncertain driver. Recognize it?

The house was old and somehow out-of-place: two storeys with a spacious glassed-in porch, all hiding within the depths of a chilly bare garden as if it were slightly embarrassed by its vulnerability. There was neither a tall fence nor a screeching cur on a chain nor a kitchen garden, only a path of damp, round pebbles and the bare branches left from last year's golden glow flowers, passionately entwined like skeletons, effectively serving as a hedge for the owners. The house was totally on its own: Ensk hurriedly retreated toward the east, enticing half-destroyed little neighboring wooden houses to follow. From the west came the inevitable advance of a pine forest that now looked, in April, especially severe and transparent, as if it had been sketched in ink on a wet, delicate, tautly stretched sky.

The taxi driver killed the engine, climbed out of the car, and lit a cigarette. 'Go 'head, honey, don't be afraid, I'll wait,' he promised. 'You couldn't even get out of here on reindeer. How could I not understand that!' Galina Petrovna quickly walked along the path toward the damp, dark steps, crunching the ice. She knocked, not noticing a porcelain doorbell, and her heart pounded just like before exams, as if it were a whole lifetime ago. 'I'll hang myself if even this doesn't help,' she thought decisively.

'Then you are a fool,' someone said in a mocking tone, and the door swung open.

On the doorstep stood a tall women in a stunning robe of dense silk woven with flowing dragons that looked like fantastical flowers. The dragons were fiery with a coppery shimmer; the same copper burned in the woman's thick hair, piled in a smooth bun on the back of her head.

'What?' Galina Petrovna asked, frightened.

'I'm saying you're a fool, my dear, if ever I did see one,' the woman repeated, enunciating. And then she laughed, showing rounded, white, smooth teeth like a movie actress on a postcard. Her neck was just as perfect, white, and smooth, and a twisted strand of gold chain with a heavy pendant dove from her neck into a plunging neckline, toward taut, ripe, molded breasts. Just as heavy were the earrings—golden clusters of grapes—that slightly pulled at her large, tender earlobes. She smelled of something almost edibly sweet, and all of her resembled a festive New Year's tree: dressed up, slightly glistening, and buxom.

Galina Petrovna suddenly saw herself as if from afar—in

her skimpy wide-open old coat with telltale spots of dried milk on her blouse, and a disheveled braid hastily secured with a black rubber band from the pharmacy—and for a moment she desperately wanted a robe just as beautiful, and earrings like grapes, and high, ideally curved brows over laughing eyes.

'Well, now you're thinking all the right things,' the woman praised. 'Come on in or you'll chill my oleander.'

Galina Petrovna strode into a spacious entryway that was dark and solemn, with a plump low padded stool and heavy coat racks. She felt thoroughly flustered when her glance caught a flirty little Arctic fox fur jacket and a long red coat with a huge silver fox collar. 'Excuse me, I must have confused the address,' she mumbled. 'I'm here to see the wise woman.'

'I am the wise woman,' the woman said calmly, with a laugh as melodious, youthful, distinct, and ominous as a mallet running along a xylophone's metal keys.

Oddly enough, Lindt was the only one who didn't notice the change in Galina Petrovna. Nothing, not even his young wife's hysterics, whims, or increasingly severe indolence that progressed as fast as a cancerous tumor could dull his adoration, but his opinion was, really, the only one that counted. Now almost twenty, Galina Petrovna had become a true nobleman's wife, in all the fine grandeur of a concept that's velvety but slightly worn around the edges these days. She acquired a set of full-fledged menials who hated and adored their mistress to the point of primitive groveling, imagined kisses on a plump little shoulder, and an almost fetishistic inclination toward aristocratic behaviors and clothing. This didn't limit itself to the usual complement of housekeepers or personal chauffeurs approved from above, however, since dozens of people depended on Galina Petrovna's moods, dreams, and menstrual cycles: furriers and cooks, jewelers, tailors, doctors, graduate students, and professors, all of whom were adults, family people with children, people who'd lived a little and seen their share of suffering before falling into servitude under this young girl.

Galina Petrovna, however, was no longer a young girl: all access to academician Lindt's body, telephone number, archive, or soul now went only through her. It was with her decree and volition that new articles were published and presidiums and conferences were chosen, and it was she who set and cancelled his formal meetings, and squandered nerves and money. And oh Lord, what money! Lindt's gold reserves, previously dead weight, came to life, stirred like a melting glacier and set sail, flashing their quick, round zeros in the sun. Galina Petrovna spent nearly all Lindt's Stalin Prize money renovating and furnishing their enormous apartment but then Lindt, who'd barely even noticed all the antique heaps of stained oak and Karelian birch, promptly received the Lenin Prize and his capital doubled again, as if the devil had beckoned.

This was all just as the wise woman had promised: the more Galina Petrovna spent, the more money she had, the better she took care of herself, and the more she could tolerate the sufferings in her everyday life. A perfectly fair deal. Zoya the visiting nurse had told the truth, so Galina Petrovna tested the conditions of the agreement on Zoya first. When Zoya came to the Lindt's for a scheduled visit (and a million thrilling questions) a week after the memorable trip to the clinic, it was Boris's dandling old nanny with the moustache who went out to see Zoya instead of Galina Petrovna. That nanny was the first in an endless series of serfs Galina Petrovna learned to hire and fire with the same mindless knack as a peasant woman sorting potatoes, indifferently tossing aside what's rotten or just small. Zoya was sent to that same pile of rejects: all it took was one call for the poor woman to be exiled from the prestigious paradise of the elite Fourth Division and banished for the ages to a regional clinic, vaccinating screeching proletarian offspring against fatal maladies. Galina Petrovna herself was pleasantly surprised at the pleasure she experienced from that fairly insignificant event. It's a lie that revenge is a dish generally best served cold: it satisfies hunger much better when it's fresh from the oven. And it's even more delicious when you retaliate for the sake of it, just for fun, without any reason or even malice. As if you're God.

The wise woman had said that, too.

Galina Petrovna quickly set up the household in marvelously grand style: her unexpected talent for appreciating nice things was rather like the flip side of her indifference to people, though the conventional wisdom in matters of décor is that it's the result that counts, not reasons or even consequences. In Galina Petrovna's hands, even blatant cultch from the flea market seemed to acquire meaning and turn out to be a rare antique knickknack. Beyond that, she had no qualms about seeking advice and wasn't shy about asking questions, a rare and precious quality almost unbelievable for a young woman who didn't know what else she should want. Nikolayich could only clutch at his head over the deranged old collectors reeking of Dostoyevsky who frequented the house, but Galina Petrovna came to love whiling away hours on the sofa, paging through thick catalogues and albums about art and swinging her rosy, round, impeccably groomed heels. Lindt nearly wept from emotion when he kissed her smooth feet, their itty-bitty nails decorated with thick scarlet polish, just like little berries, I swear. Manicurist once a week, cosmetician twice a week, hair styled every morning, little indoor shoes on a low heel, silk robe with dragons woven in. Seven silk robes, one for each day of the week.

The housekeeper, an oaken village woman who obediently responded to Nikitichna (she was actually Natalya Nikolayevna on her birth certificate, a light, dizzying hint that promised almost nothing, a lot like a puffy, Pushkinesque branch outside a half painted-over bathroom window) went through Galina Petrovna's laundry with trembling hands. She might have been sorting, might have been telling fortunes, might have been offering up a prayer of praise to her Mordovian spirits who succored and scurried, and now here she was, Natashka Duplishcheva—once a snotty-nosed, bare-bellied, rickety girl—an ignorant fool standing in a spacious master bedroom up to her elbows in what's forbidden, voluptuous, soft, and lacy.

Oh, those slick silk slips, icy on the outside but electrically hot on the inside where the silk sticks to the hips and caresses the long, smooth small of the back and vertebrae set like a little road of young stones. These indecent, nearly see-through panties smelled of the delicate and mysterious life of a young, pampered body—even after being worn, even with yellowish spots and the whitish slime on the gusset, even soaked in the crotch with the old academician's sperm—and that intermittent, almost petal-like aroma blended with the smooth smell of the imported pink soap Galina Petrovna had ordered placed in all the lingerie drawers of her endless wardrobes.

And brassieres? Lacy, with thin straps: the breasts lie in them as if they were in an open basket, all molded and taut, and you don't know whether to pinch them, avert your eyes, or plunge a pin with a bright, round little head like a drop of blood into that firm, golden skin with all your might.

Nikitichna-Nikolayevna shook her head hard, shooing away a dark, nasty thought, and then she turned everything inside out, folded it along the seams, and laundered it all in a thick, sputtering lather for the whole, entire day: one nylon stocking was in the bedroom, the other on the windowsill in the office, a mother-of-pearl button had popped off, the dishes were covered with streams of congealed fat that glistened like mica, and there was book dust, clothing dust, floor dust, undersofa dust… But this still wasn't work: it was a frantic festival of arousal that made her feel all warm and fluttery down there in her belly because every carelessly thrown dress and all the heaps of wadded bed linens (to be changed every day, ironed on both sides, starched, never blued, no matter what, did you get that? repeat it!) exuded Galina Petrovna herself, someone incomprehensible and thus especially desirable to the cloddish plebeian mind.

A year passed and then another, smooth, rich, carefree, and empty. Lindt was given yet another medal, Borik hatched out of his swaddling unnoticed and turned into a fat, malleable little boy whose first little tooth and first little step gave joy to no one but the nanny who, as it happens, was soon fired. They brought in another nanny and so on, moving down a temperamental list from the always-dissatisfied lady of the house. Galina Petrovna's social gatherings became fashionable: she'd met all the necessary people in the city (the rest were either unnecessary or not people), come to love diamonds, and then emeralds, but returned to diamonds which, as they say, go with everything, unlike emeralds, for which you have to choose an appropriate mood or dress.

Galina Petrovna, however, suddenly became despondent again in 1964. She was twenty-three years old, with five years of marriage and a husband of sixty-four, but nothing changed because time stood still: the formidable gulf between her and Lindt couldn't and wouldn't close, so she wasn't even getting older. He would always be forty-one years older. Until his actual death. The wise woman had said, be patient, your academician will die and then everything will change right away. But being patient was unbearable, and it was impossible to do anything about it (and what 'it' could she have done, anyway? suffocate him with a pillow at night?) and Lindt didn't intend to die anyway. It was as if he'd even stopped aging: he was tiny, odious, and sucking her young blood to his heart's content.

And so, one gloomy spring morning, Galina Petrovna went to see the academician in his office and, pulling the belt of a silk robe tight around her perfect waist, announced that she wanted to go back to school. Excellent, Lindt said, livening up. An excellent idea. It's great you thought of this, *feygele*, going to school. I'm completely for it, completely. After all, we have equality of the sexes and it would be a sin not to take advantage of it, if only out of curiosity. Galina Petrovna didn't even smile, and the little joke hung pathetically in the air, immediately turning foolish, flat, and humorless right in front of them. So what do you want to study, sweetie? Lindt heroically paid no mind to the awkward pause: family life, after all, isn't a simple thing and Marusya, as it happened, had also chewed out Chaldonov in the most beastly ways. A pathetic justification, of course, but he had nothing else. I'd been planning to go to the polytechnic institute, Galina Petrovna said, offended. Ah, Lindt nodded, satisfied, that means physics and mathematics, a bad student's best friends. Let's crack them open right now!

Lindt pulled a little notebook out of somewhere, laid it on the desk, and perched on his knees in the chair, like a little boy. He quickly wrote something on an empty page and then, with the deft motion of a card magician, beaming and incomprehensibly satisfied, tossed the notebook to Galina Petrovna. The monster. Galina Petrovna ran her eyes along the lines and pondered: she'd already gotten completely used to Lindt's squiggles but unfortunately she'd altogether forgotten everything the Judaic grad student had pounded into her head. Go ahead, sweetie, Lindt gently hurried her, as if he were lightly pushing a child into a doctor's office. 'The problem's very simple.'

The problem really was for children, and not just from the perspective of Lindt, problem tester for the All-Union Schoolchildren's Physics Olympiad, which had just been founded, brand-new, in 1962. If Lindt mulled longer than a minute over a problem destined to be cracked by brilliant Soviet babes, the problem was simply eliminated from the list as insoluble. They didn't run into many of those, though: it wasn't easy to force the academician to mull over physics for schoolchildren. The corner of Lindt's eye caught the gloomy ebony wall clock's minute hand: three and a half minutes for something so ridiculously simple. Then again. It seemed nothing would be like it was then, back in 1918 when he and Chaldonov practically ripped the notebook away from each other, racing each other as they solved problems: that was their first meeting and it was also their joy and vow and faith and a promise of everything. Lindt began laughing mirthlessly: How about that, practically all the promises really did come true, though it was another matter how, exactly, that happened. Galina Petrovna blushed hard when she heard him chuckle, then suddenly blotted out Lindt's little letters and signs with such anger that she tore the paper.

'What is this for?' she asked with the throaty, rough fury all her menials knew so well. 'I said I want to go back to school, not play idiotic games.'

The bewildered Lindt crawled off the chair and tried to take his wife by the arm. Galina Petrovna tore away and left the room, smashing at the door as she did, hard, flatly, and sharply as if she were slapping someone in the face.

It was only toward autumn that Lindt was able to procure an engineering degree with a specialty in water supply and sewers. He had to call in serious favors but according to the diploma (no, there's no need for honors, I implore you!) inside the dark blue cover, it emerged that Galina Petrovna Lindt, born in 1941, had studied at Ensk Polytechnic for exactly the five years of her marriage, as the document testified with a row of genuine figures and letters that had been entered in all the rolls. The document was rock-solid, you couldn't find fault.

'You spoil your wife far too much, Lazar Iosifovich,' chided general Sedlov, the KGB head for the Ensk region. Even Lindt wouldn't have dared pull off the shady diploma deal without Sedlov's permission. Sometimes you can (and even must) bite the hand that feeds you, but Lindt was too smart to spit in it.

'No, no, she didn't ask, it was my idea,' he said, trying to justify himself, though he didn't sound very convincing.

'Your idea? That's even worse!' the general hooted. He was a tall handsome man who resembled an opera singer and had a nicely groomed old-style moustache that lent him a lighthearted, even slightly comical look. Completely misleading. Sedlov wasn't stupid (that's almost brilliance, for a general) and he was certainly carnivorous. 'You can't give women freedom, they can't handle it,' he spake edifyingly and then changed the topic, deciding Lindt had had enough. 'They say your wife's an incredible beauty.'

Lindt keenly picked up on a microscopic pause and the general quickly received a kind invitation to an upcoming gathering, No, no, there's no occasion, just the usual informal get-together with friends.

Sedlov arrived at the get-together with a case of twenty-year-old Armenian Nairi cognac and behaved like a true charmer and life of the party, meaning he drank horrendous quantities without damaging his professional reputation in the slightest, sang impassioned renditions of classical romance songs befitting his appearance, and flirted with all the ladies in turn, including the housekeeper, causing a dish with a saddle of lamb to land on the floor with a bang and a passionate shriek when she was overtaken between the kitchen and a hard place. Sedlov was flawless and very quickly became a regular at the Lindt home, such a regular, in fact, that seven years later, in 1971, Galina Petrovna couldn't hold back and resolved to ask him about the fate of citizen Nikolay Ivanovich Mashkov.

It would be stupid to think she'd forgotten Nikolenka: as if anyone could forget something like that! In the beginning, after Nikolayich had frightened her, Galina Petrovna didn't even dare telephone Mashkov at the department or let a single word slip that any such person had been a part of her life. Galina Petrovna bit on her trembling little fist so she wouldn't burst into tears, then swallowed and swallowed again. Maybe her parents had told him everything? No, no, would they really dare? She just had to behave herself, then they wouldn't ever touch Nikolenka: a child's fears, a child's assurances, and a child's dreams of braiding a rope out of sheets, out of her own hair, to escape the bewitched castle. It was all over when she got pregnant and there was nowhere to run: she was defiled, potbellied, and bow-legged, no longer worthy of her fairytale prince.

The wise woman had said, forget it, don't mess with the past, you can't change anything, it's just corpses. She must have been a devotee of systemic psychotherapy.

Of course at times it's the corpses that are hardest to forget.

Nikolay Ivanovich Mashkov, you said, sweets? General Sedlov rolled his eyes toward the heavens, memorizing; like many others working in national security, he'd become paranoid long, long ago and didn't trust paper, people, or even himself. An occupational hazard. Like varicose veins for hairdressers and waiters. Of course we'll find him. And even deliver him, if need be. You need him dead or alive? Galina Petrovna began laughing and lightly slapped the general on the lips, her bracelets jingling a gentle melody. She was thirty: the peak of health, youth, and beauty, and her high-ranking marriage had brought her more pleasures than someone else could possibly have devoured in a whole century. It had also taught her to be so wily that she could easily grace any spy service. Or so she thought, anyhow. Don't deliver anyone, dear. I'm just curious.

The general juicily kissed the hand that had disciplined him—finger by finger, knuckle by knuckle, January, February,

March, April. Galina Petrovna had attempted to seduce him in the very beginning, shortly after they'd met. She was completely unsuccessful, but they'd become fast friends, such fast friends that the general sometimes even regretted being such a Joseph the Dreamer. Daaaamn this job!

'You're a very beautiful woman, Galina Petrovna, but please button up,' he'd said back then, so firmly that Galina Petrovna sobered up instantly.

It was a cold October evening, but it was warm, even stuffy, in the general's Volga, which he drove himself, only himself because he didn't trust anyone else, All ears are unnecessary ears. Keep quiet, the enemy's listening. He was old school. The windows in the car perspired a little as if they'd teared up from Galina Petrovna's aromatic, cognacky breath and her breasts—the large, round, heavy breasts of a young woman who'd birthed and fed a baby, more than one if you counted the others from the maternity hospital, even if she didn't feed them herself—shone white, indistinctly, and for naught in the dark car. Plaintive bluish veins ran from her tender pink nipples, hiding under thin skin.

'Why?' she asked gloomily, slowly starting to button her dress.

'Because you, Galina Petrovna, are married.'

'Everyone's married, damn it, and they all have lovers! Why am I the only one who can't?' Galina Petrovna bit her lip so she wouldn't burst into tears. The humiliation was unexpectedly strong.

'Because not everybody is married to academician Lindt.'

The general lit two cigarettes and held one out to Galina Petrovna. Despite his training, his hands jumped treacherously and a huge, painfully swollen bulge throbbed in his pants. Galina Petrovna inhaled so strongly that the cigarette scattered crackling Christmassy sparks.

'And you, sweets,' said Sedlov, unexpectedly switching to the familiar form of 'you,' 'and even I, are trivial shit compared with Lindt. That may be insulting but it's the truth. Your husband decides the kind of issues for the government that you and I can't even fit in our heads, which is why I won't let you worry him. So don't ask. You won't have any lovers, I'll see to that, don't worry. And in general, keep in mind that you were being watched before, but they apparently did a shitty job. Now they'll watch well. I'll be watching myself.'

Galina Petrovna inhaled again and then slowly, with gusto, drove the hot cigarette into the Volga's upholstery. The imitation leather reeked as it melted and a hideous, uneven wound slithered along the upholstery. The general began laughing and opened the window.

'Well, you are a hot one, sweets!' he said, amused. 'Here, why don't I teach you to drive a car instead, huh? You won't believe the freedom! When you're driving 120, the steam lets itself off, you'll see.'

Galina Petrovna blinked away her tears and laughed, too.

'Let's,' she said, also switching to the informal 'you.' 'Teach me,' she said, then jokingly added, 'Sweets.'

Sedlov brought the promised information a week later, though he'd learned everything he needed within an hour: this Nikolay Ivanovich Mashkov turned out not to be such a big fish. Galina Petrovna took the skinny cardboard folder and smiled, thinking she looked completely carefree. 'Coffee? I'll make it myself.'

'Then I definitely don't need any,' the general laughed. 'Just don't pine away, read it, there's nothing criminal in there.'

When Galina Petrovna smiled again, it came out like a tortured grin because she'd forgotten she was already smiling. I'll have to keep an eye on this half-wit, Sedlov decided as he quickly conquered one flight of stairs after another like a young man, mentally jingling his spurs. Old relationships are like old wounds. They keep quiet a hundred years and then, oops, you're already in the great beyond.

The general hadn't even left the stairwell before Galina Petrovna knew Nikolenka hadn't gone anywhere, hadn't been convicted or exiled, hadn't even moved away. He'd been perfectly safe, living in Ensk all those years in a little two-room, government-issued apartment (Trudovoi Lane, 14/1, apt. 12)... Galina Petrovna stood, paced around the room, and sat back down. Right, it was 1959. When she married... No, when she was given to Lindt. Nikolay Ivanovich Mashkov defended his dissertation unusually quickly and successfully (not one black mark) in that very same 1959 and received a corresponding raise in salary and a position as deputy head of the Chemistry and Natural Compounds Department, and not at the institute, either, but at the university, a colossal jump forward, practically a shift in social strata. At present, Mashkov lived at the specified address with his wife, citizen Natalya Ivanovna Mashkova, a librarian, and two daughters, Anya, age eight, and Yekaterina, age four.

And so he'd been bought off back then just like her parents, simply bought off. Galina Petrovna closed the folder and tried to imagine Nikolenka's wife, home, and little girls, but she couldn't see anything beyond her own fuzzy reflection in the sideboard glass. Agate goblets with silver trim, Russia, seventeenth century. Silver, onyx, gilding, carving. She'd just recently begun collecting Petrine-era tableware and there was already a disastrous shortage of space. She needed to look for another china cabinet, it would nice to find something carved, but not openwork, Galina Petrovna thought, surprised herself at how little pain she felt.

Lindt looked into the dining room. You busy, *feygele*? They're offering me tickets to the Bolshoy, on tour. It's *Swan Lake*, no masterpiece, of course, but they say Plisetskaya herself is in it. Want to go to the ballet? Galina Petrovna nodded and smiled, unexpectedly, almost tenderly. Ballet sounds wonderful, she said. She'd always hated ballet. Of course I want to. And then to the Central, right? We'll drink till we drop!

Lindt beamed and quickly kissed his wife, as if pecking her, and disappeared right then, like a little demon. Galina Petrovna's gaze followed her husband and she reflexively wiped off her cheek with her shoulder, wiping away the damp trail.

All that was left now was to wait until he died.

But at least now she'd enjoy the wait.

And that's how it worked out: the nine years from 1971 through 1979 were most certainly the most placid, if not the happiest, in Galina Petrovna's entire life. The Soviet Union—at least Galina Petrovna's Soviet Union—was rich, self-confident, and great like never before, like a carefree nobleman who's had a little too much to drink and doesn't yet suspect some petty thugs will relieve him of his excellent polecat fur coat after a couple more back streets and then let him go, whooping and hollering, as he runs through the cold in just his drawers, pathetic, humiliated, and messy, with a bloody soup running out his broken nose. Even the all-knowing Lindt couldn't foresee an outcome like that.

He went to his institute ever more rarely, staying to work at home, which irritated Galina Petrovna ever more rarely. After living out successive material passions for antique dishware, furniture, and jewelry, she'd finally made her way to books and you couldn't find a better advisor for books in Ensk than Lindt. They even started something like a mid-day ritual: Galina Petrovna went to her husband's office with a glass of tea in a heavy silver holder made by Khlebnikov (not the same crazy one who called himself chairman of the entire globe but the honest Moscow merchant of the first guild, Ivan Petrovich Khlebnikov, well-known throughout all Russia for his jewelry factory on Shvivaya Gorka near Taganka in Moscow) and Lindt enjoyed pushing away papers, something he'd wearied of during his life, so he could tuck into lunch and a conversation, all as Galina Petrovna surreptitiously ate up all the cookies she'd brought her husband.

Eat, eat, sweetie. I'm glad you like it. So of course you have to take the Golubinsky, you couldn't get *History of the Russian Church* even before the revolution, not to mention that now it's even in four volumes!? Is it in good condition? Ah, foxing, that's nothing, it's fixable. You know he was a professor at the Moscow Theological Academy, that Golubinsky, a very splendid old man and a very unfortunate fate. He fought with Pobedonotsev all his life. And he went blind in his old age, too. But he was kind, unusually so. Lindt fell silent, reminiscing about Marusya's voice: warm little bells, not soulless silver bells but the woodsy bells of flowers on a thin strand of a stem, like suede inside, purple and pink. And her stories about Golubinsky, who'd been to the Pitovranovs' house even in her maidenly years, pre-Chaldonov.

Good Lord, just think, I hadn't even been born then!

Galina Petrovna patiently waited for Lindt to stop his lyrical mental spasms—Golubinsky's fate didn't concern her in the least, but the condition of the binding was another matter. Lindt checked himself and returned to the present, and that was how they'd spend an hour, sometimes longer, chatting until Galina Petrovna finally remembered they were expecting her at the beauty salon or seamstress's. Sometimes she even gave her husband a kiss when she left. It was so much like a normal family that it wouldn't have been a sin to mistakenly think it was.

Galina Petrovna had grown much calmer: she tyrannized the servants less and she rarely went into her hysterical fits, which were horrible, tedious, and cold as thunderstorms, with screaming and broken dishes, though she never smashed anything valuable. She was almost happy and she herself practically forgot to notice that 'almost.' Her life fully suited her and she could handle or reconcile herself with her circumstances, whether that meant a favorite earring sliding down the drain or Borik's hasty marriage.

Borik, whose parents noticed him no more frequently than some piece of the furnishings—Oh, Lord, where did we get that horrid vase? Ah, right, the Liskovs gave it to us—grew into a splendid fellow, despite all the usual laws of pedagogy and human nature. Borik was a bit of a drip, but he would have been of no interest whatsoever to psychotherapists, making him yet another example of how comfortable prosperity mutilates a child's soul far less than deep, dark poverty on society's margins. Boris was just as wonderfully indifferent to his mother and father as they were to him and his indifference was cheery and polite, the indifference of a well-bred young man forced to share his shelter with people who were barely familiar and just a tad bit irksome. Borik had reddish hair, a fat butt, and the ability to laugh, and he didn't inherit either Lindt's aptitudes or Galina Petrovna's beauty. It was unclear, though, where he'd gotten his cleverly intelligent hands; he spent much of his time in his room, gluing together model sailing ships that were as beautiful and fragile as dried-out butterflies.

Sometimes Borik's friends came over: they were nice, lazy, rich, coddled boys, just like him. They argued often and passionately about the future of the world and the Cold War, listened to American records and traded horrible carbon copies of dissident manuscripts generally written so badly that they should have been burned as well as forbidden. These were typical endearing little games for the boys, an adolescent inoculation of freethinking without which it would have been too difficult later to plod through unenviable lives as Soviet trade representatives and attachés.

Borik graduated from high school with decent grades, perhaps because Galina Petrovna always forgot what class he was in. His modest diploma, however, was plenty for getting into the university's machine engineering department: Borik's surname and patronymic had an exhilarating effect on any admissions committee in Ensk. Lindt didn't even need to call anyone, though to be honest, he hadn't planned to.

At the end of his second year, Borik brought home a skinny, flustered girl and announced to his parents that he intended to marry soon. Galina Petrovna assessed the girl with a glance: cheap little dress, plastic clip earrings, eyelashes looking at the floor, and a dark ponytail on the back of her neck.

'You pregnant?' she immediately asked.

The girl finally looked up, her eyes as tawny as a little mutt's.

And she was a little mutt. A stray.

'No,' she said, for some reason adding, 'Sorry.'

'Then why get married?' Galina Petrovna reasonably asked, enjoying the feeling that all of her—beginning with her slightly raised, ideal brows and ending with the sleek stockings on her slender calves—was a hundred times better and of higher quality than this empty little thing who couldn't even use her youth sensibly. Her nails were bitten off and the skin on the bridge of her nose was flaking. A cheap thing.

'Presumably the word "love" doesn't say anything to you, Mama?' Borik glared out from under his brow and Galina Petrovna acknowledged for the first time that she'd given birth to a man, a real adult man who grew sharp stubble before morning, had thick veins on his forearms and, from the look of things, had filled out the front of his pants with everything he needed. For some reason that thought was unpleasant.

'Don't speak out of turn,' she said, calmly putting her son in his place. 'You and I will talk later. Bridegroom.' Boris jerked his head as if he'd been slapped but Galina Petrovna was already turning to the girl. 'And of course you're planning to build your family nest here? Or do you have your own mansion? As you can see, we don't have much room here.'

The girl looked around the living room and blushed.

'I live in the dormitory,' she said quietly. 'With the girls. But they give separate rooms to married couples.' She blushed even more and corrected herself. 'Can give them. They promised us, Boris asked at the dean's office.'

'Our Borya is a no-nonsense guy,' Galina Petrovna agreed with an acidic tone. 'A splendid go-getter. You're lucky, what can I say.'

Finally unable to take it any longer, Borik stood and pulled his mutt off the chair as if she were a jacket on a coat hanger.

'Let's go,' he said, 'Let's go, there's nothing else for us to do here. She lost her mind over collectibles. And my father's simply lost his mind. I did warn you.'

The girl obediently went toward the door, neither asking nor objecting, and Boris held her by the hand as if she were a little girl and because of how firmly and trustingly their fingers intertwined and because of how they left, in step, without having to confer about anything, it was clear that this was love, of course it was love, love without any ulterior motives, without cause, even without any rationale. Even Galina Petrovna understood that.

'And don't you count on me registering your little cur in this apartment!' she yelled after them but the door had already slammed. Good luck and good riddance.

Lindt didn't notice his son's absence until the third day.

'Did Borik go away or something?' he asked at lunch, taking a bowl of thick chicken noodle soup.

'No, he got married,' Galina Petrovna gloomily said.

'Well, that's lovely,' Lindt said indifferently, stirring his soup. 'This soup is outrageously hot! The temperature of food should be the same as the human body's, meaning exactly thirty-six point six Celsius! Then the body can digest it properly.'

Galina Petrovna smiled sociably and quickly shut down her brain. She couldn't tolerate her husband's conversations about 'smart things.'

Borik didn't show up, not in a week, and not in two, but Galina Petrovna wasn't, honestly, particularly concerned. Faithful general Sedlov reported every now and then about the situation on the battlefield: they'd registered the marriage, gotten a room in the dorm, split the cost for a party for the whole class, what's with you, why so stubborn, sweets, really? She truly is a nice girl, not some slut on the make. An orphan, her parents died, good student, socially active. Make up with them, you'll calm down. I have no intention of being concerned about this kind of shit, Galina Petrovna said. That's it, I don't want to hear anything more about that tart. The general shrugged, just try and understand women. You could snap off your head trying to figure out they're thinking.

Borik and his young wife spent their honeymoon on a construction brigade that lasted the whole summer. They came back in September, thin, tanned, and happy after building cowsheds and earning the fantastic sum of two thousand rubles. Between the two of them. Borik went to see his father at the institute and came home with five hundred more in his pocket. I'll pay you back, Papa, he promised. I'll work and pay you back, just don't tell Mama anything. Lindt shook his head, maybe agreeing, maybe objecting. Borik thought he seemed absolutely, completely old and somehow sluggish.

The money went toward a deposit on a cooperative apartment. Two thousand five hundred was exactly enough for a small apartment, but it was three rooms. They got the paperwork just before New Year's, so the holiday was loud, fun, and double: and just as it should be, lucky third-year student Boris Lazarevich Lindt carried his laughing young wife over the threshold of a new apartment that was totally empty but all theirs. They made a racket, shot Soviet champagne at the ceiling, and hosted guests, students just like them, grad students, young and happy Soviet dolts, children of a great country that was slowly and solemnly entering its own great death throes. The television they'd rented just for the holiday said, heartfelt,

'Happy New Year, 1980!' And Borik vigilantly made sure there was enough beet salad and boiled chicken for all who wanted it. They'd hoped to make potato salad á la Olivier but hadn't been able to get green peas. To hell with that, though, they were unbelievably, magically, wonderfully happy anyway.

'And what are you bourgeois going to put in that little room? An office?' asked one of their tipsy guests, attempting to tap cigarette ashes into a tea cup but getting them on his own pants each time instead. Borik, all flustered, happy, and redheaded, caught his wife's eye. She smiled and nodded, go ahead, it's okay now.

'We'll have a nursery in the little room,' Borik said firmly, and everybody started shouting and jumping even louder, for new strength, a new year, and new happiness. Right then and there they passed a hat around the circle for donations from impoverished students and appointed the soberest messenger to visit the taxi drivers selling warm vodka, and then the party bounced on toward morning at triple strength, like a ball that gets an unexpected kick. They sang Makarevich and Vysotsky, kissed, and danced to the cassette player, shaking their heads, shimmying, laughing, and not going home until about six in the morning, almost at dawn.

Borik closed the door behind the last guest and looked into the room they'd already designated as their own bedroom. His wife, his girl, his sunshine, his happiness, was quietly sleeping on the foldout bed, gently pressing her hands to her still unnoticeable belly. Borik covered her legs with a coat that had slipped off, blinked, then blinked again and went to the kitchen to wash dishes. The water was cold and rusty—plumbers are people, too, and they celebrate the New Year, too. If it's a boy, we'll call him... No, we won't call him anything. No boys.

Borik raised his head to the ceiling, demanding, as if he instinctively felt God was there. I want a little girl, he requested, glad he knew what to ask for this first time in his life. Please. A little girl. A little girl named Lidochka. The faucet snorted and spat out a twisty spurt of hot water. Borik smiled and nodded gratefully, as if he'd truly gotten an answer.

And Lidochka Lindt was born in June 1980.

Chapter Six: Lidochka

Of course Lidochka didn't have worms, and Galina Petrovna lost all interest in the little girl. A five-year-old child also proved to be a cross that's both heavy and surprisingly cumbersome to bear. Lidochka couldn't just be wrapped up in tissue paper and put somewhere in a distant cabinet, and dealing with inopportunely torn tights and even less opportune questions hadn't entered Galina Petrovna's plans at all. And how about all that touching, smooth-as-honey coo-chi coo-chi coo that everyone and his brother bestowed on Lidochka? Oh, your little granddaughter is such a little doll, oh, Galinochka Petrovna, she really has your eyes!

In the first place, Galina Petrovna didn't need any little granddaughter: she, as it so happened, had just turned forty-four, though she barely looked thirty-five. In the second place—and this was the big thing—the eyes, the habits, and that quick turn of the head and even, oh, God, the way Lidochka pulled her plate closer… After four years of widowhood, Galina Petrovna had almost forgotten the animate, animal loathing her husband had elicited and so she watched with hatred, as if she were in a nightmare, as this cute, lively little girl's chubby, happy little body exuded Lazar Lindt. She had his frown, his smile, his hands, the phalanges on his fingers, the angular little bone on his wrist, his manner of quickly, almost furtively touching her hip, all of which made disgust physically shoot through Galina Petrovna, just like when you knock that vulnerable, lively, and electric little edge of your elbow on a corner.

Go on, leave me alone, you'll wrinkle my dress!

Lidochka huddled, frightened, after awkwardly attempting affection, her head shrinking into her shoulders and looking around with dark, pathetic eyes that were just like Lindt's. Good God, of course it wasn't the child's fault, but how could it be Galina Petrovna's fault?

Raising Borik had been far, far simpler but then again, everything's simpler when you're nineteen. Beyond that, Borik was great at entertaining himself but Lidochka, who hadn't yet grown unaccustomed to the parental love Borik never knew, attached herself to Galina Petrovna completely by instinct, like a baby animal that's easiest to calm not with a word but with a comforting hip, familiar scent, and warm breathing, everything Galina Petrovna lacked and was categorically not to be had for money. The nannies were all just as arrogant, brainless, and dilatory as they'd been during Borik's childhood: for set recompense they were prepared to wipe Lidochka's butt and make sure she chewed with her mouth closed, but they certainly didn't want to love her. Nobody loved her anymore and Lidochka came to realize that, ever more clearly, with each passing day.

Of course it's probably not accurate to say she 'realized': how much did she understand at five? She'd simply grown accustomed to it, like a flower that's been on a windowsill where there'd been sun, a mild breeze, and a pretty blue watering can with sweet water that's stood for a while. But then the flower gets moved to a faraway corner that's painfully unbearable compared with that former paradise, yet not so dark the flower can just allow itself to die. The cruelest thing was that the memory of the paradise hadn't withered away like everything else: it had grown instead and filled with such lush, painful force that Lidochka would begin, again, to sob for no reason at all, even shrieking at such high notes it was almost as intolerable as the sound of a circular saw. To no good effect whatsoever. The nanny, who was used to children's hysterics, simply left the room, justifiably thinking her nerves were too valuable and nobody'd ever screamed their way to a hernia. Galina Petrovna, however, once caught Lidochka at the peak of an auditory fit and socked her with an indifferent, high-caliber slap. Lidochka's teeth chattered and she fell silent. Nobody had hit her before. Ever. Anyone.

The hardest part was that nobody talked with her, not counting, of course, the most basic communications: come here, give it to me, set it down, go to bed. Stop it. Back off. Leave me alone. Don't touch. Mamochka had always said lots of interesting things. And Papa, too. Lidochka remembered how cozy it had been to sit between her parents on the couch, feeling her mother's soft hand as cool as milk on her cheek, and sneakily pulling a very interesting and colorful thread out of Papa's sweater. Her mother was worried, do you think they'll give us a vacation trip? How could they avoid it, Papa said. I'll hammer away at the local union committee if they don't. What happens if you hammer at them, Lidochka asked. She'd perked up quickly, leaping on the word as if she were a kitten pouncing on a rustling newspaper bow. Then they're smashed. What's smashed? Lidochka forgot about her thread, stumped and her mouth agape. Not 'what' but 'who.' They are, from all kinds of vodka and other alcohol they put down their throats. It means they drink a lot for no good reason. Means they're alcoholics. And then it dawned on Lidochka: Does that mean they're all alcoholics at the union committee? Mamochka softly collapsed into the couch from laughter. See how even a child can understand everything! There won't be any vacations for us!

No, there will! You'll see! Papa even stood up but then he came right back, like a beetle Lidochka had caught with the thread, and then he started buzzing like a beetle, too, pulling at his kicking daughter. Oh, you, Barbariska! What a troublemaker! Why did you unravel my sweater? You decided to send your dear father out into the world naked? Lidochka kicked and screeched, fending him off with fat little feet. Don't tug at her like that, she won't sleep, Mamochka interceded, sorry, too, about the damaged sweater. Look at the mess you've made, huh? How did you manage to pull it like that? And why did you need that yarn? It's pretty, Lidochka said, trying to catch her breath but not the tiniest bit scared. It really is pretty, her mother said. See how colorful? It's called variegated. And so there was another word and another story and they kept coming and kept coming until the hammered people at the local union committee finally gave Papa his vacation trip. And they went to the Black Sea.

Lidochka gave a start when a book slipped off her knees and quietly thudded to the floor after her daydream: she still had trouble telling memory from reality and Mamochka had vanished right then, as if she'd never existed. Lidochka sighed and crawled down from the couch after the book and settled in with it on the floor, trying not to crackle the pages. No noise was allowed at Galina Petrovna's. It also wasn't allowed to run, jump, or build a house under the table by stretching the tablecloth so it made a secret, dim, and exceptionally cozy hideout with golden sunny streaks that swarmed with gnat-like dust motes. Lidochka mentally counted on her fingers: play with a ball, gallop, pick at upholstery and wallpaper. Smudge everything with markers. Ask for a pastry before lunchtime. Also not allowed. That was rough. Very rough.

Lidochka essentially lived like a pedigreed lapdog. She was served proper food four times a day on translucent vintage china, and after her breakfast (tea, oatmeal with preserves, hot roll, yellow butter, hard cheese) and before her snack (milk, crunchy cookie, a couple apples or a banana) she was taken out to play in the courtyard, a quiet place outside an apartment building for officials that was separated from the real world by a forged fence with cast iron decorations and spikes. Lidochka could run around a little or swing on squeaky metal swings, under the supervision, of course, of not just one but an entire dozen nannies, each of whom enviously watched after the kidlet entrusted to her, who had to be plumper, livelier, and more appealing than the rest. The nannies shelled sunflower seeds and bragged about their masters' wealth and the children's antics and naughtiness: And mine, oh, mine, oh hooow he lets me have it on the head with that bucket! 'Mine' was there, right close by, all round, self-important, dressed in imported clothes, and sniffling as he tried to uproot a hawthorn shrub that had gone reddish from autumnal shame. They didn't forbid the children anything, at least nothing indecorous. They apparently just didn't notice anything good because there was so little of it. After rifling the contents of the manorial cabinets, they inevitably moved on to the refrigerators, breathlessly reporting back on what they'd tried and when, what they'd pilfered or thought unworthy. They detested cooks and housekeepers as second-class citizens, menials, and floor washers. They never lowered themselves to cleaning up. Got worked up with stories about food, snagged packages out of shopping bags, wailed when they called to their charges, stuck caviar sandwiches, soft rolls, and slices of aromatic baked ham into greasy mouths that gaped like baby birds.' Quickly swallowed up the scraps. Never shared with each other. And didn't allow the children to share. That's all we need! As if they don't have anything to eat at home! These well-fed offspring of officials, by the way, weren't in any hurry to do good deeds: the building was filled with either obnoxious, spoiled, fat-faced little noblemen or taciturn, weak little degenerates, the pathetic, sickly offspring of powerful family lines, overindulged more than a plump landowner's son but deprived by nature of even the most elementary instincts and survival skills.

Lidochka didn't like going out to play.

Or sitting at home.

That left only books: they didn't demand or forbid anything, and she could talk with them. As much as she wanted. If only to herself. Once Galina Petrovna was convinced Lidochka had quickly conquered all the insignificant children's landmarks, beginning with the simple-minded Doctor Aibolit and ending with Pushkin's wonderful, sly *Ruslan and Lyudmila*, she pondered a bit and decided she could yield on one of her principled positions, if only for her own peace. She brought Lidochka to one of the tightly locked bookcases, turned a scratchy key, and put it away in her pocket. You can root around in these all you like, she graciously said, pointing at the lower shelf. But don't even think about the higher shelves. Lidochka began nodding a little, amazed at the tattered treasures revealed to her.

That's how she inherited her grandfather's books.

These weren't, of course, all the books from Lazar Lindt's huge, valuable library, just minor second-hand rubbish Galina Petrovna didn't know how to identify but decided not to throw away; this wasn't, of course, to hold onto memories of her deceased husband but because she was afraid of making a mistake. Book fads changed almost as unpredictably and frequently as skirt length and lapel width, so everyone might be hunting one minute for simple-minded editions of Ivan Dmitriyevich Sytin, but then suddenly take to collecting first editions of futurists, plunking down as much for a ridiculous sewn-together brochure of a book that was practically made of wallpaper as a regular Soviet citizen would be prepared to pay for a lusted-after Romanian cabinet and shelf suite for the living room. So Galina Petrovna had gathered up annual sets of *Niva* journals bound together back in the nineteenth century, crumbling arithmetic textbooks, and simple-hearted little issues of *Ladies' Reading for the Heart and Mind*, and banished them to one shelf, mentally wondering why the demanding Lindt even found this worthless biblidiocy necessary.

Lidochka sat down on the parquet floor in front of the bookcase, sprawling out bare legs that had lost, forever, their sweetly touching baby fat during her year living with Galina Petrovna. She was six years old, completely grownup, considering all the circumstances of the time and place. Can I really? She asked again before extending her arm, because Galina Petrovna could change her mind at any moment and she could get a mighty fine tongue-lashing tomorrow for what was allowed today. Lidochka knew this. She generally knew a lot more than a person her age should know. Good Lord, yes, read, said Galina Petrovna, giving her permission. Just don't tear anything or color anything with markers. Lidochka nodded again and flawlessly pulled the most tattered volume out of the crowded, slightly scruffy array of books. It was Elena Molokhovets's *A Gift to Young Housewives; or a Means of Reducing Household Expenses* and it might have even been a little warm.

Lidochka settled in more comfortably and the book opened itself right up, as if in greeting, to someone's very favorite spot: it was much-read and even slightly greasy. 'Ice cream is prepared in the following manner,' Lidochka read as if it were a magical folktale. She rushed on, following a cozy, inaudible voice that hid an inoffensively humorous tone: take the freshest cream, not too thick or, thus, too fatty, and use whole milk if you don't have enough; beat egg yolks with finely sifted sugar until they're white, mix with the cream and put in a pan over the fire, stir until it thickens but do not boil. 'But do not boil,' Lidochka repeated. She'd never had any inkling that ice cream was prepared at all, particularly in that surprising following manner. She thought ice cream came into the world in frosty paper wrappers or, at the very least, in a waffle cone that quickly turned mushy, making it especially delicious.

'Test with a spatula,' the voice warned, and Lidochka immediately turned back to the book. If it doesn't drip cleanly off the spatula but clings, like thin sour cream, that means it's cooked enough, so let it cool, stirring; strain through a sieve into a tin that should first be carefully dried; cover with paper and a lid and rotate it over ice. Lidochka forgot everything else on earth as she imagined the ice cream rotating on ice, skating like Natalya Bestemyanova, strong and plump-legged, with a luxuriant hat of springy hair that looked trained, too. And the voice—cozy and unbelievably dear—explained everything about how to wipe off the top of the tin, how to beat the resulting mass with a spatula until the ice cream turns into a thick and sweet mass resembling Chukhonsky butter, and here the word 'Chukhonsky' was also like a fairytale that needed no explanation and now, for the first time in many, many months, Lidochka didn't think about Mamochka and was completely happy for the first time.

'The more frequently the ice cream is mixed with a wooden spatula, the better it will be: therein lies the secret of good ice cream,' Marusya finally finished and quietly began laughing. This was her shelf and these were her books that Lindt took when Chaldonov passed away, when everything passed away except memory, except voice, except that laugh that just couldn't die, except this book. Maybe her very favorite on earth. Now it was Lidochka's favorite book. Elena Molokhovets.

For the next six months, Lidochka only let *Gift to a Young Housewife* out of her hands to take a bath or sleep but even then Molokhovets lay close by, on the nightstand because Galina Petrovna wouldn't allow her under the pillow. This was a very peaceful half-year, at least for Galina Petrovna, because Lidochka sat in a chair for days at a time, unseen and unheard, with the tattered volume on her knees. Galina Petrovna sometimes even forgot there was a child living in the house—what could you say, even the fussy old ficus living in the corner of the living room and lazily imitating a winter garden demanded more attention and care.

The idyll ended, as is typical, with a bloody Sunday that was bloody in the most literal sense of the word. It was a wonderful day—clear, with frost in the air—and Galina Petrovna was hurrying to finish up her earthly daytime chores because she was planning to go on a lovely visit that evening. 'Here, wash your hands right now and eat,' she ordered Lidochka, who was, as usual, sunk halfway down in the chair. Lidochka raised her pale little face, obediently nodded, and then a heavy, thick, nearly black drop plopped onto the yellowed page, right on the recipe for cream wafers (bake like little horns, serve with coffee or tea). Lidochka, scared, smudged it with her finger, slid down from the chair, took a few uncertain steps, and lost consciousness, splotching blood from her nose on the rug, her own sweater, and Galina Petrovna's brand-new, snow-white, pure cashmere jersey. The spots would never come out for anything and of course there would be no visit and no lovely evening, oh, how that little girl can ruin things! Absolutely unbelievable!

The ambulance came in about ten minutes and Lidochka was brought to the hospital even though she'd already completely come to and washed up. The doctor wouldn't hear of anything else when he heard about her faint: We're taking her, there won't be any discussion, who knows what might have happened to the child, what are you talking about! Galina Petrovna began running around the apartment gathering up Lidochka's things and realizing to her horror that she didn't know where anything was, that damned nanny, I'll fire her tomorrow, what a slovenly mess she's made, the lazy bitch! Where are your tights, she asked Lidochka, and the doctor looked surprised, but it was none of her damned business after all, who is she to me, anyway, like she's a big shot, and with looks like that, who the hell does she think she is criticizing me? Galina Petrovna dropped her purse, picked it up, and dropped it again. Only then did she realize how scared she was.

It was Sunday so there was just a duty doctor in pediatric neurology, a harsh thin guy with sharp cheekbones who'd gotten so exhausted over the last day that he'd completely lost his manners, an unbelievable situation for the Fourth Division where fawning over patients was the most important thing, even more important than treatment outcomes; that's right, treating wasn't nearly as important as obliging. But this duty doctor had thirty full beds and an isolation room on his hands, and a little ten-year-old boy was melting away in an encephalitic hell in that isolation room, it was completely hopeless, completely, and the duty doctor had sat by his bedside the whole night, helplessly checking the already-unnecessary IV every now and then and dreaming of just one thing: for death throes to begin so they'd come for the boy and bring him to the emergency room, to heaven, wherever they liked, just as long as he didn't have to see his parched mouth, sunken eye sockets, and those drawn-out convulsions that twisted at his worn-out little body. Welcome to pediatrics, sonny. He could have gone into dentistry. Mama said the smart person always looks for the warmest place.

The duty doctor deftly examined Lidochka, who was lying spread-eagled on the exam table; he methodically ruled out muscular rigidity, a symptom of positive SLR, let's look at your eyes, follow my finger, okay, let's see, stick out your tongue, give me a grin, good, now stand up, arms in front of you. Okay, a stable Romberg posture. Good job. She's just pale, but not even to the point of bluish skin, that's worse, and she's as weak as a potato sprout, it's as if she's been growing in a basement, not a wealthy home with plenty of food. The duty doctor looked with hatred at Galina Petrovna, plump, beautiful, legs crossed, patent leather boots gently pressing her calves, high spike heels, you won't find yourself wearing those in the winter unless you only have five steps from the car to the front door. A manor lady. And the child looks like she's from a concentration camp. What a snake! They're all despicable, only think about themselves.

For a moment the duty doctor was afraid he'd said that out loud but no, the exam room came back with a jolt, gleaming with indifferent nickel and glass. Some coffee would be nice now, three spoonfuls for a cup, rounded spoonfuls. And a smoke.

'So what's wrong with her, doctor?' Galina Petrovna asked, impatient. Her hysterical, ashamed fear for Lidochka had nearly passed and now she was just uncomfortable and desperately wanting to go home where it was warm and light, so she could be far, far away from this skinny guy with the completely deranged eyes.

'Orthostatic collapse,' the doctor coldly said. 'Plus low mobility, emotional tension. Low body mass, do you ever feed her at all? And do you let her outside?'

He'd finally had enough and lost it: his large heart was booming in his ears, pounding faster, out of exhaustion and fury. Galina Petrovna's cheeks turned into bright spots that were almost abstract, like in a Joan Miró painting.

'What do you think you're doing?' she asked quietly then stood. 'I'm going to write up a complaint about you. I'll have you out of here at the count of two.'

'Go ahead,' the duty doctor said, suddenly happy. He jumped up, too. 'Write it up, be ever so kind. Just don't forget to include that you weren't able to answer a single one of my questions. You don't know the child's illnesses or the what and when of her vaccinations, Ah, I'm uninformed about her, a head injury, how should I know? Your parental rights should be terminated or, better yet, you should be taken to court.

What a snake!' The little word finally escaped and it circled the exam room like an ill-mannered top, giving the duty doctor sudden relief, as if he'd heaved an unliftable sack containing something alive, putrid, and weakly squirming off his back.

Galina Petrovna silently watched him with wide eyes, taken aback by such unheard-of insolence.

A nurse looked in the door.

'Third isolation room right away, Nikolay Ivanovich,' she said.

'It started?' he asked. The nurse nodded. 'Call the emergency room, I'll be there in a minute,' he said.

The nurse nodded again and disappeared, clicking down the corridor with quick feet, a sure sign everything had taken a scary turn. They only run in a hospital ward when someone's dying. The living can certainly wait. The duty doctor rubbed his face hard with his palms, straightened his lab coat, and patted Lidochka on the head: she'd been standing by the exam table the whole time, arms hanging limply, mouth half-open.

'Bring her to an ENT just in case,' the doctor calmly recommended, as if nothing had happened. 'And sign the little girl up for some kind of sports or something. So she doesn't forget how to walk. Good day.'

'Good day,' Galina Petrovna mechanically repeated. And Lidochka, her mouth stretched, suddenly began crying, desperately and completely silently.

Curiously enough, Galina Petrovna didn't even think of complaining about anybody and simply swallowed a bitter pill that turned out to have a thoroughly curative effect: Galina Petrovna was ashamed. No matter how you looked at it, Lidochka was her granddaughter: she was still family, even if she was aggravating, barely familiar, and unpleasant. Those alien little veins contained parts of Galina Petrovna's own chromosomal composition and a shadow of her own blood. Of course Galina Petrovna knew it was impossible to command the heart, but it was possible to get used to Lidochka, resign herself, and adapt, something she also knew about, probably better than most other people. In any case, it would have been despicable to abandon a lonely little six-year-old girl for effect, and Galina Petrovna might have been unbalanced, spoiled, lonely, cruel, and unfortunate, but no, she was not despicable. Anything but despicable. She brought Lidochka to an ENT, a neuropathologist, and even (by pulling lots of strings), a private, semi-underground, and unbelievably expensive homeopath, and all the Aesculapians confirmed in unison the furious duty doctor's diagnosis and recommendation. More exercise and then she'll have an appetite; more interaction and then the emotional tension will disappear. And no more binge reading!

Galina Petrovna locked the bookcase with the key again but Lidochka pressed Molokhovets to her chest in such a desperate, completely unchildlike gesture that Galina Petrovna just waved it off, fine, fine, go ahead, just no more than an hour a day and keep in mind I'll check on you myself. Lidochka nodded, gratefully smiling through huge tears just waiting to flow. Galina Petrovna saw her own dimple on Lidochka's cheek for the first time and felt as if she'd looked into the past for a moment, into a childhood long overrun with dust and cobwebs. 'Would you like to go the circus together?' she asked Lidochka, surprising even herself. Then she pulled the little girl close, feeling almost affectionate (or at least not disgusted) for the first time. Lidochka inhaled the suffocating aroma of jasmine and tuberose—a huge, huge bouquet of them, a basketful even, where black currents, big and freshly picked, lay on the bottom, interlaid with damp tree bark, all awaiting the patient explorer—and then gave a funny, mouse-like sneeze. Estée Lauder's Beautiful perfume, born in 1986; Galina Petrovna never missed the latest thing.

Of course they didn't go to the circus. But the sweetness and warmth of that promise fed Lidochka's hungry heart for a long, long time.

Sports activities were immediately rejected: Galina Petrovna was categorically against girls with oars and similar abominable caryatids. Little girls should be little girls. And so it was decided to supply the missing activity by signing Lidochka up for dance lessons at, of course, the very best place, the Central Palace of Young Pioneers: Galina Petrovna's snobbery didn't tolerate anything unworthy, even in trivial matters. She drove Lidochka to her first class herself in the Volga, not such a big sacrifice if you consider that her new fur coat (just received from the special elite Party atelier) was just clamoring for its first outing. Yes, she'd had to work with a clueless seamstress who'd kept trying to put vulgar, tacky tails on the hem, but Galina Petrovna had stood her ground and the fur coat had come into being, though it wasn't even a fur coat, exactly, but a light thin coat made of iridescent black astrakhan with moiré swirls where the unborn lambs would have developed tight, babyish curls later on. The lining was made from the most genuine silk and it had an improbable, almost imperial shade. It's so impractical if it gets torn or soiled! exhorted the seamstress, an idiot, a quadruple village idiot, because all Galina Petrovna had to do was touch her hands to her hair or open the flap on the coat—which was as withdrawn, impenetrable, and strict as a nun's habit—for the coat to suddenly let the world know it had a mysterious, restless, and fevered reverse side that transformed it into something particularly stricken, vulnerable, and improbable, almost as if it were alive.

A huge collar of silver fox touched with a grayish frost, roomy sleeves, lots of little buttons on her high, tautly covered bust... Galina Petrovna got out of the car, squeaking in the tidy, freshly fallen snow. There was a scent of imminent twilight, approaching thaw, and a tiny bit of just-cut hothouse cucumber. The misshapen Soviet moms waiting for their offspring at the Pioneer Palace jealously pursed their lips when they caught sight of the exotic lady, and Galina Petrovna felt like either the heroine of a library novel forgotten on a park bench or a faded, damp, and wonderful decal, so blurry it was impossible to remember exactly where it had first flashed outside your memory's window. Galina Petrovna buried her lips in the ticklish fur, inhaled the delicate, slightly frosty air, and suddenly felt very silly, very young, and very lucky.

'Shall we go?' she cheerily said to Lidochka, who obediently began taking small steps, ungainly beside Galina Petrovna in her checked quilted coat and stocking cap with a yellow pompom that looked like a shaggy lemon run amok. 'I need to order her a sheepskin coat and a bonnet with ties right away,' Galina Petrovna thought in passing, and Lidochka hesitated, flustered, as if she'd sensed those thoughts. She dropped a mitten and her whole body softly tumbled after it, as only small children can tumble. Galina Petrovna sighed and stopped, come on, get up by yourself, yourself, and she understood right then that something elusive had been impeding her all this time, not the gnat-like snow, not the icy sidewalk that her heels sunk into with a pleasant sugary crunch, but the tall guy standing on the front steps of the Pioneer Palace wearing a jacket made from crackly sounding water-repellent Soviet fabric. There was something familiar and thus alarming about him: reddish, gloveless hands beginning to feel the cold, a slight slouch, tousled light hair, a foolish knitted hat sticking out of his pocket like a traitor, now there's a fop, he must be waiting for a girl. And just then the girl appeared, jumping out onto the steps, red-cheeked and laughing in a black leotard and short satiny skirt that barely covered a round little rear end that didn't look the slightest like a Young Pioneer girl's: by all appearances, they were happy to have all kinds, not just inquisitive little children, under this hallowed roof. Out in the cold, the girl immediately started steaming like a warm lathered horse and even flung herself on her awkward Romeo's neck with a precious little whinny. He quickly pressed her to himself and opened his cheap jacket, trying to completely envelop his little treasure, you'll freeze, you silly, I love you so much, you can't even imagine! The girl started laughing even louder, kicking her solid little feet and surfacing from under the jacket as she nimbly pulled her flustered guy into the lobby. A dense and tangible light glowed for a few more seconds on the steps—the living imprints of living human love. Only when the light finally went out did Galina Petrovna realize the guy looked like Nikolenka. 'He brought me to the banqueting house, and his banner over me was love,' she thought in someone else's unbelievably distant words and then she suddenly felt a stiff wave of swooning exhaustion, also from a distance, from a diligently forgotten past, and it licked away at life's color and dissolved her energy, making everything—the fur coat, the joy, and the evening—instantly disappear, leaving only a regular life that was ordinary, usual, endless, and thus no longer very tolerable.

Galina Petrovna realized she was about to either burst into tears or faint. That's it, you go the rest of the way yourself. Room twenty-eight, second floor, she ordered, forcing herself as she pushed Lidochka—who'd already gotten up and even fully dusted herself off—toward the gates of a cloistered golden childhood. The nanny will pick you up in an hour. Wait in there, don't hang around outside. Lidochka looked at her, frightened, and snuffled her nose, but she recovered and trudged off toward a huge door the height of three people. Oh, how she drags her feet, good Lord, why does she need dancing, she probably doesn't have an ear for music at all, why am I being punished like this, I'll unbutton this damned coat. And oops! A disobedient button popped off, clattered against the windshield, and flew away somewhere under the passenger seat.

Only in the elevator was she able to fully deal with the astrakhan fur, which now felt like a heavy burden. The housekeeper, who'd cooked up the idea of making *pirozhki* to celebrate the dance debut, sprang out of the kitchen and raised her flour-sprinkled hands to the heavens. 'They didn't take her?' she gasped, shaken up as her round eyes searched for Lidochka.

'They even take legless Down syndrome kids there,' Galina Petrovna snapped and testily cast the fur coat on the floor, inside out and flayed, now definitively and unalterably dead. 'Tell Lyusya to go pick her up there at six. And don't shout like that, for God's sake. I have a migraine.'

The housekeeper wanted to ask something but Galina Petrovna just shook her head, 'I said leave me alone!' and loudly slammed a door right in the servant's face, another in a series of closed doors, God only knows how many there were in this family's history, if anyone's counting.

Galina Petrovna herself didn't know why she'd come into Lindt's office but everything was in the same places as before—the big desk, the files with papers, an old leather glasses case he'd loved very much, a covered typewriter he couldn't stand—and she herself had ordered that nobody dare touch anything. It was like a little museum, sterilely clean and completely unnecessary because after Lazar Lindt died—right here, as it happened, right on that sofa that's too roomy even for death throes—hardly anyone had come into the office. Particularly not Lindt himself.

Galina Petrovna went up to the desk and ran a finger over her own face in a wooden frame: she was about sixteen in the picture, a cute, clueless girl quick to laugh, and it was Lindt's favorite photograph, perhaps because she'd never laughed like that with him. Next to it was some grayed old lady in the same kind of frame, maybe kin, maybe a friend; in all their twenty-three years of family life, Galina Petrovna had never gotten around to asking who she was. It was too late. And thank God.

'Everything should have been different,' she quietly said. 'Everything, absolutely everything. Was I really like that?' Lindt was silent, lying shrunken on the huge sofa, pulling his knees up to his wrinkly, empty mouth in the exact same pose he died in, the exact same pose he'd been in before birth. 'It's you who wrecked my whole life. You mutilated every bit of me.'

Galina Petrovna sensed rumbling tears arriving from a distance, perhaps even from as far away as childhood, but Lindt was still lying there, not turning, and she suddenly knew he wasn't silent at all but mumbling something melodious, unintelligible, and unconnected that was barely perceptible and strained the auditory nerve's capacity. It was like something in a dream: each individual word is completely alive and round as a bead that's threaded against another bead that's just as comprehensible, but when all the beads come together they twist into a tangled, messy clump devoid of all meaning, making them especially terrifying.

'It won't be long now, Galina Petrovna,' the doctor had said sympathetically. Judging from his eyes, he wanted to pat her on the shoulder but didn't dare. 'You go, at least get a little sleep. I'll spell the nurse in the morning.'

Galina Petrovna nodded obediently but didn't move from her place, as if she couldn't tear herself away from the slow, spellbinding, almost ceremonial death throes. Plastic knitting needles clicked quietly and precisely in the taciturn, elderly nurse's hands, and the old Lenzkirch floor clock, all oak with bronze castings and gold-plated hands, ticked just as quietly and precisely. Lindt mumbled in time with them, exhaling shallowly and frightfully. *Amol iz geven a mayse. Un di mayse iz gor nit freylekh.* And then again: *Amol iz geven a mayse.*

'What's he saying?' Galina Petrovna asked. 'What's he saying? Do you understand?'

'No,' the doctor said. 'It probably doesn't mean anything at all. His brain is probably more than half-dead. You go. You don't need to see all this.'

Galina Petrovna stood and only then did she feel how horribly numb her legs and back were after sitting so many hours. It was true. She had to sleep. Or at least lie down for a little while. She stopped short on the threshold and asked with a strange intonation, will he definitely not get better? The doctor guiltily tossed up his hands. Galina Petrovna left and then they could hear constrained howling sounds in the hallway.

'Poor thing,' the doctor said to the nurse, who was as indifferent as a sphinx. 'It's good she's at least begun crying, I'd already been thinking we'd even have to get out the Valium for her.'

Galina Petrovna wiped her wet eyes and inhaled deeper to calm herself but then couldn't bear it and burst out in uncontrollable laughter again, pressing her mouth with both hands.

It had begun in 1979. Or at least Galina Petrovna first noticed it in seventy-nine: God only knows how long Lindt himself had been living with it, and even God probably didn't know how frightened Lindt was. Lindt was already nearly eighty, and he'd formally been a pensioner for a long time, honorary, meritorious, who the hell knows what all else, but he did, in fact, still go to his institute, maybe not every day but several times a week, even if there wasn't anything formal about his visits. He was as venomously witty as before, grasped things with the same paradoxical speed as before, still monitored tons of projects and tended countless grad students and young scientists like sheep (more accurately: sadistically drove them to despair), and was zealously finishing yet another monograph.

They'd been married twenty years, but Galina Petrovna still tried not to call Lindt by name. It was easier to walk a few dozen meters, feeling how a new velvet dress smartly flowed over her hips, open one door, then another, and a third, and reproachfully raise her eyebrows. Lindt was standing, small and stooped, in the middle of the bedroom in just a snow-white shirt, and his withered, bowed legs—child-sized but covered in grown-up bald spots and purplish veins—stuck out underneath as if he were wearing a nightshirt. On the bed in front of him lay a pressed suit with wonderful dark plum tints, welcomingly opened in an embrace and with a modest little row of laureate medals on the right side and a bulky service ribbon bar on the left.

'What's going on? We're late!' Galina Petrovna said.

Lindt started, gaped vacantly, glanced at Galina Petrovna, and focused again on the suit. His head quivered finely, barely noticeably, as if it were a rundown mechanism trying very hard to move from its place.

'We're late!' Galina Petrovna repeated, dissatisfied.

'For what?' Lindt asked, confused, and for the first time in her life Galina Petrovna heard something like fear in his voice. She suddenly realized, with a quiet and distinct horror, that her husband didn't seem to understand anything. Neither what was lying in front of him nor the reason she was dissatisfied. That hanging senile jaw, the cloudy yellowness pooling in his unseeing eyes… It was fully possible he didn't even recognize her. Well, good Lord, of course he was almost eighty. She'd have to phone the Nikitskys right away, Lyalya said she knew a neuropathologist. Though what did nerves have to do with it? Lindt had probably gone out of his own great mind long ago and she hadn't even noticed.

'What? You don't remember?' Galina Petrovna cautiously asked, as if she were speaking with an unruly lunatic who might grab an efficient, purplish open-blade razor at any second. 'We were invited to Andrikov's, it's his birthday. The car's already been downstairs for half an hour. Or don't you feel well? Should we stay home?'

'Oh don't be silly!' Lindt said, suddenly lively and enjoying himself as he nimbly jumped into his suit pants. 'What do you mean stay home?! Besides, the Andrikovs always have good food, it would be a sin not to have some chow if they're serving it up.' He laughed an absolutely abnormal laugh that sounded more like a howl, scaring Galina Petrovna so savagely for a second that she felt weak and sweaty, as if she were a little girl, a total child who'd been mercilessly, even joyfully, abandoned in the woods by the one and only adult she knew.

'Looks a little like you overpowdered yourself, Mother, you're white all over, like a snowman,' Lindt said. He was dissatisfied and attempting to deal with the fly of his pants, which was also absolutely abnormal: he'd never called her Mother, and he'd never criticized her, not even in his thoughts, Galina Petrovna knew that for sure, she could be covered in soot, in feathers, or even in shit itself. And he'd never had any problems whatsoever with his fly, either. Now that's where everything had always been excellent for Lindt.

The evening at the Andrikovs' went impeccably nevertheless: Lindt was even more brilliant than usual, scattering paradoxical witticisms and dancing the ladies around, all to such a degree that Galina Petrovna mentally called herself a psychopath and hysteric more than once. For several long months everything remained as ordinary and livable as before, but somehow she just couldn't calm down. She stealthily observed Lindt with a wary, tense feeling, as if she were following a one-of-a-kind insect that was moving, off in the distance, along a trajectory that wasn't yet dangerous but God knows what might pop into its head the next minute. And was there anything in that huge unsightly head all dotted with elderly brownish liver spots?

Everything was the same as usual, though Lindt might have been more frequently aggravated, plus he'd begun to eat in unusual quantities and even with quirks and idiosyncrasies, something that had never happened before. Or had it? Galina Petrovna watched over every little piece of smoked beluga that Lindt dipped first in horseradish, then in cornel jam as he expounded on the appropriate activization of taste receptors. Or had he always eaten that way? Good God, what a fool, she'd lived twenty years alongside him and hadn't noticed anything at all!

But the oddities with food, which were initially barely noticeable, continued, and Lindt began dropping pieces of food, laughing at himself and his old man's infirmities, Look, *feygele*, soon you'll have to feed me with a spoon. One day the knife malfunctioned and after that the fork disobeyed and then the spoon was no joke at all, though for now Lindt operated it perfectly well, shoveling and mixing everything together in a deep soup bowl: meat soup with olives and lemon pieces, new potatoes, and the veal cutlet the housekeeper had prudently cut into small pieces. All this unappetizing glop was warmed to a temperature of thirty-six point six degrees Celsius and sent into his mouth with a lip-smacking smusk: according to Lindt's latest theory, this was the most effective method for digesting all food's nutrients.

The day Lindt poured a glass of sweet tea into his dish of Hungarian goulash, braised cabbage, and steamed chicken croquette was the day Galina Petrovna had a definitive epiphany. Lindt stirred at the disgusting slurry with a spoon, thought a bit, and then began crumbling in Berlin cookies, too, with a sneaky grin. The housekeeper crossed herself unnoticed and headed to the kitchen. Galina Petrovna swallowed a nauseating lump. It wasn't abhorrence, no. It was fear.

There was no doubt. Lazar Iosifovich Lindt, academician of the Academy of Sciences of the USSR, laureate, member, and *honoris causa* of everything possible, had definitively and irrevocably gone round the bend.

This still had to be proven, however. Lindt, who had never tolerated doctors, had now became completely unmanageable, but there could be no discussion of examinations, and of course Galina Petrovna couldn't call for a padded ambulance. For the first time in her life, she despairingly regretted that she herself had driven Nikolayich out of the house with such a bang so many years ago: Nikolayich could probably have at least sweet-talked, if not forced, his master into something. But it was too late now, too late, so much time had already passed that you'd never find him and it had already been ten years since General Sedlov said in passing, your former major domo left the agency and is, so they say, drinking horribly but firmly holding his tongue. And that's what real training will do. Nikolayich, who'd hung himself long ago at the apex of a hangover in his lonely one-room cell of an apartment, nodded jauntily, proud he hadn't betrayed his old comrades. He'd lived an odious but honest life. Like a true Chekist.

Out of desperation, Galina Petrovna invited a psychiatrist for a visit: she'd procured a full professor through friends, a fat, round man resembling a merry Easter egg. The professor happily accepted the invitation and had tea with the academician for a couple hours, nimbly and inconspicuously asking questions and chasing Lindt into all manner of logical dead ends like a tomcat, but Lindt was irreproachable, as if out of spite: he didn't mix his foodstuffs and he beat back all his interlocutor's verbal shots with an ease worthy of himself. The professor, who'd quoted a hundred rubles for the visit, kissed Galina Petrovna's lovely little hand and assured her in parting that Lazar Iosifovich was completely healthy, psychologically speaking, and besides a true genius has the right to certain quirks, particularly at such a venerable age so, well, trust my experience, everything is more than fine. Galina Petrovna wiped her hand on her hem for effect and gave the professor fifty rubles instead of the promised hundred. Just so he'd know, the dickhead.

A few months later, however, even the bright spots like the one the psychiatrist hit grew rarer. Lindt began sleeping poorly and he often trailed off in the middle of a sentence, his whole saggy, frozen face gazing off into a time and space known only to him. Once, when he was looking out the window, he said with surprise, now that is a line, oh, my dear mother! He opened the window with a creak and cheerily yelled, hey, guys, don't even get in that line, there won't be enough potatoes for everyone anyway! Galina Petrovna drew aside the thin, creamy lace curtain: the courtyard was completely empty but for an aging yard worker rustling around with a broom and a long, fluffy, fiery-red cat gliding along the edge of the shrubs.

It resembled a slow immersion. It was as if Lindt was walking step by step, unhurriedly, into stagnant black water, losing what little humanness was ever in him. Nobody stopped him or cried, and nobody begged him to return. Nobody at all. Astonishing though it was, he continued working improbably hard, spending at least four hours a day at his desk, sometimes talking quietly, sometimes furiously. One time Galina Petrovna couldn't bear it when the academician had begun boisterously arguing with some Sergey Alexandrovich and showering him with horrible, prison camp cusses. When she looked into his office, Lindt was conversing with the clock.

Each time yet another grad student received a packet of

papers covered with notes in Lindt's trademark academician's squiggles—which had now gotten even larger and more horrendous—Galina Petrovna waited for a call with frightened questions asking where she'd gotten this claptrap. Of course there were calls, but they were completely different: Ah, that's just brilliant, completely staggering calculations, tell Lazar Iosifovich they sent a grateful telegram from *Physics of Plasmas*, they're just ecstatic about his last article and you know, I want to tell you a secret, Galina Petrovna, this whole thing might just smell of a Nobel!

Galina Petrovna hung up the phone and her gaze followed the future Nobel laureate, withered, tiny, and wrapped up in a robe soiled and unrecognizable from stains, as he shuffled down the hall. He jumped before turning into his office, flapping imaginary wings with a sonorous cock-a-doodle-doo. The telephone rang again. Galina Petrovna picked up the still-warm receiver and said in a tired voice, 'Fuck off, you idiot! And don't ever call again, I've had enough.'

Borik blushed and jumped out of the phone booth as if he'd been scalded. 'Let's go,' he said to his wife, who was pushing a baby carriage where their tightly swaddled newborn Lidochka slept, looking like a very pretty little sausage. 'There's nobody at home. I'll call later. Another time.' But of course another time never came. Two weeks later, Lazar Lindt fell ill with a flu that had wandered in from who knew where. The ambulance crew that came for his forty-degree temperature suggested hospitalization but Galina Petrovna refused. Fine, said the sharp, disciplined, and accommodating lady doctor. Considering the patient's position and age, I think we can easily organize round-the-clock care at home.

The Fourth Division stood on its head in the literal sense of the term and Lindt was on the road to recovery about ten days later. More specifically, the flu began slowly retreating, like a flood, leaving behind crockery shards, debris, and the bloated corpses of pets as well as the stench of damp, death, and rot. The internist (with, of course, the highest qualifications) who visited the high-ranking patient every day took Galina Petrovna aside and delicately asked if she hadn't noticed any oddities in her spouse's behavior.

'He's a genius,' Galina Petrovna fiercely said. 'He's always been a little off, what do you want from me?'

'Courage most of all,' the internist said, admiring himself from afar for a small fraction of a second. 'I should tell you that, from the look of things, Lazar Iosifovich Lindt has Alzheimer's disease.'

Lindt died on December 25, 1981, two months after the doctor announced his sentence. He spent his last three weeks in a state of delirium filled with indistinct muttering that was unintelligible to everyone. Lindt was still alive when a special division of the central 'Ritual' funeral service company finished making huge spiky wreathes, stored thousands of tender double carnations in special refrigeration rooms, lost count setting out velvet pillows to display medals and awards, and placed a coffin with bronze handles in a corner: it was completely ready, bright, varnished, almost cheerful, and too large for its intended person.

It was loud, crowded, and even bustling at the Lindt home, as if a big, long-awaited celebration was approaching. The housekeeper was running her legs off serving canapés and open-faced sandwiches, and Galina Petrovna, who'd lost weight and gotten even prettier, received visitor after visitor with dignity. The director of Lindt's institute discussed the script for the funeral, delicately and with a thousand apologies since, this is a large-scale government event after all, they even formed a special government commission, you understand this yourself! Galina Petrovna understood and didn't object to either a farewell at the Central House of the Soviet Army or having the first secretary of Ensk's Regional Committee of the Communist Party of the Soviet Union in the honor guard. Her hands were endlessly kissed, condolences were expressed, and people backed away from her when they took their leave, wiping their eyes with hankies. But Lindt just wasn't dying: he lay in the fetal position mumbling his quiet gibberish as if he were hanging between two worlds on invisible but sound strands. That had been going on so long that everyone—including Lindt himself—was, finally, tired of waiting.

Galina Petrovna looked in on Lindt in his office on the twenty-fifth of December at four o'clock in the afternoon, as she always looked in hourly, nodding to dismiss the nursing aide, who'd been delicately gnawing at a plain Jubilee cookie in the corner. Go ahead, have something hot to eat, I'll sit for a while. The nurse disappeared with a grateful murmur and Galina Petrovna remained one-on-one in the dusky blue room with her shriveled, nearly vanished, husband. *Amol iz geven a meylekh*, he muttered quietly over and over. *Der meylekh hot gehat a malke...* Galina Petrovna went to the window and drew the brocade curtain back a bit: a heavy, silent, solemn snow was falling, a snow that only comes on Christmas, and the whole courtyard, the whole city, and the whole world was filled with that snow and with a light that was pale, alive, and real, a light that only comes once a year, at Christmas. The muttering suddenly subsided and Galina Petrovna turned around, frightened. It was almost dark, and there was a fusty, heavy smell of medicines, pain, and an elderly person's tortured body. It was as if all the objects in the office had pressed themselves into the corners and tightly closed their eyes. And only the former Lazar Lindt looked at her, from the bed, his eyes lively, tired, and completely human.

'*Feygele*,' he said affectionately, 'It's you. And I kept thinking Mama was singing.' And then he quietly and very precisely sang in Yiddish, '*Lyulinke mayn feygele, Lyulinke mayn kind*,' an ancient lullaby that was older than Lindt himself, the very same one he'd been repeating with his unsteady, hardened tongue for three long weeks.

Galina Petrovna herself didn't understand how she ended up on her knees beside the sofa. 'You,' she mumbled, shaken. 'You, are you really...'

'My head hurts,' Lindt complained and placed his wife's large hot hand on his own huge forehead. 'Did I fall or what? I don't remember anything.'

He looked around the office, attempting to sit up a little but couldn't. Without expecting it herself, Galina Petrovna sobbed as loudly as a simple village woman and then bit her jumpy lower lip.

'What's happening to me?' Lindt asked, insistent. Right then his eyes widened and froze for an instant, as if he'd caught a glimpse of something intended neither for himself, nor any other person.

He knew.

'Oh, so that's what it is,' he said huskily. 'And I thought I'd fallen.'

Frightened, he clenched Galina Petrovna's fingers as if he

were a little boy, as if she could help, as if something could be done, but he immediately caught himself and let her hand go.

'It's nothing,' he muttered, 'It's nothing, *feygele*, don't be afraid. If you think about it, it's no more than an experiment, and a very intriguing one at that.'

Galina Petrovna wanted to answer, to at least say something, but all the words she'd prepared escaped her: she'd been waiting and preparing for years, after all, imagining thousands of times how she'd curse him before he died, how she'd get everything out, telling him there'd been a rotten lump in her throat for the twenty-three long years of her nightmarish marriage. She nestled her forehead into the edge of the sofa and began sobbing, racked as if she were vomiting.

Labored, Lindt lifted his hand and stroked his wife's warm, living hair.

'Don't cry, *feygele*,' he quietly said, making the request but not hoping for anything, just as he had asked her for things their whole life: bread, a look, love, compassion. 'I am so… grateful to you for everything,' he said, then fell silent, collecting himself. 'There was nothing better than you. My whole life.'

Galina Petrovna raised her wet face, her forehead emblazoned with a mark from the sofa. Lindt gratefully and tenderly smiled at her with all his strength.

'I'd like to… turn over, my dear,' he said, and Galina Petrovna jumped up, bustling around, and began settling her husband in more comfortably with her own clumsy hands, just as the sated nursing aide hurried back into the office, oh, what are you doing, you don't need to, Galina Petrovna, I'll do it myself. The two women's hips bumped as they turned the academician's body, which had withered to darkness, and then Galina Petrovna picked up his emaciated, parchment-like hand, which had slipped, and for a second everything took on a Biblical power and simplicity.

She laid her husband's huge gray head on the pillow, looked him in the eyes, and recoiled.

Lazar Iosifovich Lindt was no more.

After they'd carried the neat, fully covered bundle out on a stretcher, Galina Petrovna drove everyone out—doctors, those who'd arrived to witness the death, KGB officers who'd shown up out of deference, practical nurses, and the sniveling housekeeper—and was absolutely alone for the first time in many months. She walked through the entire gigantic five-room apartment, looking in all the corners for some reason, as if she were hoping to find or understand something. But she didn't find anything, and then she suddenly began wailing, low and terrifyingly, like a dying animal, like a dog hit by an indifferent wheel (everything was dead below the crushed waist, but the soul still just couldn't tear itself out of the fractured ribcage into a quiet, predawn serenity). She wailed, swaying, not understanding herself what she was doing, until the downstairs neighbors—a general and his wife, a meek couple of very advanced age—began pummeling the iron radiators so they boomed, and she wailed until about a dozen fists pounded on the front door and a pair of hatchets painfully mutilated and broke it. Then some other unfamiliar people began flitting around and an ambulance began braying outside the window, its short blue flashes driving away the timid, dusky souls of the deceased who'd arrived to welcome the new guy. The strangers shook Galina Petrovna by the shoulders and shoved a glass of reeking valerian at her face but she kept wailing and wailing until the doctor poked her plump forearm with a gleaming needle, as if it were biting her. And the room immediately began spinning softly around the grandiose chandelier with the faceted Bohemian pendalogues, carrying Galina Petrovna into a solitary oblivion where she continued wailing anyway, plaintively and terrifyingly, on one note.

Now, though, nobody could hear her.

She woke up about two hours later because the deceased Lindt was softly calling '*feygele*' into her ear in a young, affectionate whisper. Galina Petrovna lay for an entire minute, all damp from horror, eyes tightly shut, and her mouth stale and bitter from the tranquilizer until she realized it was all just a dream, only a dream, not even a nightmare. All the nightmares in her life were over, gone along with Lindt, who was now apparently standing in the anteroom of the heavenly registry office: he smoothed his gray lion's mane of hair, blew on a pocket comb filled with dandruff, grinned, and anticipated the conclusion of a most fascinating argument, and so, my dear man, on that particular question I will be forced to contradict you, even now. Galina Petrovna painstakingly imagined the metal table at the morgue for officials, her deceased husband's tiny little body all shriveled from old age and passion, and then an impassive coroner who for some reason had large kitchen scissors, the same kind the housekeeper usually used to split a chicken for lunch, the serrated jaws nimbly cutting through pale, bloodless flesh.

Only then did she finally make up her mind to open her eyes.

She was lying in the quiet, dim living room on a huge leather couch so shocked by its mistress's attention—it had never seen her before—that it didn't dare stir. For a while, Galina Petrovna looked mindlessly at a motionless, dark chandelier spreading its bronze arms like a giant lurking spider ready to jump right on prey that was paralyzed with horror. I'll replace that hideousness tomorrow, she thought, and the word 'tomorrow' reverberated in her head with a sad, vague clang, as if a bugle had been dropped somewhere far away, maybe in childhood, by a small Young Pioneer who was always tired from heroics and looked like a tortured toy that had finally wound down or maybe an angel who'd grown up too fast.

Galina Petrovna awkwardly tried to sit up but the sedative had made the world as soft and addled as an unfinished scarf that had partially fallen off knitting needles. Only then did she notice she wasn't alone in the living room. Dozing by the table in a pool of light that barely seeped out from under the shade of a small lamp was a medical attendant, one might even say a little baby medical attendant of about twenty, with his disobedient head lowered over his large paws: he'd apparently been left there so the distinguished widow wouldn't get into more trouble as she celebrated. The little attendant's wrists were as wide as a pedigreed puppy's and a touching little hole gleamed on his sock right next to his big toe, like a newborn's bellybutton. A well-bred guy. Took off his shoes. Didn't risk defiling the manor's parquet floor with dirty boots.

'Hey!' Galina Petrovna quietly said.

The little attendant jolted, threw his head in the air, and smiled stupidly and joyfully, maybe from unexpectedness or maybe from youth, but it was exactly like Borik smiled when he was small and half-awake. But this one was younger than Borik. And his mother's probably younger than me. The little attendant wiped his eyes hard and anxiously asked Galina Petrovna, are you all right?

'Completely,' Galina Petrovna responded and opened her robe, softly lighting the room with her bluish naked body. 'Come over here.'

The little attendant swallowed and looked behind himself, flustered, as if someone older and experienced could give him a hint about what to do.

'Come here, come here, don't be afraid,' Galina Petrovna mockingly repeated, feeling a wild, stupid joy engulf her face and breasts because everything had finally happened, everything was over, she'd finally waited it out.

Everything truly was over in five minutes, including the joy, and Galina Petrovna didn't feel a thing beyond a sharp desire to wash up (the same as with Lindt, only a thousand times worse) after she'd closed the door behind the bewildered and desperately flustered guy.

In the first half-year of her widowhood she went through no fewer than ten lovers, young and not so young, insolent, self-confident, quiet, and bashful of everything on earth, but nothing happened with any of them other than damp and detestable bodily bother that lacked even a shadow of the love and tenderness that, as it turned out, had filled every minute of her life with Lindt. Everything had been different with him. Absolutely everything.

And now that the fairytale she'd thought was so scary had ended, Galina Petrovna suddenly discovered that the spoiled, youthful, beloved little girl she was used to seeing herself as twenty-three years ago had turned into a pumpkin: an ordinary forty-year-old widow without, of course, any material problems, but with the beginning of a double chin. There was a rush of contenders to sleep with her and eat her food, but nobody would say 'my sunshine' at night without waking up, and nobody remembered she liked her apples so hard they crunched but preferred her pears overripe, and nobody was touched that she licked her sticky fingers like a little girl after eating a messy pear. And nobody thought of her as a little girl any longer, either.

Galina Petrovna drove off the lovers and even had fallings-out with the few girlfriends who could tolerate her shenanigans and diamonds, My son, you say? Well, that little pig contrived not to come to his own father's funeral! Galina Petrovna replaced the wardrobe and furniture in the bedroom, bought a new car, and realized there wasn't really any reason to leave the house.

It was horrendous. But it was freedom.

Lidochka made it to room twenty-eight on the second floor without any misadventures. She could see a hall of Cyclopean magnitude through a half-open door: a mirrored wall reflected parquet polished to an equally mirrored finish, which itself reflected the mirrored wall in a strange way. A sequence of reflections in every direction ran up against a dangerous infinity and the ever-shrinking chandelier faded like a greasy yellow spot in the center of each infinity. A very simple problem, Lazar Lindt responded. If you take the speed of light into account and suppose the distance between the mirrored surfaces is two meters, then you can see nine billion reflections of the chandelier during an experiment with a one-minute duration. Lidochka began counting, her mouth half-open. An important condition, Lindt continued—and again it was impossible to understand if he was joking or had died long ago—is that the observer should be completely transparent so as not to block the row of reflections.

'Are you new?' asked a voice behind Lidochka's back. The voice was so sharp Lidochka jumped a little and lost count. 'What's your name?'

'Lindt. Lidia Lindt,' Lidochka admitted, not turning but trying to speak distinctly, as Galina Petrovna had taught her, you have a name worthy of pride, so get used to pronouncing all its consonants intelligibly, Li-di-a Li-n-d-t.

'Lazar Iosifovich's granddaughter?' The voice behind her back warmed noticeably. 'But why aren't you facing me when you speak?'

Lidochka caught her breath and turned around; nothing awful, nobody awful, just a ropy older woman with gnawed-at chicken bones instead of clavicles and calves like bottles, strangely twisted out.

'I'm Anna Nikolayevna, artistic director of the Little Bells dance club,' the woman said, ceremoniously introducing herself. 'Do you like to dance?' she asked, noticeably concerned.

Lidochka was at a loss, unsure what to say: she'd never actually danced, other than brief round dances with Mamochka around the holiday tree that only lasted until Papa started laughing or said, stop it, girls, my head's already spinning, let's do some serious work on the cake instead! But at Galina Petrovna's there were no holiday trees and nobody did any round dances, sang, or danced any other way. Lidochka wasn't even allowed to speak loudly.

'Fine,' Anna Nikolayevna said, taking pity and grasping Lidochka firmly by the hand. 'We'll figure everything out now. Let's go.'

And the huge door into room twenty-eight flung open.

A year or so later, seven-year-old Lidochka had already danced everything she could with the Little Bells: the mazurka, Russian folk dances, and a czardas that was obviously too spicy. They'd discovered she had perfect pitch, too, (No surprise, I sang beautifully when I was a child, Galina Petrovna shrugged enviously), and an exceptional physical gift: the fortunate muscular agility that allows the mortal human body to move according to laws from another dimension, perhaps even another time. Anna Nikolayevna doted on the astute little girl who didn't need to be shown twice, unlike most clumsy adolescents: Lidochka never lost count or confused the rows, and she could repeat any *pas*, even the most complex, with the deceptive ease that assumes the existence of tremendous abilities and perhaps even talent.

The paleness and faints were forgotten: Lidochka now had plenty of physical activity to go around. She'd lost weight and grown more spindly, though now her leanness was dexterous and slender instead of sickly, and she had luxuriant hair and large eyes, too. Lidochka promised to become a real beauty with time, a promise that threatened to come true in literally just a few years. She now resembled Lindt even more but in a feminine incarnation where everything Galina Petrovna had found hideous in her dead husband became oddly lovely in Lidochka, annoying Galina Petrovna even more, almost unbearably. They rarely communicated, inasmuch as that was possible living in the same apartment. It should be noted that Galina Petrovna faithfully fulfilled her grandmotherly duties: Lidochka ate (finally with an appetite) the same as Galina Petrovna, meaning everything was the very best and freshest; dressed beautifully in expensive and tasteful imported clothes; had her own bedroom; and was, thank God, completely healthy. Nothing else had any meaning, at least not for Galina Petrovna. Nobody asked Lidochka's opinion, just as nobody bothered to ask again if she liked to dance. She didn't. She faithfully attended Little Bells three times a week nevertheless, not missing a single lesson.

Within just a few months she'd moved from the back rows—where inexperienced little newcomers jumped like goat kids—into the forward, almost front, line of dance that holds demanding viewers and picky pedagogues rapt. Anna Nikolayevna even staged a special solo dance for Lidochka—a Russian 'gypsy' folk dance—and though there was something deeply abnormal and even tragic in how the cute, dark-skinned little girl bent languidly, moved her thin shoulders, and raised the cloud of her colorful starched skirts over her head, nobody noticed that. Nobody at all. 'Smile,' Anna Nikolayevna whispered from behind the curtain. 'I'm begging you. Smile.' But Lidochka only knitted her thin dark brows even harder, casting quick, gloomy glances at the simple-minded, applauding public, just like a real gypsy. Later she didn't smile for a long time at dance school when she danced, either, but they beat you for that at dance school, and not just for that, of course. Just one more little leap and the curved little foot almost touches the back of the head, the too-heavy necklaces jingle, the too-loud, completely drunk music jingles. Over. Finally over. 'Take a bow, Lida, and an encore, encore, as long as they're asking,' Anna Nikolayevna said, banishing all her own innumerable unsuccessful-dancer complexes along with Lidochka as she tried to push the sweaty little girl onto the stage again. 'I'm late,' Lidochka said, but she ended up in the square of wooden light again, leaping again, invitingly twisting her hips and wrists, counting out the beat, and looking gloomily into the hall. She truly was late because the home economics club started at six, she'd be picked up at six-thirty, and it was almost six-fifteen now so they'd already taken fifteen whole minutes of her stolen time!

When they finally let Lidochka go, she runs along the huge staircase, not changing her clothes and gathering up her stage skirts like a movie Cinderella, only you can't lose dance shoes with strong straps so easily, nor can you find a prince or your fate so easily. Home economics was always in room five, where the old lock had been broken long ago; the usual dirty rag was stuffed in the little hole. Lidochka sits down right on the floor and quietly pulls out the rag. 'Floors should be washed at least once or twice a week, not missing any corners.' Miss Alechka's fat, cozy voice wafts to Lidochka, inoculating the bored girls with the foundations of future family happiness. 'A washed floor will dry faster if a window is open.' Lidochka closes her eyes and smiles, imagining a window flung open, the sun swimming in a bucket, and a damp trail on dark, freshly wiped boards. A home! Her own home. Finally.

Five more minutes and she'll have to get up, go back to the dressing room, change clothes, and go out to the nanny who, thank God, is always late but those five minutes are all Lidochka's, nobody else's. She's at home for those five minutes. 'Why'd you sit on the floor, little girl, you'll catch cold!' says some dissatisfied unfamiliar lady, one of those who always has something to say about absolutely everything. Lidochka obediently gets up. She's growing up to be an amenable, cheerful child, qualities that go hand in hand far more frequently than we think. 'Food and groceries should be kept in closed containers, and there should be a special pail with a lid for refuse,' Miss Alechka tells her just then, edifyingly, not suspecting her most faithful little student sits outside the door three times a week and hasn't been able to hear any of these classes all the way to the end. You could say Lidochka only goes to dance because of home economics.

She'd tried to hint that there was another club but Galina Petrovna wouldn't hear of it. And who's going to do your homework for you? Lidochka guiltily lowered her head—she was already eight so she'd been going to school for a year, the best one in Ensk, of course, with a focus on everything all at once—English, math, and music—but she only got mediocre grades, how could that be, you're the granddaughter of Lazar Iosifovich himself but you can't solve this simple problem! Lidochka doesn't like school, either. She hasn't liked it since the very first day of school in her life, which was attended by everyone's parents, grandmothers, grandfathers, cameras, and even video cameras. But Lidochka, pale from anxiety and equipped with a formidable bouquet of damp pink gladiolas, was handed over to the teacher by a nanny who headed right off to do her own errands. Why're you by yourself, are you from the orphanage or something, asked a large-cheeked little boy with the affectionate, impudent eyes of a future rogue. And then the nickname 'Khasye the Orphan,' as cold and sticky as a spitball, was imprinted on Lidochka's life, a life already lacking the joys children need. She tolerated it as long as she could, but one night she couldn't stand it, got up, and headed off in search of the truth, her bare feet slapping the floor.

She found Galina Petrovna in the kitchen. She was sitting on a chair, her hair loose and face au naturel, quickly filling out some sort of receipt, taking a big drag on a cigarette from time to time and then placing it on the edge of a filled ashtray.

'Why aren't you sleeping, it's already late,' she said, dissatisfied, dispersing the layered smoke with her palm. Lidochka was surprised to see glasses on Galina Petrovna's nose: they were totally elderly and human, with black frames. As if she were a real-for-real grandmother.

'Am I an orphan?' Lidochka asked. Galina Petrovna was silent. 'Mama died, right, didn't she?' Lidochka prompted Galina Petrovna, who confirmed it. Yes. Died.

Lidochka wasn't giving in, 'But where's Papa?'

'Your father went away. You've already asked about this a hundred times. Isn't that enough?'

'Did he abandon me?' Lidochka felt imminent tears shifting deep in her nose; they were ticklish, like the little bubbles in soda.

'Come here,' Galina Petrovna called her over. 'Here, look.' She moved the receipts aside and pulled a little gray cardboard book out from underneath them. 'This is your bank book. See? It says Lidia Borisovna Lindt. Every month your father wires you a hundred rubles. To this very bank book. And as soon as you turn eighteen, you can do whatever you like with that money. And you say he abandoned you.'

Lidochka looked incuriously at the bank book. A hundred rubles meant nothing to her, it meant even less than 'nothing.' She wanted to know the important thing.

'But why doesn't he visit?' she asked. 'He doesn't love me anymore, does he?'

Galina Petrovna took off her glasses and rubbed the red, wound-like indentation on the bridge of her nose. Her eyes were suddenly wet and vulnerable.

'Go get some sleep, okay? I'll tell you absolutely everything tomorrow.'

But the next day Galina Petrovna, all made up and inaccessible in a high hairdo, looked so little like her quiet, nighttime, glasses-wearing self that Lidochka didn't risk asking more questions. Everything went back to the way it had been, like always: school, dancing, stolen home economics, dancing again.

Lidochka finished second grade and then third, an important landmark, by the way, not just for her but for the country since it was 1989 and the huge country was going downhill, gathering so much speed that the coming changes had already begun jolting the smartest, most sensitive people and giving them motion sickness. Anna Nikolayevna staged another solo dance for Lidochka, an unintelligible composition of her own creation that forced Lidochka to freeze in awkward and uncomfortable poses, but Anna Nikolayevna was very satisfied, so satisfied she even asked for a meeting with Galina Petrovna, where she explained for a long time, all muddled, about high callings and the dance world.

'What do you want from me?' asked Galina Petrovna, annoyed.

'The girl absolutely must be signed up for ballet school, she has talent, tremendous talent,' Anna Nikolayevna said, overwrought and pressing her flat breasts with hands that were also flat but huge, too, like some fossilized sea creature's flippers.

'Talent, you say?' Galina Petrovna drawled. She snickered unpleasantly, 'That's the last thing I need.'

Anna Nikolayevna looked imploring, like a dog.

'You don't understand,' she said, 'You don't understand. Ballet is an entire life.'

'I hate ballet,' Galina Petrovna said, repeating words she'd said at one time, and history, true to Hegel, made yet another loop, overcoming the phases of tragedy and farce and finally rising to the level of irony.

Right after finishing third grade, nine-year-old Lidochka easily beat out tough competition—a hundred fifty children for each spot—and was accepted at Ensk's nationally famous ballet school. She was a year younger than the rule: they only took ballet students starting at age ten but made an exception (for the first time without any Lindt or connections) for this unbelievably promising little girl. Anna Nikolayevna was as exultant as if she'd been accepted herself—an idle joy since she'd been dismissed from the same school ages and ages ago, a whole sad lifetime ago—and she brought Lidochka to her very first ballet as a reward.

The performance was *Giselle* and Lidochka felt sick from excitement, the too-tight collar on her new dress, and Anna Nikolayevna's vinegary breath: she bent down to Lidochka's ear, her eyes completely insane and flashing in the dark, and whispered something about great devotion and that everything in Lidochka's life was about to change. And that was the unvarnished truth. A cardboard door flung open on the stage and a little ballerina fluttered out of a prop on the left, her springy sinews all atangle and her face grinning with the tension of a person forced to hold an inordinate, overwhelming burden on her shoulders. The public limply splashed applause and the little ballerina held her little muslin skirt and leapt, tossing up muscular legs and landing on the wooden floor with a distinct, dreadful clatter. The tension in her neck and groin tendons and her doll-like false eyelashes, quivering from effort, were perfectly visible from the eighth row.

Lidochka bit her lip, sniffling. The schedule of lessons Anna

Nikolayevna had neatly copied out for her didn't leave even the slightest hope that Lidochka would find time in the next eight years for home economics, even if it were stolen and eavesdropped, sitting outside a closed door that would also remain on the opposite end of Ensk. I knew, I just knew you'd understand everything; Anna Nikolayevna was getting agitated and began crying, too, uncomfortably clutching Lidochka to her bony rib cage. Each bemoaned something impossible that hadn't come true, and a tired Giselle silently cried inside in time with them, then slipped on a *balloté* yet again, for the three thousand twenty-first time, the brainless cow, she's a talentless, talentless, old jade unfit for anything!

It was a forty-five-minute drive from Galina Petrovna's house to the school and classes started at eight, sometimes ending late in the evening. A future specialist with the qualification of 'ballet performer' was obviously also required to master playing the piano and other special disciplines in addition to the usual comprehensive school subjects. Classical dance, classical dance in pairs, folk dance for the stage, historical-vernacular dance, contemporary choreography, acting skills, gymnastics, and makeup. Galina Petrovna tolerated this outrage for a couple months—wakeups at six in the morning and obligatory exercises at home on the weekends—before going to meet with the ballet school's director. If there was anything Galina Petrovna could do, it was kick up a fuss. Despite a lack of spots in the dormitory and the presence of living space and a residence permit in Ensk, first-year student Lidia Borisovna Lindt was accepted for full room and board at the dorm for out-of-town students. It was fifty meters from the school building and offered five meals a day, round-the-clock caregivers, and a medical unit with physiotherapy and an infirmary. Galina Petrovna, who'd just opened a second antique shop with general Sedlov's help, took responsibility for renovating the bathrooms and fully furnishing the physiotherapy room with the most up-to-the-minute equipment.

'I think it's an honest deal,' she coldly said, 'Besides, I'm planning to bring the girl home every other weekend. And you can use her bed as much as you want.'

Lidochka entered a room as narrow as a coffin: two beds, a little rug with trampled teddy bears, and a window all cracked and covered with multiple strata of oil paint. Desolate, she inhaled the unlived-in dorm aura. It wasn't home this time, either. Again. A colorless little girl, not even a little girl but a girlet, was hanging around by the window, her mousy hair pulled into a loose ballet bun, her little face a grimace of cautious politeness. The huge eyes of an emaciated little owlet. Buchenwald.

'What's your name?'
'Lida.'
'I'm Lyusya.'

A half-year later, everyone at the school called them LyuLi. LyuLi's here. Lida and Lyusya. Lindt and Zhukova. The snoot and the suckerfish. The princess and the pea. LyuLi, can I have your Russian homework to copy? Lidochka looks at Lyusya, Lyusya looks at Lidochka. Then they nod in agreement with round, smooth, ballet heads—the strands of their parts, the knots of adultish swept-up hair over thin childish little necks—sharp shoulder blades, school uniform aprons, horsy tendons, and the articulation of overworked vertebrae. Yes, you can have it! And so Lyusya's notebook is sent sailing across other kids' desks. Lidochka had already copied everything from it, back in their room: Russian and math aren't her friends but she's friends with Lyusya Zhukova and Elena Molokhovets.

They don't need anyone else when the three of them all finally get together in the evenings. Lyusya lies right on the floor, spreading her small hips, one knee thrust under the cast iron radiator. Lidochka stands on the other, keeping herself balanced as she holds the huge Molokhovets tome in her hands. This exercise is called 'the frog.'

'One veal liver cut in thin slices, one eighth of a pound of lard, one diced onion, placed in a saucepan, add English pepper, bay leaf, salt, place covered over a high flame, watching that it doesn't scorch,' Lidochka sings out. The sound of Lyusya's guardian angel's hungry mouth watering is audible in Lidochka's pauses. 'When the liver is ready, meaning lightly browned, drain the fat, place on the table, cut into small pieces, grind everything together in a mortar, adding a spoonful of washed butter and a quarter of a French roll, soaked and squeezed out, then grind again, press through a sieve, pour in a shot of Madeira...'

'Is it much longer?' Lyusya moans, her hair stuck to her temples with tears as the stretched tendons in her groin silently scrape, but Lyusya, who's looking at the ceiling from the depths of her pain, doesn't even notice she's crying. She has poor turnout and has to work on it, is forced to work on it, everything's painful in ballet, no matter what you touch. It's all one never-ending pain.

'Don't interrupt!' Lidochka says, angry. 'Another ten minutes. I'll tell you. So, add a shot of Madeira, one spoonful of good rum, sprinkle in nutmeg and salt, and stuff into baked horn-shaped puff-pastry shells, put in the oven for about five minutes...'

The weakened Lyusya closes her eyes, attempting to imagine horn-shaped pastries or even just the little pies her grandmother made: fried, greasy, and covered with golden-brown blisters. With cabbage. Or apples. Or—Lyusya's favorites—with mushrooms and coarsely chopped hard-boiled eggs. Maybe not even her grandmother's but ordinary ones, rubbery ones from a cafeteria in an aluminum tank labeled with the bold inscription 'SocNutr.' If you bite the taut side of a pie like that it scalds the hungry roof of the mouth with an empty warmish sigh: the kitchen was stingy with the filling again, the freeloaders!

The ballet school's kitchen, however, wasn't stingy with the filling and they also weren't stingy in their feelings for the dancers, who looked away as they carried their greasy half-empty plastic trays past those pies, dear reader, past. Doughy server ladies dipped ladles into gigantic saucepans with tempting, steaming proteins, fats, and carbohydrates, but all in vain because—despite the hellish physical burden and the ration calculated by dieticians—the future ballerinas hysterically feared, to the point of hungry faints, gaining even a gram and losing the favor of their all-mighty god forever.

Mandatory weigh-ins every six months were Judgment Day: this was when the sun, moon, and light fixtures darkened and fell from the swaying ceiling, and the ceiling itself rolled up like a scroll. The dancers—paler than even the palest horse and deafened by angels and a trumpet-like intestinal voice—crowded the corridor in front of the medical office, pressing their quivering shoulder blades against the wall and using their last strength to suck in nonexistent bellies. The norm of 'minus one hundred fifteen' was a matter of mathematics: if a girl was one hundred forty centimeters tall, she had no right to weigh more than twenty-seven kilograms. But twenty-five kilograms—the actual norm, reached by subtracting one hundred fifteen from her height—was better. Twenty-three was very good. In the upper grades, 'minus one hundred fifteen' transformed to a full 'minus one hundred twenty.' A meter and a half tall and weighing thirty-five kilos instead of thirty? Who's going to lift you, you fat cow? Don't eat, go smoke instead!

They started smoking from about thirteen, smoking desperately, selflessly, and hungrily, with their teachers' blessing and encouragement. They gulped the salvatory, satiating smoke—this is for Mama, this is for Papa, this is for the legendary Galina Sergeyevna Ulanova, and their jealous, envious eyes pawed their girlfriends' hips and ribs—Tanya has such a horrendous ass, they already tossed her off the center barre, she'll have to dance under the piano before you know it, they should kick her out, dear God, kick her out, please, just not me! Tanya looked at the frightening medical office with eyes white from desperation, crushed by her inescapably impending femininity. She knew herself she was doomed, her ass was one thing but—just think, so disgusting, get away, have mercy and let me squeak by, get away—some breasts had also begun taking shape, a weak bulge, nature's pathetic attempt to take back a slab of life-giving fat from ballet, if only a millimeter.

The exhausted pubertarians dieted on buckwheat and kefir before weigh-ins or exams; this was a way to shed up to fifteen kilos in three months and say goodbye to your pancreas forever. Furosemide was the ballet dancer's best friend and gallbladder removal was the most fashionable operation (only torn ligaments were more common), but without a gallbladder you'll be even lighter, lacier, and airier, you Sylphide. No fiber the week before the weigh-in, then a curative fast the two last days, and if you really get the urge to eat, well, all it takes is two quick fingers to a resistant pharynx for all the calories and hopes to erupt with a hoarse roar and a spray into the toilet's maw.

Yes, girls, the main thing is not to drink anything, no liquids, because we're drying out our muscles, tossing off the ballast, enema in the morning, enema in the evening, fainting spell, toilet again. A teeny little square of chocolate in the morning before Golgotha, so as not to collapse right at the impassive doctor's feet. Your weight's on track but that height isn't good for anything, a couple more centimeters and you're out, sweetie pie. Sweetie pie's nearly inhuman adult eyes dance with fanatical flashes from a fire stoked by either self-sacrifice or the executioner: she's ready to chop off half her head, or even her whole head, if that's what it takes to prepare for the next weigh-in. Anything but her sharply, roundly arched feet, we're raising our insteps, raising our insteps, hens, we don't feel sorry for ourselves. And they don't.

Defective Tanya with the nonballet ass is consoled in the hallway by her fortunate, chittering friends, who are dying from relief: it's not me, not me! Tanya isn't even crying and she'd die if she could stop her heart through sheer force of will, but they only do that kind of high-level character work in the upper grades and Tanya was screened out too early, much too early, so she's just biting on her little fists with all her might, so hard her teeth leave even white marks that slowly fill with a fire that starts off reddish then turns to a thick, festive plum color. Her gallbladder is saved and her life is over, but even twenty years later she'll feel an inner howl when she sees four haggard, nodding, feathery swan heads floating along her television and hears the whistle of a dark wind tearing away a playbill without her name printed on it. Tanya clicks the remote, cutting off the white act of *Swan Lake* in midnote, and leaves the room, aged, grayed, and hopelessly dead since fourteen. 'Ma, where're you going?' her youngest son yells after her but Tanya doesn't answer. (Thank God they're both sons, she'd sign a daughter up for dance school anyway, carry her in her own arms and throw her on the altar.) Her back still couldn't be straighter and her shoulder blades are tightly contracted in a knot of iron muscles that don't know how to relax. This correct back, always in position, is known as aplomb among dancers. They have no other aplomb.

It's worth noting that Ensk's ballet school was outstanding thanks to the war, which in its day brought nearly the entire Leningrad ballet there. To complement the shipment of cold-sensitive ballerinas from the Kirov, they sent the USSR's best ballet school, too, meaning the one that now carries the name of Agrippina Vaganova. Of course back in 1941, Vaganova was a live, imperious biddy and her name wasn't yet on any memorial plaques, but she already had all the titles you can ransack the encyclopedias for now: eminent Russian ballerina, pedagogue, ballet choreographer, keeper of centuries-old traditions of imperial Russian ballet, people's artist of the Russian Soviet Federative Socialist Republic, and blah, blah, blah. Something else was important: when the ballet returned to Petersburg from evacuation, they left behind more than just nice memories, they also left half the pedagogical staff and an entire class of newly selected, skinny, ballet-obsessed wartime children. They were the foundation of the future Ensk theater and future ballet school, which quickly won laurels across the Soviet Union for tough drills and ideal body position. The

Ensk school is immediately obvious, moaned balletomanes as they feasted on little ballerinas flying across the stage: *glissade, glissade, preparation*, ah! What *ballon*, oh mercy! What *ballon*!

There are things it's best not to think about. Or maybe not even know in the first place.

Let's say you try walking off the street into a military barracks, a camp barracks, a torture chamber, or a totalitarian sect's meeting. Nobody will let you in, just as a curious observer won't be let into a ballet school: mere mortals leading easy, empty, everyday lives could never understand the solemn horror that permeates the essence of truly closed societies. The ideal parallelepiped of the military or camp barracks. A dance class drenched in light and sweat. The complexest of rituals: delightful drills where the only purpose is to shut off reason forever, to never think, never worry about anything, never decide anything, and submit to a universal way of the world, dissolving and ceasing to be yourself so you can be incarnated on a higher level, with a blissful, plural number. Pain, humiliation, brutal hazing, hunger, and the happiness of complete submission. And pain again.

Now imagine soldiers who've turned to tin from zeal and are fanatically in love with their drills. Prisoners who begin preparing their mutilated bodies for torture long before their daily interrogation by voluntarily stretching on the rack and methodically breaking one joint after another. Hear out this lecture about your own lack of talent as you stand stretched en pointe, know you're a hopeless freak unfit for anything: Don't hang on the barre, don't droop, don't droop, hold that heel, the heel, who am I talking to? You'll get a riding crop to your calves or a palm slapping a cheek so catch the rhythm, pull in your belly and butt at the same time, and acknowledge everything little children feel when they run down the ballet school stairs in one lovely, loud little herd. Now weigh, on one side, everything they've voluntarily chucked out of their lives: pastries, bedtime stories, friendship, first love, fried potatoes with homemade cutlets, and trust in grownups, kids their age, and themselves. On the other side weigh just one thing: the opportunity to run onto the stage and take a low, affected, and drawn-out bow for the public.

Make your choice.

Don't ever regret it.

Now you know what ballet is.

Lidochka was used to inconspicuously mediocre grades at her regular school, but at ballet school she almost immediately became an acknowledged queen. Her qualifications, which were nearly ideal, even impressed the worldly viewing commission during the first round of the application process. The selection rules are, honestly, more reminiscent of descriptions of breed characteristics for show dogs or horses, and the screening was tough, even severe. 'Negative characteristics are: unproportionally large head, head with angular form, large lower jaw, large chin, jutting corners of jaw, incorrect or malformed shape of nose or ear, deformation of front teeth, abnormal (improper) bite. Children with a short and broad neck are contraindicated for admission. Children with inordinately long necks or a protruding Adam's apple are also not for the stage.' And so on, ten terse, typed pages of material only likely to hearten someone already crazed from Nazi eugenics.

Lidochka, however, turned out to be perfection—proportion of height standing to height sitting, length of neck, thinness of ankles and wrists—and it was as if everything about her was completely made for ballet, which tolerates no imperfection, even in the small things. Lidochka bent wonderfully in all directions, raised her little foot forward, back, and to the side with ease as she displayed wonderful extension, briskly drummed out a little polka on the floor, neither overwhelming nor ruining one single light note. Musicality, dance sense, rhythm, and physical health, everything was tops.

The only thing that disturbed the pedagogues a bit was that the skinny, dark-skinned little girl in the shiny white panties didn't even attempt to make them like her. All the others had groveled, crawled on their bellies, and grinned with jackal-like little faces to simulate sweet smiles. They gazed slave-like into eyes, prepared in advance to do anything—and even more—for the sake of ballet. Anything that others desired. But Lidochka just looked gloomily off to the side, not even seeming particularly happy about her undeniable success. The commission put their laurelled ballet heads together to confer and decided she must just be stupid. Stupid was very apropos in ballet. Stupid, that was good.

By the time she was almost fourteen, Lidochka had definitively acquired the status of best student at the school and learned to mechanically react with a smile to even the worst pain. Smiling was what was expected: a ballerina needed to control her face and do something beautiful for the public so that even the weakest-sighted provincial in the third row of the balcony could recognize all the sweet, fortunate completeness and fullness that comes from contact with Beauty. It also became obvious at about that same age that Lidochka had another very rare talent that went beyond her undeniable and even frightening physical gifts: she turned out to be an ideal victim.

Psychologists, psychiatrists, and criminologists have all expounded cluelessly and at length on the nature of victimhood, talking rubbish, as is so often wont to happen, and piling up lots of short skirts, loose morals, atrocious upbringings, and congenital character weaknesses. None of that applied in the slightest to Lidochka, who was as strong-willed and well-schooled as a show poodle: anyone has the right to hike up its stubby, cropped tail and feel its anal glands. Lidochka had muscles of steel and her nerves were exactly the same; she didn't wear pathetic clothes that were see-through, skimpy, or likely to evoke pathetic desires; and when she was outside she didn't toss around the come-hither looks of a pubertarian rendered stupid by her own hormones. She barely looked up, preferring to gaze at the spat-on asphalt that quickly and smoothly slid by under her small but already professionally turned-out feet. Still, if there was just one abnormal, drunk, or simply broken-hearted person in the region, he was quickly drawn to Lidochka by some strange, gloomy power that was insurmountable, both for him and, even more so, for Lidochka. They were dejected, pathetic, and tenacious as they mumbled their insufferable stories, aggressively demanding attention and sympathy, and begging, too: Lidochka could never keep money in her wallet, though even she didn't suspect she gave from fear rather than compassion.

Of course Lidochka's victimhood came in part from a unique combination of outer attractiveness and an inner softness that was a sort of unrecognized rejection of evolution, when a living being voluntarily chooses self-destruction rather than fight or flight. That, however, wasn't the main thing:

Lazar Lindt's fourteen-year-old granddaughter actually possessed the innate and rare ability to see the world's other side, that dreary, seamy side that's usually only noticed by priests and, of course, doctors, and only after many long years of work. To be sure, priests and doctors can usually at least do something for the unfortunate people that life endlessly sends their way, but Lidochka was forced to just watch. Just watch. Not spurning, not covering her eyes, and not resisting. She couldn't help anyone but she SAW the pain of others, saw it without flinching, tightly squeezing her eyes shut, or even trying to step away. As befits the ideal victim, Lidochka considered herself obligated to do anything that people around her needed, even if she found it unpleasant or even disgusting. Ballet taught her that. And that was ballet. Lidochka Lindt's ballet. Her individual calling.

It was especially difficult to see old people that nobody but Lidochka seemed to notice. In 1996 Ensk, elderly people who'd once built a great country were now indigent and alone, and they'd nearly gone out of their minds rummaging around in the country's wreckage, like Job among the ashes. Because Lidochka had submitted to her own morbid gift, she didn't notice the abundance of glowing shop windows that filled Ensk or the slick foreign cars or the colorful clothes gussying up city dwellers that youthful Russian capitalism had suddenly transformed into a horde of deceptively amiable and entrepreneurial bastards capable of anything. There was a blossoming world of young, healthy, and audacious people all around Lidochka but she—who was also young and healthy, not to mention provided for beyond all possible demands thanks to Galina Petrovna, who was wealthy under any political system—noticed only wrinkles and tatters.

The old between-season coat from the seventies on an elderly woman digging around in a garbage bin, an old man wearing strips of medals and decorations that stuck out sharply when he knocked coins around his calloused, shaking palm, hoping he could save money on something, No, there's not enough, eh... Then beat it, gramps, why're you hanging around in the road! Lidochka stuck paper money that wouldn't change anything into the old man's pocket and watched powerlessly, following his stooped, woeful, and helpless back. Elderly poverty was frightening, it was the most frightening poverty on earth, something nobody needed: meek eyes puffed with whitish gunk, gaps in toothless mouths, holes on sweaters mended by disobedient fingers, shameful crooked patches on clothing. And good Lord, how Lidochka feared those old people, how she feared old age itself, something unavoidable and horrible, more horrible than death itself, which seemed like a long-awaited and hard-won relief after that humiliating, decrepit powerlessness. It was a strange and difficult fear because Lidochka didn't know any old people other than the wretched people, all strangers to her, she saw on the street. Everybody around her—Galina Petrovna, girlfriends from school, pedagogues, even Mama and Papa, even Mama's mother and father, and Lazar Iosifovich Lindt in the photo in the office, all soot-black and phosphoric white—was young, strong, and immortal, as if they were here forever, even if they were long dead. But the fear grew stronger and sharper instead of leaving, and there was no salvation from her intolerable fear of old age, just as there was no salvation from classical dance.

Maybe, Lidochka timidly thought, just maybe, if she had a home... her own home, filled with warmth and children. Maybe things would be a little easier then? Fence herself away from old age, make old age livable, care for grandchildren, take out the garbage with a grunt, and help so at least someone would need her right down to the last second. At least do something. At least embrace someone. She'd come to love walking to the square near the school: graced with a sandbox and a wooden slide, the little park was a cloister of carefree motherhood. Restless pigeons, sedate moms taking their babbling tots for walks... Lidochka sat for hours on a bench, sating her eyes and ears, and trying on for herself someone else's ripe unhurried pregnancy or cute little toddler, or mentally borrowing some gawking mom's manner of calling her child over without interrupting her jabber with the other moms, then quickly and agilely wiping the child's completely dry little nose or straightening his jacket, all to show herself and everyone else that's her own child, her very own, a relation, even if she's deathly tired of him. Lidochka wanted to have something of her own, too. That was redemption. She knew this for sure. No, she believed it, which was much stronger.

Even the old people at the square weren't so scary—placid grandmothers and grandfathers surrounded by love that saved them—but everything ended ruthlessly, irrevocably, and instantly, as was usual in Lidochka's life. An unfamiliar, ugly, and unwanted old man sat down on the bench next to her, taking three laborious moves to do so and then taking so much time and agony to get something out of his pocket that Lidochka even jolted as if to help him but no, he did it himself, thank God, all by himself. He pulled out some sort of paper, smoothed it with gnarled fingers, broken nails, and the fusty whiff of unkempt, unloved, aged flesh. The old man read the paper—apparently something official because some kind of purple stamp flashed, there was a sweeping indifferent signature, and the computerized letters were as even as grain—and then he sat for a long, long time, bristling like a sick pigeon except that silent, cloudy tears flowed out from under his wrinkled red eyelids. Then he sighed, firmly wiped his face with his palms, and bitterly said to himself, And there's what your own children will do. Lidochka kept watching the poor old man even as he was walking away, wondering what his children had done to him. Taken his apartment? Sent him to a nursing home? Moved away to America forever? Maybe they'd just died, suddenly and unscrupulously leaving him totally, absolutely alone?

She stopped going to the square: she was afraid of seeing the old man again and afraid to admit to herself that the children and grandchildren she dreamed about so desperately and so specifically weren't at all required to love her back. The funny round tots at the playground weren't a guarantee of avoiding either a lonely old age or death. They weren't a pension fund and they weren't a long-term, high-interest deposit account you can add money to. They were just children, independent people with no other purpose. This was the truth and reconciling with it essentially meant losing everything, and Lidochka wasn't ready for that. She was already forced to lose far too much in 1997.

Lyusya Zhukova was expelled at the end of the school year: she wasn't even allowed to continue into her next and final year so she could at least feel like a graduate for a while. No, they tossed her out, not even waiting for exams, all because, well, sweetie pie, if you want to dance you have no business lying around the sick ward with pneumonia for a month and a half. Ballerinas don't get sick and if they're sick they don't miss classes and if they miss then they study on their own, oh, the doctor forbid any stress?! Your problem, dearie. They always began using the formal 'you' at the school when they crossed someone off the list of the living. Lyusya didn't even try to contest it: she was as pale as a maggot, looked horrible from her desperation, and was still fighting the weakness of pneumonia. Why bother? It didn't concern anyone that she'd contracted pneumonia in a classroom icy-cold from drafts, where she'd been working for hours at a time on the *grand pas de chat*, a giant cat leap that just wouldn't come. Her legs came up higher than ninety degrees, her arms fell out of third position, and her torso bent backwards. Boom. Another near-failing grade.

Lidochka had faithfully done her feline duty for her best friend, faithfully going to see her at the sick ward and reading Molokhovets, just sitting a while on the institutional flannel coverlet and swinging her legs consolingly. She also made the rounds of all the pedagogues, begging and promising to give Lyusya a helping hand (or at least a leg up!), but it was all for nothing. The director, whom Lidochka visited by appointment, like an adult, was also implacable: the school doesn't need mediocrities. And you, Lindt, why waste your time on dead weight like this, you'd be better off going to rehearse. Or don't you understand the responsibility you have? Lidochka understood. As soon as she began her last year of school, she, at seventeen, would dance the first Giselle of her life at the Ensk theater on a real grownup stage, an unheard-of, rare opportunity bestowed only on future primas. Giselle was an honor. Get to work, the director summed up, and the obedient and steadfast Lidochka turned and left, like a tin soldier.

Lyusya was taken home by her mother, a fat village woman from a horrible rusty factory city in the Southern Urals where people had no greater joy than getting shitfaced into total oblivion from the day they were born. 'Just don't you wail. You'll graduate from a normal school and I'll get you a job in ac-coun-ting,' she went on, bundling up Lyusya's things, her eyes shooting around the room so as not to forget anything important and useful for the household. 'Flapping naked legs around! It's a disgrace, anyway, not an occupation.' Lyusya sat on the edge of a chair as straight as a stick, not wailing, just mechanically, out of habit, flexing feet nobody needed anymore. Lidochka sat down next to her and rubbed her nose on her girlfriend's skinny shoulder as she always did when she wanted to be affectionate: they'd cried so much together, revealed so many funny childish secrets that were especially frightful because they were childish, laughed so much, muffled, after lights out, daydreamed so much, fallen asleep together in one bed, lean, chilly, small, and only ever finding a drop of compassion and warmth in each other. I'll come visit you for all the vacations. And I'll write every, every single day, Lidochka promised as passionately and bitterly as if she were making an oath. Lyusya jolted as if she'd just been woken up and looked at Lidochka with dry eyes that appeared almost hot. 'You can stick your letters up your ass, you idiot!' she suddenly shouted so loudly her mother dropped a bundle that gasped dully as it hit the floor. 'I hate you, I always hated you! Idiot! Rat! Crooked-legged freak! Stinker!' Her mother crossed herself, shrugged it off, and gloomily said, 'Don't waste your nerves, honey. It's not worth it. Don't let it get to you, let's go home.'

Lidochka was all alone after Lyusya left. All she got in memory of her best friend was sole use of the dorm room (tribute to a queen, plus yet another financial tranche from

Galina Petrovna) as well as a new habit of taking a scalding, wheezy, long shower whenever it was convenient. The word 'stinker,' however, remained, along with a smell of sweat that was elusive, unseen, and intangible to everyone except Lidochka: everyone stank in ballet. Absolutely everyone.

The summer vacation before her final year felt especially long to Lidochka. She stayed in the dorm with Galina Petrovna's tacit approval: they saw less and less of one other and, odd though that sounds, they almost completely reconciled as a result. Lidochka went to visit Lindt's apartment every other weekend like clockwork and found some nice bauble in her room each time: a fluffy new sweater in a package as crackly as ice, a music player that looked like a portable cobblestone smoothed by the sea, and even the most difficult-to-find Grishko pointe shoes ordered from New York. Galina Petrovna had always been best of all with relationships built on commodities and money; she supplied Lidochka with pocket money every month, never asking for a spending report, and showed accurate bank statements testifying to the impeccable condition of Lidochka's accounts. The bank had recently become Galina Petrovna's property so Papa's hundred monthly rubles had been converted into conditional currency units that were just as conditional as her father's congratulatory telegrams, which had become just as infrequent as Lidochka's questions about him.

By the time she was almost seventeen, Lidochka had reconciled herself with being a total orphan.

Lidochka could be grateful, too: Galina Petrovna had no difficulties with her and could even be proud of her, when she got the urge. Galina Petrovna didn't have any real urge, however, and was just as painfully and passionately enthralled by business as she'd once been with used books and antiques. She didn't even come to the school for the final shows where Lidochka always soloed with the same steady, indifferent, and magnificent brilliance that differentiates a genuine diamond from a simple faceted crystal.

Lidochka spent endless summer weeks in endless rehearsals and endless wandering around the city: she got to know Ensk in the finest detail for the first time during that vacation. Around that corner there's a bench where you can have a rest, and over there, among those broken, pissed-on ninebark bushes, there's a small plaster bust of Lenin languishing in exile, daubed with paint and mutilated by teenagers to total unrecognizability, which made it seem completely human and alive. At first, Lidochka roamed the streets completely aimlessly, but then she snooped around a beautiful old front-yard garden on the outskirts with its fence painted a lemony color—audaciously and not in a northern way—and mentally laid a paved road to it from a another part of town entirely, adding a huge crimson maple she'd only ever seen in a magazine photo.

This game turned out to be ridiculously interesting, so Lidochka began deliberately taking walks: now she was inventing and assembling her ideal home.

Absolutely everything was important: color, light, stone texture, the shape of the roof, even the smells. Especially the smells! When she was searching for the aroma she needed for the entryway (floor polish, wood, and a little vanilla), Lidochka somehow wandered into a little grove of late-Soviet apartment buildings that looked like broken macaroni. She suddenly stopped in the middle of the yard. The crooked carousel for children squeaked mournfully and rustily, and the birches might have grown but they were still the same, the left one's crooked like a squiggle, Mamochka had said. Lidochka sat on a bench and felt her chest for a nonexistent key on a ribbon that had been thrown away long ago and quickly mumbled, just like when she was little, something that turned out to have set in her head for the ages: Usievich Street, No. 14, Apt. 128. It was her old yard. The building where Mamochka and Papa's apartment still was. It was absolutely unbelievable she hadn't thought of coming here herself.

Lidochka went into the entryway, which remembered her as a five-year-old: tap-tap, little legs, an elevator that was often shut off, stairs that seemed high and endless, unforgotten sagging paint on the railings, unforgotten and unforgettable smells and lights. It's the sixth floor, you'll get tired. How about a piggyback ride? Papa scooched down, all ready, and presented his neck but Lidochka wasn't tempted by the opportunity to pull on his ears, (Steering left! And now steering right!), so she stubbornly rushed up all by herself. Mamochka always said, you have to do everything yourself. As if it were a prophesy. Of the Black Sea.

Lidochka stopped in front of the door; at one time she'd barely even reached the handle but now, there you have it, here she is and it turns out even the doorbell Papa had to lift her for back then—all laughing, her legs squirming—wasn't so high, either. Lidochka raised her arm, intending to ring, but the elevator's mechanical bones rumbled next to her and she hurried off down the stairs, two at a time.

She came back the next day, not even knowing why herself, and then the next day, and the day after, too. She'd sit for a long time on the windowsill in the stairwell, hugging her knees and not thinking about anything, just sensing that even if her parents themselves weren't right there with her, at least their apartment was. It was a pleasant, even cozy, feeling that people often experience in a cemetery long after they've come to terms with a loss, even a formidable loss. It's probably just like coming to terms with an amputation or hopeless infertility by beginning to find a quiet pleasure in the absence of a leg or children, something few others understand. Galina Petrovna didn't go to the cemetery herself, though, and she didn't bring Lidochka there, so this feeling was new and so strange for Lidochka that she wasn't even surprised when one fine day the door to her parents' apartment slowly and suddenly opened a little then immediately closed again with a sharp squeak. Lidochka calmed herself, thinking she'd imagined it but then the door opened a little again after a few minutes of tense mutual expectation. Two perplexed little children's faces—a girl and a boy—appeared in the doorway instead of ghosts from the past.

'Who are you, auntie?' the boy asked. Judging by his voice and nose, he was no older than about ten. Lidochka jumped off the windowsill, not knowing what to say.

'I... I...,' she said, flustered. 'I live here. I mean, I lived here. A long time ago.'

The boy and girl looked at each other and the girl confidently handed down her judgment. 'We live here, auntie. You go away. Or we'll call the police.'

'You are so stupid.' The boy was upset. Judging from the noise behind the door, he'd cuffed the girl on the back of her neck. 'You can't talk to grownups that way. And how is she your aunt anyway? Our aunt is Alya and she lives in Biisk, we go see her every summer.'

The last sentence was obviously an invitation to dialogue

and Lidochka had to admit she'd never been to Biisk and she didn't have an aunt, either Alya or anyone else. The little boy, as a man should, felt his superiority and quickly grew kinder and more lenient. He opened the door a little wider and bragged as he jingled the security chain, 'And our father's a candidate of sciences! And Mama's going to be, too. How about that!'

'Well, my mother died,' Lidochka unexpectedly said, admitting it and, oddly, hardly feeling any pain about it for the first time in her life. It was simply a fact. A fact in her biography. The children looked at each other again.

'What about your father?' the girl asked, very seriously.

'Papa...'

Lidochka thought for a moment then realized she couldn't even explain the story about the cards and telegrams to herself. 'I don't have a father, either,' she said. 'For a long time now. I hardly remember him or my mother.'

The boy slammed the door hard, as if he'd struck Lidochka in the face, and of course that was the right thing to do. What an idiot, she'd found just the thing to talk about with little children! For the many-thousandth time, as was her habit, Lidochka took all the blame for what happened, then she brushed off her jeans and slowly walked down the stairs. She'd visited the past and that was enough. It was time to rehearse, work, stretch her muscles, repeat the same movement over and over hundreds of times. The paradox was that one could become a great scholar, fabulous composer, or major writer. But you couldn't become a great ballerina. You could only be one, fatiguing yourself every day with the exact same barre exercises that even the most awkward and ridiculous little beginners do. It was just that Lidochka really didn't want to either become or be a ballerina. Not a great ballerina or an ordinary ballerina. She wanted to have a home. A home and children. And nothing else.

The little boy didn't catch up to her until the third floor. He was dark-haired and skinny, with the very straight shoulders of a future officer.

'Here,' he said, catching his breath and holding half a loaf of bread out to Lidochka. 'Take it. You're probably hungry since your mother…' He wanted to say 'died' but couldn't and guiltily added, 'We have potatoes, too, but they're raw.'

Lidochka took the bread and sniffed the soft, aromatic flesh.

'Thank you,' she said. 'Thank you, really. Are the potatoes red or yellow?'

'I don't know,' the boy said, surprised. 'What's the difference?'

'A big difference,' Lidochka said. 'If they're red, you can cook them with sour cream, there are two ways. If they're yellow they're good for dumplings. Have you ever had potato dumplings?'

The potatoes turned out to be neither red nor yellow, just disgusting, all covered with eyes and pale sprouts, plus there wasn't sour cream, flour, or even eggs in the house, though there were a few little carrots and as many expired spices in old-fashioned paper packets as anyone might want.

'It won't work, will it?' asked the disappointed girl, who'd turned out to be very quick and very ugly. But of course everything worked for them.

When the Tsarevs came home from their scientific research institute at around six that evening, they found nearly authentic Italian bruschetta with rosemary, excellent tea, boiled potatoes with a surprisingly orange color and a flavor reminiscent of a real pastry, and Lidochka, who'd gotten ten-year-old Romka and six-year-old Veronichka to fall irrevocably in love with her within a couple hours.

'This is absolutely incredible!' Mr. Tsarev mumbled, stuffing a whole potato into his mouth at once and waving his hands in delight. 'How did you make this, Lida?'

'It's very simple,' Lidochka said, flustered, 'you have to boil them in the skin and put one carrot, one onion, and a couple allspice berries in the water right away...'

Mrs. Tsareva quickly grasped her by the arm, how many berries, and when do you salt it, and so that's all? Really? No, Volodya, no, what are you doing, like a little boy? At least leave a bit for the children!

The next day Lidochka came to the Tsarevs' and brought two huge bags filled with groceries that Molokhovets herself would have envied. By the end of vacation, hardly any recipes from *Gift to a Young Housewife*, which Lidochka knew by heart, remained untried. Lidochka's hands turned out to be just as talented as her feet and her inner cook overshadowed the ballerina ever more confidently. The Tsarevs—who were absentminded and destitute, as befits science's martyrs—gained weight, had pinker cheeks, and even took on an oily sheen, like yeasty *bliny*. But Lidochka herself, who secretly dreamed expulsion would save her from school, didn't gain a gram: she'd inherited Lindt's insane metabolism, with a gluttonous cellular furnace that could instantly incinerate a hundred *pelmeny*. During breaks between culinary research projects, Lidochka, Veronichka, and Romka eagerly learned macramé and embroidery using good-natured and confusing recommendations from old issues of women's magazines. The elder Tsarevs couldn't have been happier, though they—tempered by Soviet upbringing and an innate optimism—were happy about anything that didn't kill them. And killing these tight-knit, cheerful, and unpretentious people wouldn't have been easy, just as it's not easy to kill people who really, truly have faith in something with all their hearts.

The Tsarevs had believed in the Soviet government's power their whole lives. Not in real Soviet power, of course, but in the ideal, book-based, and correct Soviet power that should (at least in theory) have compensated everyone according to his work, after first pumping out all his abilities. The Tsarevs fulfilled their side of the bargain honestly and didn't begrudge their hands or brains, so the humiliating lines and shortages of everything from children's tights to subscriptions for volumes of Dostoyevsky galled them. They despised the real, daily, here-it-is Soviet power just as you despise a mother who drinks a lot and tries to act younger: she's impossible and pathetic, but she's still yours. Of course that's just another of love's variations.

The Tsarevs thought that if the Soviet people were to exert certain additional efforts—burying Lenin, forgetting Stalin, or allowing Solzhenitsyn back—then everything would somehow magically change and crystal-clear rays of happiness would begin sparkling for everyone. They wanted to improve without toppling, leaving what's good from the old and adding the best from the new. They believed Soviet power was completely compatible with democracy, like an abundance of tanks with a surplus of toilet paper, and that freedom of speech… Well, excuse me, but that's already written in the Constitution. The Tsarevs diligently devoured all the dissident manuscripts and banned books they could get their hands on and were even more naively surprised about why the books were banned; they also listened to crackly, hoarse radio voices of America, Stockholm, and London, and criticized the party and the government in whispers, with a shot of vodka. Despite all that, in essence they remained completely Soviet people.

They were wonderful, these Tsarevs: honest, hard-working, kind, completely ordinary people. There were millions of these Tsarevs and they were the best of what Soviet power had managed to accomplish in all its years of existence. Everything else, including missiles, lathes, and ballet, was breaking, aging morally, falling to pieces, and not meeting the expectations entrusted in them. But people stayed the same. People. When perestroika finally burst in, the Tsarevs, like everyone else, were as happy as children jumping in front of a door where there's a celebration and a decorated tree on the other side. They got addicted to Korotich and his magazine *Ogonyok* like heroin junkies, trudged off to protests and barricades, voted, adored Yeltsin, applauded Sakharov, and even nestled up against each other after they went to bed at night to debate in passionate whispers about what would happen tomorrow...

'Tomorrow' it turned out the Soviet power the Tsarevs had so frantically wanted to change had been the only truly happy and stable thing in their lives. Halcyon childhood and free education, a blue quartz lamp in a nice new clinic and a matinee about Chapayev. Student construction battalion songs, pastries for twenty-two kopecks, and sticky-sweet port wine for two rubles twenty kopecks (you could redeem the empty bottle for seventeen kopecks!), advances and salaries, a bonus, belief in equality and brotherhood, and a happy life that unfurled before them like a silk rug, a life filled with the wonderful milestones and habitual rituals that make human happiness possible. A May Day demonstration everyone shirks, but then the drinks and food go down marvelously afterward at someone's loud house party; a trip to the Eternal Flame for May Ninth, the Victory Parade, and watching TV in the evening: Iosif Kobson crooning and a concert that blends wonderfully with the Beatles and Stones living in the tape player; the underground *Cancer Ward* and the pulpy Maurice Druon, procured with equal effort and read with equal pleasure. Strong army, kind police, cold hands, warm heart, sober head. It's too bad it all collapsed. It's too bad we will never, ever be young again.

In the end, Soviet power gave the Tsarevs each other: they met back when they were students and they'd already married by the end of their first year at the institute. Young engineers, young arguments, young and awkward sex, dorm, wedding, grad school, floating in kayaks every summer, mosquitoes, the most delicious tea drunk from a meat tin with pine needles and little dots of golden grease, and two children. They were perfectly happy together, these Tsarevs: Elenochka Romanovna was a round, dishy woman easily amused, and Vladimir Sergeyevich was as skinny, cheery, and woolly as a Yeti but with huge early bald spots over his animated wrinkled forehead. Only negligent and wanton mothers have children this lucky. Soviet power was negligent. Even after shamelessly abandoning the Tsarevs forever without looking back, they never stopped being good people. And they never stopped believing that was right.

They took to Lidochka with the very same happy geniality they took to everything life sent them or their children dragged home: kin from the provinces, guests who stayed too late, chickenpox, or a pigeon with a broken foot. At first Lidochka decided to keep her visits to the Tsarevs a secret, not because she wanted to conceal something, but simply because most of her life was obviously of no interest to Galina Petrovna. But then too many questions and too many revelations came up, and Lidochka voluntarily missed an outing with Romka and Veronichka to make an unplanned visit to the widowed empress.

'You pregnant? Sick?' Galina Petrovna quickly asked, applying lipstick at the mirror. She was always hurrying lately, there was no time for life, life was interesting, business demanded fast-paced decisions, and fast-paced decisions demanded big money: one thing attracted another, just like the children's toy where the little wooden man and the little wooden bear take turns knocking fake little axes on a little anvil.

It turned out Lidochka was healthy and not pregnant. Meaning, as they say, thank God. What else do you need? You need money? Take what's on the table.

'I wanted to ask about the apartment,' Lidochka quietly said, used to not raising her voice at Galina Petrovna's.

'About what apartment?'

'Oh, the one where I lived with Mama and Papa. When they, when I...' Lidochka stumbled on her words like a cripple who doesn't know the right name for his own injury. To say it honestly and directly, or so other people can bear to hear it.

'Safe and sound, it's still standing,' Galina Petrovna said, putting an earring with a dangerously spiky diamond of a very rare, cognac color into a round earlobe that hadn't aged an instant. 'Why do you ask?'

Lidochka stumbled on her words again: she always felt particularly ungainly and stupid in Galina Petrovna's presence.

This was the same place where fear and being in love come in such close contact they could hardly be distinguished from one other.

'I was there, well, I just went to look in, and…'

'Ah, so you met the tenants. The what-are-their-names? I don't remember. Utter idiots. But they're paying promptly for now. Were they rude to you or something? Just say so. We'll find someone new.'

Lidochka began shaking her head, 'No. They weren't rude. But that apartment, whose is it?'

Galina Petrovna began laughing, 'So you somehow got smarter? That's commendable. It's your apartment, yours. Don't worry. It's privatized, registered in your name, and the money they pay is put in your account, you can use it when you turn eighteen. And move then, too. Or are you intending to settle on my neck and leech off me your whole life? I wouldn't have that if you paid me.'

Lidochka nodded. Galina Petrovna's neck didn't seem to her like a very convenient place, either, even if it was still beautiful and adorned with a strand of select Tahitian pearls. Lidochka's audience was finished; there was no point in asking about financial relief for the Tsarevs. As revenge, Lidochka stopped even going to see her grandmother every other weekend, a needless effort nobody noticed. Galina Petrovna knew perfectly well that bad news travels fast so she'd be notified quickly if anything untoward happened; if everything was okay, there was no reason to worry. She didn't have to come if she didn't want. And Lidochka didn't want to. She liked it at the Tsarevs', paradoxical as it may sound, precisely because they were absentminded and happy and had driven the ghosts out of the house. Nobody and nothing in the old apartment reminded

Lidochka of her parents anymore. That was surprising and untroubling.

But the children were the main thing. Romka and Veronichka. They made messes and argued, asked impossible questions and didn't obey, spilled flour, stained their clothes, banged their knees, listened with mouths agape, and interrupted every other word. Being with them wasn't easy, but being without them turned out to be totally impossible. Every time Lidochka showed up at the door, Veronichka's ugly little face and Romka's unbelievably correct features, which seemed to mock his sister, flashed with such selfless gushing joy that Lidochka couldn't believe she herself was the reason for the joy.

Everything, including the weather, went bad and got more complicated when the new school year started. Lidochka was again busy from morning until she collapsed, and then there were *Giselle* rehearsals, an empty dorm room, and an Ensk autumn that was icy, damp, and filled with lingering sinus troubles and embittered pedestrians. Romka and Veronichka were trapped at school, too, and life from Monday through Friday would have lost all meaning if daydreaming about a home hadn't occupied all Lidochka's mental and inner energies. She spent the weekends with the Tsarevs, as before. And she didn't even notice she hadn't seen Galina Petrovna for at least two months.

Before classical dance class, Lidochka was lingering in the hell that was the school hallway. If she'd closed her eyes, she would have heard the usual school din—totally childish, noisy, and joyful—but you couldn't fool Lidochka, who was frozen still next to a windowsill (outside there was a sourish sky and a gimpy maple as raggedy and water-logged as a city beggar; September in Ensk was more hopeless than any November in the middle latitudes) with a warm rehearsal jersey stretched over her shoulders. She knew all she had to do was turn around and the din would disappear and dissolve into ballet's harsh speechlessness: there's a big-eared second-year student over there by the wall doing a split right on the floor, stretching her little tendons one by one, simultaneously clutching a geometry textbook in her little paws, her soundless lips moving because you can be kicked out for things other than a poor extension.

And there's the unwieldy Ksyusha, leggy, big-boned, and struggling with her turnout, they'll boot her out even before it's clear no torture could remake her hip socket: she'll be booted out just because she'll grow to unliftable dimensions and no male dancer could possibly figure out even the simplest support for this lanky girl. But Lidochka's hip socket is impeccable: Lidochka's hip joint turns as if she had the double-jointed frame of a forest elf under her skin instead of human ligaments. No, Lidochka hurts, too, like everyone else sentenced to a life in ballet, but at least her pain has a visible result. Phenomenal physical qualifications, say the teachers, shaking their heads, are a precious rarity, a future prima, no doubt about it! Lidochka will never be kicked out. They'll never set her free.

She has a God-given talent.

Never in her life did she ask God for any gifts.

Lidochka watches as the wind first rudely pulls at the maple outside the window by the arm, then cuffs the tree on the nape of the neck as if it were moralizing to a disobedient teenager who's pressed, immobilized, between two unyielding knees.

Give me a full answer! The maple turns away from yet another jab and looks to the side, as if persecuted and searching out a suitable alleyway for escape. You can't get away, whispers the sympathetic Lidochka, as she mechanically stretches one calf muscle after another under woolen leggings, warming up before classical. How many more of these classes does she have left?

Lidochka made an honest attempt to count but lost track somewhere around one hundred, sped up her mental pace, and then finally ran off, one hand tightening her rehearsal jersey over her chest, the other deflecting from her face taut branches of pale-leafed shrubs she'd not yet invented or fully thought through.

The house hadn't gone anywhere: it was standing on a little hill and this time it was made of bricks deliciously baked a reddish-brown. Lidochka pondered and the bricks obediently lightened as she bit her bottom lip like an owner, transforming them into sawed pieces of coquina limestone, all porous and cheery as sugar. Lidochka walked up to the door—was it light? dark? light? fine, let it be dark walnut—plus two curved lamps with cast-iron shades and a doorbell that gazed at visitors with a welcoming but rather silly pearlescent button.

Lidochka rushed through the entryway, squeezing her eyes shut—it still wasn't even clear if the entryway was large or small, but that was for later, now I'll definitely think something up for next time!—and didn't open her eyes until she was in the huge kitchen she adored and had nearly fully furnished, right down to shining brass and copper gadgets, all lovingly polished clean. Lidochka hurriedly counted the earthenware cups again—I forgot everything on the table last time!—three, four, six, and then next to them there's an earthenware pitcher the color of rough terra cotta, too, and it's almost unsightly but totally wonderful, retaining the unknown potter's fingerprints on its uneven sides. Milk will always stay cold in crockery like that, even in the fiercest heat wave.

Everything in the kitchen had stayed the same, thank God. Sunny sighing curtains. A huge cooktop. Underfoot was a rough wooden country floor soaked with summer, and a little mouse as light and transparent as a house spirit's shadow will crawl out of that little hole under the baseboard. Lidochka will never forget to leave the mouse a small but properly served dinner by the table leg: a couple little slices of cheese and a heel of bread on a soft paper napkin. Mice should, without a doubt, live in the house because the children would sleep poorly without them quietly crunching on dried bread, and there would be cats, too, a whole pack of independent and stealthy colorful cats who'd become one breedless lump long ago because of their tangled, forgotten bloodlines.

And there should definitely be a dog, too, a huge outdoor dog, and whenever there's rain or snow everybody will convince each other at dinner that the dog is very warm and comfortable in her roomy doghouse filled with hay. And then, after all the lamps and nightlights have gone out, one by one in all the rooms, Lidochka will put the last plate, wiped until it squeaks, in the buffet and go to the door to sneakily let the dog in. And she'll smile when she hears the flustered and cheerful knock of a dog tail in the darkness: someone had already taken the trouble before Lidochka. Children's hearts grow faster than the children themselves when there are lots of animals in the house but oh, children, children why are you in such a hurry?! Toward spring they'll buy new shoes again for everyone, there'll be cheerful arguments again over the cardboard boxes, indignant shrieks from the youngest, and rustling soft, wrinkled paper mixed with the strong scent of black rubber heels and unworn leather. Lidochka saw every squiggle on the soles and sensed the warmth of every felt insole but then the children's faces darkened and faded, and the children were nothing but birdlike voices, a close and affectionate squawk, and her husband had remained completely unseen and Lidochka could only catch the warm movement of agitated air, no matter how much she hurried around the rooms. It was as if someone had drawn open an invisible drape and popped Lidochka in the face with a heavy stream woven from scents, from scents… Lidochka felt lost, not knowing how her husband would smell and not understanding what she could call out to him. 'Sweetie?' she asked as she stood, lost, on the threshold of an empty, floating, and unsteady room as a whole series of similarly vague expanses streamed in front of her: it was as if someone had dropped a strand of vibrating, flowing beads on the bottom of a stream. The house, so firm and so real, began to darken and lose its physical outlines, and then Lidochka guiltily squeezed her eyes shut, returning to the kitchen she'd dreamed about most, more often than anything, as if it were the meaning and light of her future life.

She caught her breath in the kitchen and set the table for tea—teaspoons in the upper right-hand drawer, ramekins for the preserves in the buffet, on the left-hand side—and quietly promised herself not to hurry anymore, not to chase ghosts or rush them to show themselves in the flesh. You shouldn't rush anyway: strength is in the ability to give yourself over to particulars and life is, well, life is made up of little things. And only by gathering those little things into one unbroken pattern, only by smoothly locking one detail in with another can you hope that a house will someday transform itself from an endless stream of imagination into the realest truth.

Which is why it was so important not to make mistakes with the details. Lidochka, for example, knew absolutely for sure that she would certainly serve something home-baked with tea: cream puffs, almond cookies, or, at the very least, a mazurka cake, the one Molokhovets simply called 'very tasty.' Lidochka, who'd memorized the cherished volume long ago, quickly mumbled the recipe like a prayer, beat a half pound of butter until it's white, add a half pound of sugar, six egg yolks, a quarter cup of bitter and a quarter cup of sweet ground almonds, six beaten egg whites, and a half pound of flour, pour into a flat, buttered paper pan, and bake.

'Don't take the mazurka off the paper until it's cooled,' Marusya sternly cautioned, and right then and there, in a softer tone, she advised, 'Can be glazed on the top or decorated if desired, or sprinkled with cinnamon, sugar, or almonds.' Lidochka obediently nodded: she had no idea how bitter and sweet almonds differed but that wasn't important. The only important thing was the warm aroma of batter permeating the kitchen and children happily and furiously bustling around the table for the right to be the first to take the mazurka out from under the towel. But then the children faded again, first looking like Romka, then like Veronichka, then like strangers' children who were very wonderful but still someone else's, and Lidochka sighed, realizing something wasn't right today, which meant it was time to get ready to go back to a real life that felt less and less real to Lidochka than the house with every passing day.

'But you're real to me,' she said to the dog, 'You understand that, right, Naida?' And Naida knocked her thick woolly tail on the floor in agreement and shyly started to smile again. Lidochka bent to scratch the dog behind a soft, warm ear and took such a hard blow under the ribs that she flew out of her daydream without even having the chance to drink her tea, walk through the rooms, or see if the big old-fashioned pink silk lampshade with the insufferable, touching, and marvelously bourgeois fringe would go well on the glassed-in porch.

The school hadn't gone anywhere. There were even a couple minutes, quivery from tension, left before the bell—like all slaves of daily routine it had been a long time since Lidochka needed a watch to know that. There was no reason whatsoever to run and push. Nevertheless, a scrawny, ungainly little first-year didn't just shove Lidochka in the side with all her strength, she actually stepped hard on her foot—her foot!—the precious foot of the school's best female student, a foot that was small, firm, and maimed as if it belonged to a Little Mermaid that an evil, impotent storyteller had forced to walk on knife edges for years. No love involved, just for his own feeble enjoyment.

During breaks, the ballet dancers could push and shove, jump like goats, play regular children's tag, and even fight. But feet, well, feet were sacred, a tool for work, something only an insanely envious competitor would dare encroach on. The tricks here were floors rubbed with something slippery (go on, witch, break your neck!) or ground glass in the pointe shoes, and this wasn't some anecdotal glass but real, true light bulbs ground into the finest powdery dust. One diagonal pass across the stage and living human toes are transformed into wet, bloody little cushions for invisible pins. Once was all it took for Lidochka to acquire the permanent habit of feeling inside her ballet slippers with a split-second palpitating motion that was almost medical. She began checking all her shoes just as mechanically and carefully: slippers, shoes with embryonically tiny heels (so as not to overwork worn-out legs), and big fur boots that looked like ungainly puppies.

Lidochka grabbed the first-year by her hot, transparent ear and jerked it discernibly but not too hard, as punishment. That was completely ineffective, however, because the other girl didn't notice anything, neither the princess's crushed foot nor the princess's disciplinary gesture. She was essentially a little zombie: soft, lacking will, and completely focused on one point invisible to others but wildly painful nevertheless. Lidochka mechanically followed the first-year girl's gaze and the icy needle that had once pierced Galina Petrovna's fate now passed, with quiet, uneven effort, through the fabric of Lidochka's life, securely joining two pieces of embroidered fabric there was no one to admire.

And then a god was walking down the hallway, swinging a gym bag. He was all milk, honey, and gold: dark honey, warm gold, and baked milk. Like Molokhovets's torte from Ulm, Lidochka thought, shaken, and then the first-year, pressing her blazing cheek against Lidochka's side, mumbled in a whiny voice, 'Look, look, it's him…'

'And who is he?' Lidochka asked, keenly sensing how the world—the world she was accustomed to and thought indestructible, even if it was hateful—flipped in one incredibly smooth, round movement, after having been painfully and awkwardly upside down for so long.

'Vitkovsky,' the first-year said. 'Alexey Vitkovsky, they sent him here from Moscow.'

Lidochka nodded as if she understood, pushed the spellbound little girl aside, and followed after the one now known as god, not noticing the silent, unhurried falling of wreckage and bursting of unseen straps and seams around her. She made a few more unmemorable but important steps: this was the first time in her many years at ballet school that she'd done anything within these walls—simply moved—on her own initiative rather than someone else's. But then Lidochka stopped when the leash had fully unwound. Even the end of the world—and that included apocalypse and first love—isn't a valid excuse if we're talking about tardiness for classical dance class.

Lidochka tossed her head like a tired mare and turned back.

Ninel Danilovna—Big Ninel—didn't tolerate tardiness. She'd been a legendary Ensk prima a million years ago, a divine Odette and a devilish Odile, but now she was just a heavyset, mean old woman with iron fingers and an equally iron gullet. It was something to see the fragile, lovely, unbelievably youthful gesture she used to fix the bun of red hennaed hair on the fatty, lumpy nape of her neck or the precise, fiery blow with which she permanently frightened female students by knocking their slack shoulder blades and knees into place. Straight rows of stretched, frantic little necks, whitened fingers grasping the barre, rounded eyes trembling from tension. Raggedy woolen jerseys and snagged, stretched leg warmers lay in a destitute pile in the corner: it was pitiful, this dance school fashion statement that rehearsal clothes had to be torn, a barely perceptible gulp of freedom of no interest to anyone, a tiny right to self-determination. Prisoners slash their veins with sharpened spoons for the same reason. They ought to try exercises at the barre or stretches on the floor.

'*Grand battement jeté!*' Ninel snapped, and the little marionettes obediently hoisted their lower extremities. 'Fifth position, right leg front, two *jetés* front, *piqué*, close. Two *jetés* to the side, *piqué*, close back. Two *jetés* back, *piqué*, close. Two slow *balançoires* and two quick, close back and *en dedans*. Lindt!' she suddenly shouted in a way that even the seventh-years, who were used to everything, flinched. 'Tuck in your ass, where did it go? And what's with your back? That's not a back, it's a trough!'

The accompanist, a small old woman resembling a shriveled doll everyone thought was mechanical, stopped, leaving her hands raised above the keyboard and her indifferent, empty eyes looking straight ahead. Lidochka jolted from the harsh blow and, still smiling, obediently straightened her back, which was already extended to the limit. The distinct mark of the pedagogical hand blazed on the bare skin between her shoulder blades. The girls exchanged furtive, joyful looks: Ninel hadn't thrashed the school's best student since her fourth year, and Lidochka's shameful return to the status of everyone else held promise for many very enjoyable breaks between classes.

'Again! *Grand battement jeté*! And agaaaaain! Lead with the foot, you idiots! The foot, not the hip! My God, why am I wasting my nerves on you!? You should have been strangled back when you were in diapers, every one of you!'

This time Lidochka's foot soared higher than everyone else's, as it was supposed to. But that wasn't important. Nothing was important. Ninel called Lidochka in after class. Are you feeling okay, she asked, and felt Lidochka's sweat-varnished forehead with a clumsy hand not accustomed to affection. Yes, I'm fine, Lidochka nodded. But that wasn't true: the world in front of her just floated on and on, swaying and overflowing with gold and honey, honey and milk.

Poor Lidochka, who'd grown up in a world of great, absolute nonlove, really did decide, initially, that she was sick. That feverish agitation, that wild, spinning excitement that had settled in below her belly, that inordinate chattiness, and that strange shiftiness when you just don't know what to do with your anxious hands: isn't that actually an illness? Icy wet palms, hot cheeks, insomnia, and neurasthenic restrained laughter with a little bell signaling approaching tears distinctly pounding in its depths. The school doctor, who was as ruddy and fat-bellied as a Pushkin critic, felt each of Lidochka's joints with dexterous, soulless fingers, as if he were a gypsy asking the price of a suitable old nag. He prescribed valerian. 'You, Lidia Borisovna, are as healthy as can be. Inasmuch as your ballet sickness can be called healthy. But worrying like that about some performance, I hear you're dancing Giselle, right? Congratulations, that's a big honor for a graduating girl but worrying about it, well, forgive me but you really don't have nearly enough health to worry about what is, in essence, shit like that. Take the drops at night and it will resolve itself.'

Lidochka took the drops, but nothing resolved itself.

Of course valerian root tincture in the evenings and many years of muscle weariness knocked Lidochka hard into her bed, but it was such a soulless institutional dormitory bed that even the undemanding night fairies shunned it, justifiably presuming that normal dreams require at least a miniscule drop of homey warmth. After lying a few hours facedown in the depths of an impenetrable oblivion, Lidochka shuddered close to dawn as if an uneasy adult hand were shaking her by the shoulder. Each time, her cheap little alarm clock with the square Chinese face showed three o'clock and a few insignificant minutes in the morning: a time for full universal peace and quiet when starved lovers unclasp embraces, street killers calm, and even the most hopeless patients set death throes aside until morning.

Lidochka sat up in bed, pulled a flannelette blanket stamped with institutional insignias over her shoulders, and stared straight ahead until morning, seeing nothing, not feeling the cold, and smiling weakly and slightly luminously in the dark.

Alexey Vitkovsky.

She went faint from how the brittle, icy, crown prince name of Alexey transformed into the soft epic poetry name of Alyosha with one soft motion of lips parched from agitation. Alyoshenka. It was like you were kissing the bronzed, warm back of a round little raisin roll.

A-lyo-shen-ka.

He was so gorgeous Lidochka couldn't look at him for more than a few seconds, just like the sun. She immediately felt dizzy and the world moved in dark, fiery spots that took a long time to cool. She had to content herself with small things: dark rings of hair on a swarthy young neck, a mole on a cheekbone, a habit of raising his eyebrows slightly, as if surprised. His brows were silky with shiny sparks, like a mink pelt, and those eyes, were they dark blue or black? Lidochka didn't know. She didn't dare know. One time Vitkovsky walked down the hallway so closely she could feel his warmth, something as impossible and desired as the existence of God. Lidochka faltered, intending to finally at least say something but she strode by yet again without raising her eyelashes—her haughty back, raised chin, and queenly bearing could only have fooled someone who'd never gone to dance school.

By falling in love, Lidochka, who'd already been so unsure of herself, was now, in fact, totally adrift. There wasn't anyone to just talk with, let alone ask for advice: Lyusya Zhukova hadn't answered any of Lidochka's letters after her exile from paradise, distracting the elder Tsarevs from their diligent efforts at survival would have been shameful, and the children were just children. They gave her a little strength but took a lot of time in return. That left only Galina Petrovna, but could she talk with her about love? Lidochka would have had equal success looking for sympathy from the box of rosin where the dancers kicked their pointe shoes around before running on stage, so they wouldn't slip off into another dimension forevermore or snap a neck.

Lidochka had a particularly difficult time handling the endless rapturous racket in classes and dressing rooms: everyone from first-years through alumnae had fallen in love with the handsome new upperclassman, as was to be expected. It was a thirsty, silly, hysterical adoration that could only bloom in closed societies: schools, military barracks, even prisons. Discussions of the wonderful prince's shirts (oh, he's wearing pink today!) and his ancestry (I'm telling you, girls, his father's a diplomat!) felt to Lidochka like a humiliating parody of her own feelings. The right to daydream about Vitkovsky and interpret his glances, smiles, and even gestures belonged to her and nobody else. Despite all Lidochka's efforts to preserve at least some semblance of independence, she frequently caught herself feeding on the very same pathetic crumbs at the communal table as everyone else: as long as Alexey Vitkovsky was the subject, Lidochka thirstily soaked up every word and every foolish story when she was sewing ribbons on pointe shoes, pinning up her hair, or standing under the shower among other naked wet skeletons like herself.

Only very naïve people could presume that in ballet all feelings are platonic and all suffering is lofty. The reigning moral licentiousness at dance schools can only be excused because the majority of students simply don't know things might be different somewhere else. Tight ballet leotards, habitual changes of clothes in everyone's view, lifted naked arms and legs, communal bathing, endless tending of bodies but not souls: all this leaves no place for either imagination or romantic daydreaming. Flesh is just flesh for any ballet dancer, a working tool for occasional use in a friendly quickie but nothing more. There's just no energy for anything more. The girls in the upper classes gossiped a lot about the lovers grownup ballerinas take but they usually emphasized the material side of matters. One beau, for example, gave a lucky girl two pairs of leather boots—black and salmon-colored—at once and that was the highest triumph of male-female relations. Nobody knew about any other relations between a man and a woman. That included Lidochka.

Of course there were birds and bees, dogs and cats, couples embracing on benches, Ritka Komova had quit school because she was young, crazy, and in trouble, and once a page torn out of some medical book had floated under the school desks, with a black-and-white drawing and the horrifying caption 'penis in slit'… Take a look and pass it on. Lidochka looked and passed it on. And thus concluded her sex education.

When lessons in duet dance began, it turned out you could have a relationship with your partner, too. It was easier for two to fight for a place in the repertoire, it was more convenient to rehearse in twos, and in the end a partner was 'your' person and you didn't have to waste time on explanations about why you couldn't have children or how to knead an aching muscle.

The dancers who chose partners were either the stubbornest fanatics or dancers whose looks were so hideous that boots the color of salmon didn't glimmer in their futures. But there was nothing—or almost nothing—human in those pairs, either. They were marriages of production necessity. There was no need to worry about romantic feelings after two skinny, sweat-soaked adolescents had spent several hours in a row working on arm lifts or swinging the girl in the 'fish' pose with a turn. Injuries, falls, nasty smells, sweat, spit, shortness of breath, someone else's slippery hands indifferently feeling you up… the only way you could end up in one bed after that was if you'd had a terrible drinking bout. Or a terrible bout of despondence.

Lidochka grasped all that as soon as she acquired her own partner, Lyonya Belyaev, a pale, stubborn boy hung up on ballet and his own butt. He wore himself out for hours on end with exercises, achieving some sort of special gluteal curve—and even when he lifted Lidochka on a stretched arm slightly trembling from tension he contrived a way to angle his eyes so he could see his own butt on the mirrored walls. His touch was as cold and sticky as semolina porridge, and it aroused nothing in Lidochka, not even disgust. He rarely dropped her, so thanks for that.

Everything was different with Vitkovsky. Lidochka's whole body felt him, even from a distance, and that was a wonderful, vivid, and nervous feeling most resembling the pain from a burn.

This was real. This was love.

By the end of autumn, Lidochka had lost so much weight that it was even noticeable for ballet school, but nobody considered worrying: they all wrote it off to *Giselle*, finally scheduled to premiere at the end of January, meaning Lidochka had supplemental lessons with the men's class in addition to regular classes and rehearsals. Ulanova was probably no fool for rehearsing with the guys, so leap, Lindt, leap, ordered Big Ninel. There's no great ballerina without great *ballon*. Lidochka obediently leapt, barely noticing gravity and easily outdoing the guys with the longest legs and best leaps. And then for another hour after classes. And more. An empty hall, *jeté interlacé, interlacé, interlacé!* Up! Up! Up! She leapt for the last time, clattering her pointe shoes horribly, then hung on the barre, spent, and relaxed her overworked, humming muscles as she felt a stream of cool sweat run between her shoulder blades.

'Cool,' someone said behind her in genuine amazement. 'I've never seen girls leap like that in my life.'

Lidochka turned.

Vitkovsky stood in the doorway, dark-haired and slight, his shirt open at the chest. A white shirt, girls, today it's white.

'Your name's Lida, isn't it?'

Lidochka nodded.

'Listen, do people drink coffee here? In your Ensk?'

Lidochka nodded again and Vitkovsky began laughing.

'They told me you're mute,' he said cheerfully. 'But I thought they were lying. Listen, could you just show me one decent coffee shop, huh? I haven't had a cappuccino since Moscow and you won't believe this but I'm already starting to go into withdrawal. Will you show me?'

Lidochka nodded a third time and then they both started laughing like children, uncontrollably and voraciously nudging each other with gazes.

A week later everyone knew Vitkovsky and Lindt had started seeing each other.

Nobody even envied Lidochka: they just reconciled themselves to the idea that the princess got the prince yet again. As if she hadn't slaved away with everyone else, as their equal, working even harder. As if that endless autumn hadn't existed and nearly gobbled up all of Lidochka along with a love that went unnoticed, unrequited, and mute. Unlike the others, Lidochka couldn't quite bring herself to believe her own happiness, like when you dream you're flying—you're flying!—but you still know for certain that it's not real. It just can't be real. It has no right to be.

They walked around a lot together, along the same streets and lanes Galochka Batalova once wandered as a young girl, holding her wonderful storybook prince's hand: if you looked carefully, you could still see weakly glowing imprints of their confused tracks here and there, but Lidochka was so completely engrossed by Vitkovsky that she didn't notice anything. His eyes turned out to be dark blue. Dark, dark blue, an incredible, almost unnatural shade that looked like what happens when you rinse a sable paint brush daubed with ultramarine in a glass of water. The penetrating Ensk cold constantly chased Lidochka and Vitkovsky into one little café or another, where they talked for ages in an artificial dimness, illuminated by the tiny fire of a cigarette they'd lit for two. It was actually Vitkovsky who talked, to Lidochka's quiet joy, about himself, always about himself.

She fed on those stories like children feed on a fairytale they're hearing for the first time, when it's still completely new and truly magical, and a wondrous, unexplored world seems to arise and imprint itself right on the heart with each plot turn and each pause the storyteller takes to catch his breath. As usually happens with legends, it turned out the tall tales of Vitkovsky's diplomat papa didn't so much embellish as distort a wonderful reality.

Vitkovsky had indeed transferred to Ensk from Moscow; this wasn't exactly unheard-of at the school, but it wasn't unique, either. The three most established ballet schools in the country—Vaganovka in Petersburg, the Bolshoy Academy in Moscow, and Ensk—jealously followed each other's successes and traded scandals, pedagogues, and students from time to time. Nevertheless, graduates like Alexey Vitkovsky usually aspired to go to Moscow rather than leave it, to be closer to the prized Bolshoy Theatre, that Mecca of the ballet world famous for meager salaries, horrendous hazing, and classical repertoire that had remained absolutely the same for decades, as had the primas, the *pas*, the applause, and the swinish snouts of the government figures in the tsar's loge.

Alexey Vitkovsky, however, threw away all those tempting prospects and vaulted ceilings to finish his ballet education in Ensk. The word at the school was he'd followed his father, a big functionary that the ruling party at the time, known as 'Our Home Is Russia,' had sent to the far reaches of the Motherland to take one for the team and strengthen the provincial electorate's faith in 'market reforms and robust conservatism.' In reality, Vitkovsky's father was a heavy-drinking choleric and former secretary of one of Moscow's regional party committees, meaning everybody was already so pissed off by his benders and quirks that he was simply sent as far away as possible.

Vitkovsky didn't feel the slightest bit shy as he told Lidochka all about it with the artless directness of a coddled child certain he'll be forgiven any nasty transgression, even if it belonged to his parents and was thus particularly irremediable.

What about your mother? Lidochka suddenly looked up, her huge eyes brimming with compassion. Vitkovsky nonchalantly shrugged his strong shoulders. He didn't remember his mother, she might have left them or might have died; his father's drunken stories differed, though one thing always remained the same: his hoarse affected sobbing and the little puddles of acrid reeking puke that marked the party functionary's path to his own bedroom. He was, incidentally, not a bad father and though he hated everything about ballet, he preferred voluntarily going where his son could continue his idiotic education over heading to sunny Krasnodar.

'You probably miss it,' Lidochka quietly said, meaning the love of her beloved's mysterious vanished mother. She was suffering his orphandom a thousand times worse than her own, which was as distant and familiar as a dislocated joint. Vitkovsky nodded, missing the point, yes, life's crappy without Moscow, this place is, forgive me, the asshole of the world, you might as well just hang yourself. He finished off the muddy dregs in the bottom of his coffee cup with a swallow and called the bored waiter over with a dandified flick of his fingers.

'Did you warm up?' he asked Lidochka. 'Want anything else? No? Then I'll go to the john and we'll get moving.'

The waiter finally reached their table, shuffling his feet and sneering derisively as he observed Lidochka watching Vitkovsky's retreating back with tender, thirsty adoration and blindly reaching an awkward hand into her purse for her wallet. She always paid for both of them in cafes but never noticed, just as she never noticed his slightly rude and pushy tone or how he'd never once really asked her anything about herself or their future together. He'd also never touched her, not once, though Lidochka's open swooning heart was hoping, at every moment, for his kiss.

They went out onto a black, icy street barely illuminated by the icy, fragile glow of a lozenge-like streetlight.

'All right, old girl,' Vitkovsky said and then, just like in the movies, he lifted the collar of a trench coat that looked movie-like, too, with its quilting and bright checked lining. 'Time to go home. Ta ta!'

'See you tomorrow,' Lidochka quietly said, smitten by the silvery snowy dust that just barely touched his dark hair, not even thinking about how she now had to go back to the dorm alone along winding, thoroughly frozen night streets. She truly didn't notice anything: not the checks she paid, that she in essence saw Vitkovsky home every day, that all he ever called her was 'old girl,' nor the thousands of other horrible unrelenting little things that would have unequivocally torn at her heart had she not been temporarily endowed with the lofty and divine blindness customarily known as love.

Ensk saw in the new year—1998—with unheard-of weather anomalies. A sudden, full-fledged thaw at the end of December brought the realest of babbling brooks, unhurried dripping from sunny eaves, and a vociferous clamor of sparrows crazy with joy. By early January, those same sparrows were sprawled out on icy sidewalks, frozen, fragile, and bound together by an unhurried nocturnal and musical death. Yard workers bundled in enormous sheepskin coats gathered up the weightless little sparrow bodies and tossed them in rubbish bins; Lidochka thought you'd certainly hear a frozen chirruping trill inside the remains if you were to gently shake one of the feathered little corpses near your ear.

There were only a few weeks left before *Giselle*—two and a half weeks, to be exact—and the premiere had been postponed from January 25 to February 1. Lidochka could only gasp when she heard the long-awaited date, pressing her palms to her flaming cheeks, and running out, which cut rehearsal short, in mid-bar. 'Nerves,' Big Ninel grumbled apologetically and picked up a hairpin Lidochka had dropped. Prince Albert, a lanky grownup dancer from the Ensk opera and ballet theater, went over to the window, dissatisfied and bouncing his chilly over-inflated shanks.

'Everybody's nervous,' he drawled. 'Everybody. But I'm the only one who has to work like a galley slave. I haven't been paid since October, by the way!'

Ninel cut him off, 'Get work as a manual laborer if it's not enough money.' She remembered the prince as a jug-eared student with acne on his forehead and atrocious turnout. 'You, you dickhead, may only be remembered because you danced this premiere with Lidka.' She waved a fat hand sprinkled with age spots and grunted as she went to the door; the staccato clicking of the runaway Giselle had faded outside. 'And don't stand there like a post, work. Fucking Baryshnikov.'

Lidochka turned up in the first-floor girls' room, a much-loved oasis of tears, woes, and gossip for generations of ballet students. Lidochka lifted her head when she saw Big Ninel, quickly wiped her tears, and lit up the peeling, smelly bathroom with such an unbelievable, glowing, timid smile that Ninel smiled back from surprise.

'And what a head case you are after all,' she honked out, taking a squashed pack of cheap cigarettes out of her pocket.

'Here, have a cigarette and calm down.'

Lidochka drew in her tender cheeks, leaned over the pale flame of a match and coughed gratefully, acknowledging the huge honor granted her: smoking one of Ninel's unbearable Vatras with her as an equal, adult to adult, ballerina to ballerina.

'Why'd you run away? You scared?' Ninel asked, releasing enormous reeking tusks of smoke through her nostrils.

Lidochka smiled again, guiltily this time, not even trying to explain anything. February first wasn't just the day of the premiere, it was also Vitkovsky's birthday. His day. Lidochka had decided long ago to declare her love to Vitkovsky on February first but now… Now that declaration had taken on special meaning. It couldn't be coincidence. It was fate. Fate had turned its sunny, ceremonial, joyous side toward Lidochka for the first time.

'I'm ready, Ninel Danilovna,' she firmly said, strongly inhaling again and tossing the sizzling cigarette butt into the toilet.

'And good for you,' Ninel grumbled. 'Then go to the classroom, I'll catch up.' Her gaze followed Lidochka out and she tossed her own cigarette into the same toilet. After thinking a bit, she hiked up voluminous, thoroughly old-lady skirts. A stream of urine hit the old Soviet porcelain, whipping up a firm yellow froth. 'There's no way I'm not sending that girl to Moscow,' she mumbled. 'It may be the only way I sneak my way into the encyclopedia.'

Ninel straightened up, pulled down the bottom of her skirt, and tugged decisively on the toilet's chain, flushing away all the innumerable woes and sins that had collected during her long, affectionless and, essentially, completely unhappy life.

After Lidochka had quickly dressed in the completely empty, echoing dressing room (school was out for vacation, with strict instructions to remember daily exercises, as if anyone could forget), she ran to the front steps and looked around for a familiar tall figure tied at the narrow waist of his coat by a belt, but her face fell right then and there: Vitkovsky had gone to Moscow for vacation (without saying goodbye! without saying goodbye!). So they wouldn't be getting together. Well, fine, it wasn't long until February first. Lidochka wrapped herself a little tighter in her fur and hurried off to the dorm, enjoying the feel of the loud, starchy crust of ice crunching underfoot. I'll roll myself up in a blanket, she promised herself, and sleep, sleep, sleep, and when I wake up, Alyosha will already be back! She pulled affably on a snowy branch of a familiar fat fir tree and began laughing as she stuck her mittens under the sweet little snowstorm she'd created herself.

'Lidia Borisovna,' someone called out behind her. 'Lida! Wait a minute!'

Lidochka turned, still smiling and beaming with a round dimple on a pale, slightly dark-skinned cheek and her wet tangled lashes. It's just like before, oh Lord, just like it, just like before, thought Luzhbin, understanding from the surprised nuances of Lidochka's smile that she hadn't recognized him. And then he suddenly lost his balance and, to his shame, thudded on the smooth ice of a soaring sidewalk.

Lidochka greeted the new year with the Tsarevs, politely informing Galina Petrovna in advance, leaving her none the worse for wear. 'Will they at least feed you there?' was all she'd asked Lidochka. And Lidochka, who planned to bring to life no fewer than a dozen beloved pages from Elena Molokhovets, honestly answered that there'd be food. 'Well then, happy upcoming New Year,' the indifferent Galina Petrovna wished her; only the dial tone heard Lidochka say 'You, too.'

This was the first happy New Year holiday of her life, the first since the last one she'd spent with her parents. After sampling all the delicacies and singing all their folk songs, the Tsarevs and Lidochka slept a few short hours that were just as hectic and cheery as New Year's eve night; when they awoke they discovered a completely Pushkinesque morning outside the window: sunny and blinding, with a slight touch of cheery frost.

'Do you know what we're going to do now?' asked Tsarev, who'd grown an incredible, almost scampish, cheery, blue-tinged stubble. 'We're going to the dacha now!'

It should be noted that 'dacha' was just a word here. What the Tsarevs owned was, in fact, a small, awkward slice of a former collective farm's tilled land, hopelessly undernourished by the ownership's socialist management methods even during the five-year-plan before Lidochka was born. The run of the Tsarevs' property was bordered on one side by a pine forest that gradually scrambled its way up a low, round hill; on the other side, well, there just weren't any other sides because the tilled land had all been sliced up to benefit the clueless great unwashed of the scientific research institute, who'd never had either the money for fences or the obnoxious proletarian spirit for scandalous behavior. And so the Tsarevs, for example, recognized their land by a tool shed Sergey Vladimirovich had knocked together himself out of ammunition boxes and carefully secured with a giant, almost antique, barn lock.

The little tool shed was intended for agricultural tools but could hold, when the need arose, a fold-out bed hospitably ready to take a weary wayfarer into its springy, sagging bosom. The Tsarevs didn't stay overnight at the dacha, though, so they generally only used the fold-out bed to pick over mushrooms they'd gathered in the nearby woods: first slightly snotty suilluses, then saffron milk caps. Thanks to an inherited habit from their village kin, the elder Tsarevs went out of their way to take only exceptionally young mushrooms with caps no larger than half a fingernail but Romka and Veronichka, overcome with primeval passion, even rooted out giant, crumbly russulas eaten through by sneaky translucent worms and plastered with dead pine needles. Lots of short-lived arguments flared in the family because of the russulas but of course experience and authority won out and only the obviously edible mushrooms were sent on for mushroom caviar and salting.

In the winter—in the absence of mushrooms—there was absolutely nothing to do at the dacha but decorate a tree and throw snowballs. The Tsarevs began throwing snowballs after realizing they'd have to tromp almost half a kilometer through fresh snow to the nearest fir tree. They divided into teams at first but started fighting every man for himself when they began enjoying themselves: Lidochka screamed and jumped louder than anyone, all decked out for the dacha in Romka's old fur-trimmed jacket with mismatched buttons and a totally torn-off pocket. Her light, trained body brought her joy instead of pain for the first time in her life, and when she pasted the enemy with yet another glistening, well-aimed snowball, she managed not only to dodge incoming artillery but even produce a jubilant Indian whooping she'd learnt from Veronichka. The Tsarevs initially trembled in the face of this danger but then they craftily joined forces as one loud family cohort and drove Lidochka, who shrieked and continued fighting them off, into a huge snow bank. Aha, she said, indignantly. So that's how it is, panting from laughter and trying to break free, Aha, ganging up on me! Now I'll show you! And she quickly molded a snowball and launched it with all her might into the elder Tsarev as he performed a victory dance.

That's how Luzhbin saw her the first time: a slight, almost nonexistent girl, unkempt and laughing, kneeling in a snow bank and wearing a little boy's short coat, her face shining with wet snow. She gathered entire mittens full of snow and suddenly raised her eyes—they were unbelievable, dark, deep golden, and sunny all through, with lively coffee-colored sparkles at the very depths of a joyous, half-childlike gaze—and Luzhbin suddenly sensed he'd flown face-first and at full speed into an invisible but indestructible wall. And the girl in the silent, unmoving snapshot that surrounded him swung so the snowball, which still retained the shape of her little palms, launched forward. And as it flew, flying for so, so long, all glowing and round, Luzhbin immediately grasped how happy he'd be with this girl, how irreparably, unprecedentedly, and fantastically happy, and he felt the taste of her lips and the weight of her pregnant belly, he lived an entire long, joyful life with her, just like the first summer vacation in someone's life, and he died exactly a week after her death because she shouldn't grieve, shouldn't be left alone, and everything was over and done with by the time the snowball finally slapped into the shoulder of the elder Tsarev, who was dying of laughter.

And Romka happily shouted, 'Hello! Hello, Uncle Vanya!'

Ivan Luzhbin was local, born in Ensk in 1961. He was born into a simple Soviet family renowned for decency and borscht, graduated from an undistinguished school on the outskirts with good, solid grades, calmly did his army duty, and entered Ensk's technical institute without the slightest visible effort, graduating without any ostentatious brilliance though he held five patents for thingies of huge use to the Motherland, so two academic departments and half of Ensk's development labs nearly came to blows over him after he'd defended his thesis project.

Of course that kind of stir was understandable: it was 1986 and the very concept of 'engineer' had long ago turned into a synonym for an idiot-loser who sat around in cheap, wrinkled pants at a shabby scientific research institute that had been trying for God knows how many five-year plans to invent a new chain for the tank of the legendary, eternally dripping Soviet toilet. Institutions of higher education all around the country graduated brainless girls dreaming of marriage—they just couldn't wait—as well as listless young men who'd already reconciled themselves to the fate of a destitute character in a popular joke, somewhere in jokedom's middle rungs, between the hapless Vasily Ivanovich and the totally moronic Chukchi. With the simple fact of his existence, the calm, sluggish, and even, perhaps, slightly sleepy Luzhbin had returned forgotten and deserved glory to the word 'engineer.'

Luzhbin had a clear, cynical head, stubborn character, feline curiosity, and absolutely incredible hands. There was no equipment he couldn't bring back to life after a bit of reflection but—and this was far more important—there wasn't any law of physics he couldn't demonstrate by thinking up and assembling a thingy that hummed, squeaked, or scattered sparks. This wasn't just a rarity but an obvious talent even if it was, in and of itself, not at all showy. Luzhbin was destined for a good academic future but he chose one of the development labs after a bit of reflection: it wasn't the most promising in terms of professional growth but it was the most generous at the current moment since he'd immediately have a more-than-decent salary plus his own apartment within six months. That was important, very important, even it wasn't for him but for Olga, although if it was for her that meant it was for him, too. Olga was the most important and best thing in Luzhbin's life. She was even more than that: she was the only and best woman on earth. There were no other women at all. At least not for Luzhbin.

Luzhbin fell in love with Olga in his first year at the institute and then patiently waited until he graduated, not because he was unsure of himself but because he wanted to offer her only what was truly the very best: he'd never displayed his feelings, only observed her with surprising calm as she had numerous (but short-term) flings and romances. Then, as soon as his work papers had settled into the sacred safe at the right design lab, Luzhbin calmly went first to the barber, then to the florist, and finally to Olga at the dorm, where, in his quiet, expressionless voice, he made a proposal he felt sure she couldn't refuse. And she didn't refuse.

They had a loud and expensive wedding that met Olga's standards and requests, and when Luzhbin lifted a bridal veil sprinkled with tiny spiky rhinestones from her excited, pretty face, he never regretted for a second the debts he'd taken on to arrange this celebration for her at the central banquet hall with one hundred fifty drunk, feasting guests, most of whom he didn't know. Or that lacy, snow-white dress with the train carried by a five-year-old boy Luzhbin also didn't know: the boy wore a little velvet suit sewn especially for the occasion but was less preoccupied with his page duties than the very interesting thick greenish snot he kept releasing from his nose and then swiftly sniffing back. There was also an out-of-tune vocal and instrumental group that had asked two hundred rubles for the evening. There was sturgeon in aspic, too, but the cost for all this was piddling compared to the happiness that awaited him and Olga.

They got their promised apartment a half-year later and Luzhbin paid off all his debts, right down to the kopeck, in another three months. Olga never found out he'd taken on extra work to do that, working overtime in his regular job and part-time as a janitor, too, washing floors, emptying waste baskets, and dusting window sills at the design lab in the evenings as swiftly and adeptly as he did everything, never ceasing to smile at the very corner of his firm, strongly curved mouth. Why would she need to know anyway? What of it: the floors. Honestly, Luzhbin would have done anything for his wife. Anything. He'd've killed, betrayed the Motherland. By all means. She was his Motherland. Olga. Only her. And he wouldn't ever betray her under any circumstances.

In 1991, Olga dumped him like you dump a sticky ice cream wrapper into a bin, and she left town with a visiting lancer. Maybe she was following the flighty behest of her literary name, or maybe she'd truly succumbed to the charm of an outsider from distant shores who was generous, dandified, and handsome, with a luxuriant moustache permanently sprinkled with the red pepper of a little joke that's always smutty and told at just the right moment.

As his wife packed her suitcases (the lancer tactfully waited outside the front door in an indistinctly rumbling taxi) and her nimble, pretty legs stepped over items trying to be saved,

Luzhbin silently sat, dazed and examining his shaking hands, in a corner on a stool that had wandered in from who knew where. The blow, which he'd missed, turned out to have such an anesthetizing power that Luzhbin didn't even feel pain, only a quiet bewilderment bordering on madness. It was as if he was on his way to receive a general buzz of cheery approval and a well-deserved award that's waiting on a little crimson pillow, but then the corridor he's confidently walking through suddenly ends on a silent city square: a gallows stands in the center, so black it looks charred, and an executioner who hasn't slept off last night paces from boredom in his baggy, dirty, dreary, pre-dawn clothing.

When the last zipper on the last bag had screeched, Luzhbin was still attempting to understand what he'd done wrong, what he was guilty of, where he'd made the wicked mistake that forced his wife to casually tear their five years of happy—it was happy!—absolutely happy marriage out of her life, just like that. Olga was attempting to remove her own past from its established place but it had difficulty fitting into one indecently distended suitcase and three gym bags of varying size. She couldn't move everything and so flung an angry ash-green lightning-like glare at Luzhbin, help me already, you dolt! He obediently stood, took the things out of the apartment, and neatly arranged them on the stair landing. And turned.

'I'll go the rest of the way myself,' Olga graciously dismissed him as she wrapped, tied, and wound a very long bright-red scarf around her neck. Ensk was cold in April and her weak throat always suffered from endless ailments in the spring and autumn. A sleepy Luzhbin had always brought her scruffy-looking boiled cranberry drinks at night and she'd mumble something in a hot, hoarse whisper then fall back asleep, pressing against him with her whole body, fiery from heat and damp, and impossibly desired. Impossibly.

'Olya,' he said, scaring himself when he heard his own voice. 'Olya, why?'

She thought honestly for a moment—smoky, greenish eyes, mercilessly bleached bangs, lively pink reflections on her cheeks from the scarf, from joy, from life, and from the joy of life—and simply said, 'Because I love someone else.'

Luzhbin nodded as if he'd understood, as if that really was an irrefutable reason impossible to argue with: well, of course you love another person and it turns out he, Luzhbin, isn't even a person. The anesthesia wore off then and physical pain of such crude insurmountable power descended that he blindly closed the door, which was itself gasping from despair. He blindly wandered through the orphaned apartment, tripping with all his weight on the mewing cat (who'd spent the entire packing time hiding who knew where and not even condescending to come out and say goodbye) and only when Luzhbin ran into the stool he'd risen from a few minutes earlier did he finally began to weep. Not because he'd had his ribs broken—precisely cracked—one by one en route to his heart but because he'd bumped his injured knee, the one he'd pulled two weeks ago when he and Olga went outside the city to ski on the last heavy snow. They'd gotten lost and then figured out where they were and wound up kissing themselves into a stupor in a copse while half-empty local trains rumbled and screeched behind them, and he'd pressed Olga's back against a pine tree and frenziedly torn his way through her jacket and sweater, gathering melting grains of snow from her delicate, cool cheekbones with his lips, and the snow already tasted completely alive and completely like spring and he hurried so clumsily, so like a boy, that he twisted his leg and Olga had alternately laughed and gasped the whole way home, complaining to the other female passengers, the chatty, cozy old women sitting near them, that her husband was disabled now and how could you leave a man like that. You couldn't leave him. People wouldn't understand.

When the cat's silent paw knocked a jingly little hair clip with a fake dark-blue stone out from under the couch a year later, Luzhbin had already recovered enough that he was almost calm fingering this silly little feminine thing that had somehow become so attached to the house (or to Luzhbin himself?) that it wanted to stay and so found its way to the dustiest, most distant corner and lay there a full twelve months, fearful not only to take a breath but even to glisten. Luzhbin caught a random ray of sun with the clip and projected a slippery toy-like rainbow onto the wall. He'd tried with such fierce fury to forget his wife for twelve months that he'd simultaneously utterly destroyed his own life, rendering it into unrecoverable dust, copious ashes. He no longer hurt. Nothing at all hurt. Not anything. Do you want to play with it, Matryona, he asked the cat, but Matryona just shifted her grayish fur coat in disgust and retreated regally. That's the right decision, Luzhbin mumbled, the right thing, you'd just hurt your paw. And he chucked the hair clip as hard as he could through an open, chirpy springlike window.

It was actually the cat who didn't allow him to either drink himself stupid, totally lose his mind, or sink into the apathetic, mirthless paralysis that so easily crushes the will of even the strongest Russian men when there's a woman involved. The cat needed to be fed the fish he procured and cooked, fresh water had to be poured into a china cup with a broken-off handle; and newspapers had to be finely torn and placed in an old pot adapted into a simple cat toilet. He also had to talk with the cat, which became necessary because ever since Olga left, the cat had been ruthlessly tearing the wallpaper and disemboweling the couch as a way of displaying the finest sides of her character. And all those petty, insignificant efforts caring for a creature that was essentially clueless, ill-mannered, and irrational settled on Luzhbin's calloused human grief like a balm, inconspicuously lubricating and moistening his painful scabs. The scabs fell off themselves when the time came and he discovered that the skin underneath was pale and weak but very smooth and alive.

It took another year for Luzhbin to realize he'd survived and pulled himself out of the hole. The scariest part was behind him and the cat. Luzhbin left his design lab as soon as he realized that, and he didn't listen when the director bawled and mewled, mourning the loss of his best employee. Everyone around was involved in business and some were even successful, so Luzhbin decided to try, too: after all, he'd already lost everything he held dear so there was nothing left to fear. After thinking a bit, he decided to get into computers, first purchasing (he had to descend into debt again) and then assembling. Losing his wife hadn't affected Luzhbin's professional skills at all, so his assembly work turned out to be not only cheaper than Asian assembly work, but also better. Initially there was a lot of money, then there was an awful lot, and in a couple years Luzhbin discovered with surprise that he was rich by even the most capitalistic of standards. He thought about shutting down the company, too, but the hungry, pathetic, mean little worm inside him wouldn't quiet down, so Luzhbin decided it would be short-sighted to toss away a business that had just gotten on its feet. In truth, he also wanted to prove to Olga—who'd irrevocably melted away into who knew what time and place—that he was better. Because he'd realized long, long ago why she left him. He'd realized it, but still couldn't admit it to himself. It was all just about money. Money he didn't have, money the lancer did have, although maybe the lancer didn't have it either, at least not in the quantities Olga needed, but it was money, and money is power. Power that men and women reckoned with. And now Luzhbin was part of that power, too.

Of course, nothing got easier because of that and Luzhbin was all alone after the cat died. Neither his rapidly developing business nor the positive flow of incoming money, nor the entertaining chitchat with gangsters, nor the first bank credits… nothing brought relief or filled the horrible emptiness inside. Luzhbin got a new office and even renovated the old apartment in a faddish way—high-tech—but then it was unbearable to even be at home, let alone spend the night. Luzhbin agonized for a couple weeks, then sold his apartment and moved in at work, using a five-square-meter break room hidden behind his office. A couch, easy chair, TV and video unit, microscopic little bathroom with a shower, and a dozen shirts on a clothes rod were all he had. He found he didn't need more anyway. His inert but unattractive and not-so-young secretary brought his shirts to the laundry, but Luzhbin learned how to order his own pizza.

He suffered horribly from loneliness, in a totally physical way, like dull, long-term pain in the joints haunts other people. And of course only warmth—from a woman or at least a cat—could save him from the pain, but Luzhbin had given up inside, no longer believing in either women or cats. If those two—his only ones, his most beloved—had totally abandoned him, was there any point in waiting for compassion from anyone else?

Luzhbin's friends despaired of trying to introduce him to their sisters, sisters of sisters, or friends of wives (what's with you, Vanya, just come, she's a great girl!), so tried to at least turn him on to pornography (or you'll totally lose it, bud, God is my witness, you'll just totally lose it!). Fortunately Ensk now had a whole slew of kiosks and simple tables that sold videocassettes: just one naughty wink would send the salesman to dredge up the right box from the detritus of action movies (all of which spoke with a distinct Chinese accent at the time) and melodramas where grandiose intentions and the frills on the main heroine's dresses more than compensated for lame, unwieldy plots. Pornography cost twice as much as the usual cinematic fare but it was a child of the nineties, too: ludicrous and unsophisticated with pockmarked rugs instead of backdrops as well as an impassive cameraman's ever-present shadow, which always found the most inappropriate moment to lie down on characters sweaty from sexual exertion, momentarily distracting a viewer who was also jacked-up and sweaty because of an approaching and predictable finale.

The things you'll do for your friends: Luzhbin made an honest effort and watched about ten jolly cassettes with garish naked torsos on the boxes but didn't even get the expected physiological relief. Alas! It turned out he possessed an innate and rare gift for seeing humanness in even the most inhuman things. Instead of following the back-and-forth development of an artless plot, Luzhbin might notice some touching, completely mechanical, and very female gesture that a porno actress used to adjust her hair, even though she was barely discernable behind a fence of erect members. Or maybe some sexy hunk, his back sweaty from exertion, would suddenly extend his lips toward his partner's lips, trustingly and almost tenderly, out of some habit that even such scummy work apparently hadn't beaten out of him, but then the woman would sharply deflect him and they'd stare into each other's eyes for a whole second with frightened and absolutely human eyes, never ever ceasing their bestial, awkward, and almost mechanical body movements.

A couple times after getting very drunk and not regaining consciousness, Luzhbin slept with some stray hussies who might not have even been so bad; one even called him a couple weeks in a row, tempting him with home-baked goods, sex at no cost, and the comforts of home. But Luzhbin imagined everything that would happen when the sex and pastries were done: he'd have to get up, talk about something, do something, entertain someone he hardly even knew, and deal with her opinions that weren't interesting to anyone, including herself.

No, save me.

He completely stopped drinking, just in case.

In 1997, six years after Olga left, he was still single but had already reconciled himself to that. Yes, he'd had to move out of his break room, under pressure from friends and partners, but the deal turned out to be advantageous: by pure chance, Luzhbin bought a big house on the outskirts of Ensk. It was abandoned, old, and so obviously in need of care—like a person—that Luzhbin couldn't resist and so he took on the rebuilding, redoing, and repairing, like a bird starts weaving a nest long before it's found a mate. The house turned out to be surprisingly responsive and with his tinkering Luzhbin began regaining his own heart, starting off slowly, just a little, a millimeter at a time, without even noticing it himself.

He greeted the new year—1998—with his house rather than alone, and that was a glorious, warm, and long-forgotten feeling. He walked through all the rooms at midnight, clinking a glass of mineral water that was loudly losing its fizz against the furniture, lintels, and windowsills, then went to bed, feeling strong, healthy, and surprisingly young for the first time in ages.

And the next morning he saw Lidochka for the first time.

That was the beginning of a new era, he knew it for sure. A happy new era that would go on for a long, long time, an entire life. And Luzhbin was certain he wasn't wrong this time.

He put lots of thought into getting ready for his second meeting with Lidochka, more than he'd ever prepared for a business meeting. He got a huge torte and went to visit the Tsarevs: he'd known them forever, since construction brigades in their student years, and he asked so much about Lidochka that the Tsarevs began giving each other looks.

'The girl's seventeen, Vanya,' Mrs. Tsareva said with a barely perceptible shadow in her voice. 'Did you come to the wrong door by any chance?'

Luzhbin went quiet, weighing something inside and then firmly, as if he were speaking with Lidochka's parents instead of the Tsarevs, said, 'No, there's no mistake. I want her to be… No, that's not it. She will be my wife. And it's not a problem if I have to wait a year, ten years, twenty-five years.'

The Tsarevs looked at each other again.

'Well, if she's going to be your wife,' Tsarev said, stretching out his words and thinking. 'If she's going to be your wife, I think we should drink to that. What do you say, Vanya?'

Luzhbin smiled, radiantly, flustered, and joyfully, as he hadn't smiled in many, many years.

'Drink to that—now you're thinking,' he said. 'An excellent idea. I vote for that with both hands!'

Lidochka truly didn't recognize Luzhbin, who'd been standing watch by her dormitory for several hours. To be honest, he'd barely registered in her memory the first time they met: some friend of the Tsarevs' had come and kept them from playing in the snow, a dull, drab guy with an expressionless face. Like a boiled potato. For Lidochka, at seventeen, he seemed like he was really getting on in years, though anyone older than twenty-five seemed pitiful and elderly to her. Luzhbin had quietly discussed something with the Tsarevs, looking all the while at Lidochka with such strange expressions of his eyes and lips that she was confused, as she was always confused when she saw people she didn't know. Lidochka was overjoyed when he left, squeaking off in the snow, his fists stuffed into the pockets of an expensive straw-colored sheepskin coat. She quickly put him out of her head so thoroughly that now she couldn't remember his patronymic or even his first name.

'Ah,' she mumbled, helping Luzhbin get up off the sidewalk, 'You're not hurt are you?'

'Ivan Vasilevich, you can just call me Ivan,' Luzhbin said, immediately grasping Lidochka's situation and introducing himself. He suddenly realized he could feel all of her from a distance, not like a man, no, but probably the way a mother feels her new-born child.

'I remember, of course I do,' Lidochka said, lying and apologizing with her eyes for the lie. 'You sure you didn't hurt yourself?'

'No,' said Luzhbin, 'Not at all. A very pleasant way to meet, isn't it? Do you live here?'

Lidochka nodded. Tiny live beads of melting snow glistened on her eyebrows and lashes. Luzhbin felt breathless.

'Seryozha, uh, I mean Sergey Vladimirovich, said you're a ballerina? Is that right?'

Lidochka began laughing, 'Oh, come on! It's really hard to become a ballerina, it doesn't work out for everybody. It's like a title. There's lots of dancers but only a few ballerinas. I'm just a student at the dance school.'

'Do you like to dance?' Luzhbin asked. A long, dark shadow ran along Lidochka's face, instantly snatching away both the twinkle in her eye and her smile.

'Yes, very much,' she said, lying again, though this time she wanted to get rid of him rather than be polite.

She's going to leave now, Luzhbin realized, grasping feverishly at one, then another shard of the rapidly deteriorating conversation.

'You have a premiere coming up soon, don't you? I don't honestly know much about… but I'd like… if it's possible…' He pathetically threw up his hands, not knowing what to say. Lidochka's eyes warmed a little.

'Of course you can,' she said. 'The performance will be on February first and I think there are still tickets but I can get a comp ticket for you if you want.'

'I'll buy one,' Luzhbin assured her. 'I'll definitely buy one.'

But Lidochka didn't smile.

'Goodbye,' she said and headed toward the dorm doors, trying not to notice how Luzhbin was watching her. Sleep, sleep. Roll up in the blanket and sleep. When I wake up, Alyoshenka will already be back!

Lidochka didn't sleep the night before the premiere and then the next day she couldn't pacify an evil little vein that was finely twitching under her left eyelid right until evening, the first harbinger of a serious future tic, it's nothing, Lidochka, nothing, just don't make a mistake, that's the big thing, Big Ninel wailed as she styled Lidochka's hair herself in the dressing room. Lidochka nodded without understanding a single word, looking as drawn and yellow as a very sick patient just released from the hospital. A hideous wax doll who had trouble raising her enormous butterfly-like false eyelashes looked out of the mirror at Lidochka. The premiere didn't worry her in the slightest: Lidochka was more afraid than anything that she wouldn't see Vitkovsky. I love you, I love you, loveyouloveyouloveyouloveyou, she mumbled inside, practicing.

The 'To stage' light blinked and Ninel straightened Lidochka's bodice. That's it, there you go, kiddo. God be with you. Lidochka stood. Just don't make a mistake, got it? Big Ninel implored again, rummaging in her roomy purse for her vial of Validol. I won't, Lidochka promised, heading toward the left curtain, her pointe shoes loudly, distinctly clacking.

She danced the first act so superbly that the guests Big Ninel had invited from Moscow—all sitting in the best seats of the best row for the view—could only blissfully press their lips together as if they were rubbing smooth bursting little beads of caviar on the roofs of their mouths. The hall was filled, something that hadn't happened in the Ensk theater for an offensively long time, and Lidochka was unusually expressive and also unusually technical, though after the mad scene she flew back behind the curtains and moaned 'A basin!' Big Ninel turned out to be at her very best and was—even more importantly—hovering, so Lidochka twice vomited frothy bile into a vessel extended at just the right moment, meaning the public got their delicate melting dancer back, fortunate the aromas of perspiration and vomit would never even reach the parterre.

She had to change costumes before the second act, into the snow-white romantic tutu and smooth hair of a stupid village girl about to be reborn as a witch, but Lidochka was thinking about something else entirely. Vitkovsky was nowhere to be found! 'Ninel Danilovna, did you happen to see…' she began, and Big Ninel waddled in like rising dough gone wild, I saw them, saw them, Lidka, everyone from the Bolshoy's here, everyone they need for decisions. 'Don't get all self-important but don't sell yourself short, either. You're invaluable, they already know that, but now you have to know that.' Ninel convulsively sighed. 'Don't forget this old woman when you're gone, do you promise?' Big Ninel abruptly pressed Lidochka's round and glittery head to her limp bosom and began crying weak tears more like a puppy's than a child's. Lidochka extricated herself from the enormous stifling embraces and flung herself out of the dressing room.

She didn't even run, she was borne, as a sheet of rice paper is borne by the wind: the translucent layers of her tutu fluttered toward the dim lights, the shadows of ballet ghosts dashed after her, and Lidochka truly would have believed she'd died and come back as a Wili if it hadn't been for the horrifying clatter of her heart and pointe shoes. Judging from the buzz in the auditorium, not much time was left before the beginning of the second act; Lidochka turned, turned again, and finally saw a burning contraband cigarette under the dusty stairs and heard quiet voices, one of which she would have recognized even in her sleep, even if she were dead. She stopped, gathered her breath, and peered into the unsteady duskiness. 'Go on, run, old boy, you're on soon,' said Vitkovsky's voice, and the cigarette embers went out. Lidochka took a step forward, hoping the dancer she couldn't see would notice her and go away but right then she blinked from impossible, unbearable horror the likes of which no living person can bear. IloveyouIloveyouIloveyou pounded in her head, Iloveyou, Iloveyou, I…

It's not true, calm down. It's not true.

Lidochka opened her eyes. Prince Albert and Vitkovsky were kissing. She could seem them perfectly distinctly, especially Vitkovsky's closed eyes and dark eyelashes, slightly curled, like a perfect girl student's, and a beautiful boyish hand with a little bone on a broad wrist, stroking Lidochka's partner's butt.

'I love you,' Lidochka suddenly yelled so loudly it even scared her. Vitkovsky started, opening foggy eyes that looked as if they'd been filled with milk fresh from the cow.

'What are you doing here, old girl?' he asked, flustered and pushing the prince away.

The prince turned and indignantly looked Lidochka up and down. 'What kind of manners are those?' he slowly said through clenched teeth. 'Why aren't you on stage? They recruit a bunch of sniveling little girls from the school and I have to coddle them.'

He chucked Vitkovsky on the neck and walked past Lidochka, simultaneously tensing his nostrils and long jowls like an angry horse.

And so Lidochka was left standing under the stairs, dropping thin arms that were drowning in her ethereal tutu. Her mouth limply opened up part-way, as if she were feeble-minded.

'So what is it, old girl, what? You a little kid or something?' Vitkovsky babbled, rubbing his elbows with his palms and wincing as if his joints pained him terribly.

Lidochka was quiet for a moment and then repeated the one phrase that kept ringing in her head, 'I love you.'

Vitkovsky's handsome face flashed for an instant with the sort of compassion that most likely leads God to forgive many transgressions. Many but not all.

'Lida,' he said, calling Lidochka by name for the first time. 'Lida, what, you really didn't know? I'm gay, don't you understand? I've never ever liked chicks, never in my life, can you believe that?'

'But what about... So why did you... with me?...'

'You're hilarious and you dance well.' Vitkovsky guiltily smiled his honest, almost childish smile. 'Besides, you were the only girl who didn't come after me! Girls make me nauseous, don't you get it!'

Lidochka turned as if she were mechanical and headed for the stage.

'Just don't tell anyone, huh?' Vitkovsky yelled after her. He sighed and took another cigarette out of the pack. She'll blab it to everyone anyway. Those chicks, nothing but problems.

There's a reason they say professional skills die last: Lidochka danced the second act just as impeccably as the first and all the critics' reviews mentioned her hardened, dead face—the face of a dead Wili turning into a witch—as a big artistic coup, unexpected in the arsenal of such a youthful and very promising ballerina. It's a shame nobody noticed that Lidochka came out for bows with the same dead face and that Prince Albert squeezed her icy, damp palm and poked Lidochka in the ribs with his elbow, perceptibly but unnoticed. Smile, you idiot, he hissed, stretching his made-up mouth in a grateful grin. Smile! Lidochka didn't even hear him, just as she didn't hear either the ovations or the cries of 'Bravo!' She was struck by a strange blinddeafmuteness that didn't allow her to see anyone in the applauding crowd, neither the jubilant Tsarevs (Veronichka even tried to stand in her seat but was scolded) nor Galina Petrovna nor Luzhbin shoving toward the stage with an enormous basket of white roses that nearly made the balletomanes choke on their own venom, so very tacky, just imagine! How tacky! Luzhbin placed the basket right under Lidochka's feet and immediately pushed his way back through the babbling crowd when he couldn't catch her gaze.

Everyone wanted to speak with Lidochka, interview her, kiss her hand, and express their admiration, but she disappeared as soon as the curtains closed, as if she'd never been there. Those who wanted to see her had to content themselves with Big Ninel who believed in the end—after the agitation she'd experienced and cognac she'd secretly drunk—that it was she who'd danced her very first Giselle at seventeen so magically, frantically, and ravishingly.

Luzhbin drove his car up to the back entrance and got out, leaving the engine to warm up. It was so penetratingly and ringingly cold that it seemed as if the huge, spiky stars hanging low over night-time Ensk were creating that clear, frosty sound. Luzhbin waited for Lidochka because he knew she'd come out; it was if he'd been told in advance what she'd do, though he still missed the moment she appeared, seeming not to have walked out the door but simply emerged from frosty puffs of his own breaths, thin, bare-armed, and bare-legged, wearing a weightless white dress that looked to Luzhbin as if it froze for an instant in that horrible cold and was also mournfully, thinly ringing along with the stars, the air, and his own heart.

Luzhbin looked at Lidochka for a few seconds as if he didn't believe she was real then immediately tore off his sheepskin coat and rushed to the back door.

They drove around Ensk in the car for a long time that night, just riding around, and for the first time in his life Luzhbin was consciously glad he'd made a pile of money: his brand-new Volvo was warm and smelled good, soft comfortable seats caressed their backs, and soft comfortable music successfully filled the silence. Lidochka never said what happened; she didn't really say anything but she didn't cry either. She stopped quivering later, too, and when day broke, she even shifted lightly, getting more comfortable and then Luzhbin knew the crisis—whatever it was—had passed and he could say something, though his big concern was coming up with what, exactly, to say. And then Luzhbin said exactly what he needed to, with the far-sightedness of an adult person in love. 'Do you want to go outside the city, Lidia Borisovna? I have a wonderful house, it's old. There's pine trees and fresh air. You can sleep things off and calm down, then I'll take you wherever you'd like.'

Lidochka looked up with grateful eyes and nodded a few times with a head still decorated in a Wili's frightful little snow-white wreath.

Even without opening her eyes Lidochka could see the grand, brazen pink bodies of the pines piercing Ensk's low, shaggy sky. It smelled of pitch, close heavy snow, and an approaching dusk that was unclear, quiet, and filled with the sound of dogs ceremonially calling out to one another, almost like church bells.

Lidochka was sitting on the porch, swathed up to her neck in a plaid blanket. She'd slept almost all day and when she woke up she discovered her romantic tutu on a coat hanger and neatly folded men's jeans and a sweater lying at the foot of the bed. Of course you'll have to turn up the sleeves, Luzhbin babbled, jumping up when she came into the living room, holding up the falling jeans with both hands—but those trousers—hold on a second... He got a belt, an awl, and huge tailor's scissors from somewhere and quickly bored holes in the belt. And then he knelt in front of Lidochka and cut off the jeans with a neat, careful rustle, so they wouldn't drag on the floor. His hands shook slightly but noticeably.

He gave Lidochka some strong, burning-hot bouillon to drink and apologized for a long time that it was made from cubes, but at least it was hot, cooking's not my forte, Lidia Borisovna, forgive me but I can do everything else, don't worry. Here, let me show you the house, huh? There's a lot here that hasn't been finished but for the most part... Lidochka put the cup on the huge table and looked around the spacious kitchen. Show me, please.

The house turned out to be almost exactly what she'd dreamt of, maybe even better, but the big thing was that it was tranquil, so tranquil Lidochka suddenly began believing everything that happened last night, no, everything—her whole past life—was just a nightmare, a sinister dark episode from which she was slowly beginning to recover. Luzhbin brought her from room to room, waving his arms around and getting excited, and then he dragged a rocking chair on the porch, gave Lidochka some small felt boots that were almost a child's size (they were here in the store room, I couldn't bring myself to throw them out, it would have been too bad) and wrapped Lidochka up in the blanket himself, you sit here a while, get some air, and I'll bring you some tea. Don't worry, I make good tea.

Lidochka pressed a felt boot into the porch floorboards and lightly rocked the chair. She was five the last time anyone—her parents—had loved her and she'd completely forgotten what that was like. The Tsarevs didn't count because they were so stuffed to the gills with proper Soviet morality, half-digested forbidden literature, and an inborn amiability that they loved absolutely everything: the Motherland, titmice, Ensk, Solzhenitsyn, and each other. Lidochka got lost in the sugary whirlwind of their universal, undiscriminating adoration. It was the same as warming yourself up in a pile of half-familiar stirring bodies: very warm, a little disgusting, and completely unfocused. But now Luzhbin specifically liked her, something that was even clear in how he carried the cup of tea for her and how he watched her drink, reflexively reaching with his lips as if he was either trying to help or afraid she'd burn herself. He was taking care of her. And that turned out to be an unbelievable feeling, when someone takes care of you. It was warm.

Luzhbin looked out on the porch as if he'd been drawn by those thoughts.

'Don't need anything?' he asked, 'You're probably hungry. We can go somewhere for dinner.' He even pulled his head into his shoulders a little, afraid of a refusal.

'Ivan Vasilevich, please carry me into the house,' Lidochka said.

Luzhbin looked at her with an almost animal horror, as if

he were a stray (scrawny, the whole body just hoops of hungry ribs) who'd gotten so used to shouting and hard kicks since puppyhood that he didn't recognize an affectionate human hand.

'Into the house?' he hoarsely repeated.

'Yes, please,' Lidochka said. She worked her arms out from under the blanket and extended them.

When Luzhbin awkwardly picked her up, Lidochka mechanically tensed her muscles like she did for lifts, to ease her partner's difficult lyrical lot. She was a 'convenient' ballerina who never hung on a partner's arms like an impassive burden or a limp assortment of tendons, meatless bones, and prickly, staticky nylon that her partner's extended arms had to raise to exalted heights—up toward the dusty theater ceiling, artificial stars, and listless faces of lighting technicians whose heads were permanently messed up after witnessing endless torrents of the beautiful. But Luzhbin was so taken with her elfin weightlessness—she barely weighed forty-five kilos even in the felt boots and wrapped like a doll in the thick blanket—that he didn't even notice her muscular exertions.

'So light... like a flower,' Luzhbin mumbled, clutching Lidochka to himself, as you clutch a sick child who's weakened, delirious, and semi-conscious from a horrible night-time fever. As if you're sending your ten-year-old daughter to the hospital. Three steps to the door. Four unseen, bumpy flights of stairs, a tired doctor's morose back in front of you, don't drop her, don't drop her, don't... shhhh, be patient, Sunshine, it'll all be better soon. A weak kick at the door into the entryway, hold it with your shoulder so it doesn't slam, doesn't hit. The old ambulance's open rear end, its insides icy-cold and vibrating. Don't cry, sweetie, Papa's here. He'll never leave you. I'll never leave you. You hear me? Never.

Lidochka suddenly embraced Luzhbin around the neck as if she'd heard that fear and then poked her nose somewhere between his clavicle and shoulder, and he could feel her soft, cool lips up close, almost on his skin.

'Lidia Bor… Lidushka,' he said in a muffled voice, pressing her to himself.

One small felt boot had already fallen on the porch and the other fell in the living room but neither of them noticed because they were struck at how close they were to one another—just a few hours ago they were barely acquainted, hadn't even known one another.

And then Luzhbin suddenly ended up having a hundred hands, and all hundred were simultaneously everywhere, tangled up in buttons, sleeves, and all kinds of unexpected straps. And he mumbled the whole time, too—my little girl, little girl, little girl, my little girl—with soft, hot, wet lips and the lips were everywhere, too, so for a second it seemed to Lidochka, whose eyes were shut tight, that Luzhbin would just swallow her up right then, absorb her with a quiet smacking sound as if she were a piece of macaroni soaked in a greasy cheese sauce. She tried to help a little but didn't honestly know what she should do so just lifted her arms like a child and bent her knees so it was easier to pull off all the endless clothing, and Luzhbin mumbled the whole time, little girl, little girl, and then finally the clothes were gone from both of them and all of Lidochka's skin suddenly sensed someone else's naked body: heated, heavy, and as unpleasantly prickly as wool in some places.

She opened her eyes out of fear and unexpectedness, and saw Luzhbin's face a millimeter away from her own, almost insane with a tension she couldn't comprehend, his lips bloated as if they were blurred and faded. Lidochka's glance caught a gigantic wrinkle on a wet forehead, reddish stubble, unseeing pupils, a brush of short and colorless lashes, and saliva boiling at the corner of a trembling mouth, and then she squinted again, all covered in instant blue-gray goose bumps.

'Is it cold?' whispered Luzhbin, frightened and sensing Lidochka's quick, firm goose bumps under his palms. For an instant he stopped squeezing and kneading her as if she were dough taken from the ice box.

Lidochka shook her head for no without opening her eyes; her ballet bun came loose after losing its last hairpins and Luzhbin's lips delved into warm, live, smooth hair with the light scent of piny air, fresh cucumbers, and a funny, ticklish bit of tobacco dust. Luzhbin quietly gasped as if he'd choked on the aroma and then got going even stronger and this time Lidochka finally caught the vector of his hurried strivings, and everything immediately got easier, as if a reasonable—albeit deformed and chaotic but still comprehensible—picture had emerged from an incoherent combination of ungainly movements. Almost like dance.

'But I'll have a house,' Lidochka thought inopportunely. Then she obediently spread her trained knees into a *plié*, as if she were in class.

Luzhbin, all distorted, clenched, and frightening, raised himself over her on extended, convulsive arms and Lidochka experienced the horrid, bizarre, and crowded sensation of having something inside that didn't belong to her, and then she began weeping, unable to contain herself when she suddenly saw Vitkovsky's face very, very clearly: happy, dear, and wonderful, with the little mole on his firm, hot cheekbone. And right then all of Luzhbin contorted and tensed, making

Lidochka afraid he'd die and she'd have to get back to the city God knows how, on a winter night through snowy, fairytale-like mountains and dales that were dark blue, purple, and totally mute. She attempted to break free but Luzhbin moaned in a childlike, almost crying voice—Oh, God, I can't hold it!—and then he jolted and then again and again. And Lidochka understood it was all over.

The darkening bedroom smelled of sweat and something else that was unfamiliar, strange, and thickening. Luzhbin sat on the edge of the bed dangling reddish legs that looked as if they were wearing itchy woolen stockings, and it was even obvious from his naked, stooped back that something horrible had happened. Lidochka didn't know what to do now, either, so she kept lying on her back, just in case, not budging except to wipe her tears and put her open knees back together, like a butterfly folding its thin, dark wings.

'Do you hurt?' Luzhbin asked, without turning. He used the informal 'you' with Lidochka for the first time, as if sweat and all their mixed fluids gave him the right to a special closeness. His voice was as crumpled as a used handkerchief.

Lidochka listened to herself honestly: her injured meniscus ached a little (snow had likely started or would start any minute) and there was a strange round feeling between her legs as if she'd been punched there at full force or she'd had to ride on a horse for a long time, a whole eternity. But dancing a performance on bloody toes cut to a pulp after her girlfriends had sprinkled glass in her pointe shoes—that was pain. Lidochka remembered a wave of the electric, live boiling water her ankle had descended into with each lacy leap and quietly said, no, it doesn't hurt.

'Please forgive me,' Luzhbin said, as if he'd truly done something awful. 'It shouldn't have been like this at all. Not at all, don't you see!'

Lidochka was silent.

Luzhbin suddenly turned to her with his whole body and Lidochka immediately turned away when she saw, between his legs, what she hadn't even wanted to see or understand. He understood right away and pulled the edge of the bunched-up blanket over himself, blushing deeply.

'Marry me,' he said quietly. 'I beg you. Marry me, please.'

They held the wedding in June, as soon as Lidochka turned eighteen (Galina Petrovna's condition) and right after final exams at the school (a condition from Luzhbin, who'd prevailed upon Lidochka to finish things out, not leave school, and then 'Whatever you want, whatever you want, sweetie, honest'). Lidochka didn't have any conditions, at least nothing feasible. Of course she would have preferred a quiet civil registration of the marriage but Galina Petrovna and Luzhbin's businesses required them to observe all sorts of merchant politesses, meaning Lidochka had to tolerate a dress ordered from Paris, a limousine with the traditional dollies on the grille, placing flowers at the eternal flame, and a wedding banquet. Luzhbin felt nauseous, too, just remembering his previous wedding: it might not have been as rich but it was just as ridiculous. What tormented him most, though, was that Lidochka didn't love him. He could sense she didn't love him. He understood he was rushing into things but he understood even better that he couldn't not rush into things. Time works wonders, said some glib bimbo at the registration office, when she saw how Lidochka barely moved her pale lips as she pronounced her 'Yes.' That's a lie, said Galina Petrovna, interrupting with such malice that the bimbo recoiled and gaped with a garish made-up mouth.

Galina Petrovna barely waited until the end of the ceremony to walk up to Lidochka, pull her by the arm as if she wanted to tear it off, and then whisper right in her face, furiously, as if she were hissing, 'Listen, young lady, I stand guilty before you, don't argue, I'm guilty, and you don't even know the half of it.' Galina Petrovna caught her breath for an instant and remembered the wise woman she'd gone to right after giving birth to Borik, how stupid she'd been, so stupid, and there hadn't even been anyone to tell her she was stupid! The woman had honestly asked her, and why aren't you asking who'll pay for this, sweetie? And the big thing: How? It'll all land on your children and your grandchildren. Galina Petrovna had closed her eyes and heard her own voice say, fine and let them pay, what does it matter to me? The frighteningly even teeth inside the woman's head began laughing again and she said, good for you, I love it!

Lidochka—all pale, even paler than her dress—looked at her, not understanding, and only the diamonds on her neck and in her ears burned with a lively, ravenous, and fabulous light. Galina Petrovna didn't begrudge her generosity in giving her granddaughter her best stones for her wedding. But that didn't make it easier. 'Don't put up with it if things get unbearable or you want a younger man, do you hear me? Don't let it drive you to sin. Leave your husband and live however you have to.'

'I don't understand,' Lidochka admitted.

'That's fine, you'll understand soon,' Galina Petrovna promised. She unexpectedly laughed a strange, short, and almost sobbing laugh. It was as if she'd gagged on Lidochka's wedding and just couldn't clear her throat.

'There'll be another gift from me, just wait,' she finally said and then quickly turned and left the registry office.

When the never-ending wedding finally ended, the Luzhbins went home, outside the city, an immediate relief for both of them. The summer turned out to be unexpectedly good and warm, and Lidochka and Luzhbin worked tirelessly on the property and the house, cautiously growing closer to one another even as they kept a distance. By the time Luzhbin heard his wife quietly singing in the kitchen in late July while concocting a dinner, he even believed Lidochka would come to love him very, very soon, instead of someday.

He even felt adrift when Galina Petrovna called to summon him to see her at the bank. She could have handled someone's well-being by telephone and Luzhbin had no financial business with Lindt's widow and didn't intend to, out of principle. It would have been unwise, though, to quarrel with Lidochka's only relative, so Luzhbin dropped everything and went to see her when and where he was bidden. Galina Petrovna was waiting for him in a huge office and Luzhbin was once again staggered at how beautiful she was, how abnormally beautiful and youthful she was for her years. It was unpleasant. Next to her was a fawning, weaselly little character who looked like a used tampon a dog had slobbered on.

'So,' Galina Petrovna said without greeting Luzhbin. 'Here's a buyer for your house. He'll pay good money and he wants to move in before fall, meaning fast.'

'What?' Luzhbin couldn't believe his ears. 'What buyer? What house?'

'Your house,' Galina Petrovna repeated, 'What's not to understand?'

'What about us?' Luzhbin still didn't understand.

'You're going to Moscow.'

'But why Moscow?' Everything that was happening was so ridiculous Luzhbin couldn't even get angry.

'Because the Bolshoy Theatre's in Moscow, you idiot.' Galina Petrovna took a stack of papers off the desk and shook them. 'Here, look: laureates, delegates, and some other fuckheads and people in the arts. They're all writing petitions: Lidochka has to dance and they're gnawing their own balls off at the Bolshoy because she didn't go there. They say she has talent, a huge talent, a second Pavlova, blah, blah, blah.' Galina Petrovna shook the papers again, squeamishly squirming, 'I hate ballet. It's filthy. But I can't do anything about that.'

She fell silent; they all fell silent, though the tampon man nervously cracked his knuckles.

'You should have enough for an apartment but if it's not enough, I'll add some. I'll also help with your business. It's my final gift to Lida,' Galina Petrovna finally said. 'I hope I've settled my accounts with her now. That's it, you're free to go, fuck off.'

Luzhbin turned and got the hell out. He didn't like ballet, either, but he didn't intend to let his wife's talent molder. At first he wanted to go back to the office but then he decided to go home instead. Lidochka was in the kitchen, as always, and long waves of tempting aromas mingled as they spread.

'Lidusha!' Luzhbin yelled from the threshold. 'It's me!'

Lidochka peered out. Her cheeks were rosy from standing over the stove and she wore a short sundress: she looked very much like a young girl. So much for eighteen: she barely looked fourteen.

'Why're you back so early?' she asked, frightened. 'Did something happen?'

'No,' said Luzhbin, 'Well, yes, something happened but it's good. Galina Petrovna has a gift for you, like she promised.'

Lidochka's face changed even more and Luzhbin unexpectedly sensed he was doing something awful and irreparable, maybe making the very biggest mistake of his life.

'What smells so good?' he asked. 'That aroma—it's making my head spin.'

'Royal soup and Viennese sausages,' Lidochka reluctantly told him. 'So what's with Galina Petrovna? What's the gift?'

Luzhbin inhaled a full chest of air and confessed, 'We're moving to Moscow. You'll dance at the Bolshoy, they're already expecting you, they're even preparing a repertoire.'

Lidochka was silent and her face slowly deadened and froze like melting candle wax, transforming into the grimace of a dead Wili, the face of the girl in the tutu who'd turned to stone on the frozen steps of the theater that night. Luzhbin could even feel cold issuing from her, that same horrible ringing cold from inside her.

'And the house?' said Lidochka.

'We'll sell the house, it's already as good as sold. We'll sign the papers tomorrow and then we can pack.'

Lidochka was quiet another minute and then said in an even voice, 'Fine. Take off your jacket, wash your hands, and we'll eat.'

Lidochka woke up in the middle of the night as if something had jolted her. For some time she couldn't fathom much about the person lying next to her: the close-cropped, whitish back of the head, the deep crease on the neck, the cadenced inhales and exhales of the blanket. She recognized the house right away, though, even before she'd opened her eyes: it was exactly what she'd dreamed of, only better, and completely hers. And it wanted to say goodbye.

Lidochka cautiously sat up and her feet reached for fluffy slippers that were too new and too unfamiliar, just like her little pajamas with the silly appliqué, like the wedding ring, like her entire life now, the life she'd attached so much hope to, though of course none of it could have come true. She quietly walked through the dark rooms, making no mistakes and not confusing anything. Lidochka knew this house in advance, by heart, even without any lights: that pitchy burl under her caressing hand, that welcomingly squeaky floor board, that scent that was the sleepy, pure breath of her future, and those stairs to the second floor that seemed to sing quietly but purely, like an old singing teacher who'd worn out her vocal cords during the course of her life but was still bashfully and unrequitedly in love with music, if only for herself.

Of course Luzhbin had redone a lot—surprisingly dexterously and well—without disturbing either the essence or the substance of the house itself. Lidochka quietly rejoiced as she walked through three completely new rooms they'd recently added, happy her husband had done such a nice job and arranged everything so properly, particularly the second back porch that went right into the woods so you could run down the stairs in the morning, cut some wild flowers before breakfast and maybe, someday, some mushrooms for a fresh little sauté, too: they'd even planned to cultivate saffron milk caps and chanterelles by the steps. And why not, it was actually fairly easy, the big thing was to muster the patience and stay away from white mushrooms, which are moody and die in even relative captivity. They'd also planned to tame squirrels: Luzhbin said there were plenty of them in the forest and Lidochka was worried in advance about conflict between the squirrels and the cats—very possibly an armed conflict—but at least the children would thoroughly enjoy the squirrels. Luzhbin had just laughed because neither children nor cats were in the plans just yet besides, the squirrels, Lidushka, aren't exactly rushing to our house yet, you can see that yourself. But don't worry, they'll come running—en masse—as soon as we finish renovating. They'll puff your future cats' fur coats right up! Lidochka awkwardly laughed in response, still hesitant, and Luzhbin pressed her to himself uncomfortably, mumbling iloveyouIohLordmyGodhowIloveyou like an incantation. He had a funny name for her, Lidushka, and it came out sounding almost as affectionate and cheerful as her parents' Barbariska. Of course she could get used to that. She'd absolutely get used to it, Luzhbin was a good guy and Lidochka knew how to tell good from bad. Even so, she'd married this house, not Luzhbin.

Lidochka stroked the smooth, freshly planed banister on the porch: it was warm and absolutely human to the touch and the house sighed as it accepted her affection, simultaneously assessing and coming to terms with the circumstances before they parted. It was more dusky than dark and Lidochka suddenly began crying as she stood in the warm, translucent pudding of the dim northern night. She cried, consciously cried, like she hadn't cried in ages; tears were the simplest, most everyday and ordinary thing in the frightening ballet world she'd grown up in, so they hardly cost anything. Everyone cried at school—from pain you just couldn't get used to, from humiliation because there's no ballet without humiliation, from fear of being kicked out, from offenses, from rage, and then from pain again—but the everydayness of those tears deprived them of all meaning and significance, transforming crying into a habitual physiological act that automatically excluded misery and commiseration. Her tears now were completely different: heavy, slow, and so real Lidochka thought they were even steaming a little.

She cried a long time before she realized crying was completely hopeless, too: everything was decided so she had to wash up, blow her nose, go back to bed, endure until dawn, then pack her things herself, and get ready to leave for Moscow, a place everyone dreamed about that was, for Lidochka, just a flat picture from a children's book, meaningless, soulless, and garish. She had to keep living and dancing. Oh God, dancing again!

Lidochka went back into the house, and entered the bathroom—Luzhbin had added and furnished it, too—without disturbing so much as a floorboard. The bathroom was roomy with little country rugs, a wicker basket for laundry, and ultramodern fixtures that slyly pretended to be old-fashioned: the round-sided bathtub on curved legs alone had cost an entire fortune. There was a window, too, a most genuinely large window that Lidochka quickly flung open, letting in several old apple trees that had run wild plus the ghost of the former future garden she'd been planning to start next spring: apples, pears, definitely a couple plums, and even cherries (sand and Nanking), since they overwinter well and the jam is delicious, and for pastries, too, and then when the grandchildren start to come... but Lidochka caught herself and looked at the bathroom with lost eyes.

What grandchildren?

Total strangers will be living here in another week.

She opened the medicine cabinet for some reason and

looked over all the little jars and vials, most of them Luzhbin's, and then a razor caught her eye: it was old, from the Soviet era, with a heavy ivory handle and removable blades. Papa'd shaved with one of those way back. Lidochka smiled at Luzhbin's weakness for old things that he pitied as if they were alive: it was something else they had in common, a dormant bud that could grow into a nice strong branch over time. Maybe even into love. But there had to be a home for that. This home. Her home.

Lidochka slammed the cabinet shut and turned on hot water that tautly and hoarsely struck the bottom of the bathtub. She had to take a bath. Had to go. Had to dance. Had to. Had to. Had to. It never occurred to her that she could refuse. Just say, no, we're not going anywhere. I won't. I just don't want to. But Lidochka had ended up in ballet as a child, and 'No' was only used there with a command. No, you'll do it! No, you'll leap. No, you can do it. That was a completely different 'No,' and Lidochka simply didn't know the others.

She slipped off her pajamas in front of a huge mirror that ran almost to the ceiling and her cold eyes sized up her reflection as if she were scrutinizing an unknown, unpleasant person: turned-out feet, scrawny arms, clumsy bones sticking out of hips gnawed away by hunger and exercises, and ugly yellowish skin over the strong, lean muscles of a track athlete. A combination for producing ridiculous bodily motions. A freak. A fool. A pathetic, freakish fool.

She truly didn't see anything of what drove Luzhbin crazy and made other men gaze after her with eyes that were almost rapturously frightened: not the barely noticeable but still lovely breasts, nor the mole on her fragile high neck, nor the wavy hair gathered high, nor the line of her shoulders, a line as pure and expressive as Georgy Ivanov's late poetry, when he was already hopeless, dying, and bitter. Send salted cucumbers and Russian herring, if you can find it, George is begging for them. He's doing worse.

    Lidochka mechanically leaned on the edge of the sink as if it were a ballet barre and her body—all drilled and mustered into shape, completely alien and abhorrent—immediately took on the familiar position. Lidochka herself didn't understand how she straightened even more and then, with such mechanical agility it was as if she'd been possessed by evil spirits, suddenly made a quick and unusually elegant *battement tendu* from the first and fifth positions in all directions and then a superb *grand battement* to the side and froze again in front of the mirror with a waxy welcoming face, as if she were expecting applause. She did all this so quickly it frightened her: this was the first time in her life she'd actually felt as if a horrible, external demonic power had come over her, a power capable of forcing her into submission at any moment, in the most literal and physical sense. Even her body, which had been nurtured in hatred and servitude, was against her. It was horrifying. Truly horrifying.

    Lidochka opened the medicine cabinet again and her shaking hands unscrewed Luzhbin's razor handle and knocked the blade—purplish, with 'Leningrad' written on it and a tiny little rust spot on a very sharp, dangerous edge that was almost invisible—onto her palm. Her fingertips immediately became cold and clammy. 'As it should be,' Lidochka quickly said, afraid she'd reconsider. 'I should have done this ages ago. We're not going to any Moscow. Let's go to Leningrad instead. Leningrad, Leningrad, buy nice clothes so you'll be clad! Bright red! Dark blue! Or like sky! Choose what you want, just don't be shy!' She squeezed her eyes shut and even hissed quietly, but it wasn't painful at all. So, that's it, she said, calming herself because there was nobody else to calm her. So that's it. And she quickly lay in the nearly filled bathtub without opening her eyes.

Warm water quietly splashed around her neck as if its smooth, bare gums nipped at her skin. Her ankles and wrists felt almost pleasantly ticklish, and a barely perceptible, caressing, and thoroughly summery breeze came through the open window in faint waves. Wafts of tiredness swooped in, too, like after a long, happy walk—for the whole day—through the woods, when your hair is filled with sunlight and dry pine needles, and there's a slightly squeaky basket pulling on your arm because it's heavy with mushrooms you'll need to wash and trim before nightfall so you can braise a whole pot of them with nutmeg, parsley, and sour cream the next day, and your eyes droop, and your lashes are so heavy, and there's such a heavy aroma of damp underbrush, ferns, and sun-warmed bark swirling in your head, no, don't sleep, don't sleep, don't sleep, would a good housewife go into the bedroom without finishing up everything in the kitchen?

The little knife slipped out of her twitching fingers, clanging on the bottom of the sink, and Lidochka woke up with a frightened start.

It was very bright and somehow cold. She quickly pulled her pajamas right onto her wet, unruly body, groped for the door and found herself not where she'd expected to be—a hallway lined in lightly scented, golden wood paneling—but on the threshold of a totally unfamiliar room that was empty, white, and somehow unlived in, as if it had just been renovated. There was another door ahead and Lidochka hurried to it, more surprised than frightened, leaving smooth, naked, wet tracks on a floor lightly powdered with dust. Yes, it had been renovated. And those workers, they hadn't even swept up!

This door yielded as easily as the first and Lidochka knew after just one step that the next room wasn't any different from the last: they all had the same lime-splotched sawhorses in the corners, the very same smooth windowless walls, and even the door ahead of her was the same. A nice new imported door. Oak veneer. Gold-tone hardware. And behind that door was another and then another. An enfilade.

Lidochka walked faster but the rooms floated by, opening up one after another and not changing: light, empty, and identical. Not frightening, no. Just strange and thus unpleasant. Lidochka tried counting them but quickly lost track and so just walked and walked, using her shoulders to part air that was just as smooth, bright, and stale as everything else.

After opening yet another door, she suddenly felt she'd begun to tire and right then it seemed as if the tiredness might be taking on a physical form: she noticed there was more dust in the room and the sawhorses had darkened and seemed to sag. Lidochka stopped and looked around as if she wanted to ask someone about deviating from this route. But it was empty behind her and doors gaped as far as the eye could see, getting smaller and more distant. Lidochka cautiously went up to sawhorses and touched their squeaky, cracked boards. Only now, up close, did she see that the walls, which had been whitewashed and smooth before, were covered with a barely noticeable web of thin, thin cracks.

Lidochka looked around again and sensed drifting fear rustling in her hair like a silent paw. She wanted to scream and call for someone but imagined her voice going silent and rolling through the endless echoing rooms so kept quiet, using all her strength to convince herself to calm down. They're just rooms. Lots of rooms. I'm just sleeping. That's exactly it, I'm sleeping. But of course she wasn't sleeping.

Lidochka touched the sawhorses again and a nail, mournfully bent, rusty, and red-headed, fell out with a soft clang. She bent to pick it up and even choked when she saw her hand stretch toward the nail: it was an old woman's hand, thin with dry, wrinkled skin stretched over bones.

Her own hand.

She ran through several rooms, squinting, groping, and not hearing anything except whistling in her own bronchial tubes. Doors slammed with a frightening echo, her heart pounded in her temples and throat with a frightening echo, and Lidochka thought her heart was getting larger and larger with each step as her body, meanwhile, withered, tightened, and turned into a mummy, into a dense and rigid chrysalis, into dust.

Lidochka stopped and opened her eyes when there was finally nothing left to breathe. The room was the same, just more dilapidated. There were large, silent clumps of dust in the corners, and a sawhorse went to its knees, quietly and very humanly sighing when one of its legs collapsed with an inaudible crack. Lidochka frantically felt at her face and hair but didn't understand anything so put her hands to her eyes again. No, she wasn't imagining things. She'd aged. With each room. With each step. She was getting older. No, she wasn't aging. She was dying.

Lidochka suddenly grasped that with absolute clarity and the fear that had haunted her so long and so persistently—the fear of growing old—immediately disappeared, as if the only thing that could consume that nightmare was old age itself. Now that she'd gotten there, there was simply nothing left to fear. Lidochka stood for a bit, not knowing what to do next, then suddenly pulled herself together and continued on, ahead, slowly moving her heavy, deformed feet, the feet of a professional ballerina, feet that swelled with each step and were simply turning into an old woman's bare, ugly feet. She no longer turned around because she knew for sure there *was* something behind her: she knew that invisible but palpable something was heavily and lazily pressing her, chasing her forward. It was hard to walk, her vision grew worse and worse, and more and more age spots kept appearing on hands that were all wrinkled, pathetic, and shaking. There was also less light and more dust, and when the sawhorses in the corner finally became a heap of nearly rotted trash, Lidochka knew the door in front of her was the last.

Now I'll die, she thought, completely calmly, and then used her last strength to turn an ancient doorknob darkened from age.

A street glistened—it was as wet and black as a licked liquorice candy.

Gleaming watery drizzle quivered in a thick column of light from a streetlamp, and there were scents of recent rain, hot donuts, and strong coffee from a white-hot copper cezve. A car slowly turned, rustling along the liquid, glistening cobblestones, its bulging sides reflecting short neon flashes, floaty windows, and curved pink tubes that blinked the words 'Coffee Shop.' A herd of teenagers in short crackly raincoats ran along the sidewalk, and the last girl smiled broadly instead of excusing herself when she grazed Lidochka with her damp shoulder. Her teeth sparkled: they were damp, round, and smooth, too, like beach stones and pebbles from childhood. From the Black Sea.

Lidochka mechanically smiled in response but the girls, their tights-covered knees all jumbled, had already turned the corner, taking with them a cloud of hurried half-childish clamor and an almost physically tangible happiness. Only as Lidochka watched them did she realize she was standing on a completely unfamiliar street—alive, eighteen, wearing yellow pajamas with a paunchy cat sewn just above the heart—and the evening was cautiously placing first one, then another chilly, wet palm on her back. It's autumn, Lidochka thought, not at all surprised. Early autumn. Or late spring. But it's summer at home.

Another pedestrian walked past her, a hefty graying man with a huge German shepherd on a leash. The dog's cordial leathery nose casually poked at Lidochka. You should be ashamed! The man quietly scolded the dog first and then calmed Lidochka. Don't be afraid, he doesn't bite. I'm not afraid, Lidochka said and stretched to pat the dog's head, as hefty and warm as a child's, but the dignified dog shunned her, leaving Lidochka's hand hanging in the air, young, slender, and full of strong, live, hot blood.

'Barbariska!'

A resonant voice cracking a little from nervousness—a voice almost forgotten but still unbelievably and physically dear—raced down the wet street, bouncing like a ball off pavement, streetlamps, and damp walls that looked as if they were covered with goose bumps.

'Barbariska!'

Lidochka frantically turned her head and yes, a woman

was running along the sidewalk toward her, wide open in the happy cross of an embrace: she was curly-haired, not too tall, wearing a thin, squeaky blue-gray raincoat almost like cellophane, the very same as… Lidochka stepped toward her, pressing her clenched, unbelieving hands to her chest as if she were trying to cover the appliquéd cat's eyes.

'Ma!' she called out in a husky, soundless voice. 'Ma.'

Her slippers, soaked by the black night's dampness, squelched quietly but distinctly.

'Mamochka!'

'Barbariska!'

They nearly fell as they embraced, and Lidochka banged her shoulder hard but barely noticed, knocking like a little girl, as if she were blind, into familiar and tender warmth, the only warmth: there were Mama's cheeks, Mama's earlobe all aflame and translucent with a simple little gold earring that was always trying to get lost, Mama's laughter, and Mamochka's scent, which was unique, familiar, and not at all wanting to die, gone even from memory but living a long, long time in the cabinet now occupied by the Tsarevs, where Lidochka sometimes secretly opened the doors and inhaled everything all at once with her eyes squeezed shut: pain, yearning, fading traces, and the last molecules of her own childhood, but that was rare, very, very rare. She was afraid to breathe up all her mother's scent and be left completely and definitively alone. Mamochka, Mamochka, God, Mamochka, how did I, without you, all that time I've!…

Mamochka kissed Lidochka wherever her hot, happy lips landed and then she suddenly began pulling at her and feeling her, as if Lidochka had tumbled from some horrible height and she now had to determine she was in one piece: her bones, muscles, ligaments, even that her tights hadn't torn. Good girl, just don't you ever go up in the storage loft again! Promise? You've gotten so scrawny, Mamochka whispered into Lidochka's collarbone, her voice rough from approaching tears. All scrawny. All that's left is bones. Lidochka wanted to say something but couldn't, and then they both, suddenly and simultaneously, began laughing and crying as only women can, and then they started hugging and squeezing each other, completely forgetting they were standing in the middle of the street. And they just kept repeating the whole time: But how are you? How are you? Oh God! Mamochka! Barbariska! Were you okay without me? What about you? What about you? And?

They calmed down simultaneously, too, as if they'd suddenly switched off from each other, and Lidochka immediately sensed she was freezing. Her shoulders shuddered and Mamochka hugged her again right away, pulling her toward herself, under her wing, under the skirt of her raincoat, which also turned out to be lined with an unforgotten, dear, tender, and slightly stuffy warmth she hadn't forgotten. Pani Walewska: a vial of intoxicatingly dark-blue glass, the white-blond curly head of a frivolous Polish beauty on the side. Lidochka breathed in the unpretentious scent—it had only two notes—and blissfully closed her eyes, pressing so firmly with her whole body that she couldn't tell where it was her heart beating and where it was Mamochka's. My little daughter, Mamochka joyfully said, rubbing her cheek in Lidochka's hair. Let's go. Papa misses you horribly, too.

'Papa?' Lidochka wriggled out from under the raincoat and stepped away, looking incredulous, as if she were a little girl watching from below, though she and Mamochka were now the same height. Lidochka might even be taller, 'What do you mean, Papa? Is he really…' Lidochka wanted to say 'dead, too' but couldn't. It was impossible to believe. Even now. Even here.

'Yes, Papa,' Mamochka raised her brows, dumbfounded, but then she suddenly understood and gasped in disappointment, pressing her mouth with her hands. Her familiar wedding ring flashed, thick as a barrel with a yellowish little diamond squeezed into gold dough. 'What, didn't your grandmother say anything to you?'

Lidochka shook her head, no, nothing. Well, of course she said something, that Papa went away. To earn money. He didn't? But he sent me cards for all the holidays. Lidochka remembered the little box where she'd neatly placed all the little pieces of cardboard decorated with flowers, teddy bears, and balloons. Bright stamps. Hurried, sweeping handwriting. 'My dear little daughter! Congratulations! Do well in school, listen to your grandmother. Your papa.' The ink was either blue or black. Illegible postmarks. No return address. Ever.

Mamochka gasped again.

'Oh, come on, what cards! He really did leave but… Well, yes, almost right after my funeral. Just think, he went back to Adler, well, the place we were at the sea, remember? Of course someone was already in our room but somehow he… Anyway, they let him spend the night in the next room and he, what a fool… Oh, I let him have it, you can't even imagine! Leaving you all alone! But what could I do by then? They didn't find him until morning. You know how it is. It was too late.'

'But what about the money?' Lidochka asked, still not believing her. 'The money. Papa wired me money every month.

Galina Petrovna showed me. It went into my bank book. She transferred it all to her bank later so nothing got lost, not even a kopeck, even in the default.'

'It didn't get lost because that was her money,' Mamochka said. 'She was the one wiring you money. Of course it's really strange she didn't tell you anything, but then…' Mamochka thought for a moment and then happily shook her curly head. 'But maybe that's all for the best, who knows. Come on, let's go, good Lord, you'll get completely soaked. You can tell Papa and me all about everything.'

'Just like when I was little?' Lidochka asked, 'Every little thing?'

'Every little thing,' Mamochka said, laughing. 'We don't know anything about you! Everything here is just like where you are. Lies in the newspapers, just soapy series on TV. You only get news from your friends. And you have to wait so long for them, too, those friends! And then they don't all tell the truth, you know how that goes, some of them just gossip. Just like when… Oh, there's no point in getting into it. Here, let's go home.'

'Home,' Lidochka repeated, disbelieving.

Home. Finally, home.

Mamochka hugged her around the shoulders again, pulling her, and right then the night street floated off to the side with a tremble and completely spread and swelled, as if it were ready to overflow at any moment and ceremoniously crawl across a cheek, like a snail. Mamochka's face was distorted for an instant, too, bursting at invisible seams, growing deformed and unfamiliar, even unhuman for a moment.

Lidochka stepped away, shuddering.

'What is it, Barbariska?' Mamochka affectionately asked

and Lidochka tried to smile, quickly blinking away the moisture. She suddenly began quivering from within, a fine, incessant shivering. Only wearing her pajamas. In the evening. In an unfamiliar place. In the rain. What was this, anyway? Where? What? How did I get here?

She didn't look at her mother any longer. She was afraid.

'Barbariska.'

Lidochka was quiet and looked straight ahead. The door of the coffee shop across from them slammed. A bus glided along the roadway, lighted inside and filled with gesturing, soundless people, like in a silent movie.

'Barbariska!'

Discontent that was as thin and bluish as steel rang out near the depths of Mamochka's voice, as always when Lidochka didn't obey.

'Don't you even think about going anywhere,' Lazar Lindt calmly said, closing and shaking out an umbrella all covered in lively mercurial drops. He looked so much like his own photograph that Lidochka wasn't even surprised. Mamochka. Papa. And now here he was, too. She wondered if she could call Lindt 'Grandfather' or if she'd have to observe formalities, like with Galina Petrovna.

Lindt began laughing as if he'd read her mind and stood on tiptoe to kiss Lidochka's cheek. He smelled delicious, like strong, real coffee with foam and a cinnamon stick.

'What formalities could there be here?' he said. 'It's too bad you cooked all this up. Go on, get home right now.'

'Home,' Mamochka called out, echoing him, and Lidochka mechanically strode over to her, still afraid to look, but still headed for Mamochka. Lindt scowled and blocked her way with an unexpectedly young and quick motion.

'I said go back. Get out. I don't want to see you here any more.'

Something blue flashed behind him, rustling, and Lindt winced, throwing up his hands and keeping Mamochka from getting by.

'Go on, right now,' he said, hurrying Lidochka. 'What, don't you know where your home is?'

'No,' Lidochka honestly replied. 'I don't know.'

'Look back,' Lindt ordered her.

And Lidochka looked back.

Behind her was a window, an ordinary window on the first floor of a house that wasn't new, though of course there should have been a door, that same last door she'd come through as she aged in the enfilade in her dream. On a windowsill inside the glass—on the other side, the side where Lidochka knew for sure there wasn't anything but a procession of empty, dilapidated rooms—sat children, festively lighted, like in a theater. A boy and a girl. No more than a year apart in age. The girl was about seven, with a snub nose and a big polka dot bow nestled into sweet curls like a dragonfly on a flower—the light-hearted bow was obviously the work of a female adult's loving and indulgent hand. The little girl was angrily rebuking the little boy, a large, gloomy chucklehead of a boy in a tight colorful shirt, and because the boy was listening inattentively and taking offense, it was obvious—despite his firm cheeks and a height advantage—that he was hopelessly younger, maybe even by a whole year, but did not intend to reconcile himself with that, oh no, he didn't intend to! The dissatisfied little girl poked at his round shoulder with her little fist and then looked into the darkness outside the window, tensely, seriously, almost like an adult, as if she'd sensed Lidochka's gaze.

'Who are they?' Lidochka asked, frightened.

Lindt chuckled coldly behind her. 'Oh, come on,' he said, 'Think. Guess.'

Lidochka looked closely and then the children's faces suddenly broke into separate, familiar features as if someone had turned the tube of a kaleidoscope: Lindt's jet-black curls, Mamochka's smile, Luzhbin's square forehead, the little boy's cheek with her own dimple, the one that formerly belonged to Galina Petrovna and to someone else before that, someone nameless and long forgotten but still related. Mixing blood pounded in Lidochka's temples and wrists, reverberating in the boy's chest and filling the girl's lips and eyelids with a bright pink color and pulsing all at once in a million veins past, present, and future.

Those are my grandchildren, Lidochka understood. It's not all over. Not at all. It's all continuing. But what now? And why? She strode over to the window as if she wanted to knock but right then her mother began screaming frightfully behind her back.

'I won't let you! No, I won't let you! Barbariska!'

Lidochka looked behind her.

'Quick,' Lindt said, 'Go on, quick!'

Something was beating in his hands with all its might and breaking away, something frightful, but it wasn't Mamochka, no, and the grimacing Lindt held on firmly, so firmly that Lidochka sensed her muscles tightening under her dry skin as strong male arms squeezed at her and everything around her flooded with light, purpose, and a triumphant splash. Heavy warm water was already flowing off her rather than through her, Come on, come on, quick, Lindt shouted, I'm holding her, go back, go on, go back, and Lidochka smashed on the window glass with both hands: everything around her seemed to freeze for a second then it exploded and shattered into a million crunchy, glistening shards, and she ran back after the laughing children, running through rooms that were now perfectly alive and filled with wonderful people, friendly dogs, and amiable old furniture. The smells of floor polish, apple pastry, and juniper branches grew stronger, and a blinding, dense, milky light rapidly drew closer, filled with such joy that Lidochka began laughing too, and the light kept coming nearer and nearer until it hit her on the face like a strong hot hand. And then again. And then again. And again.

'Come on!' Luzhbin yelled right next to her, just above her ear.

'Come on, girl, come on!'

And Lidochka woke up.

Luzhbin knelt over her and his face wasn't even pale but dark blue, jumping, shaking all over, and quivering: his distorted lips and chin shook, and his cheek twitched, disfigured by a tic.

'You,' he said, as if he weren't recognizing or believing Lidochka had come back or that she'd even been able to try to leave. You...

Lidochka wanted to answer but her lips only murmured without responding, and water filled with her blood murmured, too, as it whirled down the drain. Her back hurt a lot for some reason, and her wrists and ankles ached a little, too, the long way, all tightly wrapped in sheets torn into bandages, what a good job he did after all that, so smart. Vanya. He knew. He saved me… He saved me… Thank you.

Luzhbin bent down, trying to hear, and Lidochka forced her voice out with all her strength, whispering, I… I… Want…

'What do you want Lidushka?' Luzhbin raised her up a little by the shoulders. 'Something to drink? Maybe some water? The ambulance will be here soon, they're coming, hang on, my dear. They'll be right here. Right away.'

Lidochka stubbornly shook her head and finally finished what she had to say, 'I want to stay,' she firmly pronounced, surprised at herself because she'd never in her life spoken like that and never in her life had she wanted anything for herself, never dared, and it turned out to be so simple, you just have to gather up a full chest of air and say it. Just say it.

'I want to stay,' Lidochka repeated, and Luzhbin understood right away what she meant: the house, him, all of life, which from that second on had finally become, forever, a common life for both of them, just as he'd wanted it and as she, Lidochka, now wanted it, too. She'd made her choice, and for the first time someone had chosen him, how about that, consciously and for real, and Luzhbin began to weep, gasping from gratitude and nestling his face into Lidochka's hollow, almost child-like stomach, which already concealed within its golden darknesses a chapter not yet read or known to anyone.

An ambulance dissatisfied with the early call screamed shrilly outside the gate and a doctor gray from pre-dawn exhaustion tried to put out a cigarette he'd smoked right down to the filter of its spit-soaked end, but he missed the overflowing ashtray. Good Lord, take a look, what a palace, Vasya, how is it these bourgeois just can't deal with life, I hate these suicidals, it's the fourth case this week and they're all total hysterics, I'd stuff them all in the nut house, the nut house, honest, I would, without the right to correspondence, and if just one of those bastards would cut their veins like you should, not across but lengthwise, lengthwise, lengthwise, but no, saving those bastards for this salary, well, fine, go ahead and brake, there you go, back it up, back it up, or we'll never shove the stretcher in.

The doctor jumped out of the ambulance, which was parked so its tire pressed against some of the golden glow flowers Marusya had planted. He headed toward the house along the same path the young Galina Petrovna once walked to see her witch, and everything had truly, finally, come untangled, resolved itself, and come together, but this time it was for forever: there was love, which wandered through this story for so long, unable for so long to get in sync, and there was that house, and the delicious cold air, and a round pink sun, slowly emerging from behind pines that were pink, too, and that sun was so huge that Lazar Lindt began laughing with joy somewhere far, far away.

He began laughing and kissed Marusya's warm little immortal hand.

List of Main Characters

Non-Russian readers of Russian books often have trouble with 'all those names'. Those names frequently take very different forms: Alexander, Sasha, Shura, and Sanya are just a few variations for 'one and the same' boy or man. These forms indicate varying levels of formality and informality, and might denote pet names, teasing, or status. To help familiarize the reader with this world, we've added the following list of the most important characters in *The Women of Lazarus*, with variations on their names.

Maria Nikitichna Chaldonova (née Pitovranova)
Marusya—a cosy-sounding diminutive
Mama Masha

Lazar Iosifovich Lindt
Lesik—Marusya's nickname for Lindt
LazarIosich—a nickname invented by Lindt's assistant, Nikolayich
'Lazar' is a Russian equivalent for 'Lazarus'

Sergey Alexandrovich Chaldonov
Seryozha

Galina Petrovna Lindt (née Batalova)
Galochka
Galyunya
Galya

Lidia Borisovna Lindt
Lida
Lidochka
Barbariska—a lozenge-shaped candy flavored with barberry
Lidusha
Lidushka

Secondary Characters With Notable or Changing Names

Ivan Vasilevich Luzhbin
Vanya

Isaak
Isa
Isochka

Valentina Tulyaeva
Valya

Elvira Tulyaeva
Elya
Elechka

Vasily Nikolaevich Samokhov
Generally known by an elided form of his patronymic:
    Nikolayich

Ninel Danilovna
'Big Ninel'—the name 'Ninel' is 'Lenin' in reverse

Several historical figures appear in the book as minor characters, including:
Lavrenty Beria
Abram Ioffe
Nikolai Zhukovsky

A Few Place Names Worth Mentioning…
- Ensk isn't a real place: it takes its name from the letter N
- There is a place called Elban. Its name sounds rather like a swear word.
- Semipalatinsk, which is in Kazakhstan and has been renamed Semey, really was used for nuclear testing.

For more information or to receive our newsletter,
please contact us at: info@worldeditions.org